THE
LONDON
MONSTER

Donna Scott

The scariest monsters are the ones that lurk within our souls.

—Edgar Allan Poe

It is of a Monster I mean for to write,
Who in stabbing of Ladies took great delight;
If he caught them alone in the street after dark,
In their Hips or their Thighs, he'd be sure to cut a mark.

—The Monster Represented, an illustrated collection of verses, July 1790

A Note

August 1789

I have little patience for misinformation. First of all, I did not attack a Miss Kitty Wheeler in the Ranelagh pleasure garden. I only whispered some indelicacies in her ear. There were far too many people meandering about on that enchanted summer night, so I would never have been so reckless as to draw my knife. I am not a fool, after all.

But the papers always manage to get it wrong. Or perhaps it's the women. I have been described as a thin, vulgar-looking man with ugly legs and feet. How would they know the true nature of my legs and feet? Do I go about without stockings and shoes? I think not! Some accounts describe me as short with a villainous, narrow face, yet others paint me as a small, big-nosed man with curly hair, a tall man of regular features, or foreign-looking with a dark complexion. I have been said to wear all-black clothing, a brown greatcoat and striped waistcoat, or a blue silk coat with ruffled details and blue and white stockings. They say I have long slicked hair, plaited behind and turned up, or loose curls and a round or cocked hat with or without a cockade. Essentially, I look like everyone or no one at all.

The Morning Chronicle *has often referred to me as a 'miscreant' or a 'wretch'. The* Oracle *is less judgmental and therefore uses terms like 'attacker' and 'perpetrator'. But the* World *is the most accurate of the papers, for it portrays the women as the real monsters. They are the ones whose histrionics and featherbrained ways have placed all men in danger, for any innocent man can be accused of being me with one wrong look or harmless suggestion.*

And that is how I do it. First, with a kind word or two, and then with a proposition. The circumstances—whether the object of my affection sways her hips when she walks or strides forward with impatience and arrogance—will determine how I choose my words. The lady who entertains me first with the rhythmic swish of her skirts as I follow behind her will always get the kinder introduction. Perhaps a compliment before I express my true wishes. But it is the haughty jilt who will take the brunt of it. I might whisper a vulgarity in her delicate pink ear, comment on my growing arousal or the bounce of her breasts. What brings me the most pleasure is that first gasp, the initial moment of shock which registers in her raised brow and parted lips, a sure sign I have offended. After that, it is not exactly pleasure I feel, but anger that burns my chest—a building rage. Every desire I've ever had spills freely from my tongue and coats her like the soot on a hearth's bricks. She might fight to get away—most of them do—but I am stronger, faster. And it is only then that I draw my blade.

Part One

Chapter 1

September 1789
Newgate Prison, London

Even as he stood atop the wooden cart with his hands bound and a rope around his neck, Thomas Hayes didn't regret what he had done. Only three people knew the truth of it, of course—the lady involved, her assailant, and him. But without the victim coming forth, no one would believe Tom's pleas of innocence.

Behind him, a chandler stirred the boiling tallow that was meant to cover Tom's dead body when the deed was done. The unpleasant odour of rancid lard filled his nostrils, yet strangely made him awfully hungry at the same time. He should have been hanged in the morning, but as the hours passed and no one came to retrieve him, he thought they'd reconsidered and decided the best way of death would be from starvation. He hadn't eaten in two days, either because his gaolers forgot to feed him or because they simply thought it unnecessary. Either way, his mouth watered and stomach growled in what was to be the last day of his two and twenty years of life.

He imagined his father's expression when he finally read the news from the *Morning Herald* or the *Public Ledger: Son of Candidate Joseph Hayes Hanged at Newgate for Attempted Murder*. His father's face would drop into his hands, his head shaking with disappointment, and his dreams of becoming a member of the House of Commons turning to ash with each blazing written word.

The two men awaiting execution to Tom's left mumbled their prayers. Tom had said his that morning as he took the sacrament from the chaplain, having satisfied the man's religious estimation that he was truly repentant. But he wasn't. He'd do it all again if presented with the same circumstances.

The gibbet stood only a foot higher than his head, and the ground little more than three feet below him. He wore the same clothes he had been wearing the night he had attended the party at Apsley House and knew with certainty that had his brothers been informed of his fate—another reason to curse him for ruining their family name—they would purchase his clothing and shoes back from the executioner once he was hanged. They were plain but beautifully made, his coat and breeches of the finest worsted wool and his shirt of white linen, now stained from weeks lying on the dirt floor of his cell. Sadly, his recently purchased cocked hat was nowhere to be found. The two men beside him were less formally dressed, both in crudely made hemp clothing, their brown forms slumped and feeble. From the look on the spectators' faces, he knew that he stood out like a peacock on parade.

The constable beside him nodded, and the executioner covered Tom's bare head and face with a coarse white linen sack. "There you go, lad."

The bag scratched the skin on the bridge of his nose, so he tried to wriggle it away as best he could, considering the rope pressed tightly against his throat. He was to be hanged in chains once he was declared dead—as were all felons, particularly those accused of attempted murder—and placed on display as carrion for nearby birds looking to feast on his remains. That part bothered him the most. He thanked God that his mother wasn't alive to see it.

The crowd suddenly hushed, telling him he had only seconds left to live. He took a deep breath through his mouth to avoid the tallow stench and relaxed as much as he could. The sound of a bare hand slapping the horse's hindquarters, then the jingling of its tack registered in his mind as the last sounds he would ever hear. The cart below him shifted forward, and he stumbled to stay atop, but the flooring disappeared, and the noose jerked him upright unforgivingly. It was the last thing he remembered.

He awoke facedown in the dirt, a searing pain above his brow and between his eyes. Someone had loosened the rope from around his neck, but the sack remained over his head. His throat burned and jaw ached.

"'Tis God's will that he live. 'Tis God's will!" He recognized the chaplain's voice full of excitement. Multiple hands flipped him onto his back, and fingers worked frantically to remove his hood. Although his eyesight was blurry, he could make out the dark shapes of several heads hovering over him, gasps and mumblings about God's intervention stemming from their direction.

"It broke right through!"

"Thomas, can you hear me?" the chaplain asked.

Tom tried to clear his throat to speak but only managed a guttural sound.

"I think he's trying to say something."

Someone grasped his hand and rubbed it briskly. "Can you hear us, lad?"

He blinked, the realization that he was still alive finally striking him. In the near distance, the horse jingled its tack and snorted.

"Lift him up."

A group of hands forced him into a sitting position, causing the pain in his brow to worsen. Someone slipped the noose over his head and set it on his lap. The rope was heavy, sturdy, and in one piece. He rubbed the top of his head, which already had a nice goose egg forming on it.

"What happened?" he croaked.

The chaplain leaned over him, his face slowly coming into focus. "The gibbet snapped. 'Twasn't meant to be."

So that's what had struck his head. Three other men crouched around him, waving back the throng. One of them held up the splintered wood. Even with faulty vision, Tom could see that woodworm had eaten it through.

"God has spared you, my son."

"We should call the magistrate." The constable, still holding his pike, frowned. "Lucky fop."

<hr />

It was a short walk to the Old Bailey, but the best walk of his life. The bright blue of the cloudless sky above and the crunch of the gravel beneath his feet suddenly seemed extraordinary. Tom inhaled through his nose, taking in the sweaty stench of stabled horses mixed with the tangy odours of a nearby butchery. Nothing had ever smelled better.

With the constable's tight grip on his arm, he entered through the gate in the brick wall, occasionally wriggling his fingers and touching the sensitive flesh around his neck to ensure he was truly alive. He had survived his own hanging.

The courtroom looked nothing like it had at his trial. This time, due to the late hour, the four brass chandeliers were lit, casting dull yellow light on the heavy wooden benches and semicircular mahogany table in the centre. Except for a sprinkling of the few spectators who followed them in, the room was mostly empty.

The chaplain spoke first, his eyes round with excitement. "He should be set free! God has spoken!"

Tom stood at the bar between the chaplain and the constable, facing the judge. He was a serious-looking man, his forehead high and framed by the cascading curls of his white peruke. He scratched the side of his nose with a long finger. "And you say the victim never filed a complaint?"

"No, milord," Tom replied in a scratchy voice, the pounding in his forehead becoming more prominent with every word spoken. "He fled when . . . the crowd arrived."

"*He?* I thought the victim was a woman."

Tom took a deep breath, his throat searing from the effort. "He had attacked a woman and then I attacked him . . . well, not *attacked,* exactly. . ."

The judge stared at him sideways. "Then who filed the complaint against you?"

"A constable, I believe." Tom had been through all this before. The dark street. The woman calling out for help. A well-dressed man pointing a knife at her hip. The struggle. And then a swarm of onlookers holding him facedown on the cobbles, his nose bloodied and throbbing. Much of the attack had even been written about in the papers, although highly inaccurate. "You see . . . I was defending the woman . . . from the London Monster, and—"

"The London Monster?" the judge asked incredulously. "Did you see him? Could you identify him?"

To his right, a young clerk of sorts scribbled notes on paper. He couldn't have been more than thirteen or so, for he hadn't a sign of a single hair on his chin.

"I only know . . . that he was tall . . . and thin with light brown hair," he answered gruffly.

"Well, that narrows it down to half the men in England." The judge scrawled something on a piece of paper.

"It was . . . dark, you see."

The chaplain approached, recognizing Tom was struggling to speak. "'Twas all a misunderstanding. The crowd thought he was the one who attacked the lady. But he was coming to her aid, milord. An honourable behaviour."

"And you know this how?"

"His confession."

"It sounds as if he confessed naught."

The chaplain lowered his head. "Well, there were other sins, but . . . none of which pertain to this matter."

Tom wanted to smile, but it hurt too much.

"Indeed," the judge said, squinting his dark eyes. "I am not here to retry his case, sir. This is a highly unusual circumstance that requires careful deliberation and good judgment. A failed hanging does not guarantee freedom."

"Yet it is clear God has had a hand in this, milord." The chaplain elbowed Tom to speak.

Tom cleared his throat. "I am most grateful . . . for any consideration you might give me, milord."

"I will review the facts and then make my recommendation." The judge left the room, turning back once only to harrumph.

Tom sat on a wobbly stool for the rest of the afternoon, awaiting word of his fate. He could be hanged again, transported to America, or set free. He hoped for the latter of the three possibilities, considering death and indentured servitude didn't seem particularly appealing. Not that his brothers would mind. Either result would keep him out of their lives, rendering him incapable of further soiling their good family name. It would break his father's heart, though. He always took the news of Tom's unfortunate 'misadventures' personally, as if it were Tom's intention all along to destroy his father's efforts to gain the respect of those who never had to engage in the 'dirty' business of commerce in order to feed their families.

The young clerk sat quietly against the wall, occasionally shooting Tom a quick smile. Of compassion or amusement, he couldn't tell. Nevertheless, it was unsettling.

Just before dusk, the judge returned, his brow furrowed and the corners of his mouth caked with breadcrumbs. Tom's stomach growled, reminding him of his hunger.

The judge readjusted his periwig with a quick tug over his forehead. "Thomas Hayes, I am recommending you be set free."

"Bless you, milord! Bless you." The chaplain nodded, his hands pressed together in prayer. "God will remember—"

"Quiet, please." The judge held up one bony finger that wagged in Tom's direction. "You are not absolved of the offense, however. Before your release, you will be branded, so as to mark you for your crime."

Tom imagined what his brothers would say about him being forever marked as a criminal. Perhaps a hanging might be better after all.

———————◆————◄◦►————►———

He walked the first three miles out of London, then caught a ride on the back of a cabbage cart the rest of the way home. His palm ached intensely, a clear

M branded into his skin. The sharp tang of his burnt flesh still clouded his senses. The wound was raw and red, and although he knew it would eventually turn pale, at the moment it screamed of his crime of attempted murder.

He had been given a second chance and was determined now more than ever to rid the streets of London of the vermin who preyed upon women too weak to fight back. Especially the man who'd sent him to his death. The London Monster. His brothers and father wouldn't like it, but it was who he was. Who he was meant to be.

He thanked the cabbage farmer for the ride, then skirted around the wall to the side of his home and over to the servants' entrance. If his brothers were to see him, his disheveled state was sure to elicit questions.

He blew on the fleshy pad at the base of his thumb to cool the burn, but it only made it worse, as if he were blowing on hot embers to restart a flame.

He eased open the servants' door and surveyed the entrance. Crates filled with vegetables sat stacked along the wall, partially obstructing his view to the kitchens. He stepped inside, carefully closing the door behind him. Cook stood at the far end near the hearth, her ample bottom blocking whatever she was preparing. Tom inhaled the delicious mix of aromas of yeasty bread and roasting mutton. He tiptoed over to the long wooden table where three covered baskets sat and reached his good hand inside, his fingers pressing into the soft freshly baked bread.

"There you are!" Henry, his oldest brother, appeared from nowhere, his hands on his hips and his mouth in full scowl. "Good God! You reek of rotten cabbage! But I imagine with a bloody nose, you cannot smell yourself. Where have you been?"

Tom shoved a good bit of bread into his mouth, ignored Henry's question, then made for the stairs.

Henry grabbed his coat sleeve and pulled him back. "No, you don't! You go missing for weeks and expect my question to go unanswered?"

Henry took a step back and waved his hand before his nose. He scanned Tom's clothing and general appearance with disapproval. "My guess is you've either been deep in your cups at a brothel or sleeping in an alley full of rubbish. Which is it?"

Tom swallowed his bread with a bit of effort, his throat still sore but much improved since the hanging. It was the best thing he'd ever eaten. Bread. Who would've thought? He grabbed another roll and began climbing the stairs. "I'll take the brothel. Now if you'll excuse me, I'd like to wash up."

Henry called after him. "I hope no one saw you like this. Why must you insist on embarrassing our family with such behaviour? This has got to stop, Thomas."

Tom paused on the stairs. A mere hundred or so spectators were in attendance, none of whom seemed familiar, but Henry needn't know that. "No one saw anything, Henry."

"That is what you said when you punched Bolingbrook's son at their estate, and we were never invited back. Father has not forgot about that, and neither have I."

"Well, he deserved it," he said, continuing up the stairs. Why Henry had to bring up something that had happened half a dozen years ago was beyond Tom. But that was what he and Roger always did—remind him of all the scuffles he had ever been in, only a few of which were his fault.

"Look who decided to return for supper." Roger, three years older and two feet wider, blocked the entire stairway with his girth, making Tom's escape impossible. "Days of whoring made you hungry, lad?"

The truth was, Tom occasionally spent time at Parker's Place, a bawdy house just outside of London proper, but not necessarily for the delights in the upper rooms. It was the only place he could find a respite away from his brothers' constant intrusions and criticism. Not to mention a good, friendly fight with the bullyboy and a decent tot of brandy. The conversation was also much lighter, the women happy to have someone more interested in their thoughts than what was hidden beneath their skirts.

He didn't bother explaining the events of the past week. They wouldn't believe him anyway. At least, not about his innocence in the circumstances.

Roger continued down the stairs, forcing Tom back to the bottom. "Your behaviour is reprehensible, Tom. If you insist on whoring, you should take your pleasure in more reputable establishments. Not ones that leave you stinking like the Thames in high summer."

Tom speared him with his eyes and nudged him away with the back of his hand. "I will remember that next time. Thank you for your counsel, Roger. Now step aside."

"Wait." Roger's gaze fell to Tom's palm. He grabbed his wrist, sending scorching pain to the little red M. "What is this?"

Tom yanked his hand away, but it was too late. Both Roger and Henry saw it.

Henry stepped closer, his face suddenly void of colour. "Good God, lad. What have you done now?"

7

Chapter 2

Sophie hurried home to change her clothes before Mother returned from visiting Aunt Lydia on Bridge Street. It was just after noon, so the servants would be dining belowstairs, but just in case, she peeked through a side window to check. All of them were seated around a long table, heads bowed and hands clasped in prayer. Perfect!

She entered through the front door and quietly climbed the stairs to her chambers. Quickly, she peeled off her coat, waistcoat, and breeches, folding them in such a way that they could be easily hidden in the bottom of her stored portmanteau. She slipped her shift over her head, then stepped into her petticoats and skirt. Putting on her corset would've proven impossible without help, so she avoided it altogether, hoping no one would notice the missing garment under her bodice.

She sat in front of her dressing table and removed the black ribbon from her hair, allowing her brown tresses to flow freely over her shoulders. She studied herself in the mirror and smiled, satisfied she'd done a good job of looking like a perfectly respectable woman. After one last look at the accused's name written in the notes she'd taken at the Old Bailey, she tucked the paper into her journal, then shoved it between her bedstead and mattress. She had to find Thomas Hayes soon before word got out that he had actually seen the real London Monster. It would only send a myriad of journalists after him and rob her of a great story.

"I thought I heard you up here," Peg said. Sophie's maid entered the room, grabbed the hairbrush, and gestured at Sophie's hair. "May I?"

Sophie smiled. "I thought you were below with the others."

"I was, but I saw you on the lawn and thought it might be a good idea to see if you needed my assistance."

"Did anyone else see me?"

Peg dragged the brush through her hair. "Not that I am aware. But you should really take more care in how you traipse about the property. It is only a matter of time before someone discovers what you're up to."

"You would never tell, would you?"

"I might not have to, my dear. Your carelessness will expose your secrets."

The last thing Sophie wanted was to be discovered by her mother, or anyone else for that matter. If she couldn't disguise herself, how would she complete her investigations? "You wouldn't believe what I witnessed today."

"I can only imagine." Peg set down the brush and gave Sophie that familiar look of doubt, her head tilted to the left, her mouth gathered to one side.

"A man was to be hanged today for attempted murder, but the gibbet snapped, and he fell to the ground. The judge released him."

"That is extraordinary."

"But that is not what is important."

"I imagine it is to *him!*" Peg laughed.

"Of course, of course." Sophie remembered the man's bloodied nose, already turning purple from the fall. Although he was worse for wear, he stood tall and somewhat unaffected by the miracle that had saved his life. "What I mean is, he claimed to have seen the London Monster."

Peg gasped, her hand covering her mouth.

"I was hoping to interview him upon his release, but the judge had him taken away to be branded before I could get to him."

"Branded?" The corners of Peg's mouth turned down in distaste.

"Oh, you know. His thumb." She tapped the fleshy pad on her palm to indicate the location. "I spoke to the constable afterward about the incident. He said a woman was attacked on Dean Street by a man with a knife. He said horrid things to her, apparently, before he stabbed her in the hip with his blade."

"Oh dear! And this man saw it happen?"

Sophie nodded once. "He tried to stop it, but a mob approached and mistook him for the assailant. The villain managed to escape in the confusion, and the poor man was arrested."

"That is *his* story, I imagine."

"What are you saying?"

"Perhaps *he* is the London Monster."

He could be, she supposed. No one came forward saying they'd seen anyone fleeing from the scene. But she'd watched the man's eyes as he spoke to the judge, and he never averted his gaze as liars often did. Lips could lie, but eyes never did.

"I'm worried about you, dear. This monster is on the loose! You simply cannot go about the streets alone. You could be his next victim!"

Sophie had considered that, but she never left her home unescorted—unless she was dressed as a man.

Peg reached into Sophie's wardrobe. "They say he attacks only beautiful women."

"So I've heard."

"Imagine what he would do to a beautiful woman not wearing a corset." Peg snatched the omitted garment off the bed, then untied Sophie's bodice.

"You noticed?"

"A blind man would notice, my dear."

Two days later, Sophie hired a hackney to take her to Parker's Place. She pulled her brown wool cocked hat low on her forehead, careful to remain hidden from her fellow travelers. She had one task to complete before she went in search of Thomas Hayes.

The hackney dropped her off at the coach stand a street north of the bawdy house where she had befriended a prostitute named Maeve. She was likely in her early to mid twenties but wore lines of experience and hardship around her eyes that made her seem older. The first time they met was outside of a theatre in the West End when Sophie, dressed as a man, hid behind a staircase, drawing rough sketches of the women who paraded out front, offering their bodies for a few shillings. Maeve had approached her from behind, her fingers grazing Sophie's neck above her collar.

"Smooth." Maeve's finger traced the outline of Sophie's ear. "You're too young to be out here shopping for love. A lad of twelve? Thirteen, are you?"

Sophie froze, afraid to turn around and be discovered as a woman. She clutched her journal to her chest and cleared her voice, hoping to sound masculine. "I'm waiting for my master."

"Is that so?" Maeve asked, her hand now pulling the book from Sophie's grip. "Then what is this?"

Maeve held it open in front of her, scanning the drawing. It was of two women flanking a gentleman, his face caught in mid sneer, his eyes ogling the brunette's breasts.

"Are you spying on that man? Perhaps for his wife? Or do you plan to use it in other ways? Offer it in exchange for a bit of his sterling, will you?" She dangled the journal in front of Sophie's face, wiggling it between her two fingers.

Sophie grabbed it from her. "Neither. I'm simply practicing my craft."

"You're an artist?"

"Not exactly. I'm a writer," Sophie said confidently.

"Ahh. One of those hack writers from Grub Street, I imagine."

"No. A *real* writer." She rubbed a smudge of charcoal from the side of her finger. "I write and illustrate."

"You've selected a strange hour to do it. Would it not be easier in the daylight?"

"Well, I—"

"Don't bother. The truth is far from your lips." Maeve reached inside her bodice to readjust her breasts, pulling them higher over her gown's neckline. "Not a soul here knows what the truth is. We all speak the same language—flattery and deceit."

"Why?" Sophie asked.

"Why what?"

"Why do you do it? If you know there's insincerity in every word, why go along with it?"

Maeve shrugged one shoulder, primping the lace at her neckline, then twirled a lock of blond hair around her finger. "'Tis what I do."

"The money. Of course," Sophie offered.

Maeve smiled.

"But is there nothing else that comes of it?"

Maeve tilted her head to the side, considering the question. "I used to believe there was, but now . . . I know better."

Sophie sensed a story hidden in that statement. Perhaps even a publishable one. After a bit of prodding, Maeve agreed to talk. That was a week ago, and now Sophie was on her way to their first meeting.

Sophie entered Parker's Place, her hat pulled low over her brow. She felt for her purse under her waistcoat, her insides trembling with fear that she would be exposed as a woman—or worse, recognized.

Naturally, she had never been to a brothel before, so she wasn't quite sure of what to expect. The room was dark with no natural light entering the heavily curtained windows. The only light came from one large brass chandelier that hung in the centre of the room, its drip collars overflowing with wax. Red and gold velvet chairs were strewn about in no particular arrangement. The single outstanding feature was the staircase. Intricately carved cherubs and flowered vines decorated the bannister's dark wood.

A fiddler seated in the corner played a sultry tune, his head bowed and eyes closed as he ran the bow back and forth across the strings. The smells of alcohol and tobacco were only overpowered by the strong perfume worn by various ladies floating between men.

Sophie tugged on her waistcoat as she searched the room for Maeve. A large man wearing a roughly made shirt and breeches approached her, rubbing his forehead. He pointed his finger at the door. "Out you go, lad. Don't want trouble with the constables."

He grabbed Sophie's arm and practically lifted her off her feet as he shoved her towards the door.

"I'm here to meet someone," she said to him over her shoulder.

"I'm sure you are. Now get—"

"Stop! He's here for me, Connor." Maeve stood at the bottom of the staircase in only her petticoats and stays. Her blond tresses glowed under the chandelier's candlelight.

"For *you*?" He stared at Sophie questioningly. "He still suckles his mother's teat, this one."

"That shows how much you know. He's a solicitor, and if you don't let go of him, you'll soon need one yourself." Maeve winked at Connor as she gently removed his hand from Sophie's arm, then turned to Sophie. "Come now, Mr. Evans. We don't *all* mistreat our guests."

Sophie had never told Maeve her name—or any name for that matter—but she liked the sound of Evans. Sophie straightened her clothing. "Thank you for saving me from that brute."

"He's not that bad. At least he wouldn't harm you. He'd rather practice a few punches on men who are more his size."

"Good to know." Sophie couldn't imagine there being many men as large as he was. "Why did you tell him I was a solicitor?"

Maeve grinned, threading her arm through Sophie's to guide her to a set of chairs by the staircase. "Because a writer would never be able to afford my services."

"Maeve." A shapely older woman wearing an emerald gown trimmed in black lace approached, a closed fan in one hand and a glass of amber liquid in the other. "I thought your gentleman could use a drink. Only four pence." She held it out for Sophie to take, the light from the chandelier further illuminating the golden colour.

"No, thank you."

The woman raised her brow. "Perhaps Maeve should explain our policies here."

Maeve ran her hand down Sophie's arm. "Two drinks first, then we go upstairs."

Sophie's stomach turned. She hadn't thought that far ahead. Did Maeve really expect her to partake in . . . to go upstairs and . . .?

"Very well." Sophie's hand shook as she extracted the coins from her purse and dropped them in the woman's open palm.

The woman handed her the drink and slipped the coins inside her bodice. "You are fortunate to make acquaintance with Maeve. She's one of our finest. She can make all your dreams come true for a mere . . . two guineas."

Two guineas? That was a fortune! Sophie wasn't sure she'd brought that much money with her. But before she could protest, a prostitute across the room waving a white feather in their direction called out, "Mother Wharton! Come meet Lord Poltimore! He says he recently inherited an estate in the West End. Is that not lovely?"

The prostitute pressed the man into a chair and planted herself in his lap.

After Mother Wharton left, Sophie leaned in close to Maeve. "I am uncertain as to whether or not I have the currency you require. I hadn't considered we would actually . . . do anything."

"You're a peculiar fellow." Maeve looked at her sideways and laughed. "Not to worry. For a guinea, we can go upstairs and talk. Just as you said. But we can't let Mother know."

Panic left Sophie's body in a sudden burst. She stood, allowing Maeve to lead the way. When they reached the top of the stairs, Maeve turned to face her.

"However, before I tell you my story, *Mr. Evans* . . ." Maeve tipped up Sophie's chin with her forefinger. "You will tell me why you are dressed like a man."

Sophie thought about their conversation the whole ride home. She couldn't help but giggle every time Maeve stopped talking to moan amorously or bounce on the bed. Sophie had never been with a man before, but judging from the amount of noise Maeve made, it seemed a bit of a boisterous venture.

When she wasn't cooing loudly and making the bedstead squeak, Maeve had spoken freely about the man—a promising customer she thought might become her keeper—who abandoned her when he discovered she was three months pregnant with their child. He was a viscount from Hampshire and had no intention of leaving his wife and fortune for a harlot and her bastard. Maeve had the baby five months later, a sickly daughter who cried at all times of the day and night until neither Maeve nor Mother Wharton could take it any longer. They sent Emily to a family who lived a day's ride away to be cared for until Maeve had enough money to leave the brothel and support the baby's medical treatments. She thought she might rent a room some place where she could work as a washerwoman or baker's assistant. One of Parker's other girls had left two years earlier to help in an inn where she was given a clean room and food to eat in exchange for serving and cleaning up after their guests. It didn't sound like much of a life to Sophie, but to Maeve, it seemed to offer endless opportunity.

She'd told her story without emotion, insisting it was all in the past. Her child was three years old already, and the father didn't even know that he'd had a daughter. Sophie couldn't imagine all that sadness at one time. Losing a lover, having a child alone, giving up that child. All dashing her hopes of escape from a life of sin.

Sophie couldn't wait to get through the door and record all that she'd learned. Upon Maeve's insistence, she hadn't brought her journal and was forced to memorize all she'd been told. She didn't want to forget anything, so she started repeating phrases in her head from memory. *Left Ireland before she could speak. Father died of consumption less than three months later. Mother died shortly thereafter. Sent to live with relatives where she learned to read from the Bible. No food. Sent to London to work in a milliner's shop. Seduced by the owner. Sent to Parker's Place.*

It seemed as if Maeve had been *sent* everywhere. Even at the bawdy house, she was *sent* upstairs to do unspeakable things with men she didn't know.

Sophie circled around her home and peeked through the window to the parlour. Her mother and fiancé, Bertie, sat across from one another sipping from teacups. She ducked below the window ledge, her palms flush against the cold stone. How would she get upstairs and change without being seen?

She hurried to the back of the house and peered through each of the windows until she spotted Peg carrying a tray to the kitchens. She waved her arms, careful not to attract the attention of Clarice, one of the kitchen maids. After a few moments, Peg turned in her direction, a look of tempered panic on her face. Sophie motioned her outside, then pressed herself against the wall.

Peg appeared, her hand covering her heart. "You gave me a fright, you did!"

"I need to get upstairs and change into my gown. Will you help me? Mother and Mr. Needham are in the parlour."

"I am sure to burn in hell for this."

"Then I will be right there with you." Sophie grabbed Peg's shaking hands. "Please, Peg."

Peg sighed, then disappeared inside to undoubtedly create a diversion. Sophie's heart pounded wildly. How would she explain herself if she were caught? Her mother would faint at the mere sight of her in men's clothing, and her fiancé would have her committed to Bedlam Hospital for the insane.

After what seemed like an eternity but was probably only a few minutes, Peg reappeared, rushing Sophie up the stairs and into her bedchamber. She quickly peeled off her clothes and put on her gown, Peg ensuring that not a hair on Sophie's head was out of place before they went downstairs.

Her mother stood as Sophie entered the room. "I didn't hear you come home, my dear. Mr. Needham has been waiting for over an hour."

Sophie wanted to roll her eyes at her mother's insistence on referring to Bertie as Mr. Needham after all these years, especially in the absence of servants. She wouldn't even call him by his Christian name, Cuthbert.

She forced a smile. It was becoming more difficult every day to keep up the pretense of excitement over her upcoming nuptials, of which she'd already postponed twice. It wasn't that she didn't care for Bertie. She did. But they were friends. Dear friends. Outside of that, she felt nothing for him. And from what she'd seen of her own parents' sad marriage, she thought it might be a good idea if love played some part in it.

"Bertie. So sorry to have kept you waiting. I had no idea you would pay a call today. Did you send a card?" Sophie asked, knowing full well he hadn't announced his visit beforehand.

Bertie fiddled with his hat, spinning it around in his hands while he spoke. "Forgive me, Miss Sophie. I wanted to surprise you with some good news."

"Good news?" She couldn't imagine what good news he could possibly have. He never traveled. He rarely went to parties. He didn't care much for the theatre. Perhaps a pew was named after him in the church.

"I have already discussed the matter with your mother . . . and mine, of course," he said.

"The matter?"

"My dear Aunt Belva cannot make the carriage ride to London in the winter. She is getting on in age, as you know."

"Of course."

"We do not wish to cause her any discomfort, you see." Bertie's face suddenly brightened, his hazel eyes gleaming. "So . . . we agreed to move up the date for the wedding before the weather changes. Is that not wonderful news?"

Chapter 3

Mother Wharton handed Maeve another request for payment from the Hobarts, the family caring for Emily. This time, it came with a brief list of the herbs necessary to treat her daughter for her fits. Maeve settled in the small chair in the corner of her room to read it near better light. There was milk thistle needed for a tea to help with stomach pain and encourage vomiting, sacred bitters to remove ill humours, chamomile to treat her sleep disorders, and opium to calm her after a fit.

Mother Wharton huffed with impatience, her fingers absently fiddling with the keys hanging from a gold chatelaine around her waist. "Emily is a costly child, unfortunately. I'll need to keep a bit more from you this week. After the cost of food and lodging . . ." She paused to pull a small purse from her bosom and count out four shillings. "Here."

Maeve stared at the dull silver coins in her palm. She had earned over eight pounds that week. "This can't be right. What came of the pocket watch I pinched from the architect from Hertfordshire?"

"It did not fetch what I had hoped. It kept very poor time." Mother Wharton replaced her purse back inside her bodice.

"How am I to—"

"Care for your bastard?" Mother Wharton asked. "I told you what to do when you discovered your condition. You chose not to listen. So if you're complaining about your earnings, I suggest you reconsider, or you'll find yourself a bunter in Charing Cross offering threepenny uprights."

A wave of nausea crept into Maeve's throat. She would never have done to her unborn child what Mother had suggested. Never. Emily was the only beautiful thing in her life. It was hard enough placing her in someone else's care.

"Have you something further to say?" Mother Wharton asked, her eyes daring Maeve to speak.

Maeve shook her head.

"Then fix your hair and go downstairs. There's work to be done." Mother spun out of the room, leaving a strong trail of her perfume behind.

Maeve closed her eyes and took a deep breath. At this rate, she was never going to have enough money to pay off her debt and leave Parker's to raise Emily somewhere safe. She slid the small leather trunk of her belongings from under the bed, opened the lid and removed a tiny piece of pink and cream fabric. She'd snipped it from Emily's blanket the day she was taken away. She lifted it to her nose, smelling the sweet milky scent of her daughter that lingered in the tattered threads. She missed her baby. Her blond curls—much lighter than her own—and brown eyes flecked with green light. That innocent, trusting look when Maeve lifted her from the tiny box on the floor after a nap. The sweet way she curled against Maeve's chest and rested one small fist right over Maeve's heart, as if protecting the place where she lived while they were apart.

Maeve tucked the fabric back inside the trunk along with her coins, then sauntered down the stairs in no real hurry to get the day started. It was too early for the bulk of customers to arrive, yet a few lounged about drinking, smoking, and gawping at the girls. Two men sat in the back of the parlour, drinks in hand. Rosie, the new girl, flirted with both. Laughter from the gaming table suddenly erupted, and Maeve turned to face the group watching Prudence perform her specialty on the tabletop. On hands and knees, she offered her bare backside to each cull, allowing him to offer payment for the view by inserting a coin—no pennies, thank you—in whichever slot he chose. Maeve didn't care for that kind of whoring, but as she thought about the amount of money Prudence earned from that trick, her distaste for Prudence's antics softened. Perhaps she could come up with something inventive to attract more customers.

Just then, Connor burst through the door with one arm draped over Tommy, the boxer, whose clothing was rumpled although unsoiled, his nose bloodied and left cheek already turning from red to purple. She wished she knew his surname, but such intimate information was not always freely offered at Parker's.

"That's thrice in a matter of weeks that my nose has taken such a beating." Tommy stopped at the bar and wiped his face with a handkerchief. He sniffled twice, then tucked the cloth inside his waistcoat. "You caught me unawares, my good man."

Connor patted Tommy on the back casually. The two men stood equal in height, Connor outweighing him by a stone or two, much of which lay in his gut. Connor laughed as he circled around the bar. "Pour one for this sorry piece of meat, Paddy."

The bartender winked, then handed him a drink, his few white wisps of hair floating around his head as he moved.

Connor leaned on the bar. "Are you complainin', then?"

Tommy swallowed his drink in one shot, then plunked down his glass on the polished mahogany counter. He shook his head. "Simply warning you that one good turn deserves another."

"Ambushed once again?" Maeve moved closer, unsure what to make of their bizarre ritual of punching each other for sport. She pulled her own handkerchief from her bodice and handed it to Paddy. "Wet this for me, will you?"

Paddy poured water from a porcelain pitcher over the cloth, then handed it back to Maeve. She dabbed it along Tommy's cheek and the corners of his mouth to remove the traces of blood he left behind. "You're lucky I don't fancy the pretty type."

Tommy smiled at her crookedly, stirring her insides. "Ah, but *I* do."

She set the handkerchief on the bar, wishing he'd meant it about her. "Where have you been?"

"If I told you I was in gaol awaiting my own hanging, would you believe me?"

"Not at all," she replied. He was too good for that.

He fumbled in his coat for his purse, extracted a shilling, then snapped it on the counter for Paddy. "Three more brandies, if you will. One for this brute here and one for the lady."

"As much as I'd love one, the bawd is watchin'," Connor said, one eye on Mother as he walked away. Paddy slid the coin across the counter and into the till.

"Don't mind if I do." Maeve waited for Paddy to pour, then clinked her glass with Tommy's. Mother encouraged the girls to have a drink as long as it was purchased by a cull. The brandy warmed her throat. She wanted to know why he hadn't visited her in more than a fortnight, but she didn't dare ask. Not only because it was too bold a question for a harlot who worked in a bawdy house, but because she didn't want to know if he might be allowing another woman to entertain him in ways she never had. "Connor was only teaching you a lesson, Tommy. Most opponents won't wait for you to ready yourself before they throw the first punch."

He smiled behind his glass. "Calling me Tommy does not make me sound intimidating."

She'd called him that since the day they met. Although he'd argued against it, she thought it suited him, with his soft but rugged smile—reminiscent of a boy's but clearly a man's. Her decision to call him Tommy stuck once he told her she was the only person to use that form of his name.

He cocked an eyebrow. "Since when are you in the business of pugilism?"

"I know a little. Enough to at least offer some useful advice, so long as you go on aspiring to be Tom Johnson."

"You know about Tom Johnson? You never told me."

"You never asked." She sipped her brandy, clearly watered down at Mother's behest. "I know him personally."

"How is that?"

She was about to respond, but he held up his hand to stop her. "No need to answer. I suppose it matters little."

She knew what he thought, but it wasn't true. Although Johnson had visited Parker's on occasion to gamble and drink away his prize winnings, he rarely engaged in salacious affairs with any of the women. The last time Maeve had seen him was just after he returned from a fight in Banbury with a giant named Isaac Perrins. No one had expected Johnson to win, but he did, and the celebration lasted for days with Johnson dropping guineas for all of Parker's customers to drink enough to render themselves unconscious. It was during those days that he had explained some of his boxing maneuvers to Maeve. "He gave me quite the education on the art of bobbing and ducking, should I ever need it."

"Well, I hope you never do." Tommy rested his hand on Maeve's, and she held her breath to concentrate on its warmth. "Of course, you have Connor here to assuage any unwanted attention."

And you? Would you come to my defense? She managed to smile at Connor, who stood by the door. "I do."

Tommy leaned into her and spoke softly. "The London Monster remains on the prowl, Maeve. I hope you take care when . . . well, when you are . . . in town."

His words stabbed her heart. She merely did *that* when her customers were scarce. The lulls occurred when the men were caught by their wives and threatened within an inch of their lives if they ever frequented Parker's again. Even then, she only loitered around the theatre, which was always a hive of activity in the evenings. The monster wouldn't dare attempt an attack there. "I am not a streetwalker, Tommy."

"I didn't mean—"

"I believe you did."

He stared at her thoughtfully, pity in his blue eyes. She looked away quickly and cleared her throat to remove the lump growing there.

"Any word on Emily?" he asked, his voice lowered and sincere.

"The same. Her catalepsy remains." Maeve took a deep breath. "I wish I could see her."

"If you would only allow me to arrange it. I could escort—"

She held up her hand to stop him from going further. "Mother Wharton would never allow it. The travel would require me to stay overnight. She would never release me for two days and give up the coin."

"I could bring Emily here," he offered.

"What? She can't know her mother is a . . . is here." She glanced at Mother Wharton, who stood across the room with Rosie and her two culls, probably arranging a deal, and remembered what she'd said to her earlier about getting rid of the pregnancy. At the time, Maeve hadn't known what to think. Part of her had hoped that Albert would reconsider his opposition to her carrying his child and return to her, offering to set her up in a comfortable home somewhere close to his estate where he could visit regularly. But the other part of her realized that would not happen and she would end up alone, responsible for caring for their child on her own. A little more than three months in, Maeve had gone so far as to bring the teacup of laurel, madder, and hyssop to her lips that Mother had left for her in her room. But when the steam from the abortifacient reached her nose, she knew she couldn't go through with it.

"The matter is far too complicated, Tommy. My circumstances are what they are," she said resolutely.

Tommy nodded, clearly realizing there was nothing left that he could say.

"Maeve!" Mother Wharton called her name from the bottom of the stairs. "Your gentleman is here."

Maeve glanced at the door and her stomach clenched. It was that mean buck, Mr. Stone, who paid her well but often left her bruised from his unusual sexual appetite. She turned to Tommy. "I must go."

"Very well."

She started to leave, but he pulled her back.

"I almost forgot." Tommy reached into the back waistband of his breeches and extracted a small package. "This is for you. For always tending to my wounds."

"What is it?" she asked.

He smiled. "I thought it might help you with your French."

He remembered. She'd told him of her desire to learn French—an idea initiated by Mother Wharton—to sound more sophisticated months before, when she lost one of her better paying customers to another girl who could discuss the arts and speak three different languages. It was also a painful reminder of what Albert had said when she'd expressed her desire to be his mistress. *What? You? You are an ignorant girl. A whore. Not a mistress.*

She untied the twine and slipped off the cloth wrapping.

"A novel," she said. She squinted at the blurred words *Les Liaisons Dangereuses* written on the first page. At some point, she was going to have to purchase spectacles, not exactly a flattering look for a harlot. "Have you read it?"

"I have. A bit scandalous. Libertine in nature, if you will."

She glanced once more at Mr. Stone, now standing at the base of the staircase, his hand on the carved bannister. He half-smiled at her, one corner of his mouth curling upward sardonically. A libertine if she'd ever known one.

She rubbed her wrist, knowing that in a matter of minutes, this cull would once again tie the binds too tight, causing her hands to swell in pain.

He tapped the book twice with his finger. "I slipped a little something for you inside. Do not open it until you are alone."

She knew what it was. A few coins to hide from Mother Wharton, bringing her a little closer to getting out of Parker's. "Thank you, Tommy."

She swallowed hard, then joined Mr. Stone, his hand firmly on the small of her back as they climbed the stairs.

Chapter 4

Cuthbert entered the florist shop on Dover Street in search of the perfect flowers to send Sophie. She was so lovely. Hair the colour of the African coffee his father preferred to drink in winter months, skin as pale and flawless as the petals of a spring primrose, and eyes the shape and colour of a green-eyed cat's he'd once seen lounging at Queen Charlotte's feet during a party at the palace.

"Good day, sir. How may I be of assistance?" asked the clerk behind the counter. He was short in stature but had the posture and demeanor of a proud man, making him seem taller than he actually was.

Cuthbert peered at the sparse array of fresh flowers in tall wooden buckets on a long worktable behind the clerk. "Good day. I am thinking of having an arrangement sent to my betrothed. Something virginal and white, perhaps. Are these all you have?"

"Unfortunately. Fresh flowers are scarce presently, with the early arrival of the cold weather."

"Is there naught available, then?"

The clerk thought about it for a moment, pursing his lips and staring up at the ceiling. "Would you consider artificial flowers, sir?"

"Artificial?" Cuthbert asked skeptically.

"Wait here." The clerk held up his finger as if to make a point, then disappeared into the back room.

A few seconds later, he reappeared, carefully holding a long-stemmed white bloom between his fingers.

"A peony?" Cuthbert asked.

The clerk nodded. "Lovely, is it not?"

"I thought you said fresh flowers were scarce. Is that the only one you have?"

The little clerk smiled, his head tilted to the side. "You may have as many as you'd like. This beauty is artificial."

Cuthbert leaned closer to examine the bloom. It was astonishing. He reached out to touch the delicately ruffled petals cupped towards the centre in layers upon layers. "This is truly remarkable."

"Thank you, sir."

"Did *you* make this?"

The clerk nodded with pride.

"What is your name?" Cuthbert asked.

"Rhynwick Williams, sir."

"Well, Mr. Williams, can you create an arrangement ready for delivery by tomorrow?"

"Of course, sir." The clerk dipped his quill in the inkwell and scribbled all the necessary details into a ledger—Sophie's place of residence and the number, type, and colour of the flowers. They said their goodbyes, and Cuthbert left feeling more confident than ever that this would send Sophie right into his arms.

"There you are, my dear boy!" His mother welcomed him home with arms stretched wide, ready for an embrace. Her lemon-yellow gown stood in bright contrast to the walls of their pale rose parlour.

Cuthbert peered out the front window, watching Lord Greenville's carriage pull into the street, one footman stopping pedestrians while it lumbered into the thoroughfare. He was glad he missed the man's visit, Greenville's glares full of judgement and mock sympathy always directed at Cuthbert.

"Have you already paid a visit to the Fletchers?" his mother asked, breaking him away from his thoughts.

He hugged her briefly, then reached for a teacake from the silver platter on the sideboard. "I plan on paying a call this afternoon." He popped the tiny pastry into his mouth. Dalton Fletcher had been his closest friend since they were introduced over a gaming table at White's four years earlier.

"Do tell Vivian that I *adore* the sketch of the park she sent me," she said far too dramatically to be considered truthful. Cuthbert had seen the drawing sitting on her dresser beneath a book of poetry only yesterday, where it had resided for the last three weeks.

"Of course, Mother." He bowed slightly to acknowledge her request, knowing full well he probably would not see Vivian at all. She often stayed upstairs in her rooms, far from visitors, allowing him and her husband, Dalton, to carry on freely in the parlour. In the five years Vivian and Dalton had been married, Cuthbert had only seen her a handful of times. Dalton seemed to prefer it that way as well. Cuthbert felt sorry for them. They didn't seem to have the same sort of friendship and adoration he and Sophie had for one another.

He slipped another teacake into his mouth and chewed, imagining all the visitors the two of them would greet as a married couple in only a matter of months.

"You are smiling, Bertie." His mother had started calling him that after Sophie'd said it. They were children when she'd declared that his name. But he didn't want anyone else to call him Bertie. Only Sophie. Of course, he never had the heart to admit that to his mother.

"Am I?" he asked.

"What is it that has you so . . . lighthearted?"

"If you must know, I found a wonderful flower shop on Dover Street that makes arrangements using artificial flowers."

"And *that* is what is making you smile?"

"That and the fact that I ordered one of those lovely arrangements for Sophie. It should arrive tomorrow." Before she could inquire about the cost, he added, "It was quite reasonable, actually. And it will last for months."

With a nervous smile, Mother sat in her favourite chair by the hearth, then motioned for him to follow suit. "Has she warmed at all?"

Cuthbert sat across from her. This conversation always made him uneasy. It would start with far too many questions regarding his efforts to gain her affection, then change into reminders as to how important it was that he marry her. He had to combine the families' fortunes before they realized his family's was not quite what everyone thought it to be.

"She loves me, Mother." Although theirs was an arranged marriage, he felt fortunate that there was fondness between them.

"Naturally, my dear. Any woman would be lucky to have your attention." She patted his hand lightly. "You mustn't fret about her lack of affection."

"Mother!"

"I am only mentioning it because it pains me to see you so . . . unsettled when you are with her. Just remember, a man needs certain comforts that he should only take from his wife. But of course, you know that."

"This is indeed a most uncomfortable conversation to be having with my mother."

"If you cannot have it with your mother, then with whom can you possibly have it?" she asked, leaning back and folding her hands in her lap.

"I could think of at least a dozen other people," he muttered to himself. He was certain his face was flushed. How did his mother always manage to touch on the most sensitive subjects with him? It was as if she could read his mind.

He steadied his breathing to slow his heart and remove the heat that had found its way into his neck and cheeks. The truth was that he wanted more from Sophie and had often made small attempts to show her his desire, but they always ended horribly—either with her mocking him for kissing her hand a bit longer than necessary or chastising him for placing his hand too high or too low on her waist. Since that first and only innocent kiss when she was nine and he twelve, his lips had never again come within two inches of her mouth. That was eleven years ago.

If she would only let him touch her, hold her, love her. He knew it was wrong to desire her in that way, but all good sense left him when she was nearby. "We will be married in due time."

Mother tilted her head up to the heavens and closed her eyes. "November."

Bertie managed a smile. "November."

"You would never take comfort in other women, Bertie," Mother asserted confidently.

"Of course not, Mother." If only that were the truth.

When Cuthbert's carriage arrived at the Fletcher estate that afternoon, he couldn't help but feel a bit agitated. Why did he always let his mother's comments get to him so? He already felt horrible about having sex with the whores of Covent Garden and didn't need his mother's reminders about Sophie's lack of affection to compound his misery. It was hard enough being engaged to the most beautiful woman in all of England, knowing she did not share the same desires as he.

Cuthbert sat in the carriage while his footman announced his arrival. After only a few minutes, Dalton appeared, wearing a smart maroon waistcoat and jacket over fawn-coloured breeches. He entered the carriage, removed his hat, and tossed a small book in Cuthbert's lap.

"Open it." Dalton tapped the roof with his cane. The carriage eased ahead, then exited his drive to enter the main thoroughfare.

Cuthbert flipped open the worn leather cover. Instead of a title, a lewd drawing of a naked woman on her knees giving a man pleasure with her mouth covered the page. Cuthbert snapped the book shut. "Really, Dalton. Does Vivian know you have this?"

Dalton snatched the book from Cuthbert. "Of course not. It is not her business to know my business."

Cuthbert looked out the window. It was a Friday, and although the weather was quite cold, it hadn't prevented many from venturing out, for Oxford Street was bustling with people headed this way and that. The carriage eventually turned and made its way to St. James's Street, where their gentleman's club, White's, stood wedged between a haberdashery and a stately home.

They exited the carriage and adjusted their coats and cravats. Appearance was everything at White's. A missing button on one's clothing could result in scandalous talk for months.

"Do not look so glum, Cuthbert. You do not wish to have your membership revoked due to your rather dreary disposition, do you?" Dalton slipped the vulgar book inside his coat.

"You should have left that in the carriage," he whispered, glancing left and right. They walked up the short set of stairs to the entrance. "Should someone see it—"

"I would be hailed as the hero of today's entertainment." Dalton squeezed Cuthbert's shoulder. "Relax, my friend. Your uptight nature is beginning to bore me."

They selected a table in the back corner of the gaming room and ordered a bottle of claret. Smoke hung in the air just above their heads, where the smells of tobacco and roasting meat mingled delightfully. With the grey skies blocking the sun, the wall sconces had been lit to join the hearth as the dull sources of light in the room. The only other person there was Lord Greenville, a friend of Cuthbert's parents who was a regular at the club, his pinkies pointing outward as he sliced the pheasant on his plate. Although he was dressed plainly in a blue greatcoat that showed wear at the cuffs—one Cuthbert had seen him in on many occasions—he was otherwise impeccably coiffed with the curls on his periwig turned to perfection. He smiled politely at Cuthbert as they sat.

"The wine will loosen you up." Dalton poured them each a glass. "*Santé.*"

Cuthbert sipped from his glass, allowing the gentle warmth of the wine to linger in his mouth before swallowing it. He exhaled, desperately wanting his angst to dissolve with each taste. "The wedding date has been moved up."

Dalton laughed. "So *that* is what has you so bothered! You *do* know you can continue seeking outside pleasures after your nuptials."

Greenville's brow raised, his fork stalled at his lips. The last thing Cuthbert wanted was for this proper gentleman to know about such private matters. Might he divulge them to his parents? He was the authority on decorum, the judge and jury on all matters of decency, and a constant reminder to Cuthbert that he was neither decorous nor decent.

Cuthbert set down his glass and leaned in to whisper. "Please do not mention such things. Especially not here."

Dalton smiled at him mockingly, glancing briefly in Greenville's direction.

Cuthbert lightly cleared his throat. "For your information, I am delighted about our new wedding date."

"Of course you are." Dalton sipped his wine. "Well, I hope Sophie is more adventurous in the *boudoir* than Vivian."

How could a man talk about his own wife in such a manner? Poor Vivian. "I would prefer you not wonder about my fiancée's preferences with regard to intimacy, if you don't mind."

"I meant no offense, Cuthbert. It was merely commentary about my own sad state of affairs." Dalton gazed into his wine. "The truth is, I would probably continue my behaviour even if Vivian were less . . . prudish. I am a rogue at heart, I suppose."

Cuthbert had known Dalton for years and didn't doubt he would continue his dalliances with other women even if Vivian were . . . well, if Dalton were more satisfied as a husband. She was a plain girl, somewhat mousy with fair hair that didn't do much for her sallow complexion. But she was kind and genteel and appeared to manage their household quite well. But none of that seemed to matter to Dalton. He was more interested in those who were unruly and daring, two attributes Vivian would never have.

Every time he and Dalton were together, much of their talk centred around the fairer sex. Dalton had told him stories about acts he'd participated in with various women, acts that seemed improbable but were undoubtedly true, and although Cuthbert found these tales remarkably entertaining at times, he always seemed to feel soiled when they parted company. They reminded him of his own past and present indiscretions, none of which he was proud. And all of which should remain private. In his own guilt, he often asked Dalton questions he had wondered about himself. *Are you not afraid of disease? Are you not worried that you might be discovered?* But Dalton would typically shrug in response, leaving Cuthbert confused and even more despondent.

"Cuthbert. Did you hear me?" Dalton thrummed his fingers on the table impatiently.

"What's that?"

"I said, I heard women are now wearing leather coverings over the back of their petticoats for protection."

"Protection?"

Dalton held up both hands and wiggled his fingers. "From the beast. The London Monster."

"Ah, yes."

"And the coppersmith on Fleet Street said he's had over a dozen orders for copper cuirasses. He is refashioning them to fit over a woman's bottom."

Cuthbert wondered if Sophie felt the need for protection.

Dalton poured the last of the wine into both of their glasses. "Women shouldn't be out at night anyway. Looking for trouble, if you ask me."

That was true. The dark was no place for a woman. "Perhaps I should acquire one of those for Sophie."

"Perhaps. But I will not need one for Vivian."

"And why is that?"

Dalton lifted his glass. "The monster only attacks beauties."

Chapter 5

It had been more than a fortnight since Tom had been released from Newgate, yet the scar at the base of his thumb remained as inflamed and red as it had the day he was branded. His father had taken the confession about his imprisonment and near hanging poorly and accused him, red-faced, of deliberately trying to sabotage his campaign to win a seat in the House of Commons. It was all he ever talked about. Since then, Tom had felt the strain in their relationship like that noose around his neck. The only saving grace was that news of his botched hanging hadn't made the papers.

His father sat at his desk in his study, his business ledger opened before him. Tom stood quietly, watching him carefully enter numbers down the column of one page before he cleared his throat to interrupt his concentration.

Father spoke without looking up. "Be seated, Thomas."

Tom took the seat across from him, farthest from the hearth so as not to block the heat.

"I need you and Roger to help Henry with the incoming shipments while I am attending the opening of the Oxford Canal on January first."

"Of course." Tom's heart sank for Henry. Father didn't trust him with anything beyond entering numbers into ledgers and totaling them up. He felt he was too weak, too timid to do more than that.

"My presence is required there." Father set his quill on the brass stand next to the inkwell, then leaned back in his chair. "You understand the importance of this. Do you not?"

It was likely a rhetorical question, considering Tom and his brothers had been listening to Father explain the canal's importance and its impact on their profits for years. The connection was simple. Their investment in steam engines earned them enough capital to initiate a great financial interest in coal mining and shipping. Consequently, they'd made a large investment in a colliery in Northern England, where the yield had far exceeded their expectations, but couldn't be shipped out quickly enough to meet the demand in London. But now, because the Oxford Canal linked the River Thames with the Coventry Canal, that coal would reach London at a faster rate than before. "Our cost to transport coal to London will decrease due to the shorter route from the Midlands and Oxford."

Father furrowed his brow. "Is that really what you think I am asking you?"

Tom interlaced his fingers in his lap. "Sir?"

He settled both hands flat on his desk. "Pitt will be there."

Tom knew that his father had been trying to gain the ear of William Pitt, the Prime Minister, for almost a year, but hadn't had much fortune in earning an introduction. "That will be wonderful, Father."

"As it turns out, Pitt happens to be a childhood friend of Viscount Sidmouth."

The viscount, Henry Addington, was the new Speaker of the House of Commons. "So you are hoping the Prime Minister will introduce you to Viscount Sidmouth."

"Exactly. And then I can do my best to earn his support for a seat." A smile crept up on Father's face. It was a rare occurrence, one Tom hadn't witnessed since he'd returned from Newgate. "I am working very hard to secure this position, so what I need is your word that you will stay away from trouble until the elections in June. Do you think you can manage that?"

That would mean he would have to give up his boxing matches for almost nine months. He could possibly forego a few, but he couldn't surrender all of them. Not that Father knew anything about them. It would destroy him, knowing his son participated in such an ungentlemanly sport, so it had to remain secret. Father simply wouldn't understand. What he was probably referring to was all the other mischief Tom seemed to find, mostly at night. But Tom never sought out trouble. As a matter of fact, he spent all his evenings out looking to *prevent* trouble. That's when all the cowards crept out of their hideaways searching for victims. They would pounce on the unaware, the vulnerable, the young or elderly, and the women, sure to overpower them with their might and the element of surprise.

Tom knew what it was like to feel powerless and afraid, that one's fate could be determined in a matter of seconds. Ten years earlier, he and his mother had been shopping for broadcloth at Blackwell Hall. Unable to navigate through the immense throng, their coachmen and carriage had waited a few streets away. Mother hadn't minded the short walk since it was a particularly warm day for March and a welcome reprieve from the brutal winter they'd just endured. They'd finished shortly after sundown, having had difficulty arranging for the delivery of the goods with a vendor who spoke only German. As they were leaving, two well-dressed men grabbed her from behind and dragged her into an alley. Tom had followed obediently. At first, he'd been confused as to their purpose. They wore silk vests and delicate white lace at their wrists, so they didn't look the way he'd expected thieves to look. But it was only a matter of seconds before their intent was clear.

Tom may have only been a lad of twelve, but he recognized his mother's helplessness—and his own—against the brutes who had the advantage of size and strength. He tried to fight, but none of his wild blows made a difference. He punched and flailed until he realized he was hurting himself more than he was the attackers. And then it was too late. His mother lay motionless on the ground, her fingers stripped of their rings and the emerald and diamond necklace gone from around her twisted neck.

For years after that, he'd practiced punching grain bags in one of his father's warehouses, returning home with poor excuses as to why he had bloody knuckles. When he was old enough, he'd ventured into areas of London that were typically forbidden by his father to watch huge men battle each other in underground boxing circles. Tom had held his breath as they threw exacting punches that landed deftly and perfectly, sending their opponents crashing to the ground. Although he had only been a bystander, his heart had pounded as if he'd been one of those men. If he could learn how to hold his body the right way, extend his arm just enough to hit his mark yet keep his body out of harm's way, perhaps he could be one of those men declared the victor. Then he would never feel afraid again, and if he could help it, neither would anyone else near or dear to him. He would become the defender of those who couldn't defend themselves. London could be a dangerous place, after all.

"Thomas? I need your word. Will you stay out of trouble?" Father's gaze dropped to Tom's palm, where the veritable proof lay that his concerns about Tom's behaviour were legitimate.

He stared at his father. The lines etched in the corners of his eyes were deeper than weeks earlier. Tom curled his fist over the angry little M at the base of his thumb and took a deep breath. "You have my word."

Later that day, Tom walked to one of his family's warehouses on the Thames. Although there was a chill in the air, the sun shone brightly, casting a sparkling shimmer over the ripple of waves in the river and spreading warmth across his back. Walking—as if he were a commoner—was one of the things his brothers never understood.

"Why walk when there is no need?" Henry often asked.

"Why ride when the day is so glorious?" Tom always replied.

But this time, Tom wondered if he'd made an error in judgment, for someone was surely following him. It could be one of Stone's men. Ever since he'd refused to throw any more fights, Stone's hackums would show up in places unexpectedly with unfriendly reminders about how Stone had given him everything he had.

He took the most circuitous path possible to reach the warehouse. Off Lombard, he turned down Grace Church Street. Before reaching the small hill, he dashed into an alley that cut through to Pudding Lane. There, Tom slipped into a threshold and waited. Thoughts of his conversation with his father raced through his mind. How would he explain confronting the man who was following him, especially if it resulted in a bloody nose or black eye? Holding his breath, he listened for footsteps but heard none. After a quick glimpse down the lane, he hurried into a narrow alley that took him to the Thames and over to Billingsgate Dock. With so many people milling about, he was certain he'd lost the fellow following him.

But then, out of the corner of his eye, he caught sight of the man's brown cocked hat with a red feather not thirty feet away. He ducked behind a pyramid of crates and unbuttoned his coat, allowing his shoulders more movement—should he need it.

The man slowed his step, searching left and right. Tom couldn't get a good look at his face but realized he was too small for anything more than a good scare and perhaps a lecture. Just as he passed the crates, Tom grabbed his coat by the sleeve and shoved the lad against the wall.

"Let go of me!" the boy demanded, twisting and kicking to be free.

"Tell me why you're following me." Tom pressed the boy's shoulders against the wall, knocking off his feathered hat. He had seen this boy before but couldn't remember where. "Who are you?"

He speared Tom with a mean gaze. "Release me, and I will tell you."

Confident that the lad wasn't going to run—or if he did, he could easily catch him—Tom let go of his coat. The boy angrily brushed off his sleeves and straightened his clothing. He bent to pick up his hat and frowned when he saw that it had been badly soiled by the mixture of mud and food scraps at their feet. He whacked it a few times before he gave up and set the dirty cap on his head. With eyes lowered, he spoke in a defeated tone. "I am a journalist."

"How old are you?" Tom was sure this child was no more than twelve or thirteen.

The lad squared his shoulders. "Old enough to know a good story when I see one."

There was something peculiar about this lad. He couldn't quite place it, but it was as if he was an adult in a child's body. "What business do you have with me?"

"I want to know about the London Monster."

Tom straightened. He didn't want to get caught up in the hysteria again and be accused of being this beast. "That has naught to do with me."

"But you saw him. Did you not?"

Tom was about to respond, and then the realization as to where he had seen this boy before struck him. "You were in the courthouse."

The journalist removed a small book and a piece of charcoal from his coat and nodded. "Perhaps if you describe him to me, I could draw him, and we could add his likeness to the article I write about the attack you were involved in."

"Wait a moment there. You are getting far ahead of yourself, lad." Tom turned to leave and was pulled back by his coat.

"Please, sir. I need this story." The young journalist exhaled and studied him hard. "I want to be taken seriously, and the only articles I have ever published are those involving the import of Japanese soybeans or the openings of book shops and perfumeries."

Tom felt a slight pang of pity for the lad, but he couldn't risk having his name in the papers connected to the London Monster. It would send his father over the edge.

"Not interested."

"Please, Mr. Hayes." The journalist hesitated, allowing the fact that he knew Tom's name to register as threatening. "I wish to write about people. Not things. Topics readers care about but may not discuss in polite conversation. My words need to carry meaning, not simply . . . information."

Tom stared at him. It was then that he realized this was no lad. The green eyes were shaded by lashes that were far too long, the skin too smooth. "What is your name?"

"My name? Uh, Evans," she answered.

"Is it, then?" He studied her hands as she flipped open her book and prepared to draw. Her fingers were delicate and slender with no indication they had ever done anything more than lift a teacup or spread open a fan on a hot day. "So, *Mr. Evans*, how do I know you will write the truth?"

Tom knew plenty about poorly written accounts of attacks on women. He remembered the hollowed pit in his stomach when he'd read the articles about his own mother's attack ten years ago. The papers had said more about her emerald and diamond necklace than they did about the men who'd killed her.

"I am not interested in writing twaddle, Mr. Hayes," she said, with an assertive nod.

"Which paper do you work for, exactly? The *Times*? The *Morning Herald?*"

She looked down at the pencil she held carefully poised over her book, then up at him with confidence. "I work for any paper that takes my stories."

"I see." Tom pulled a string of beige burlap that clung between her bedraggled hat and her dark brown hair, then tossed it aside. "Unfortunately, I have business to attend to, so I cannot accommodate you at present."

He bowed slightly with the tip of his hat and started to walk away.

"Does that mean you will tell me what happened? When you have the time, I mean." She snapped her book closed and scampered behind him.

He looked down over his shoulder and stifled a laugh. A female reporter. Did she really believe she was capable of writing a story about such a sordid affair? There were articles about the beast in the papers almost every day. Women all around London were being attacked by this man, and the details were not pleasant. "Meet me at the east end of St. James's Park this afternoon at three, and I will tell you what you want to know. That is, of course, if you think a *lad* your age can handle it."

"Handle it?" she asked defiantly.

"Indeed." As he walked, he buttoned his coat and straightened his cravat. "I do not wish to shock you with the particulars."

She stopped him with a tug on his arm. She offered a quick nod and a smile. "I was born and raised in London. I can assure you, nothing shocks me."

Tom entered the warehouse and waited for his eyes to adjust to the darkness. After a few minutes, the stacks of crates appeared, towering almost to the ceiling. The crates to the left were mostly the raw cotton imports from America. To the right were containers filled with pottery, tea, and fabrics woven from the imported cotton, all awaiting export to the West Indies. Tom inhaled the sharp spice from the tea and the earthiness of the cotton.

He was about to call out for his brothers when he heard mumbling stemming from the back office. He made his way through the crates and waited outside the office.

"Forty pounds eight. Another eight and three . . ." his brother, Henry, muttered behind the door. "Let's see . . ."

Tom found Henry bent over a stack of invoices, meticulously entering figures into a ledger. Henry had always been fastidious with numbers. When he'd graduated from Eton, the headmaster at the time had told Father that Henry had received the highest marks in mathematics in his class, a feat Tom tried to achieve five years later but couldn't. He was beaten by George Lancaster, an overly studious lad with large ears and no sense of humour.

Henry dipped his quill in the inkwell. "Quite good. Quite good."

Tom cleared his throat. "Sorry to disturb you, brother, but Roger mentioned a shipment arriving last night. Do you know to which warehouse it was sent?"

Henry lifted his head to face Tom, one pointed finger marking the place of his last entry. "The warehouse on Harp. Roger should be there. Tell him I will be unable to meet him this evening at Brooks's."

"Have you plans?" Tom asked, hoping Henry had finally gained the courage to call on Judith Forsythe. She was perfect for him. Quiet and polite, and she enjoyed bird watching as much as he did.

"Plans?" Henry asked innocently.

"With Miss Forsythe, perhaps?"

Henry shifted uncomfortably. "Judith? We . . . no . . . I . . ."

Tom had never felt so sorry for his brother. Henry had had feelings for her as long as Tom could remember, but he froze in her presence like a rabbit under the watchful eye of a hawk. "It would do you some good to share her company. Or any woman's company, for that matter."

"What are you saying?" Henry's mouth remained agape.

"Simply that it wouldn't hurt if you were to get your feet wet, so to speak, with any woman before attempting a closer acquaintance with Miss Forsythe." Tom winked once to get his point across.

Henry looked aghast. "That may be acceptable to you and Roger, but I have higher standards. I will not entertain the idea of spending time with whores."

"You needn't do anything, Henry. I am simply suggesting that you sit in their company and engage in playful conversation. If you do more than that, well, that would be your choice." Why was his brother such a leatherhead?

"I choose nothing of the sort," he insisted, looking elsewhere to avoid Tom's eyes.

"Then, so be it. I will let Roger know you will not be meeting him at the club." Tom slipped past him, patting his brother's chest on the way out. "I, however, *do* have plans to meet a young lady this afternoon. And a rather handsome one at that."

A Note

October 1789

The Bow Street Runners are easy to avoid. They announce themselves around the streets of London without uttering a word, for they wear bright red waistcoats and carry truncheons emblazoned with authoritative bronze crests. Only a yellow cap with a peacock feather would make their uniforms more obvious.

At times, I will follow closely behind a woman when I see one of the detectives, just to feel the rush of danger course through my veins. It starts with a rapid heartbeat and quickly finds its way to my limbs, finally settling warmly in my groin. My hand might absently stroke the falls of my breeches to tamp the desire rising within me. But never in an obvious manner. It begins with the slight sweep of my fingers, which distractedly check the bottom button of my waistcoat. My hand will then slide downward, applying just the right amount of pressure to my arousal, and it ends with a curved brush over the top of my thigh. Oh, that moment! If only it lasted longer than the mere seconds it takes for us to clear the Runner and turn the corner onto a more private street.

Contrary to what the papers say, I prefer a well-lit venue, one where the streetlamps are placed on at least every corner and perhaps midway along the path. Those lit by nightfall seem to attract women like hummingbirds to blossoms filled with sweet nectar. And where they go, I follow.

Tonight should prove promising. The countess is having a party near Whitehall to honour her daughter's sixteenth birthday. Dozens of women will

DONNA SCOTT

be there, all dressed in their finest, putting on airs and flirting behind their fans. And since the wonderful occasion will take place in Lady Georgina's home situated conveniently close to the park, many of those beauties will wish to end the evening with a stroll afterward. Imagine the possibilities!

I dress myself accordingly. Although invited, this time I will not attend the event. Instead, I sit at home and wait patiently for most of London to fall asleep before I make my late-night exit.

No one knows the anguish I go through during this time. My nerves remain unsettled, keeping me on tenterhooks until I am able to venture out into the darkness. I sip brandy—sometimes port—to allay any irrational fears that may flit through my mind. Being recognized. Getting caught. I know none of that will happen, but the mind can enter dark places when one thinks too much.

The night in front of St. Anne's Church was the closest I have been to getting caught. But that was a rare exception. My nose yet aches from the memory.

At ten of the clock, I grab my hat and take one last look in the mirror. The candlelight from the sconces catches in the silver buttons on my wool coat and delicate threading of the embroidered flowers on my waistcoat. I am cleanly shaven, and my hair is tied back with a single black ribbon. I look the perfect gentleman.

I slip out of the house unnoticed and head for the park. There is a cold wind that finds its way between buildings through the alleys and onto my cheeks. I imagine it gives me a ruddy glow, a look of liveliness that young boys and over-eager costermongers often have. I temper the excitement growing inside of me with a few deep breaths, then watch the frosty air escape from my nose in white bursts.

The streetlamps are lit, illuminating the men and women who have business out so late. Except for the few bundled in brown rags, who huddle in the crooks of buildings desperate for warmth, the majority of the people are smartly dressed in hues of green, blue, and gold. I watch them carefully from a bench at the edge of the park, searching for my prey the way one selects the ripest fruit from a tree branch. She must be perfect, unmarred, and ready to be plucked.

I wait for almost an hour until finally, I spy her walking with another woman who may be her chaperone. My beauty is young, nineteen or twenty, perhaps. Her guardian is teetering on thirty—maybe forty if the light were better—and of no interest to me. The younger one wears a rose-coloured gown with a bit of white lace peeking from her cuffs and neckline. Her waist is slender, and her breasts politely spill out of the top of her bodice, just enough to be considered modest. She laughs at something her companion says, her delicate hand covering her mouth so I am unable to see her desirous lips.

I rise from the bench and slink behind a tree until they pass, then glide stealthily into place ten paces or so behind them. The young lady clings to her companion's arm, making it impossible to keep this a private affair between her and me. I follow them for a few minutes, happy that the easterly wind is blowing the stench from the cows grazing in the park away from my sensitive nose. It is just as we are about to enter onto the street when my beauty stumbles and bends slightly to adjust her slipper—her backside facing me—providing me the perfect opportunity to whisper in her ear.

I lean into her, the desire between us palpable. "What sweet treasure lies between your thighs?"

She gasps and sweeps her hand to her breast. "Dear sir! You frightened me."

I tip my hat, realizing she hasn't heard me. Her companion draws back, startled. I am about to repeat myself, then reconsider when I detect, not twenty paces away, a man wearing a red vest and carrying a truncheon. It takes all my energy to hold back my anger from this intrusion. I bow reverently, then disappear into the darkness.

Chapter 6

Sophie settled under a willow tree at the east end of St. James's Park, waiting for Thomas Hayes. It was an unusually warm day, considering the last week had brought a chill with it and the papers had all but declared winter had come early. With her legs crossed at the ankle—in the manner any fellow would lounge—she sipped the mug of fresh milk she'd purchased for a penny from a dairymaid by Whitehall. She set her cocked hat on the grass, completely unconcerned about the appearance of her hair. It was freeing to be a man in every sense of the word. Wearing breeches and no corset, for one thing, provided easier movement, and after a while, walking about without a chaperone no longer terrified but excited her.

"Waiting long, Mr. Evans?"

Sophie startled at Mr. Hayes's voice, spilling what was left of her milk onto her hat. He stood in the sunlight, outside the shade of the willow, appearing taller than she remembered. She stood to greet him, the top of her head barely reaching the height of his shoulder. Bits of his hair appeared lighter, more chestnut than the rest, and it was the first time she realized his eyes were blue. He smiled at her, and a rush of heat entered her cheeks.

"Not long at all, Mr. Hayes," she managed to say, sure she was blushing.

"You seem to have spilled your milk. Would you like me to get you another one?" He pointed at the line of cows and dairymaids near Whitehall.

"Oh." She glanced down at the mess that used to be a fine hat. "I have had quite enough, sir."

"Very well." His smile faded and his gaze grew somber. "Before we discuss what we came here for, you must agree to one thing."

Sophie picked up her book, charcoal, and pencil from the ground. "Which is?"

"You must not use my name," he insisted. "I cannot afford to have my family's name in the papers associated with unsavory incidents."

Sophie nodded once. She didn't want to lose the opportunity of landing such a good story. "I agree."

Mr. Hayes seemed to relax with those words, his smile returning. He peered up at the sky, one hand shading his eyes. "Lovely afternoon."

In a matter of seconds, he unbuttoned his coat and waistcoat, removed both, and set them on the grass. He reclined beside his clothing, leaning back on his elbows.

She didn't know what to make of it. Did men often disrobe in public like that?

He motioned at her with his chin. "Go ahead. Get comfortable. We will not have many days left like this before winter."

She froze. She couldn't take off her coat and waistcoat. That would leave her in only a shirt. He would definitely notice her breasts then. What would he think of her? Would he consider her dressing in men's clothes as degenerate, crass, vulgar? Would he refuse to speak to a woman journalist? "I am quite fine, Mr. Hayes."

"No need for formalities. Call me Tom. Please."

"Of course. Tom." She swallowed hard, her nerves suddenly on end. She remained standing, unsure of what to do.

"Ah well, suit yourself. But are you not warm in that wool coat?" He wiggled his hand in her direction.

This could be her undoing. She didn't want him to find her behaviour odd, so with fingers she desperately tried to keep from quivering, she unbuttoned her coat. He stood suddenly and helped remove it from her shoulders. Quickly, she snatched it from him, sat down, and set it on her lap in a messy heap.

"Allow me." He reached for her coat, shook it out, folded it, then set it beside her. He leaned back again, a look of delight on his face.

Sophie crossed her arms over her chest.

"So, where shall I begin?" he asked, waiting for her to respond.

Her waistcoat pressed tightly across her breasts. She curved her shoulders inward to minimize the snugness of the fabric. "At the beginning, I suppose. Where were you the night you saw the London Monster?"

He tilted his head back and took a deep breath. "Coming home from . . . an outing. I walked to—"

41

"An outing? Where?" she asked, immediately noting his discomfort in the question.

"That is hardly important. Separate the wheat from the chaff, as it were." He placed all his weight on one arm and tugged at his cravat. "I was outside of town."

He was hiding something. She was sure of it. The truth was always in the details.

"In any case, I reached St. Anne's Church in the West End when I heard a woman scream. So, I ran in that direction only to find a man standing over her—"

"She was on the ground?" Sophie's heart started to race.

"Not exactly. She was crouched over, and he was, well . . . behind her." He stood and reached for her hand. She peered up at him, then took his hand hesitantly. His gaze fell to her chest, reminding her to throw her shoulders forward. With one hand on her back and another curled around her waist, he bent her over. "Like this."

The warmth from his hand traveled through her clothes and onto her skin. His thigh pressed against her hip, the fabric of his breeches as thin as her own. Sophie could feel the tautness of his muscles. She didn't know what to make of it, having never quite felt the way she did at the moment. It was pleasant and unpleasant all the same. No man had ever touched her so roughly, yet intimately before. Certainly not Bertie, who did little more than try to kiss her cheek when her parents weren't looking. She inhaled sharply when he tightened his grip around her waist. They stayed like that for a few seconds until he loosened his grasp.

"So, I shoved him aside, then pushed him against the wall." He let go of her abruptly and stepped back. "That is when I spotted the knife in his hand."

Sophie's throat went dry. *The knife in his hand.* Her mind flashed back to a time five years earlier when she had seen the *knife in his hand.* The circumstances were different, of course, but she remembered the young man's face—the snarl, the amusement—as he casually rested his hand on the hilt of his dagger. He'd just propositioned her. She'd spent the afternoon flirting with him at a garden party she and her parents attended just outside of London. She admitted to casting smiles and offering witty remarks during their exchanges, but she hadn't thought it would lead to this—following her outside, suggesting a quick tryst behind the shrubbery, telling her she was a tease with words that were uncompromising. He hadn't pulled his dagger, but as he spoke, he'd settled his hand on the hilt, sending a strong but silent message.

"Is there something wrong?" Tom said, pulling her out of her reverie. "You've paled."

Sophie pressed her palms to her heated cheeks, shaking herself free of the memory. "Not at all. Where were we?"

"I saw him brandish a knife."

"Of course." This must have been one of the incidents where a woman was stabbed. From what she'd read, some were only assaulted with indecent language or called dreadful names.

"I hit him a few times. Twice in the gut and once in the nose, but that is all I was able to do because a crowd tore me from him and threw me to the ground."

"And the woman?"

Tom's eyes darkened. "She had been stabbed in the hip. There was blood down her skirt and on her slipper."

Sophie's hand clasped her chest. He truly was a monster. "That is . . . horrible."

Tom settled his hands on his hips, his head tilted to the side. "Are you planning to write any of this down?"

She snatched her book and pencil from the ground, having momentarily forgotten that she needed a story, a big story, to present to the papers.

"What became of her?" She held her pencil poised above the page.

"I was told she was helped home, unable to walk on her own."

"From the injury," she asserted.

Quickly, she scribbled the basic facts about the incident he'd told her in her book. He stood quietly while she recalled the details—St. Anne's Church, the scream, the man, the knife, three punches, the blood—then assumed his earlier position of lying on the ground, his arms supporting his weight and his long legs stretched out in front of him and crossed at the ankles.

He plucked a blade of grass and stuck the end of it in the corner of his mouth. The grass danced between his lips as he spoke. "I suppose you will need this for your illustration." He offered her the charcoal she'd left on the ground.

She'd forgotten about that too. Why was she suddenly so scatterbrained?

She sat next to him and drew as he described the perpetrator. Every once in a while, she presented what she'd drawn for his approval before she continued. She had managed to get the monster's clothing and stance right as he was pressed against the wall, but his facial features turned out to be a problem. Between Tom's uncertain description and her own inability to capture whatever it was he had in his mind, she ended up drawing a dark shadow over most of the features of his face, so as not to misconstrue the facts and lead the readers and authorities in the wrong direction. In the end, however, he seemed pleased with her work.

"You are quite talented for such a young lad, Mr. Evans." He sat up, his arms resting on his knees. He peered at her through squinted eyes. "You never told me your given name."

Sophie swallowed. She had never considered one. "Did I not?"

He shook his head, smiling.

She glanced at her upturned ruined hat. Sewn on the inside was a white label that said *James Lock and Company Limited.* "It is . . . James."

His brow lifted, a look of skepticism mixed with humour on his face. "James, is it?"

She nodded resolutely.

"Should I recall anything else from that night, how shall I get in touch with you, *James?*"

His question jarred her. She couldn't tell him where she—Sophie Carlisle—lived, obviously. Flustered, she gathered her belongings and stood. Besides, she had to leave before she gave herself away and her mother returned from her weekly visit to Aunt Lydia's. With a quick handshake, she headed off. "No need to look for me," she called back to him. "I will pass by your warehouse in a few days to pay a visit. You can be sure of that."

<hr/>

Sophie finished changing her clothes just as her mother's carriage pulled into the drive. Peg chatted the entire time about something or other, but Sophie wasn't able to focus on a single word. Her entire body still tingled from the excitement of the day—finding Thomas Hayes at the docks, getting him to agree to discuss the attack, hearing the details, and clinching the story. And he'd even offered to speak with her more if she needed it.

"I bent to smell them. That was the only way I knew they were not real," Peg said, shaking her head in amazement.

Sophie snapped out of her reverie. "Smell what?"

"The flowers! Have you not been listening?" Peg waved the hairbrush at Sophie as she spoke. "Whatever you were up to today has addled your mind. You'd better get yourself together so your mother doesn't suspect anything."

She was right, but she couldn't help it. She needed to sit down and write the story that was going to be the envy of all journalists. Unfortunately, with her mother downstairs, that would have to wait.

"Forgive me, Peg. My meeting with Tom has turned me inside out, I suppose."

"Tom? Did he tell you to address him in that manner?" Peg jerked back ever so slightly. "That type of familiarity will only call your reputation into question."

"He did, but only because he thought I was a man."

Peg clasped both of Sophie's hands in her own. "You are sailing awfully close to the wind, my dear."

Perhaps she was living a bit dangerously. But she liked it.

Sophie smiled. "I promise nothing untoward has happened. And it never will."

They headed downstairs together. Peg was just about to tell her something when Father called out from his study for someone to bring him his spectacles.

"They are probably right beside him," Sophie whispered.

"Or on top of his head." Peg smiled, then scooted off. "Right away, milord!"

Sophie entered the parlour to greet her mother. On the mahogany table by the window sat the largest flower arrangement she had ever seen. Out of a tall blue vase spilled at least five dozen white peonies, each in perfect bloom.

"Are they not magnificent?" Her mother stood next to them, her hands clasped under her chin, a wide smile across her lips. "They're from Mr. Needham."

Sophie stepped closer, overwhelmed by their beauty. She bent to smell them, then remembered what Peg had said about them being artificial. She traced her fingers over the soft, white petals, completely amazed at the workmanship of each bloom. It must have taken someone months to create such lovely flowers.

"Well, I think he has outdone himself this time." Her mother's hand rested softly on Sophie's back.

Although the flowers were spectacular, Sophie couldn't seem to muster the excitement they were meant to generate. Bertie was so sweet and thoughtful. Quite possibly the kindest man she'd ever known. But somehow that wasn't enough. She simply couldn't love him the way he wanted her to. And every time she admitted that to herself, her heart grew heavier as if another tiny stone was added to the pile already lodged there.

"He certainly has," she replied sadly. He probably thought she'd be elated by the extravagant gift.

Once when she was twelve and he fifteen, he had brought her three silk ribbons in different colours for her hair. With a look of trepidation, he'd handed them to her. She'd noticed his trembling fingers and the way he hid his hands behind his back as soon as she took them. Even then, she'd felt a pang in her heart for him.

Her favourite was the blue one, a robin's egg blue that shone like a beacon in her dark hair. Every time she wore it, his eyes lit up, telling her he thought she'd done it just for him and not for the love of the colour.

"You can thank him when he gets here." Mother fussed with the mound of hair that sat atop her head.

"When he gets here?"

"Any minute. For dinner, of course." She planted her hands firmly on her hips. "What is the matter with you, Sophie? We have had these plans for weeks."

Sophie had no recollection of having been told this news, but she would never admit to that because it would only draw her mother to become suspicious. "I remember. I was simply confused as to what day it was."

Bertie, Lord and Lady Needham, and the Fletchers arrived only minutes later, barely enough time for Sophie to convince herself that she was delighted they were coming. The viscount and viscountess disappeared with Mother and Father after everyone exchanged greetings. Bertie entered beaming, clearly having spotted the large flower arrangement through the door to his right. He immediately took to the parlour to inspect his gift. Sophie excused herself from Dalton and Vivian to follow him.

"Do you like them, Sophie?" he asked in a whisper, almost as if his next breath counted on her answer.

"I love them, Bertie."

Her betrothed reached for her hands, then brought them to his lips. "I do hope so. I tried to find flowers as lovely as you are."

He kissed her fingertips, then looked down at her with such longing she could barely speak. "You are always so thoughtful, Bertie."

He would make a wonderful husband someday. Just not for her.

Chapter 7

Four days after her romp with Mr. Stone, Maeve still had purple marks on her wrists. The man was intolerable, and if he didn't pay three guineas every time for her services, she would send him to hell in a handcart.

He'd paid Mother Wharton two guineas but had thrown an extra guinea on the bed before he left. She sewed the coin in the hem of her blue gown, bringing her that much closer to living a normal life with Emily. So far, that amounted to seven pounds, eight and six.

She had to do a better job at filching valuable items from her customers. But the ornery types never seemed to drink enough to render themselves unconscious, and the mild ones rarely carried anything in their fob pockets. It was getting harder and harder to turn a profit in this business.

An impatient knock at the door startled her. "What is taking so long?" It was Prudence's voice. A man said something unintelligible, and she giggled. "My cull here is eager to get started. He's holding a quid in his palm to prove it."

Maeve knew exactly to whom she was referring. She couldn't remember his name, but he was a short, portly fellow with eyebrows that curled above his eyes like two gluttonous grey kittens. A tuft of white hair stood straight out above his ears, making him appear as if he were perpetually in a fright. He'd made a habit of paying Maeve a pound if she would watch while he had his way with Prudence. Most of the time, Maeve did as she was instructed— compliment his manhood or complain she was jealous that she wasn't the lucky girl to gain his attention. But once in a while, when he was too caught up in the moment to remember her presence in the room, she'd stare out the small window and imagine being one of the ladies who walked by on the arm of her husband, smiling as they entered one of the fine shops at the other end of the street.

"Make haste, Maeve," Prudy said, adding two light taps on the door.

Maeve took a quick look in the mirror, then opened the door. Prudy and Mr. Bushy Brows stood close together, her arm around his shoulder and his nose tucked into her décolletage.

Prudy smiled. "Here she is, lovey."

Mr. Bushy Brows withdrew his nose from between Prudy's breasts. "I imagine you are distraught seeing me with another girl."

Maeve pouted—her bottom lip turned downward and her lashes aflutter—then plucked the gold coin from his hand and tucked it into her corset. "Horribly so."

He'd been her first cull of the day and the least demanding. The second required her to chase him around the room with a feather, tickling him in all his sensitive areas as foreplay. The third was more typical, requiring no unusual antics beforehand. He simply wanted the sex, and remained quiet for the most part, moaning only when the deed was done.

She was seated downstairs when, late in the afternoon, the journalist, Sophie—or Mr. Evans as she was known at Parker's—walked in. It was Tuesday, one of the two days the girl had told her she could leave home dressed like a man without being detected. It was the day when she supposedly accompanied her maid and kitchen maid to Billingsgate or Smithfield to purchase fresh fish or meat. The other day was Friday, when the girl's mother visited her sister in Westminster.

At first, Maeve didn't understand why a girl like Sophie, a girl with everything, wanted to traipse about London looking for stories to write. She was a beautiful girl, even when wearing breeches and a coat, her dark hair pulled back and tied in men's fashion. She probably had suitors from Oxfordshire to Kent. What man would dare turn away from her beguiling smile and shocking green eyes? But in the few times she and Maeve had met, Sophie had never discussed matters involving men, except to acknowledge that she was not yet married. All they seemed to talk about was her writing and desire to be recognized by the London *Times* as an accomplished journalist. That was when her eyes lit up and her hands moved about excitedly.

Maeve had never known a girl to be so animated. It was one of the things Mother Wharton frowned upon, insisting that the men who came to Parker's were men who wished for their harlots to behave as ladies, with manners and decorum. Vulgarity was meant to be reserved for parlour tricks and those things that occurred behind closed doors.

Now, after weeks of knowing Sophie, Maeve grew to realize what the girl was searching for—the desire to be valued, appreciated, respected. That was something Maeve could understand.

"Right on time," Maeve sang, waving Sophie over to the staircase.

Sophie smiled, a glass of bourbon she would never drink in her hand. "I was hoping you had not forgot our meeting."

"It happens to be the only thing I've looked forward to all day."

With a quick wink at Mother Wharton, Maeve escorted Sophie upstairs. She locked the door and they sat on her bed, Maeve with her back against the headboard and Sophie across from her with her book on her lap and pencil in hand.

"Shall we continue where we left off?" Sophie flipped a few pages, then stopped. "You were telling me about the day you were raped by the milliner . . . a Mr. Daniels, I believe—"

Maeve jerked upright. "You cannot write that! I mean his name. He was married. And I cared for his wife deeply. She would be horrified if that were to get out."

"I would never include anything against your wishes."

"Thank you." Maeve sat back. "It is only that . . . she cared for me for over a year when no one else would."

"But I thought Mrs. Daniels was the reason you came here. She sent you away," Sophie said, her forehead pinched.

"She did. But what could she do with the husband she had? He would only do it again. And she couldn't tell *him* to leave, for how would she feed her children? She had six."

"This is exactly why it is important to tell your story, Maeve. The people of London need to know," Sophie insisted earnestly.

"The people of London? Half of them are men, many of whom are my culls. I doubt they would care about my story. And their wives would care even less." They would feel no pity for her, warm and secure in their homes, bitter about her very existence.

"But there *are* people who would care."

Maeve studied her. It must be nice to believe in the goodness of others. It was something Maeve rarely saw, if ever. Her world was filled with liars, pickpockets, and cheats.

Sophie leaned closer, her gaze directed at Maeve's bruised hands that sat folded in her lap. "What happened?"

Maeve's clutched her left wrist and shrugged. The skin that had been rubbed raw was already healing but still greenish-yellow beneath the purple splotches.

Sophie frowned. "Did Mother Wharton do that to you?"

"Mother Wharton?" She was astonished that that would even be a consideration. "She is not always pleasant, but she would never lay a hand on any of us girls."

"Was it Connor, then?"

Connor may look like a brute, and he was, but only when things got out of hand in the parlour. However, almost anything was fair game once a cull began the ascent up the stairs. Maeve shook her head. "It was a . . . chap."

"I don't understand."

"Not everyone comes here for what you would imagine. Some come with other intentions." Maeve told her about Mr. Stone. The way he'd tied her up and treated her roughly, his hips pounding into her, his eyes closed, teeth clenched.

"Why do you allow him to do it? Why not turn him away?" Sophie had a look of horror on her face.

"Turn him away?" Maeve harrumphed. "He tips me a guinea each time. How can I turn my back on that?"

"Do you hear what you are saying?" Sophie asked, incredulous.

"You don't live my life, Sophie. You don't have a daughter who needs special teas and opium for her fits. Do you know how expensive they are?" Maeve closed her eyes, picturing Emily's rosy cheeks and blond curls. "I would do anything for her."

They sat in silence. Maeve wiped away a tear from her cheek. Her guilt for who she was and what she did ate at her every moment of every day. She knew her behaviour was the reason God had burdened her daughter with her condition. Why else would He do such a thing?

Sophie slid to her side and cradled her in her arms. The lump that had lodged in Maeve's throat like a pebble suddenly softened. They sat cuddled together for the remainder of the hour until they heard the jingling of the keys Mother Wharton wore around her waist, announcing her approach.

Mother knocked quickly on the door, then offered in a voice far too sweet, "Your time has elapsed, Mr. Evans. Unless, of course, you would like to extend it."

Sophie kissed Maeve on top of her head, dropped two guineas on her washstand, and left the room.

Maeve headed for the theatre that night after her last cull left. Not to earn the extra shilling or two, but to escape the confines of her own four walls. The cold wind felt good on her face, even as it caused her eyes to tear up when she headed straight into it. She didn't care that it mussed her hair or turned her nose red. It made her feel alive, able to breathe something other than tobacco smoke and the cheap perfume Mother Wharton made all the girls purchase from her for two shillings.

Drury Lane was bustling with theatregoers. Maeve watched from a small arched alcove as liveried footmen assisted dapper gentlemen and ladies draped in colourful silks and sparkling jewels out of their carriages. After they glided down from the footplate and towards the entrance of the Theatre Royal, the carriages eased away, allowing others to follow suit.

She could've been one of those ladies wrapped in a fur cloak and on the arm of an important man. If only Albert, Emily's father, had wanted more than a weekly tumble between the sheets. Would he have taken her to the theatre like those bejeweled ladies if things had been different, or hidden her away in some modest yet well-appointed townhouse on the other side of London?

Even after the disappointment of him leaving, she'd never regretted not using a pessary when they had lain together. He was the only man she did that with, and the only reason she had her beautiful daughter.

"Selling your wares, lass?" A man had approached from behind, his rank breath hot on her neck. "I have four pence to spare. Won't take but a moment."

Maeve covered her nose and mouth with a handkerchief. She didn't bother to turn around and simply waved him off with her free hand instead.

He moved away, the heat and stench of his body no longer filling the small alcove she stood in. She lingered there until the theatre let out, watching the men and women leave as a dustman shouted in the distance, marking the late hour. Only a smattering of carriages remained in line, awaiting the arrival of their occupants. There was little left to see, so Maeve flipped up the hood of her wool cloak and headed back to Parker's.

Two streetlamps on Bridge Street were unlit and, without a moon, she found it difficult to see more than ten or so feet ahead of her. She hurried her pace, watching her footing so she didn't step in night waste or anything left behind from the horses. She was almost at the end of the street when she heard someone call out to her.

"Is that you?"

The voice seemed familiar. For a second, she thought it might be Albert's, but it had been so long since she'd seen him, she couldn't be sure. She stopped and turned around, peering into the shadows, her eyesight blurry with tears from the wind. "Albert?"

A figure emerged from the darkness. Maeve blinked to try to see more clearly, but his features remained hazy. She rubbed her hands together, cold even with gloves on. "Albert?"

"Beautiful as ever." His voice seemed lower than she remembered Albert's to be. But perhaps her memory was faulty. He slowed his pace, his face hidden from view. "Let me smell you. Taste you."

Her heart jumped at the sound of his tenor. He was not Albert. "Who's there?"

"Afraid, are you? A dirty whore afraid of a gentleman?" His hand fell to the front of his breeches.

His words were sharp, slicing into her like shards of glass. She held her breath, remembering that the London Monster often spoke vulgarly to his victims before he attacked. She looked around for help but didn't see anyone, anything. She spun around and hurried as fast as she could towards the lit streetlamp at the far end of the street.

His footsteps followed closely, one long step for every two of hers. "Do your thighs tremble when you think of my caress?"

"Go away or I'll scream!" Her pulse raced, panic spreading through her chest in a violent wave.

Suddenly, she was jerked from behind, his grip on her arm unforgiving. He twirled her around, then leaned into her. "You run from me? Do you think yourself above me?"

She yanked her arm and twisted to escape his grasp, but he held fast. "Help me! Someone!"

She kicked at his shins twice but failed to make contact. He pulled her close, forcing her back against his chest and pinning her arms to her sides.

"Who goes there?" A voice arose from the dark.

Her assailant startled, his head spinning left and right.

"Help! I'm being attacked!" she screamed.

A flurry of footsteps started in their approach. The man instantly released her, sending her crashing to the ground. He ran back in the direction of the theatre and disappeared around the corner.

Three men shuffled into view and lifted her to her feet. "Are you hurt, miss?"

"I don't believe so."

"What happened?" the tall, slender one asked.

"A man followed me from the theatre and grabbed me." She rubbed her knee, which was sore from the fall.

The shortest man, still huffing from the hurry-scurry over, inched closer. "Pardon my boldness, miss, but you shouldn't be walking unescorted. Certainly not this late at night."

"I thought it would be fine. I do it all the time," she answered shakily. She readjusted her cloak neatly over her shoulders. At some point she must've lost the button at the neck. She tried to pinch it closed, afraid they would realize what she was, but it was too late. All three of them caught a clear glimpse of her overly exposed décolletage.

They shot each other knowing glances and shifted on their feet. "Ah, well. Then we shall send you on your way."

Her lip started to tremble, the shame of their recognition washing over her. She nodded as they walked away, leaving her alone once again in the darkness.

Chapter 8

"The pigeon pie is lovely, Husband. You should try it," Vivian suggested softly, the hint of a smile hidden amongst her nondescript features.

Cuthbert couldn't help but feel sorry for her. Dalton, seated next to her, hadn't spoken to her once since they all sat for supper. Although no one else at the table seemed to feel the tension between the two, Cuthbert did. His father and Lord Carlisle seemed entrenched in their own conversation at one end of the table, as did his mother and Lady Carlisle at the other.

Dalton waved her off with the flip of his hand and continued talking to Cuthbert. "The problem is that these people are inserting themselves in our government. Before you know it, Parliament will be run by blacksmiths and cobblers."

Cuthbert swallowed his bite of potato pudding, then wiped the corners of his mouth. Discussing political matters in front of women made him uncomfortable. "Industrialists, you mean."

"Call them whatever you will, but either way, they are not like us."

Lord Carlisle signaled a servant with the wiggle of his finger, then pointed to his glass. While she poured his wine, he casually unbuttoned the lowest button of his waistcoat, then relaxed in the extra space suddenly afforded him. "A catastrophe. That is what it is."

Father nodded with a grunt.

Out of the corner of his eye, Cuthbert spied a small grimace on Sophie's face.

"Where there is money, there is power. And these new men have quite a bit of both." Cuthbert knew Dalton couldn't counterargue that point. "I cannot say I necessarily find it problematic."

Dalton set his veal-laden fork on his plate. "Did I hear you correctly?"

"I am simply saying that if we were to work together, it could benefit everyone. Their commercial endeavors would help our land interests." Cuthbert smiled briefly at Sophie in an effort to smooth the displeasure from her brow that was directed at Dalton.

"Of course. But my concern lies with their ridiculous efforts to blur the lines between themselves and the gentry. Or, dare I say, noblemen." Dalton raised his wine glass, staring at the burgundy as he spoke. "After all, a handful of sterling will not hide the fact that callouses lie beneath the coins."

Sophie's fork clinked angrily on her plate, causing Vivian's jaw to freeze in mid chew and Cuthbert's throat to constrict.

"I assume you are not referring to a gentleman born and bred," Sophie said, obviously annoyed.

"Clearly." Dalton pretended a smile.

Cuthbert's stomach twisted. Sophie didn't care much for Dalton, and this argument was only going to make their relationship worse.

"Then I take issue with that, Mr. Fletcher." She sat straighter in her chair. "A man may be a gentleman regardless of his birthright. His principles and actions are what define his character."

"Ahh, but you see, you are confusing inherited rights with behaviour. 'Tis the blood that runs through a man's veins that is the determinant."

"So, you believe that an idle, morally corrupt man born of a landed or titled family is a superior over a man who lives honestly without folly and brings good to society through his business interests and actions?"

"I can see that you do not."

"As a matter of fact—"

Cuthbert cleared his throat to stop the conversation. Sophie's words had settled uncomfortably in his gut. *He* was one of those men who seemed to live with no purpose, no direction. He had no involvement in business or government. His life consisted of spending unending hours with his mother, socializing at dinner parties, or frequenting his club. But wasn't that what he was expected to do? He was both—born and bred to be idle.

And as for his morals . . . well, he'd rather not think about that. He shuddered at the memory of his most recent encounters with one of the whores in Covent Garden.

"You were right, Miss Vivian. This pigeon pie is delicious. Just lovely." He speared a piece onto his fork and held it in front of his mouth. He took a bite and smiled while he chewed. "Your cook really outdid himself, Lady Carlisle."

"I am glad you approve. He will be in charge of the wedding feast as well." Lady Carlisle gently squeezed Sophie's hand. "We are not two months away from the joyous event."

Relieved his future mother-in-law had managed to change the subject, Cuthbert relaxed, releasing the tension that inhabited his shoulders. "I have heard little of the preparations. Sophie must be the only bride in history not interested in the minutia of wedding planning."

Everyone turned to face her, awaiting a response. Sophie simply shrugged one shoulder and took another bite of veal. Cuthbert smiled uncomfortably, the tightness in his shoulders returning. She never wanted to discuss their upcoming nuptials, which were only six weeks and six days away. "Aunt Belva is pleased that we moved up the date. Her rheumatism is often aggravated by the cold weather."

Sophie suddenly appeared interested. "I thought her concern was one of travel. That she could not endure the carriage ride in the winter."

"That too," he said.

Sophie dabbed the corner of her mouth with her napkin, then set it back in her lap. "Poor Aunt Belva seems to have a list of difficulties getting to London for the wedding. November is awfully cold, Bertie. Perhaps we should postpone the wedding until the spring, when she will not need to fret about the ice and snow or her rheumatism flaring up. Why rush it? We can have a lovely wedding when the flowers are in bloom and your aunt need not worry over the weather. I know how dear she is to you, Bertie. What do you say?"

"Well, I . . ."

Mother speared him with her gaze. If he agreed to postpone the wedding, it would be longer until his family received her dowry. And that meant it would take longer to pay off their debts to more than a dozen merchants. If he disagreed, it would paint him as a heartless, uncaring nephew to his aging aunt. As much as he didn't want to postpone the date once again, he couldn't let Sophie think of him that way.

"Very well. If that is truly what you wish." His throat pinched with the thought.

"We must think of Aunt Belva." Sophie laid her hand on his, a conciliatory look in her eyes, then turned to her mother. "Do you agree?"

Lady Carlisle fiddled with her necklace, her fingers sliding back and forth over the pearls. "I must admit it gives me more time to make the arrangements. And the bluebells will be in full bloom."

Cuthbert glanced at his mother, whose lips were tight with annoyance. He was sure to get an earful when they got home.

Sophie's face brightened. "Then it is done. June, it is."

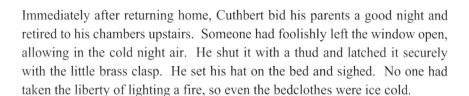

Immediately after returning home, Cuthbert bid his parents a good night and retired to his chambers upstairs. Someone had foolishly left the window open, allowing in the cold night air. He shut it with a thud and latched it securely with the little brass clasp. He set his hat on the bed and sighed. No one had taken the liberty of lighting a fire, so even the bedclothes were ice cold.

"Raymond!" he called from the door's threshold, hoping his valet had not yet retired for the night. "Raymond!"

Harried footsteps approached from the stairs, then candlelight appeared. Raymond entered fully dressed but without his periwig. His haggard features glowed oddly in the flickering light. "You called, sir?"

"Why was the fire in my room not lit?"

"Milord requested that we not light fires unnecessarily, sir." Raymond averted his gaze as he spoke.

Cuthbert tried to hide his embarrassment. He knew the reason Father had said that. The cost of wood had increased, and they already owed the fagetter eight pounds from the last year for his wood bundles.

"I need you to build a fire."

"Of course, sir."

Raymond disappeared for a minute, then returned with an armful of logs and kindling. He bent to set the wood in the hearth, his balding head peeking through thin strands of white hair. It took half a dozen times of striking the fire steel with the edge of the flint before the fire took, casting a dull golden glow around the room.

Cuthbert removed his shoes and coat and began unbuttoning his waistcoat.

"Allow me to help you with that." Raymond hurried to his side to dress him in his nightclothes. "Will that be all, sir?"

Cuthbert nodded. "Thank you. Please send someone to check on the fire throughout the night. I do not wish to catch cold."

"Of course." He slipped out the door, closing it behind him.

Cuthbert waited for the sound of Raymond's footsteps to disappear, his heart thumping steadily. Tonight, he was going to need to do something to calm his nerves. Sophie's desire to postpone the wedding had stirred a disquiet in him that he couldn't seem to temper. She hadn't even allowed a kiss on her cheek as they said their goodbyes. He wasn't sure if it was due to the prickly conversation they'd had at the dinner table or if it had to do with his unchivalrous hesitation regarding accommodating his aunt's ailments and travel fears. Or perhaps it was because her mother stood nearby and would've chastised her later for permitting his forwardness. Either way, it made his leg jog up and down the entire ride home in the carriage, drawing the attention of his father and his reproving look. Yet it was Mother's incessant chastisement of his spineless acceptance of the postponement that left him feeling as brittle as glass.

If it weren't so late, he would venture to one of his favourite bawdy houses and have one of the whores take him in her mouth. But he had promised himself that he would make a sincere effort to curb his wicked desires and refrain from frequenting them as often as he had. After all, those visits drained him of his vitality and were the cause of his angst in the first place.

He knew this because Dalton had shown him an advertisement in one of his indecent booklets about the cures available for spermatorrhoea. Of course, Dalton had shown him the ad to mock the claims that frequent self-pollution and depravity caused all types of physical problems—many of which Cuthbert endured—but Cuthbert knew the truth in its words. He suffered from irritability and anxiousness, sometimes to a point of feeling he wanted to climb out of his own skin. And there were also times that he had no desire to do anything, resolving to stay indoors all day seated next to the fire, reading a book or staring out the front parlour window, watching coaches roll past his front drive. The ad maintained those were the exact symptoms debauchery caused in the male body. And Cuthbert had them all.

He stilled his breath to listen and ensure Raymond was no longer close by. The crackling fire in the hearth was the only sound disturbing the silence. With his heart pounding, he knelt next to his bed and pried open the loose floorboard underneath. He set it aside and reached into the dark hole, his fingers groping for the little red velvet pouch that contained the contraption in the advertisement. He lifted it out, replaced the board, and hurried under his covers. Carefully, he tugged the string to open the bag and remove the piece of metal from its case. The little ring was especially cold this night, a light film of condensation covering it, likely making its intended effect event greater.

Cuthbert pulled up his nightshirt and slipped the ring over his member, making sure not to injure himself with the jagged edges in the process. When he was certain it was properly in place, he flipped the clip catch to tighten it. He sucked in his breath as it gripped him tightly. It had worked well in the past to prevent embarrassing stains on his bedclothes as he hoped it would tonight. He imagined the laundresses finding them and tittering between themselves in the morning. That possibility weighed heavily on his conscience.

He wanted to be a better man. Truly he did. He hated suffering so. But at night, as he lay in bed, all he could think about was Sophie. Her pale skin and tiny waist. Her green eyes as they peered up at him through long dark lashes. That spot on her neck that begged for the touch of his lips. It was all too much for him, knowing she could have been his in a matter of weeks. But now he would wait an interminable eight months. And all because he didn't have the courage to insist she do as he pleased.

The jugum started to tighten, squeezing him uncomfortably, so he pushed aside his thoughts and closed his eyes, begging for sleep to come.

A Note

November 1789

Most people would think my narrow escapes from the Bow Street Runners or good Samaritans would unnerve me, perhaps cause me to reconsider my ways and become the perfect gentleman. But they would be wrong.

I enjoy the closeness of danger. The excitement of almost getting caught. It energizes me. Provides me with the vigor of a man who dares stare into the mouth of a lion. That moment of uncertainty, desperation, makes my heart rattle until all I can do is react. Do I run? Do I quickly draw my blade?

A few weeks past, this very thing happened. I had found the perfect woman. One who tempted my desires in the curves of her body poorly hidden beneath her cloak. She walked alone at almost midnight. Why would a woman behave in such a manner unless she was hoping I would appear?

I cried out to her and she turned, calling the name of a friend or lover. I moved closer, my loins filling with need. I told her she was beautiful and offered to delight her with my touch. Her eyes grew large at that, but not in the shocked manner to which I am accustomed. It was more of an angry, mocking look, a look that told me she had heard worse before. And that is when I realized she was not a gentlewoman, but a lowly whore.

I considered dragging her into the alley and taking her as I pleased, but she screamed, and three arrogant fops arrived full of pomp and righteousness to save the wretch. Did it bother me? I admit it did. I would have enjoyed giving her a good taste of my cock. But the men's sudden presence posed no real threat, for none of them were armed, nor were they anywhere near my size. I fled—even more determined to make my next outing successful.

Tonight, I head over to Billingsgate, where half-dressed jilts abound by the dozens and men are too heavy with drink to stand unassisted on their own two feet. I am not particularly fond of whores, as I prefer women of good standing and gentility. There is something about a fine woman's carriage—her straight back and confident walk—that I find enticing. It speaks more to my sensibilities as a gentleman. And it poses a challenge. One I happily accept.

Even so, tonight I feel the need to settle for a barmaid or a millworker content with the five shillings a week she earns hidden in her bodice between her breasts. This type will still be shocked by my brazenness yet make for an easier target since she will likely be unescorted on her way home from work.

I wait at the end of St. Mary Hill—trying to avoid the strumpets who lounge in doorways and brazenly shout their availability as I pass by—hoping to encounter a tib as she travels up the street on her way to Eastcheap. The night air, somewhat chilly for an evening out, reeks of fish and rotting food scraps that lie in the alleyways from here to the docks. I worry that the odours may cling to my wool coat or the lace at my throat, but it is one of the small sacrifices I must make in order to partake in the desires I so crave.

In very short time, a woman approaches. Her head is bowed, rendering her unaware of her surroundings. She seems determined to make her way up the street with little or no complications. She scuttles onward, her hands holding her brown cloak tightly closed at her breast. I step in place behind her, leaving only a few feet between us. She quickens her pace. A sign she is aware of my presence.

"In a hurry, are you?" I ask, hoping to slow her steps.

She waves one hand in the air without looking back. "Go on. Go on. I'm in no need of trouble here."

Her voice is softer than I expected. My interest in her deepens and my cock grows hard as I think of the possibilities. "You have a lovely voice."

Her head jerks up and her posture straightens.

"I imagine your mouth is just as lovely." I hope this compliment will encourage her to stop.

She turns her head slightly, giving me a brief glimpse of her nose and cheekbone. There is nothing particularly striking about those features, but to be fair, it is dark, and the moment lasts for a mere second. My fingers begin to tingle as my heart races. I must work quickly, for we are almost at the end of the street, where there is a busy crossing.

"And your tongue. I yearn for its velvet caress over my cock."

At that, her shoulders jerk and her arms pull inward. I sense she is about to run. I slip my blade from inside my coat. Just as I extract it from its sheath, a man crosses ahead of us. I slide my hand back inside my coat. Something about him seems familiar.

The woman sees him too. "Leave me alone. Go on!" she cries.

He turns and faces us. It is the same man who attacked me in front of St. Anne's Church. I know who he is.

Part Two

Chapter 9

November 1789
London, England

Tom headed to Eastcheap where the usual Thursday night boxing match took place. William Futrell was scheduled to fight Jude Green, who Tom had beat in less than two minutes a few weeks before he found himself in the Old Bailey awaiting his hanging. Before their fight, Green had been considered the local champion and was favoured to win the match. But Tom defeated him quickly and effortlessly, even though he'd taken a few well-placed blows to the chin first. After that, Tom was hailed as the new champion, and the amount of his purse increased dramatically.

But now with the promise he'd made to his father that he would stay out of trouble, he could watch a fight but couldn't re-enter the ring. At least until the elections, he'd have to settle for punching bags of barley at the warehouse and sparring with Connor at Parker's Place.

The pearly moon glowed above, casting blue light over the few stragglers hurrying home for supper. Tom had mixed feelings about being out at night. Although he knew of the dangers that lurked quietly in the darkness, he enjoyed the solitude it brought.

Normally, it emptied his mind of all thoughts, but tonight one recurring reflection lingered. It was of that journalist, James Evans. He wished he knew her real name. He smiled, remembering the pluck that little beauty had when he urged her to remove her coat in the park. He couldn't believe she'd acquiesced, stripping off her coat, then spending the rest of the afternoon crossing her arms in front of her chest, trying to hide her figure underneath only two layers of fabric. But then again, she was daring enough to go about wearing breeches to impersonate a man, so he shouldn't have been surprised that she'd accepted his challenge.

He wasn't sure what had emboldened him to grab her and pull her to him. Although it wasn't the type of embrace he would've truly wished for, it brought him close enough to her to smell the perfume she likely dabbed behind her ears that morning before she ventured out as a man. *Honey and lavender*, he thought. Should he have told her that he knew about her masquerade? Nay. He would play this out a bit longer.

Tom sighed. If only he knew her real identity.

"Leave me alone. Go on!" A woman's voice rang sharp in the night, snapping him to attention.

He turned to his right and saw a young woman running towards him. Twenty paces behind her was a man in a dark cloak or greatcoat.

"Please!" she cried, springing into Tom's arms. She was shaking, gripping his coat as if she would never let go.

Tom glared at the man. He stood with his hand inside his cloak, his mouth tensed in anger. Tom's chest tightened. It was the same man he'd scrabbled with by the church. The London Monster.

The man turned to run, his hand now fully exposed, and Tom caught a glimpse of a flash of metal in the moonlight. A knife.

He tried to free himself from the woman's clutches to chase him, but she wouldn't budge.

"Please don't leave me! He said the vilest things. I can't . . ." She broke down in tears, her petite body quivering uncontrollably.

His heart hammered against his chest as he watched the man disappear around the corner. Gone again.

He escorted the woman home, then wandered through the streets, hoping to spot her assailant once more. After almost an hour he gave up, sure the monster had left the area to return home for the night. He didn't bother to head back to Eastcheap. The fight between Futrell and Green was undoubtedly over, and his mind was no longer there.

He reached his home close to midnight, too many thoughts racing through his head. He had to find that journalist and tell her what happened. This time he was sure he could give her a better description of his face.

"You are arriving awfully late."

Tom stared into the dark parlour. Seated by the window in the corner of the room was his brother Henry, moonlight illuminating the upper half of his body. Dressed in his nightclothes, he swirled a glass of ruby liquid round and round. His voice showed little concern for where Tom had been, but it was the most Henry had said to him in months outside of the warehouse.

"And you? Unable to sleep?" Tom removed his coat and draped it over the back of the sofa. He could tell by the loose set of Henry's shoulders that he wasn't well.

Henry sighed long and deep. "Judith Forsythe is to be married."

"To whom?" This was horrible. Poor Henry. If only he'd had been more forthcoming. Tom knew her family was aware of their acquaintance, but he was so timid, they probably hadn't recognized Henry's affection for her.

"Bradley Cogswell."

"Lord Chippenham?"

"The one and only."

"That toad?" Tom poured himself a glass of port and sat in the chair across from his brother. "What could she possibly see in him?"

"'Twasn't a love match, Thomas." Henry stared into his glass.

That was the spike through the heart, then. Her family had chosen a noble over Henry.

"When?" Tom asked.

"Summer, I believe." Henry finished off his port in one gulp.

Tom poured him another glass. "Then there is still time."

Henry stood, shaking his head. "'Tis no use. Both families have agreed."

"Do you love her?"

Henry moved in front of the window and stared at Tom, his silhouette framed in silver moonlight. "She is all I ever think about."

"Have you told her that?"

"Of course not!" Henry turned to face the window and lowered his voice. "We discuss other things."

He was infuriating. At seven and twenty, one would think he'd learned the art of wooing, but Henry seemed like a lost cause.

"Other things?" Tom asked.

"Birds and the theatre and . . . and . . ." He drew one hand down his face slowly. "I am not as bold as you."

Tom sipped his port, then joined him at the window. "It would not be unseemly to tell her of your feelings. I sense she feels the same."

Henry turned to face him. "You do?"

"I do."

"Even if I were to tell her, nothing would change. She and Chippenham will still marry, and I will look the fool for exposing my heart."

"If you don't, you will never know what could have been."

"Really, Thomas. Do you think her father would choose me over a noble?"

The whole of England believed that better clothes made the better man. But Tom had learned that wasn't the truth at the age of ten, when his mother's life was taken by those thieves in silk and lace. "As I understand it, Chippenham is heavily in debt. His investments in those failed banks outside of London practically ruined him. Judith's father must know that. What would he gain from that match? More debt?"

Henry chewed on his bottom lip, a habit that meant Henry was working out the facts and would only stop when he was thoroughly convinced they made sense. His face lightened a bit. "We *have* had an extremely lucrative year. The yields from our colliery alone have increased over thirty percent."

It was true. Production was at an all-time high, and now with the opening of the Oxford Canal, the London market would receive coal a lot quicker than in the past. Shipments would increase, and the returns would abound.

Tom nudged him with his elbow. "Profits could be enormous. You could support Lady Judith in the manner to which she is accustomed. More so, I imagine, than the toad."

Tom immediately regretted what he'd said. Henry's personal income was a bit of a sore spot. Father had no intention of leaving him the family business even though he was the eldest of the three of them. Although Henry was dedicated and good with numbers, Father saw him as a failure when it came to making sound investments in the world of shipping and commodities. He simply wasn't a risk taker, and Father believed those who didn't take risks never made gains.

"If you dare nothing, then nothing is what you will get," Father would say.

Henry's response would always begin with, "But what if—"

Each time it ended in an argument with Father doing a good amount of yelling and Henry cowering nervously, nodding his head in agreement.

Henry was a milksop, not a leader. Tom knew it. Father and Roger knew it. And Henry knew it.

He continued chewing his lip. "What should I do?"

"Fight for her. Prove your worth. Show her father you are better than Chippenham."

Henry paced the length of the room twice, released his lip from between his teeth, then finished his port in one deep swig. "But what if—"

Tom set down his glass and grabbed his brother by the shoulders. "Do it."

Tom searched all the papers for over a week for Evans's editorial on the London Monster. Nothing. She'd told him she would work on it and submit it right away. How long did it take for a story to get published? Surely an article exposing details regarding a man drifting through the streets of London, insulting and stabbing women would be worthy of immediate publication.

He'd worked in the warehouse every day except Sunday, hoping she would come by so he could tell her of his most recent encounter with the man. But it was already Tuesday again and still no sign of her.

He resealed the last of the crates and set his ledger inside the office, having accepted that she would once again not appear. He put on his coat and hat, shut the office door, and stepped outside of the warehouse into the fading sunlight. And there she was, hurrying over with one hand holding her hat in place and the other holding her small journal.

"So glad to have caught you!" she said, smiling. Her cheeks were rosy from the sprint, and wisps of her bound hair escaped from its ribbon. She looked as beautiful as he remembered.

"I wasn't sure I would see you again, James." He glanced at the ships in the wharf in an attempt to appear somewhat disinterested, fighting desperately to hide his delight at her presence.

"I have been quite busy. Writing, you see."

She may have been busy, but he doubted it had anything to do with writing. More likely, it involved living her life as a young woman and partaking in all those ordinary things women did, whatever they were.

"I searched for your article in the papers but couldn't seem to find it."

"That is the reason I am here. The editors insist I must divulge my source if I wish to be published. They said without it, my credibility would be diminished."

He'd made her promise not to use his name out of respect for his father. He couldn't let her use it. It would destroy his father's chances of winning that seat in Parliament. It was hard enough trying to conceal the scar on his palm that marked him as a criminal. Hiding his name printed in black and white in papers throughout the city would prove impossible.

If he had only caught the man, it might prove a different story. He would be hailed a hero and the exposure would send his father straight to the victor's seat. But until then . . .

"I apologize, but I cannot allow you to do it. My father's reputation is at stake." Truly, he felt awful for disappointing her, but he couldn't hurt his father that way.

Her face fell with disappointment. "I see. Well then, I bid you a good day, sir."

He reached for her arm when she turned to leave. "Wait. I do have something to tell you."

She stared up at him, her green eyes darkening in the dwindling light.

"I saw him again. The London Monster."

Her eyes grew wide. "When? Where?"

He tried to think. When was it? "Nine . . . no, ten days ago. Near Eastcheap."

She opened her journal and slipped a piece of charcoal from between the pages. "Did you get a good look at him?"

"I did."

They went back inside the warehouse. Tom lit the two oil lamps on top of the desk, where she sketched as he offered details of the man's nose and mouth. He stood behind her, correcting the features as she drew. Since it had been dark, Tom wasn't able to see the colour or shape of his eyes, so she shaded over them. When she was done, she sat back and waited for his approval.

He leaned over her shoulder and inhaled the smell of her perfume once again. He wanted to touch her, tuck a misplaced curl back inside her queue or accidentally graze her hand with his. But he didn't. "You have come very close to his likeness."

She tilted her head to the side. "He hardly looks like a monster."

"He is a monster, I assure you. The best disguise is a well-made coat with silver bejeweled buttons."

"I suppose I must take your word for it." She looked up at him and smiled.

How could he have ever mistaken her for a young boy? He straightened. "What will you do with it?"

"I could try again to have it published in the papers. And if they refuse, I will take it to the magistrate to help the Runners catch the fellow." She slid the charcoal into the crease of her journal. She stood to leave, and he reached for her cocked hat.

"When will I see you again?" he asked, handing it to her.

She pressed her lips together and fumbled with her hat. "I am not certain. My schedule is . . . complicated."

He couldn't let her go without a promise he'd see her soon. "Why don't we meet at the tea house at Vauxhall this Friday? I may have an idea of how we can catch him. Noon, perhaps?"

"Friday?" She pursed her lips, considering the possibility. "Very well. Noon, it is."

He was just about to reach for her hand to kiss it when he remembered he was supposed to think of her as a man. He nodded briefly, clapped her on the shoulder, and bid her farewell with the tip of his hat.

After she walked out the door, he watched her until she disappeared around a corner and out of his sight. He'd see her again in only three days, but his smile faded as he considered that the price of collaborating with her might cost him his own identity and, ultimately, his father's candidacy.

Chapter 10

Sophie raced home. The sun had already set, and the carriage sitting in the front drive indicated her mother had returned from her weekly visit to Aunt Lydia's.

Peg was waiting at the servants' entrance, wringing her hands. "I did my best to explain your whereabouts. Your mother and father are waiting upstairs to speak with you."

Sophie stepped inside and Peg led her to a small storage closet at the far end of the kitchens. Peg made a twirling gesture with her hands. "Make haste, make haste."

She undressed Sophie, then reached inside a laundry basket and pulled out a shift, two petticoats, and a gown. "I hid these in here when I realized you were not to return on time."

Sophie slipped into her clothes, the two of them bumping into the walls in the tight space with the effort. "Where did you say I was?"

"Visiting a friend. That way, your mother wouldn't question you going out without an escort. I never gave them a name, so you may tell them you were with whomever you choose."

Sophie kissed her on the cheek. "You are too good to me, Peg."

Peg swatted her hand at her. "Go on. They are waiting."

She followed the sound of her father's voice coming from the study. Mother stood next to the fireplace warming her hands and listening to Father drone on about some unfortunate matter. Sophie waited at the threshold for one of them to notice her presence.

"'Tis unnatural," Father said disapprovingly. "A woman should show more interest in her wedding."

Mother sighed. "Perhaps she is nervous. There are so many things a young girl must consider before she becomes a wife."

"At twenty, she is no longer a young girl." Father leaned back in his chair, forcing him to look across the room and right at Sophie. "Where have you been at this late hour?"

Sophie entered and kissed Mother on the cheek before answering. "I was with Vivian at the milliner's. I thought they might have some lace gloves that would be appropriate for my wedding."

All of that was a lie, of course, but she thought it might be the best way to not only divert the subject of her whereabouts to that of her impending nuptials, but also show an interest—albeit a false one—in the upcoming event.

Mother's face lit up. "I thought we could shop together for the rest of your bridal clothes."

"Forgive me, Mother. Vivian was looking for a new hat, so since we were already there, I thought there would be no harm in looking for new gloves. Now that the wedding is in June, my leather gloves would be too warm."

"Of course they would be. I hadn't thought of that." Mother smiled at Father, who rolled his eyes. She moved to brush something off his shoulder, and he swatted her hand away.

Father cleared his voice. "And since we are on the subject, your mother and I would like to tell you about the gift we wish to give you and Cuthbert once it is official."

Sophie's stomach did a small flip. Perhaps it was hearing Bertie's name that suddenly brought her into focus. If he only knew how she really felt.

Father motioned her over to his desk. A beautifully drawn sketch of a sprawling estate surrounded by sycamore trees lay on top. The home had three storeys with seven gables and oriel windows. A quaint little gatehouse stood along the great drive to the left beside a carefully planted garden.

Her father smiled broadly. "What do you think?"

"I . . . it is truly lovely. Where is it?" she asked.

"Lincolnshire."

"Lincolnshire! Why so far?" She knew she sounded ungrateful, but how could she leave London? It was her home. Even their family summer estate was in Sussex, all but a day's ride away. It would be impossible to get published living outside of London. She would have no access to the papers, and what would she write about? Bird migration and the occasional country fair?

"You don't seem pleased." Father tilted his head, his brow knitted. "'Tis the perfect place to raise your family. I cannot have my grandchildren growing up in London."

Grandchildren? She wasn't even married yet, and he was already thinking about grandchildren. The room suddenly started feeling very warm. Was her gown always so tight? She wiped away the dampness that had formed on her forehead.

"Oh, dear." Mother reached around her and guided her into a chair. "You're pale, Sophie. You do not look well."

Father stood, his fingers pressed on the polished wood of his desk, and stared down at Sophie. "Nerves. Am I right?"

Mother ran into the hall. "Smelling salts. We need smelling salts!"

Sophie took a deep breath. "Really, Mother. I am quite fine."

"She has the vapors." Mother fanned her with a folded letter from Father's desk, a look of worry and agitation mixed in her features. She faced Father. "I told you not to bother her with such matters yet. It is too soon. You should have waited until Mr. Needham was here. She would have found comfort in his presence, and then surprising her with such a grand home would have not seemed so overwhelming."

"What is overwhelming about being given an estate? You treat her like a child, Flora."

Sophie shut her eyes and took a deep breath. Her heart fluttered in her chest like a trapped bird.

"You do not understand what it means to become a wife. Taking on a home of this size requires a lot of work. She will need at least a dozen servants, a House Steward and Land Steward, nurses for the children—"

"Are you complaining? Is that what this is about?" Father grunted disapprovingly. "It is your purpose, and it will be hers as well."

Sophie shook her head. So much talk. So much to think about. "Please. I am fine."

Peg ran in with a small glass jar on a silver tray. "Milady."

Before Sophie could protest, Mother grabbed the jar and waved it under her nose. The sharp sting of hartshorn caused her eyes to water and instantly filled her head with heat. "Everyone stop! I am simply tired from being out all day. Perhaps I should lie down."

She was about to stand when she spotted an envelope sticking out from the pile where her mother had withdrawn the letter she used as a fan. On the front, the name *James Evans* was scrawled in scratchy penmanship. She sucked in her breath. Peg was supposed to intercept all letters that came to the house with Sophie's pseudonym on them. How did this one make it through?

Sophie slid the drawing of the country estate over the letter and leaned over the desk so that the edge of the paper touched her gown. Carefully, she slipped the letter from underneath and into the bottom of her bodice. "The home is lovely, Father. I cannot thank you enough for your generosity. I am certain Bertie will feel the same."

She couldn't live there. Not as Bertie's wife. Or anyone's wife, for that matter. It simply didn't feel right. And now with the possibility that the letter hidden in her clothing was a message stating that the article she'd written about Maeve was going to be published, moving outside of London could never happen.

She stood, reached for Peg's hand, and together they climbed the stairs to her chambers. No sooner had she closed the door behind her than she pulled the letter out of her bodice and broke the small black seal to open it.

Dear Mr. Evans,

We regret to inform you that we will not be purchasing your article for publication. It is unlikely our patrons would care to read about an ill-fated lady of pleasure and her woes regarding her unfortunate employment. I should think you would concern yourself with more important matters, unless, of course, you have chosen this subject matter in order to partake in the benefits that come naturally with your research in places of ill repute. We strongly advise you to consider topics that would interest London gentlemen enough to spend two pence on a paper.

Your obliged,
Mr. Henry Foxhall, Editor of the Morning Herald

"What would they like me to write about? Missing pets or Lord So-and-So dying from griping of the guts? That would be fascinating," Sophie said acerbically. At least the last rejection she'd received had complimented her writing.

Peg peered over Sophie's shoulder to read the letter. "Perhaps he means you should write about financial matters or sports. Those are gentlemanly things."

"I know what he means. But where is the importance in that?" She tossed the letter on the dressing table and paced in front of her bed. "Those stories are present in every paper throughout London. Maeve's story is original. Exclusive. It tells the *truth* about something we all pretend doesn't exist.

Everyone walks about acting as if it doesn't matter. Well, it *does* matter, and I will be the one to thrust it into view!"

"Perhaps you should reconsider—" Peg started.

"Do not bother to admonish me, Peg. I will continue to write stories about people. Real people. And the ugliness that lies beneath polite society's view of the city."

"I do not wish to admonish you, my dear. I want to help," Peg said in a soothing voice. "You should write something that will get you published, get your name recognized first, and then you will have the freedom to write about the topics you believe are important."

Sophie stopped pacing and took a deep breath. "Go on."

"What if you were to write an article about a matter that teeters on the edge of polite society and the undesirable? Something that would satisfy both your needs and the papers'. Something gentlemen would care to read for pleasure without realizing the social implications you are making."

That could work. But what would she write about? Horseracing? What social statement might she make about that? "I suppose I could do that."

"Of course you could." Peg firmly set her hands on Sophie's shoulders to look directly into her eyes. "Promise me one thing."

"What is it?"

"This time, do your research in an establishment a little more wholesome than a brothel."

Three days later, Sophie told Maeve about the editor turning down the article. It was a difficult thing to tell her, considering she was essentially admitting that the people of London didn't care about Maeve's plight or circumstances.

"Why would they, after all?" Maeve gazed out the window of her little room, expressionless. The clop of horses in the street below marked the silence. "Normally, Friday is a busy day. Where is everyone?"

Sophie joined her. Only men seemed to be out walking, a small string of them entering and exiting the coffeehouse at the end of the street. "No women."

"'Tis the London Monster. He has everyone afraid of leaving their homes." Maeve swiped her hand over the condensation forming on the glass. "He attacked me not a week ago. At least, it may have been him."

Sophie stood dumbstruck. "What? Why have you not said anything?"

Maeve sat beside her and tipped up Sophie's chin with a gentle finger. "You dear, sweet girl. Whores are used to rough hands, either in the street or in bed. It makes no difference."

"But you should have reported it." As the words rolled off her tongue, she knew she was a fraud. She had never told anyone about the young man who had threatened to take her behind the bushes and *give her what she wanted*. She'd kept that secret close to her breast as something shameful, mostly because of her part in it. She still blamed herself, and she knew that everyone else would too.

Maeve shrugged. "You just told me that the good people of London don't care to hear about a harlot like me."

"I care."

"Of course. Your story."

"Not because of my story. Because you are my friend. One of the very few I have." Sophie hugged her to her side. "Were you injured?"

Maeve shook her head. "Not really. He grabbed me, but I screamed, and some men arrived to help."

"Thank heavens! He is awfully dangerous, you know," Sophie said, remembering the details Tom had told her about the knife he saw in the monster's grasp both times he'd encountered him. "Did you see him?"

"Not enough to give you a description. It was near midnight. The streetlamps were out."

"He needs to be caught." Sophie snatched her hat and journal from the bed. "And I am going to be the one to do it."

"What?"

"I know someone who saw him. Twice. He gave me a good description, and 'tis time I do something with it." She shoved her journal under her arm and opened the door.

"Where are you going?" Maeve called after her.

"The magistrate. If the papers will not take it, the Bow Street Runners will."

Chapter 11

Tom checked his pocket watch. It was already after one. The journalist was over an hour late.

He considered leaving Vauxhall, but he knew she wanted a story, and he was the only one who could give it to her. She had no choice but to show.

His knuckles remained sore from punching bags of grain at the warehouse earlier, and rubbing them to keep warm made the pain worse. Although he'd wrapped them in cloth so they wouldn't bleed from the impact, they were still tender from the blows. In any case, he wore gloves hiding the signs of what he'd been up to.

He ordered another cup of tea and tried to enjoy the music coming from the other side of the promenade. It was not as crowded as it usually was. Only a few warmly bundled couples strolled in front of him along the Grand Walk, arm in arm and chatting softly. Even the small creatures that burrowed below the soil or perched high in the trees were scarce. Most of the birds were gone, their chirps infrequent. An occasional squirrel made an appearance, hopping and scuttling across the lawn to another tree. It was a quiet, serene time for Vauxhall.

Tom wished he had asked the journalist to meet in the evening, which was usually much more exciting. That was when the gardens came to life. Acrobats and jugglers performed in every corner of the grounds. With a single whistle, a team of lamplighters with cotton-wool fuses would light the oil lamps hanging from low branches of the trees lining the gravel walks. It was a spectacle to witness, one that he hoped he could share one day with the lovely journalist. He could invite her to dine in one of the supper boxes and enjoy a nice bottle of wine from his father's cellar or dance in front of the orchestra to a dozen musicians gliding their bows across the strings of their violins. But he was getting ahead of himself. She had to show up for this meeting first.

"Tom! Mr. Hayes?"

Tom turned in his seat to the unmistakable voice, relieved. Evans was hurrying towards him in a clearly feminine manner, her strides too small and delicate to be a man's. He couldn't help but smile at the ridiculousness of it all. He stood and offered her the chair next to him. "I was beginning to think you would not come."

She brushed her hair from her face and sat. "I apologize for my lateness. I had a previous meeting just outside of the city and was detained longer than I had anticipated."

What business would she have outside of London that would require her to be disguised as a man? Most of the newspaper offices were located inside the city, the prisons and courts too, and so far, the London Monster's attacks had been limited to London proper.

"Outside of the city?" he asked.

She flipped her hand at him with a little flutter of her fingers. Not very manly. "I had written an article about a friend and had to deliver the unfortunate news that it would not be published."

"I am sorry to hear that." He signaled the waiter over and ordered her some tea.

"But I am not giving up. I will have one of my articles published if it is the last thing I do." She tapped her forefinger on the table resolutely. "I also delivered our sketch of the monster to the local magistrate."

He liked the fact she chose to use the word *our*. "What did he say?"

That same finger joined her others in thrumming the tabletop before she answered. "He thanked me."

"And?"

"Sent me on my way." Her mouth twisted as if trying to hold back the peppery words she really wanted to say.

"I see." Although he knew the answer to the question he was about to ask, he asked it anyway. "Was he curious as to how you managed to know what he looked like?"

"I told him that his description was given to me by someone who witnessed an assault. I never proffered a name." Her fingers stilled. "At least he took it."

He felt horrible that he forbade her to divulge his name. The elections couldn't come soon enough.

She leaned back in the chair. "But he will not send it on to the papers. He does not want to be sued for libel, just in case my source has led me astray because he wishes to implicate some poor innocent sapskull towards whom he feels ill will. His words, not mine."

"Do you think I would do such a thing?"

She shrugged, then slid her journal from inside her coat and set it on the table. "Now, what is your idea? You said you might know of a way to catch the man."

He wasn't thrilled with her ambivalent response, but he was pleased she wanted to change the subject. Knowing he was the reason she couldn't get published didn't sit well with him.

She tapped her journal. "We need to do it. I have a friend who was attacked recently. She believes it was the monster, however she was unable to give me a description."

"Was she harmed?"

She shook her head gently.

He edged his chair closer to hers. "I think we should map out his most recent attacks to discern as to whether or not there is a pattern. May I?" He reached for her journal and pencil and began drawing. A dull pain ran from his knuckles to his elbow with the effort. "We know of a dozen attacks since last year. March was the first of them, right?"

She thanked the waiter who delivered her tea, then returned her attention to him. "On Bow Lane, I believe."

He drew a curvy line and a series of rectangles with land markers in them. "This is the Thames." He pointed to the winding line across the page, then drew circles as key locations. "And these are landmarks. The palace, London Bridge, St. Paul's Cathedral, and the Theatre Royal."

"Bow Lane would be right about . . . here." She pointed to a spot above the river. "But the other attacks were on Johnson's Court, St. James's Place, Jermyn Street, Leicester Street—"

"Whoa. Slow down there." He was impressed but not surprised that she knew the locations.

She repeated each name while he marked them on the paper with little stars. When he finished, she said, "And these are only the ones that have been reported. I searched the papers for any mention of an incident the night you said you saw him again, but there was none."

"I had a feeling that woman wouldn't report it. She was too frightened." He remembered how she'd quivered in his arms as he walked her home. She could barely talk.

The journalist lowered her eyes and shook her head despondently. He could see she was wrestling with something in the way she stilled her breath.

She continued in a soft voice, her gaze averted. "And she suffered no real harm. So far, all but one woman who reported the incidents to the magistrates were injured. Stabbed."

Tom couldn't help but think of his mother. Had someone like him only been around at the time to help them, she would still be alive.

She sipped from her tea between rattling off the names of a few other streets. "As far as I know, the last reported assault was on St. Martin's Lane near Charing Cross."

He marked it on his map, then leaned closer, their shoulders almost touching. He could smell her perfume again, light and sweet. He inhaled softly, allowing the honey and lavender to flood his senses. She took her time perusing his drawing, her green eyes trying to make sense of the markings. Her lips pursed and twisted in thought. He noticed a tiny freckle on her left cheek where her pale skin was rosy from the cold.

"There doesn't seem to be a pattern here." She traced her finger over some of the landmarks.

"But we do know he mostly stays within these boundaries." He cupped his hands near the east and west ends of the drawing. "We also know that he prefers to strike in the evening on streets that are not necessarily central but lit well enough to attract pedestrians."

"It is an awfully large area for the Runners to cover."

"Exactly. That is why we must draw him to one location in order to limit the scope."

"How do you propose we do that?" she asked.

"With lures."

She jerked back, her eyes wide and mouth open in shock. "You wish to have women waiting alone at night in certain areas throughout London? You would do that?"

"Not exactly. I must speak to a friend first, but I believe we can do this without placing any women at risk."

"I would hope so." She didn't seem convinced. If anything, she appeared a bit repulsed by his idea.

Several vigilante groups in Westminster and St. Pancras had already tried and failed to hunt down the monster. But their tactics included marching in threatening groups and daring him to appear. Tom's plan was a bit more strategic.

"Please trust me. The last thing I want is for another woman to be hurt by this man." The image of his mother lying on the ground with her head at an

81

impossible angle flashed in his mind. Although her attackers had had nothing to do with the London Monster, they were still monsters. And they were all 'gentlemen'.

She stared up at him, a bit of her bottom lip caught between her teeth. He knew she was studying him. He swallowed, hoping she could sense his earnestness.

"I will work out the details as soon as I speak to my friend. When will I see you next?" he asked.

"Soon. I will come to your warehouse." She closed her journal and slid the pencil between the pages, then turned in her chair to leave.

He caught her arm, momentarily keeping her in place. He didn't want her to leave just yet. They had only been together for an hour or so. He lowered his voice and rested his hand over hers. "You should take care."

She glanced at his hand covering hers, then withdrew it quickly. "I should go."

Tom spotted a hackney ready to leave the coach stand near the entrance of the gardens.

"A ride to Parker's Place, Coppice Row? Other side of town."

The jarvey nodded with a greasy wink, and Tom climbed aboard.

The ride took longer than usual due to an overturned cart on the other side of the bridge, but it gave Tom time to think his plan through. The journalist was right. He couldn't ask a woman to act as bait and place herself in danger, even if he was nearby. And one woman wouldn't be enough. He would need several. Dozens, perhaps. But how would he protect them all? He couldn't be everywhere at once.

Eventually, the carriage pulled in front of the plain two-storey building situated on a corner. Tom fished through his leather pouch to pay the jarvey his fee, leaving him with only two shillings. He was going to have to fight soon or else he would run out of money. Father had created accounts all over town for him but provided him nothing for his purse.

"Where've you been, lad?" Connor leaned against the front door to prop it open. "No bruises? Black eyes?"

"Staying out of trouble for a while." Tom patted him on the shoulder, then slipped inside Parker's.

"Keepin' your face pretty for the ladies is what I think."

"Something like that." No one here knew exactly who he was or to whom he was related, so the less he divulged about his life, the better. "Is Maeve available?"

"Just went upstairs with one of her culls. A regular. May take an hour or so."

Damn. He didn't have an hour. He had already taken a few hours to meet the journalist at the park and had to get back to the warehouse to finish logging in the goods from Wednesday's shipment.

"Would you tell her I came by? I need to discuss something with her."

Connor tilted his head, rubbing his chin. "You need to be careful with that one."

"How do you mean?"

"Well . . . I think she's hopin' one day you'll free her from all of this."

Tom felt the weight of that every time he saw her. He wanted to help her. To reunite her with Emily and set her up some place far from Parker's or any other brothel. If only her daughter's treatments weren't so expensive, requiring most of his winnings. He could do it, though. But he'd have to fight, and right now, that could create too much scandal and upset his father's chances of winning a seat in Parliament.

"Did she tell you that?"

"She doesn't have to. I see it in the way she looks at you, lad."

Tom froze. "I plan on helping her, but not in that way, Connor. I am not . . . we are not . . ."

"That's what I'm tryin' to tell you." Connor rested his meaty hands on his hips. "She has different intentions."

Tom's mouth went dry. Maeve was his friend. Nothing more. The futility of her dreams tore at his heart. "Tell her I came by, would you?"

He started to leave, but Connor called him back. "That fellow returned lookin' for you. John? Jem?"

"The publican? George?"

"Aye. That's the one." Connor paused, his glare set on a group of men in the back of the parlour with the girl who performed tricks up on the tables. One of the men shoved another aside, and their acrimonious words started to get louder. "He wants you to fight Futrell. He beat Green too. Knocked him out only six minutes into the fight."

Six minutes. It had taken Futrell almost two minutes longer to take him down. Tom was still probably considered the local champion. That was good. "And the purse?"

"He didn't say, but I'll wager it's worth your time."

"And will you be my second?"

"That goes without sayin'."

George was the busiest boxing promoter in London and probably the only one who had enough muscle to arrange a fight as big as this one. If he took up George's offer, he was sure it would raise him in the ranks and therefore guarantee him a fatter purse. And the more money he made, the faster he could get Maeve out of Parker's and into a place of her own with her daughter. Then she would find a good fellow to care for her who could make her forget any feelings she might have for him.

Connor's attention turned to the back, where the arguing grew heated. "Damned culls. I'm gonna have to kick someone's arse in a minute."

And that's when it occurred to him that Connor could be the answer. "Connor, if I needed your help, could I count on you for it?"

"What do you have in mind?"

Tom leaned in. "I want to catch the London Monster."

Connor chuckled. "That sick cove?"

"Aye. And it is going to require you and a few of your fellow bullyboys."

One side of Connor's mouth curved upward. "Just tell me when and where, and we'll be there."

The men in the back started getting louder, with others joining in on the rumpus. Connor grumbled unintelligibly, then clapped Tom on the shoulder before crossing the room.

Tom stepped outside into the afternoon sunlight. The matter was resolved. Connor and his cronies would help him protect the women, and hopefully Maeve would agree to help him gather some of her companions to lure the beast into a trap.

But for now, he had to deal with George. He thought of the promise he'd made his father. He'd agree to this one fight somewhere outside of London proper, where no one would recognize him, and then drop out of the scene for a while. Father would never know.

He took a deep breath and headed a few streets down to the alehouse owned by George Kent.

Chapter 12

"Could it possibly get any colder outside?" Maeve bristled when a customer burst through the door, bringing the chilled air into the parlour with him. Out of the corner of her eye, she saw the fire in the hearth flicker with the breeze.

Paddy stood behind the bar, drying a wrythened ale glass with a faded red rag. "'Tis December, love. What did you expect?"

Already? She exhaled into her hands, rubbing them together for warmth. "December first?"

"Aye."

"My birthday. At least, I think it is." She smiled sadly. Not that it really mattered. It was just another Tuesday.

"Is it, then?" Paddy set two glasses on the bar, then filled them with brandy. "To the prettiest lass in all of London on her birthday."

She slowly spun the glass, wondering at how little her life had changed in the last few years.

"A touch of the melancholia, have you?" he asked teasingly.

"Perhaps." She shivered and pulled her green shawl tighter around her shoulders. "Where's Mother Wharton?"

"Locked in her parlour as usual. Probably counting her stacks of coin."

Maeve clinked her glass to his, then took a long deep drink. The burn of the dark gold liquid was just what she needed. No one she cared to spend her birthday with was around. Paddy would have to do. Emily was miles away, and Tommy hadn't returned since he'd left a message the week before that he needed to speak with her. And come to think of it, she hadn't seen Sophie in almost a fortnight.

Sophie's absence was the most surprising. Tommy came and went as he pleased, but Sophie had kept a regular schedule with her since they met months ago, appearing once a week on a Tuesday or Friday, and sometimes both. Maeve looked forward to her visits. They made her feel as if she lived a normal life, accepting a female visitor for tea and good conversation. Of course, there was no tea, and the conversation was often a depressing reminder of her circumstances. Beyond the stories of her past, she was four and twenty years old and an unmarried harlot with a sickly child. What could be worse?

"There you are." A firm hand gripped her just above the elbow, pulling her away from the bar.

Maeve startled. "Mr. Stone."

"Are you ready for me?" A sordid smile slithered across his lips, his gaze eager. His hair had been mussed by the wind, so a stray blond lock fell across his forehead. He led her over to the staircase with just enough force to keep her moving but not enough to draw Connor's attention.

"I . . . I wasn't expecting you today." She tried to smile to soften him, if only a little.

"Must I send *une carte d'adresse*? You forget yourself, my dear. You are a whore. Not a lady."

"You're hurting me." Maeve twisted against the rope that bound her hands to the bedpost. Stone lay on top of her, small beads of sweat forming on his brow like morning dew on grass.

"That is the point." He grunted with each mean thrust, banging the corner posts into the wall. "Fight me, then, *ma petite put*."

She bucked her hips under him. "How can I fight you with my hands tied together?"

His body momentarily stilled between her legs as he considered her words, but then he restarted with the same vigor as before. "Tell me you want me."

He said the same thing every time. It was ridiculous. What she truly wanted was for him to go away, never to return.

His hand came up around her throat, his fingers pressing into both sides of her neck. She knew he would never squeeze so hard as to leave a bruise, though. That was reserved for her wrists, the only acceptable location for a harlot. If he left marks on her neck, he wouldn't be permitted to return to Parker's. "Say it."

She tossed her head back and forth to try to free herself from his grip. "I want you."

"Of course you do. You're a whore." He thrust a few more times, then groaned, signaling it was finally over. He slipped off of her and sat on the edge of the bed, raking his hands through his messy blond locks.

Maeve lay still, ready for his toilet ritual to begin. It was always the same. First, he washed his face with the cloth next to the water pitcher. Then he reached for his coat that lay draped over the chair and removed a small silver snuffbox shaped like a shell with bits of mother-of-pearl inlay on the top. He flipped open the top with an exaggerated "ah", took a small pinch of the brown powder, and inhaled it sharply, leaving the light, sweet scent of apricot in the room, a smell she had grown to despise. At his leisure, he dressed, retied his hair ribbon, and studied himself in the mirror. Finally, he released the rope from around her wrists.

She slipped on her shift, wishing he would leave so she could discard the pessary—a wad of wool soaked in honey—inside of her.

He stood by the door, gripping the handle with one hand and holding a shilling with the other. "Before I take leave, I need you to do something for me."

She sat on the chair by the window, tying a garter around her stocking. "What would that be?" she asked without looking up. She was sore and tired, and if it had anything to do with any part of her body, she wasn't interested.

"I know you are friendly with the boxer. I need you to give him a message."

"The boxer?"

"The Pretty Punch."

That was Tommy's nickname. The first time she'd heard it, she thought it referred to his comely features, so she'd teased him mercilessly. He was a beautiful man, even with a nose that had been broken a few times. But her assumption about his nickname was completely wrong. He'd explained it had nothing to do with his face and everything to do with his jab.

"I haven't seen him in a while." She stepped into her petticoat and slid it up to her waist. "What do you want with him?"

"Tell him I will be at the fight on Saturday and expect him to do as I say this time."

He was being awfully vague, but based on his scowl, she figured it wouldn't be a good idea to ask him for more specifics.

He tossed the coin on the bed, but it bounced onto the floor. He tipped his hat and disappeared out the door. Her entire body loosened. She had to convince Mother Wharton to stop accepting him as a customer. It always left her broken and exhausted.

She removed the pessary and threw it into the washbasin for cleaning.

Was Stone right about Tommy? Was that why she hadn't seen him in a while? Was he fighting again? She thought he'd stopped indefinitely. At least that's what he had said only a month earlier. He'd apologized to her, concerned that he wouldn't be able to give her the extra coin for her secret cache. She remembered thinking how strange it was that he would apologize. He had no responsibility to her, no reason to think he needed to give her anything. But maybe he was softening to her. Maybe he saw past the men who came and went, past her transgressions, past the hopelessness that hovered over her, heavy and dark like a rain cloud. Maybe he wanted to help her because he realized he could love her.

Two days later, men Maeve hadn't seen in a while suddenly returned, filling the parlour with their loud voices and laughter. It was the same every year. The cold weather drove them in. The trick for Maeve was enticing them with enough brandy or rum to alter their senses, so that when they finally climbed the stairs and entered her room, they wouldn't notice that she kept the majority of her clothes on during the rumping. It was freezing, after all, and the bedclothes often fell to the floor with all their maneuvering, offering no respite from the chill that found its way through the cracks in the window frame.

Maeve stood near the foot of the stairs, watching the men talk with one another. With their frock coats unbuttoned and their hats in their hands, they eyed the women parading around the parlour. Occasionally, Rosie or Prudence would settle into one of the men's laps with the smile of a feral cat promising untamed play. It always seemed to work, for in a matter of seconds, the men would follow them upstairs wearing a hopeful grin.

"Why are you not mingling?" Mother Wharton asked, saluting a man across the room with her wine glass.

Maeve pulled her shawl tighter around her shoulders when the door opened and another customer entered. "I just finished with the gentleman from Flanders. I need a moment."

He'd been harmless, but he hadn't stopped talking, and since Maeve couldn't understand a single word of Dutch, it made for unnecessary noise.

"A moment?" Mother took a sip from her glass and scanned the room over the rim. "Do you have such luxury? With a sickly child and a dwindling number of admirers?"

"I brought in over nine pounds this week thus far and have been improving my French just as you suggested."

"That hardly provides you the luxury to stand here like an old *haridelle* wrapped in a faded shawl. You and your daughter are expensive to keep." She pulled the shawl from around Maeve's shoulders, then tossed it on the floor into a messy green heap.

Maeve knew that if she didn't pick it up, one of the other girls would keep it for her own, but she didn't dare flinch until Mother was nowhere in sight.

She peered through tapered eyes at Maeve, her gaze raking over her. Suddenly, Mother pinched both of her cheeks. Maeve bristled.

"That's better. You needed a little colour in that pale face. Now get to work." With a final scowl, she disappeared into her private parlour.

Maeve kicked her shawl behind a vase until later, then made her way over to the bar. A large crowd gathered near the door, making a fuss over one of the men entering. She stretched to look past their shoulders as they swarmed in, offering praise and well wishes. As the men parted, the familiar face she hadn't seen in a fortnight emerged. Tommy.

She stood straight, suddenly happy Mother had pinched some rosiness in her cheeks and she'd been forced to shed that faded green shawl.

Tommy edged through the crowd to get to her, his expression eager but stern. "Might I have a word with you?" He pulled her to the end of the bar, away from the others. "Did you get my message?"

"Connor told me you wished to see me." She turned to spy Mother Wharton emerging from her parlour, locking the door behind her. One would think jewels laid sprinkled over the rug in there the way she always kept it double-locked. Mother turned to her, her eyes spearing and her chin raised high with annoyance.

Maeve slowly ran her finger along Tommy's jaw. "Flirt with me, Tommy. Mother is watching."

He reached for her waist and pulled her close, their noses almost touching.

She had imagined standing with him like that hundreds of times, their mouths so close only the slightest falter would join them together. Her heart raced with his nearness.

"I need your help." He touched his forehead to hers. His skin was warm, his hair neatly bound except for a few tickly strands that had been freed by the wind. His cheek brushed hers, and his dark stubble scratched the tender skin of her temple. She leaned into him, eyes closed, ready to give him whatever he wanted. "I need some women."

She jerked back. It was the last thing she'd hoped to hear. "Beg pardon?"

His hand dropped from her waist, and he took a small step back. "As many as you can muster."

She could barely speak. Was he like all the others? Searching for twisted pleasures of the flesh?

"I have something in mind. A bit unorthodox, I must admit. But necessary, nevertheless."

She was certain all the colour had drained from her face. "Not everyone here will agree to participate in unorthodox play."

"What?" His brow furrowed.

"I am not the one to arrange such matters. You know Mother Wharton negotiates that sort of thing." His desire for a harem changed her entire opinion of him. She recoiled at the thought.

A smile crept up on his face and he laughed. "You misunderstand me. I need them to help me catch the London Monster."

Had she heard him correctly? "You want *women* to catch the monster? How do you propose they do that? With truncheons and giant nets?"

He draped his arm around her, once again pulling her close, just in a more friendly way this time. "Let me explain."

He told her his plan of using at least a dozen women at night as bait to lure the monster into St. James's Park, where he, Connor, and some of his fellow flash-men would be waiting in the shadows to capture him.

"It won't work," she said.

"And why not?"

"No woman—not even one here—would place herself in such danger."

His mouth twisted to the right. "We would be hiding nearby ready to help."

She looked at him carefully. He seemed earnest, definitely intent on catching the man. "May I ask you something?"

"Of course."

"Would you want *me* to go out there as a snare?" She tightened her stomach in anticipation of his answer.

His face softened, the hard lines in his forehead and around his mouth suddenly gone. He spoke softly. "I would not."

She closed her eyes and exhaled, relieved by his response. If only he knew how much those words meant to her. "Then I have a better plan."

She was about to explain when Mother approached, her fingers busily fumbling through her keys on the chatelaine at her waist. She glanced quickly at Connor, a stern scowl in her lips pressed thin. Would she have Tommy thrown out of Parker's? "You know our policy, sir. I have yet to see you order a drink."

Maeve rested her hand on his arm. "We were just talking, Mother."

"I know what you were doing. We are not in the business of entertaining men who do not wish for further services. He is taking you away from potential customers. *Paying* customers," she said as if Maeve needed the clarification.

Shame crept into Maeve's falsely brave smile. She had been warned about Tommy before. Mother did not appreciate that his visits never resulted in a trip upstairs.

"I understand." Tommy slipped off his gloves, extracted a shilling from his small leather pouch, then slid it across the bar to Paddy. "Three brandies. You would join us for a drink, would you not, Mother Wharton?"

"I prefer wine." She eyed Paddy, who nodded once.

Paddy prepared the drinks, and Tommy handed Maeve and Mother their glasses. "If you have no interest in Maeve, sir, there are other gentlemen here who do, so I would ask that you make your conversation short."

Tommy bowed, a scant smile in the corner of his lips. Mother harrumphed once before walking away. A wash of heat swept up Maeve's neck and across her cheeks, the embarrassment that every word spoken was always a reminder of who she was. What she did.

Tommy reached for her hand, his knuckles cut and swollen. The rumours were true. He was fighting again. "I apologize for monopolizing your time, but I know you will help me."

"You may come to me anytime," she said, her heart full of hope. She kissed the back of his hand just below where the skin was pink and swollen. "But your idea will never work. I think you should go to one of the molly houses in Holborn. You might find the *ladies* there more willing to enact your ruse."

"A molly house?" Tommy finished his brandy, his brow raised. "You think the men . . . or women . . . or what have you . . . would do it?"

"For the right price." Maeve could only imagine the faces of the men when he walked in there, all hoping he would be their next customer. "And since he only prowls at night, I believe the monster would not be able to tell the woman he is attacking is actually a man."

His face lit up. "You are brilliant."

"Wait!" She pulled him back by his sleeve. "I almost forgot. I have a message for you from Mr. Stone."

Tommy's smile faded, his jaw hardened. "What is it?"

"He said he will be at the fight on Saturday and expects you to do as he says this time." She tried to read what he was thinking, but his eyes were hard and gave nothing away.

He turned to leave, but she caught him once again. "Is something wrong? Are you in trouble? What should I tell him?"

"Tell him I answer to no one."

A Note

December 1789

"May I be of assistance, sir?"

I stare at the simpleton sitting behind a large heavy wooden desk undoubtedly meant to make him seem more powerful than he really is. He is not the magistrate, but a boyish clerk whose effort to sound like an adult is, unfortunately, in vain.

I stand in front of him wearing my scarf wrapped high on my neck so that my mouth is barely visible. "I would like to report the theft of my silver-tipped cane."

"Would you care to make a formal report?" He stands to retrieve a ledger from the counter behind him. He is no taller than my shoulder, and I wonder if he is old enough to hold a position as clerk.

I offer him a brief nod. "That is why I am here, naturally."

Of course, that is nowhere near the truth. My cane is safely stowed in the pewter stand next to the front door at home. I am only here to see the latest sketch of The Monster posted in the room. However, I don't dare look around with the clerk's eyes fixed on me as they are.

He motions for me to sit, so I do, keeping my frock coat buttoned so as not to reveal my clothing underneath just in case they match some description written in the papers. He proceeds to ask me questions, all of which I answer untruthfully. My name, my place of residence, the location of my whereabouts when the incident occurred, the description of the silver tip of my Whangee cane—having no resemblance to my own, of course. I find it terribly easy and *satisfying to create an entire scenario from the mere germ of a lie. When we are done, I thank him and turn to face the rear of the office, adjusting my coat in such a manner that it allows me the time to peruse the various sketches and notices haphazardly pinned to the wall.*

It is then that I spy the sketch I am searching for above the words, 'The London Monster. Find Him'. It looks nothing like me, except for perhaps the mouth. The nose appears a bit too long and wider than my own. There is shading over where my eyes would be, which is good since I consider them to be my most striking feature. Had the artist captured them correctly, it would surely make those who know me look twice and wonder. But I breathe a silent sigh of relief, knowing this picture speaks of no resemblance. I tip my hat and bid farewell to the addle-pate at the desk, then notice that the clothing depicted in the sketch is the ensemble I wore on the night I approached that plain woman in Billingsgate. This tells me one thing that fills my chest with fire. The description came from the man who chased me that night. The man who attacked me near St. Anne's Church. Thomas Hayes.

I know who he is, although he probably doesn't realize that. His name wasn't mentioned in the papers, but I was there at the hanging when they announced it. I also know that his father, Joseph Hayes, is running for a seat in Parliament. A family of derring-dos, as it were, hoping their mere presence in the world will help all of humanity. Never mind that the father's progressive ideas to provide London with a steady supply of coal will coincidentally line his pockets. And Thomas? He is a bit of a mystery. I have yet to discover how he manages to appear wherever I seem to be in the evenings.

He believes he can defeat me. I sense it in his determination to outsmart me. But he cannot. He will not. No one can. For only I am clever enough to walk amongst all of London, displaying the charm and gentility of a most refined gentleman. The proof is in the night he was mistaken for Mary Forster's attacker. The mob had descended upon him, not me. I had been impeccably dressed in my finest silks, much finer than his drab attire. No one even considered a man such as I would behave so dastardly.

He should learn to tread softly, for he does not wish to make an enemy of me, I can assure you.

I leave the magistrate's office breathing calmly. A tingling sensation is born in my gut. I feel powerful and free, yet a bit bothered that my last two encounters—one near Hyde Park and the other in Green Park—were botched. One would think that it would be quite simple for a man to proposition a lady in such lovely settings, but he would be wrong. It takes tremendous skill and patience to wait until a beauty is alone in order to carry out the act. Occasionally, just as I offer an honest phrase, her chaperone steps out from the crowd and makes it difficult for me to complete my seduction. What she fails to realize is that she has ruined what could have been a delightfully erotic exchange between two potential lovers. Some people are terribly rude.

But such are the vicissitudes of allurement.

I walk towards St. James's, where the streets are bustling with those determined to arrive at some intended destination. They wear layers of dark clothing appropriate for the season, allowing me to blend in beautifully in my black wool frock coat and blue breeches. Just ahead, three men start laughing, stirring me to smile. There is something about their playful manner that I find attractive. The last time I laughed like that was with my brother over a cup of tea. He'd reminded me of one of my wonderful escapades involving a young lady who had mistaken me for someone else. That night had ended quite well, especially for me, but she'd remained bitter and somewhat tarnished from the experience. But that is neither here nor there.

I stare at the trio of men and wonder if we could possibly become friends. As they pass, it occurs to me that I should be laughing too, or at the very least celebrating my latest victory of remaining anonymous. Why dwell on the two failed attempts for a rendezvous?

I quicken my pace and head to White's Club, imagining a meal of roasted grouse and smoked eel with a crisp bottle of wine. I hurry up the stairs and disappear inside with all the other men who look just like me.

Chapter 13

Cuthbert pressed his hat firmly to his head as he stepped out into the cold wind, his heart still pounding from his brief encounter with the black-haired prostitute in Covent Garden. That was his third visit to the brothel in a fortnight. Why couldn't he suppress his urges? He couldn't imagine what his mother would say if she ever discovered this part of him. It would be terribly humiliating. But even worse would be the look of disgust on Sophie's face if his true nature were ever brought to light.

He quickened his pace to the church in Westminster, trying to push away thoughts of the girl who'd wrapped her legs around his hips not thirty minutes earlier. She wasn't particularly attractive or sweet-natured, but she was agreeable enough and joined him behind the curtain of a small room where she did as he pleased. The entire ordeal lasted only a minute or two, yet it released his general restlessness and the tightness in his back and neck that he suffered from daily.

But he had to stop thinking about her and think of other things. Things that would set his mind straight and force him onto a righteous path. As he walked, he allowed the wind to sting his cheeks and didn't bother wiping away the tears that trailed out of the corners of his eyes. He needed the cold. *Think, Cuthbert, think.* He'd had breakfast that morning with Mother and Father, and they'd had a brief conversation regarding the wedding. June would be lovely, after all, he'd said. The blooms, the delightful breezes.

Privately, he dreamed of Sophie in his arms as his wife. Taking her into their marriage bed. Touching her breasts. He inhaled deeply. The prostitute had small, pert breasts with dark nipples. He shook his head to rid himself of the thought. Why couldn't he stop?

Finally, he spotted St. Martin-in-the-Fields's spire in the near distance. He was one street west of the church where he could concentrate on holy matters and not those of the flesh. He hurried, stopping only once to beg forgiveness of the woman he almost knocked over in his path. After he climbed the steps and entered the church, he breathed deeply, hoping to inhale the holiness that dwelled there. His footsteps echoed off the high arched ceiling above, and the grey winter light struggled to enter through the large window behind the altar.

He removed his hat and sat in a pew near the rear. Only a half dozen or so parishioners were there, all sitting close to the front. He edged forward and bowed his head, his hands clasped and resting on the back of the pew in front of him. "Dear Lord, I ask for your forgiveness for the wrongs I have done and the sins I have committed . . ."

When he was finished praying, he laid his head on his hands, overcome with the realization that he had fallen into a futile routine. Bedding a whore and then scurrying to church to repent was failing to rid his soul of the corruption that lay heavy and black within it. It was not bringing him closer to God, nor did it cleanse him of the filth of his actions. It only made him feel worse.

"You look troubled, my son."

Cuthbert lifted his head. The Reverend Dr. Anthony Hamilton stood before him in a black robe over his white cassock, a Bible in one hand.

Cuthbert wasn't sure how to respond. He couldn't say he was troubled because then the reverend would encourage him to divulge the details of the matter. On the other hand, he didn't want to deny he was troubled because he was certain his angst was present in all his features, and the reverend would know he was lying. He lowered his shaking hands into his lap to hide their tremor. "It is good to see you, Vicar."

The reverend smiled politely. "And you as well. But it is not Sunday."

Cuthbert hadn't missed a single Sunday in four years. The only thing that had broken his seven-year streak was when he'd contracted an awful catarrhal accompanied by a cough that had kept him away from others for more than a fortnight.

"I've noticed you have been coming more frequently than usual," he continued.

Cuthbert cleared his throat. He'd hoped he hadn't noticed, afraid word might reach his mother and she would confront him with far too many questions. "There is something about this church, this sanctuary, that fills my spirit with light."

"Ah, yes." The reverend pointed to the heavens. *"While ye have light, believe in the light, that ye may be the children of light."*

"John 12:36," Cuthbert said.

Reverend Anthony smiled broadly. "You are a child of God. That is why your soul is filled with light."

Cuthbert's throat tightened. He wasn't a child of God. At least, he didn't feel like one at the moment. He was corrupt. "I should be going. My mother is expecting me."

Cuthbert slid out of the pew, wiping the sweat from his hands on the pocket flaps of his frock coat.

"Please send her my regards. I expect I will see you both this Sunday."

"Of course." He nodded, then exited the church, shoving his hat low over his ears to keep out the cold. People were everywhere, their eyes on him, judging and condemning. He hurried his step to escape their stares, anxious to get home and shut the door behind him.

He had to stop visiting whores. Had to stop thinking about pleasures of the flesh. It was the only way to salvation and the right thing to do. He vowed to wear his jugum that night. That should help keep his vital energies in place and repress all the lewd notions stirring within him.

"Mr. Needham?"

Cuthbert startled away from his thoughts and turned to the man staring at him. He looked familiar, but he couldn't place his name.

"Remember me? I made the flower arrangement for you this past fall."

He scratched his head, then remembered. The flowers for Sophie. "Of course. Mr. . . ."

"Williams. Rhynwick Williams." He bowed with a flourish of his hand. There was something feminine about his features. Or perhaps it was something in that particular movement. "Did the lady enjoy the arrangement?"

"Very much so. She was delighted."

"I would love for you to come by the shop. I have created a new flower that I believe you will find quite extraordinary."

"Perhaps next week," he offered, thinking only of getting home and sitting in his chambers with the door closed.

"You should pass it on your way, that is, if you are continuing down Charing Cross. I'd be happy to escort you." Williams flashed a friendly smile, extending his hand in the direction of his flower shop.

He didn't want to go, but how could he walk right past the shop without entering it? "Very well."

It took only a matter of minutes to get there. Williams held open the door for Cuthbert. The shop was more comfortable than outside but by no means warm. Cuthbert waited in the dark while the florist lit some oil lamps. Carrying one lamp, Williams beckoned him through a curtain that separated the front room from the workspace in the back. The room came to life under the warm glow, every inch of space claimed by dozens of purposefully placed objects. Porcelain vases and stacked clay pots crowded one corner. On the adjacent wall, a high wooden shelf housed glass bottles of all shapes and sizes. Drawings of various flowers pinned to the opposite wall overlapped one another, leaving only a thin line of exposed wall over two large crates. Bits of blue and yellow fabric, rolls of thin wire, and odd-shaped metal tools were strewn about on the long table that lined the back wall.

"This is where I create my art." Williams proudly swept his arm, spanning the room. "It might seem a bit disorderly to you, but I know exactly where everything is."

"On the contrary. I find it incredibly organized."

"That is kind of you to say." Williams picked up a set of pincers that were curved yet pointed. "People often think of artists as scatterbrained. Flighty. And I suppose some of them are. I have known quite a few over the years from my time at the dance academy."

"You were a dancer?" That explained his perfect posture and graceful gestures.

"And a violinist. Both at the King's Theatre. Before it burnt to the ground, of course." He set down the pincers. "But that was years ago."

"Years ago? You seem quite young."

"I am three and twenty. Young enough to have plenty to look forward to, yet old enough to be settled."

"Why must they seem like opposites? Do you not look forward to being settled?" It was something Cuthbert couldn't wait for. He pictured Sophie's gentle smile and the curve of her neck where it met her shoulder.

Williams eyed him playfully. "Is it not more pleasant to enjoy the company of many women?"

Cuthbert's stomach dropped. He had just managed to forget about his indiscretions, and now they all came swirling back into his head like a dark, angry typhoon. He fumbled for words but managed to say nothing.

When he didn't respond, Williams continued. "But of course, you prefer only one. Your lady friend we sent the flowers to?"

Cuthbert exhaled. "My fiancée, you mean."

"You're betrothed, are you?" He reached under the long worktable and pulled out a bucket. "I used to be quite popular with the ladies, but ever since an unfortunate event at the theatre, I have not had the same sort of luck."

99

Cuthbert wasn't sure how to respond. He too understood what it was like not to have the attention of the ladies, or at least not from the one who meant the most.

"Well, that is neither here nor there." Williams reached into the bucket and extracted five long stems with blue and yellow flowers attached. "What do you think of these?"

"Irises? Did you make these as well?"

Williams nodded. "Much more colourful than the peonies I gave you. Perfect for this dreary winter."

Cuthbert plucked one from his hand. The petals were silky, more purple than blue, with a flame of yellow reaching out from the centre. "Will you make me an arrangement?"

"I can have it delivered tomorrow."

"At three?"

"It would be my pleasure."

Cuthbert left the shop, excited about seeing the reaction on Sophie's face when she received them. He had already sent word that he would pay her a visit tomorrow afternoon. Now he simply needed to arrive before three in order to witness the surprise. Perhaps the gift would elicit more than a smile and allow for a moment of tenderness.

"Cuthbert!"

He spun around to locate the familiar voice calling out to him. Dalton stood farther up the street, waving off a sheepish-looking group of bedraggled men. He hurried ahead with a peculiar, strangely delicate gait, his hand raised as if he were hailing a hackney.

He approached with his legs set apart, slightly out of breath. "Come with me, old boy."

"Who were those men?"

Dalton glanced behind him, unconcerned. "Beggars. They see a man in silk threads and are drawn to him like maggots to a corpse."

Dalton took a few careful steps and grimaced.

"And why are you walking like that?" Cuthbert asked.

Dalton tugged on the front of his breeches, then dismissed his question with a flip of his hand. "A bit of an inconvenient rash, as it were. Nothing a trip to the apothecary won't cure."

Cuthbert frowned, adjusting his own breeches. He could only imagine where he'd procured that rash. "Where are you headed?"

"White's. My cousin Philip is hosting a stag party there for some poor fellow about to take the marital plunge."

"I am headed home. Mother might—"

Dalton spun him around by the shoulder. "You are coming with me."

Two hours and seven—or was it nine?—brandies later, Cuthbert stood to leave, wavering once before grabbing the back of the chair to steady himself. The nearby rattling of the dice box clanged in his ears like a church bell.

Dalton pressed him back down. "Where do you think you're going?"

"I need to go—"

"Home to your mother. Yes, I know. But we cannot leave just yet. I am down one hundred and twenty pounds." Dalton reshuffled the cards in his hand.

Cuthbert shook his head to clear his senses. "One last hand and then we go."

Dalton clicked his tongue. "Don't be such a wet mop. I would like to try my hand at Hazard next."

Cuthbert noticed Lord Greenville watching him, a sincere look of pity in his kind eyes. He must think him a disaster. Why was he always present when Cuthbert felt his worst?

Someone shouted, "Ten pounds says this raggedy chap drops before the game is over."

Another challenged, "I say twenty pounds he falls off his chair."

"His head will drop on the table first. Fifty pounds says so. Who will take it?"

They were all pointing at him. Greenville forced a smile in his direction, then shook his head before venturing into a back room. It would be the end of Cuthbert if the man said a word to his parents. Why he hadn't already was truly baffling. Cuthbert considered going after him to explain but realized there was no excuse for his behaviour. What could he possibly say?

Out of the corner of his eye, he watched the steward scribbling entries in the betting book. He had become the doomed object of a bet.

"I am not going to fall. I feel fine." He didn't feel fine and silently agreed that if he didn't leave soon, he *would* fall off his chair. He turned to Dalton. "One game of Hazard and then we go."

Dalton leaned closer and lowered his voice. "The longer I stay away from home, the greater the chance that Vivian will be asleep, allowing me to escape a torrent of questions regarding my uncomfortable situation."

Cuthbert squinted at him through tired eyes. "What?"

He reached into his coat and pulled out his snuffbox. "My rash. How I happened to acquire it . . ."

Cuthbert's groin ached just thinking about it. "Fine."

Dalton pinched some powder, sniffed hard twice, then sneezed. "At least this helps."

Although Cuthbert appreciated the fruity aroma, he stayed away from the powder, for he'd read it increased sexual appetite. It was especially uncomfortable watching his father partake in snuffing, knowing its amorous effect.

They stayed another hour until Dalton had lost over two hundred pounds to various satisfied members, all losses politely entered in the betting book. On the other hand, Cuthbert had managed to remain upright the rest of the evening, making a few betting men very unhappy.

He stood to leave, his stomach roiling and head spinning from both the spirits and his losses. He did his best to bid a farewell to his fellow members on his way to the front door without looking like the town drunkard. As he approached, however, he tripped on the edge of a rug and lost his balance, only to be assisted upright by Greenville.

"Thank you, milord," Cuthbert mumbled, desperately hoping the contents of his stomach wouldn't find their way onto Greenville's polished leather shoes.

"Are you quite fine, young man?" Greenville's face was full of concern. "Perhaps you should ride with me in my carriage. I can get you home safely."

"Not necessary, although I thank you for your kindness. I would rather enjoy taking the air with my friend here." Cuthbert waved at Dalton who was already waiting out front at the bottom of the stairs. The last thing he needed was for his parents to see him arrive in the arms of Greenville, who would be sure to describe the exact nature of his condition and the circumstances in which it was achieved. He leaned close to Greenville, doing his best to maintain perfect composure. "I would appreciate it, milord, if you would keep the events of this evening a private matter."

One corner of Greenville's mouth inched up. "Of course. But may I offer a suggestion?"

"Milord?"

"If you are going to behave in such a manner, do it when no one is watching. Remember who you are." He tipped his hat and left Cuthbert standing in the entrance, his words striking at the very core of his problem. He was a fraud.

Neither he nor Dalton had any coin left to pay for a hackney, so together they walked the mile or so to Cuthbert's home. With every step creating a thundering in his head as if it were being split open with an anvil, Cuthbert had to adopt a gentler gait. He could only imagine what the two of them looked like coming come down the street, hobbling and shambling like they had just been freed from the nearby asylum.

Dalton rubbed his gloved hands together for warmth. "There's a fight Saturday night in Blackheath. We should go."

"More gambling? Have you not had enough?"

"Enough? Is there such a thing?"

Nothing was ever enough for Dalton. Not gambling. Not spirits. Not women. Cuthbert massaged circles of pressure into his pounding temples. "I am not sure I will be up to it. Up to anything, for that matter."

Dalton slapped him on the back, causing Cuthbert's ears to start ringing. "'Tis the season, old boy. Celebrations, merriment, folly." Dalton hugged him close. "That reminds me. Viscount Sidmouth will be hosting this year's Twelfth Night masque. Did you receive an invitation?"

Cuthbert remembered his mother saying something about it, but he'd forgot to respond. He never cared much for that particular holiday, for it carried with it such mischief. It almost always ended in some sort of a debacle. "I did, but I have yet to speak with Sophie about it."

"You must go. 'Tis expected to be quite the *soiree*. Do you remember what happened last year when Lord Willoughby's manservant became the Lord of Misrule?"

How could he forget? It had actually made the papers. The manservant had got a little too carried away and ordered Willoughby to fetch him some wine, and whilst he was absent, the servant planted an unchaste kiss on the lips of Lady Willoughby in front of all of London's finest. But that wasn't the worst of the scandal. The worst of it lie in the fact that Lady Willoughby kissed him back quite willingly in the same salacious manner.

Dalton shook his head with pity. "That poor fellow was marched out of London with no hope for return."

"And poor Lady Willoughby."

"That old crooked-nosed whore? She got what she deserved. Imagine your wife cuckolding you in front of all your peers. Really!"

His words rang in Cuthbert's ears. Not Sophie. Not ever.

Chapter 14

"I thought you'd never return." Maeve shut the bedroom door.

Sophie threw her hat on Maeve's bed, then flopped in the chair by the window. It felt good to get out of the cold and even better to see Maeve. "If it wasn't one thing, it was another."

"I was worried. The London Monster still roams the streets."

"You have naught to worry over with me dressed like this." Sophie brushed a hand down her brown wool coat and breeches.

She explained how Mother had decided to join her, Peg, and the kitchen maid on the last two visits to the market and how Aunty Lydia had taken ill, rendering her incapable of accepting visitors. All this prevented Sophie from the freedom she normally had on Tuesdays and Fridays to go about town pursuing possible leads for stories.

"I assumed as much," Maeve said. "I've missed your company."

Sophie smiled. "And I yours."

Maeve flicked her hand at her. "I imagine you have dozens of friends. All women like you do."

"I have acquaintances. I am not sure I would call them friends." The only real friend Sophie had was Bertie. She could count on him for anything. The others were people with whom to pass the time. "What have I missed?"

Maeve's mouth twisted in thought, a playful smirk in her lips. "Well, I had tea with Her Majesty, Queen Charlotte, last week. We had such a lovely time at the palace. She offered me one of her gowns, but I found none of them to my liking, so I refused her."

Sophie laughed. "Who would want silk gowns covered in jewels, anyhow?"

"Exactly," Maeve said, her chin raised haughtily and her lips pursed.

She liked this side of Maeve. Frivolous. Lighthearted. Sophie studied her lingering smile. There was something about it that made her look different.

Maeve looked at her sideways. "What is it? Why are you looking at me like that?"

"You seem different. Happy."

Maeve lowered her chin, smiling. "Perhaps I am."

"Is it Emily? Has Albert returned?"

"Emily is fine. As fine as she can be, I suppose." She flung her hand in the direction of the other side of the room. "And I would sooner see King George walk through that door than Albert."

"Then what is it?"

Maeve scooted to the foot of the bed, facing Sophie, her eyes twinkling. "I think I'm in love."

Sophie sucked in her breath. "In love?"

Maeve nodded. "With a boxer."

Sophie must've made an awful face because Maeve's smile faded immediately. How could she fall in love with a man who fought others for a living? A brute? "A pugilist? Please tell me he is not that awful Mr. Stone, the one who ties you up and—"

"Of course not!" Maeve said, brows raised. "Tommy is a wonderful man. Kind. Polite. And humble."

That was not how she imagined a boxer to be. All that hitting and hurting. "Does he know you are a . . ." Sophie regretted the words as soon as they tumbled from her lips.

"He knows," she said softly.

"Does he feel the same?"

Maeve hesitated. "He says he cares for me."

"Then that is wonderful." She tried to sound sincere, but she'd said it halfheartedly. What kind of life could this man—a boxer—give Maeve?

Sophie stood to embrace her. She couldn't help but feel a mixture of joy and despair at hearing talk about love. Love was not part of her own equation with Bertie. "Tell me. What exactly do you feel?"

Maeve looked at her, confused.

Sophie hesitated, embarrassed and ashamed by her thoughts. She took a deep breath. "What does love *feel* like?"

"Surely you know. You're engaged to be married."

That horrible pang Sophie always felt at the thought of marrying Bertie sat heavy in her gut. "I love him, but not in the way I always imagined love would feel. I suppose that is an awful thing to say."

Maeve sighed, patting the bed next to her. "Sit."

Sophie joined her on the edge of the bed.

"I used to think I would never love again after Albert. Perhaps I never considered it possible because I thought somehow we'd find our way back to each other. But once I realized he would not return, I surrendered that dream. It seems like such a long time ago."

"And now? You have found love again?"

Maeve exhaled in a gentle sigh. "I can actually feel my heart beat stronger when he's near. When he comes through the door, all my sadness and heartache melts away like a late spring frost." She played with the frayed yellow ribbon on the cuff of her sleeve. "He does little things for me, always striving to help me in one way or another. Sometimes I feel as giddy as a young girl, trying desperately to maintain my composure and not sound like a bumbling fool in front of him."

Sophie had never felt any of that with Bertie. He did nice things for her too. She almost wished he wouldn't. It would make it so much easier.

"And then there are other feelings. The feelings of wanting to be close to him, kiss him, feel his hands on my bare skin."

That had never crossed Sophie's mind. The more Bertie hinted at his need for affection, the more she wanted nothing to do with him.

"I want you to meet him," Maeve said, yanking her from her thoughts. "He's fighting tomorrow in Blackheath."

"Fighting? Is boxing not illegal?"

"Yes, but—"

"Tomorrow is Saturday. I will never be able to escape the watchful eyes of my family."

"Please think of a way. This could be the story that the papers will accept."

"What are you saying?"

"You told me you need to write a story that will appeal to London gentlemen yet contain a bit of grit." Maeve stood to pace the length of room. "Tommy—they call him The Pretty Punch—has defeated—"

"The Pretty Punch?" Sophie wondered if she'd heard right.

"I know. Silly, right? They say his punch is artful, always managing to land in the right spot." Maeve waved her hands in the air as she spoke. "He's fighting William Futrell, the reigning champion from Birmingham."

"How is this the story that will get me published?"

"Tommy is undefeated. It's a fight between champions. And it's one that every gentleman from London will attend."

Sophie sat back in the chair. "Every gentleman in London, you say."

Maeve crossed her arms and nodded.

Clearly, these men were betting illegally on these fights. Why else would they attend? Could this be an opportunity to expose the underworld of boxing? "Very well. I will think of a way to excuse myself from my engagements tomorrow, and then we will go meet this man of yours."

Sophie couldn't wait to tell Tom about this new idea to expose the underworld of boxing. Maeve was right. It was the perfect topic for the papers' male readership, yet she would write it with her own twist. It wouldn't simply be an article about two champions fighting one another until one of them fell. It would be about illegal gambling and the kind of people who attended such an event. She pictured them all spending their last shilling on a bet and a drink, stumbling over one another to get a better look at the fight.

It was late in the afternoon, and the winter sun was slowly fading behind heavy grey clouds. She hurried to Tom's warehouse at the wharf, edging past the stream of stevedores who flooded Billingsgate, carrying huge bags draped over their broad shoulders or rolling barrels on their sides. No one seemed to pay her any notice dressed in breeches. She smiled, proud of her ability to carry herself like a young man and fool all those around her. Especially the monster, if he was watching.

She reached the warehouse and was about to knock on the door when she noticed it was slightly ajar. She inched it open and heard Tom's voice. "Bring her something she might like."

"That would be a bit forward. A gift from a man who is not her betrothed." He sounded a lot like Tom, but his words were softer, less sure.

"She has agreed to meet you at Vauxhall without an escort, Henry. Bringing her a trinket would pale in comparison to that."

Tom's words embarrassed her. She had done the same thing—dressed as a man, of course—but nonetheless, it was a bold move.

"Very well. I know just the thing," said Henry.

They exchanged a few more words, and then a well-attired man—slightly shorter and more narrowly built than Tom—swung open the door, forcing Sophie against the wall. His gentle smile told her he was clearly Tom's relation.

"Forgive me, young man. May I be of help?" The gentleman studied her as he adjusted his hat, his eyes blue like Tom's yet with tiny creases in the corners.

She cleared her throat to lower her voice. "I am here for Mr. Thomas Hayes."

He held the door open. "Go right in. You will find him in the office."

She entered the dark warehouse and walked the narrow path between crates that led to the back, where the glow of a lamp shone through an open door. Tom was seated behind the desk reading the *Morning Chronicle*, his shirtsleeves rolled up and his gaze firmly fixed to the page. She tapped lightly on the door to get his attention.

He glanced up, and his eyes widened. "Evans. I thought . . . well, I wasn't certain I would see you again. Did my brother let you in?"

"Your brother? Ah, yes." It made perfect sense. "I hope I am not disturbing you." She suddenly felt nervous. The last time she'd seen him, he'd expressed concern about her safety and then rested his hand over hers, the heat from his skin melting into her own. It was an awkward moment, and one she was glad to have escaped quickly.

He stood and edged around the desk, the paper still in his hand. "The monster's struck again. Stabbed a woman on Dover Street."

She drew her hand to her mouth. "Is she . . ."

He shook his head. "Apparently he only managed to slice open her gown and petticoats."

He moved closer to show her the article, and she inhaled the smell of spices that clung to him from the crates from foreign lands. They filled her senses, rendering her unable to concentrate on what he was saying.

"This is why we need to act quickly," he continued. "I think there's a way to carry out our plan."

She leaned away slightly to clear her head, but her skin still tingled as if alert to his proximity. It was a strange feeling. A comfortable nervousness settled in her chest.

He spoke about men dressed as women and his friends who would trail them, ready to pounce if the monster approached. She was about to express her doubts about a man passing for a woman when she remembered her own ruse of passing for a man.

"It will be dark, I suppose." It sounded farfetched, but she had to admit it was clever. "Where will you find these men who would be willing to dress as women?"

"Do you really want to know?" One side of his mouth rose in a smile. The light from the oil lamp flickered in his blue eyes.

She nodded.

"Holborn. There are a few molly houses over there where I might have some luck."

It took a moment for the term to sink in before its meaning struck her. "I was not certain they actually existed. I imagined such talk was merely rumour."

He laughed quietly to himself.

"You must think me quite sheltered."

He set the paper on his desk, then leaned back so that he was partially seated. The wind rattled the roof shingles above and the oil lamp sputtered from the draft, causing the light to flicker behind him. It suddenly registered to her that they were alone. She fidgeted with her cravat, pulling it away from her throat.

"Sheltered?" He reached for her hand. "Women often are."

She stared at her hand in his, her skin so pale against his own. She fought to still her fingers that trembled slightly. "You . . . know."

"You could drape yourself in a flour sack and not be able to hide your beauty." His hand came around her waist and pressed into her back. He pulled her close. "I have not stopped thinking about you since we last met."

Her hip settled against his thigh, her wool breeches not thick enough to prevent his warmth from penetrating her own skin. He slipped off her hat and set it beside the discarded paper. She knew what he was about to do. And she didn't want to stop it. He bent to kiss her but hesitated. Her pulse thrummed in her ears. She was going to kiss a man who wasn't her betrothed. Before she could think of all the reasons it was the wrong thing to do, his lips touched hers, gently at first, then eagerly, sending a strange tingle down her back. His mouth was warm and hungry, yet not insistent. She followed his lead, kissing him freely. His hand traveled to the nape of her neck, releasing her hair from its ribbon. He pulled away slightly to look at her. "Tell me your name."

She caught her breath, then whispered, "Sophie."

The hint of a smile appeared on his lips. "Sophie," he whispered back, then kissed her once more.

A soft moan escaped her, and she realized her hands were around his neck, one hand tugging at his unbound hair. She felt herself growing weak and leaning further into him, but it was a wonderful feeling. Something she'd never felt before and something she wanted more of. Why was she doing this? Had Bertie tried to kiss her this way, she would've never allowed it.

"I have it! The perfect—"

Sophie froze. Henry had returned. Tom stood abruptly, shielding her from Henry's view. She squeezed her eyes shut, burying her face into his back, bits of his shirt clenched in her grip. Her first real kiss with a man, and it was witnessed by a stranger.

"You . . . he . . . I had no idea . . . I should go." Henry's words were barely audible, his discomfort present in the pauses.

From behind Tom's arm, Sophie could see that Henry's face had blanched. He was holding a small pewter frame encasing the drawing of a red bird. He turned to leave, bumping into the threshold as he exited.

Tom lurched at him. "Wait! Henry! It is not what you think."

It was all so confusing. What had she done? Sophie grabbed her hat and ran out the door past Tom and into the crowded wharf. She heard him calling out after her, but she didn't turn around. She was embarrassed. Ashamed.

When she reached Thames Street, she hired a hackney. She settled on the bench behind two horses with droopy heads and swayed backs, their master controlling the reins overhead. The coachman offered her a wool blanket for cover, but it reeked of horse sweat, so she refused it. As they left Billingsgate, cold wind affronted her from every direction, the temperature dropping with the setting of the sun. She closed her eyes as the carriage bumped along the cobblestones and thought about the way Tom had looked at her, kissed her, spoken her real name. There was something different about Tom. A confidence. A presence. It was there even when she first saw him months ago, his head in a noose and his death before him. It made him strong, yet gentle. Resolute, yet calm.

His touch had sent her to a place she'd never been before, a place of wanting and desire. As she sat freezing on the bench, she wished she was still in his arms, his chest pressed to hers, their heartbeats mingling so that one was indistinguishable from the other. Maeve's description had been right.

If that were true, did it mean that what she was feeling was love? Should she fight it? Perhaps, but something inside of her told her she couldn't.

An angry knock on Sophie's bedroom door made Peg move even faster to pin up Sophie's hair. "Sophie?" called her mother.

"Your escapades are going to be the death of me," Peg whispered, her fingers shaking and fumbling with the loose strands.

Sophie kicked her breeches under the bed. "One moment, Mother!"

Peg took a step back, studied Sophie's hair, then nodded in approval.

Sophie quickly scanned the room, searching for any evidence of her outing. Satisfied there were no signs of her spending the afternoon dressed as a man, she nodded at Peg. "Let her in, please."

Mother entered scowling and holding a calling card. "Mr. Needham waited all afternoon for you to appear. Had you forgot that he was to pay a call today?"

Sophie sucked in her breath. The sound of his name brought a torrent of guilt with it. She'd completely forgot about his visit. "Was Bertie upset?"

Mother shook her head in disgust. "Of course he was. He had arranged a special surprise for you only to have his wonderful plans dashed."

Her heart sank. How that poor man still wanted anything to do with her was a mystery. Honestly, she didn't behave so thoughtlessly on purpose. It was all the sneaking and evading that caused it. Tom's image appeared before her, and she quickly shrugged it away. "I am truly sorry, Mother, and will write him immediately to tell him so."

Mother grabbed her by the wrist and led her to the stairs. "You will have to do that after you see what that lovely man has done for you."

Sophie turned to look at Peg, who only shrugged, clearly having no idea what Mother was talking about since she had spent the day at the market as they'd arranged.

At the bottom of the stairs, Sophie glimpsed a flash of bold colour in the hall mirror before being guided into the parlour. Where the white peonies had once stood, was a huge arrangement of irises, their violet petals and long green stems illuminated by the sunlight streaming in from the front window. They were all in perfect bloom, a splash of yellow shaped like teardrops in the centre of the curved petals. They were beautiful, but it was almost January, so they couldn't be real. She stroked one of the petals. Silk.

"Are they not remarkable? They appear as real flowers, yet upon further inspection, the truth is revealed." Mother stood back in admiration.

It made her think of her relationship with Bertie. They appeared the perfect couple—betrothed since they were children, friends on all accounts, and suited for one another in every way. But if someone searched her heart and the truth behind her painted smile when she received him, one would know it was all a farce. It seemed like so many things were. "Yes, Mother. They are truly remarkable."

Chapter 15

Tom woke the next morning unsure of what to think about first. How good it felt to have Sophie in his arms. The fact his brother had thought he was kissing a man. His match against William Futrell that evening and the fat purse a victory would bring, allowing him to pay the molls to lure the monster. Or Stone's threat that he must throw the fight or there would be a price to pay. But when he sat down for his morning meal, the decision was already made, for the *Oracle* lay next to his father's plate with the headline *Birmingham Champ Arrives in London* written in bold black letters right across the top.

Tom glanced at it surreptitiously, praying his real name was not mentioned along with Futrell's in the article. Until now, Father had never put the pieces together that he was the mysterious 'Tom', otherwise known as The Pretty Punch. He had used so many false surnames and places of residence over the years, he'd angered the journalists to a point that they'd given up trying to discover his true identity. At first, they'd searched the back alleys and disreputable establishments in all of southeastern England, assuming he must be a rough, lowborn bully-huff. Naturally, they found no trace of him or anyone who knew his true identity. They'd never suspected he'd be a member of the gentry and the son of a wealthy industrialist who could potentially become a member of the House of Commons. And that suited him just fine. As a result, he was simply known as Tom, the boxer from unknown parts.

But that was before he'd fought anyone as big as Futrell. Now the hunt would ensue for his real identity.

"Did you see this?" Father jabbed the paper on the table with his forefinger, his napkin haphazardly tucked into his waistcoat. "One of the first things I plan to do in Parliament is rid this city of its ne'er-do-wells. There would be no place for them to go if these low types stopped engaging in such sport."

Father glanced at the branded M on Tom's palm as he reached into the basket for some bread. His mouth turned down in a scowl. "Be sure to wear your gloves today, son."

Tom adjusted the lace cuff of his sleeve to cover the mark. Would Father ever look at him without disappointment again? "Gentlemen attend those events, Father. Not simply ne'er-do-wells."

"Bah. They are all rogues and blacklegs, if you ask me."

Tom thought about the crowd that usually frequented the matches. It was true. Many of them were the poorer sort, but the rest of them were nobles and gentry wearing velvet coats embroidered in silk very similar to the one Father had on. "And if boxing were legal?"

"Legal? You know who that sport attracts. They would all come crawling out of the bowels of the city to attend matches. Without an appropriate number of constables, we'd never be able to keep up with the crime."

"But if it were legal, it could be taxed through licensing. Then you could use those monies for a proper constabulary."

Father speared a piece of his roast beef while shaking his head. "No need for that. Gaming is illegal, as it should be. Remove the sport and you remove the gambling. And that removes the problem." He popped the meat into his mouth, seemingly contented by his pronouncement.

"Come now, Father." Tom brushed some breadcrumbs from his sleeve. "There would still be bets on the horses. Or cards. Gaming is everywhere. You see what goes on at Brooks's. And White's is notorious for it. Everything becomes a wager. From whether or not the tea will be served hot to how many dishes of pigeon will be doled out in one seating."

"That is harmless gentlemen's play."

"Ah, yes. Gentlemen's play. Illegal for the poor. Acceptable for the rich." Tom spread a clump of butter on his bread. "I think you are looking at this all wrong, Father. Why not officially make it a gentlemen's sport? Organize it. License it. Once you do that, you control the events, and the city could benefit from the money brought in from the spectators."

Father sat back in his chair and stared at him, his eyes piercing. "Why such an interest?"

Tom did his best not to look away, to maintain his father's gaze. He enjoyed boxing and the freedom it gave him to earn his own money he could spend any way he chose. Getting him to agree would take the stigma away from the sport, and then he could box without anonymity and the worry of shaming his family. "I think it might be the platform you could use in your campaign. Legalize gaming and use the taxes to benefit the city."

Father pensively scratched his freshly shaven chin, releasing the scent of sandalwood. "I will consider it. But I doubt it will garner the support it needs from the public. 'Twill not likely be a popular notion."

Tom was about to further his case when Henry and Roger entered the room, both dressed elegantly. Tom's stomach clenched at the sight of Henry deliberately avoiding his gaze.

"You are late. Sit, sit." Father pointed at the two empty place settings across from him.

Roger tugged on his green silk waistcoat, the buttons doing their best to hold it together. A servant slipped behind him to pull out his chair. He barely sat before he had his bread in hand. Henry remained where he was, his hat tucked under his arm and the framed painting of the cardinal in his hand.

"I have matters to attend to, Father." Henry looked right past Tom, his discomfort plain in his jittery chin.

Tom stood, wiping his mouth with his napkin. He had to speak to Henry alone to address what happened in the warehouse. "Give me a moment, and I will walk out with you."

"I am in a bit of a hurry."

Tom shrugged on his coat and started to follow him out.

"Thomas! Your gloves!" Father called. But Tom's gloves were in his wardrobe upstairs. He looked back at Father and then again at Henry, who was approaching the front door. Father wiggled his finger, indicating that he head up the stairs to retrieve them. At that moment, Henry slammed the door shut, and the sound of the carriage wheels crunching the gravel followed.

Getting out that afternoon to head to Blackheath was fairly easy. Father had a meeting with a crony at Brooks's, and Roger and Henry were otherwise engaged. Even the servants were too busy to notice. So he slinked out the door dressed in his worst clothes, an old pair of brown wool breeches, a faded blue shirt, and a frock coat that once had belonged to Roger but was now too narrowly cut for his waist.

It was six miles to Blackheath but in the cold weather, even riding in a coach made it seem like it was located at the end of the earth. The match was set just before sundown in an old building that used to be a warehouse for grain storage. He had no idea how many people would attend, but George Kent, the promoter, had told him that he could expect as many as a hundred paying a guinea each. Add that to the side bets, and the purse could be as high as one hundred and twenty or thirty pounds before George took his cut. That would leave Tom with plenty of sterling to help Maeve with her daughter's expenses and pay the molls to catch the London Monster.

Tom hoped Connor remembered to meet him early at the warehouse as planned to spar before the others arrived. He was the best second in the business as far as Tom was concerned, and he trusted him implicitly.

The horses huffed as the carriage traveled past an endless heath littered with hard, prickly gorse and coarse grasses, everything a muted shade of brown and dull brass. After an hour or so, several church steeples emerged in the distance. Eventually, the town appeared, the shop signs swinging in the cold wind and a few stragglers milling about. It was a far cry from the hustle and bustle of London. George had to be wrong. Judging from the looks of it, he'd be lucky if a dozen people turned out for the fight.

When he arrived at the warehouse, he paid the jarvey and went inside. It had a dirt floor and was empty except for some broken crates, two messy coils of rope, and a few empty sacks heaped along the walls. The windows had all been broken and what was left of the glass was covered in a thick layer of grey filth. It was not what he'd expected for a fight with the reigning champ of Birmingham.

"There are more graveyards here than folks." Tom turned to find George Kent standing in front of the door, framed by the incoming light. He shook Tom's hand firmly, then pointed to the ropes against the wall. "I see no one has set up the ring."

"Are you sure people are going to show up this evening?" Tom asked.

"No need to worry, lad. Futrell draws 'em in." Kent draped his arm around Tom. "You know he's favoured nine to one."

Tom wasn't surprised. But that didn't mean he wasn't going to try to win anyway.

"Means nothin'." Connor appeared suddenly, swatting his hand in Tom's general direction. His blond hair stood on end from the wind. "We're goin' to take this fellow down before the first candle flickers."

Tom laughed, knowing that wasn't possible, but he was glad Connor had confidence in him. "I hear he's awfully quick."

"You've got more power than him. Gotta be a brawler." Connor shrugged off his coat. "Let's get a bit of practice in while we can."

Tom unbuttoned his coat and set it on top of the grain bags, then slipped his shirt over his head. The cold air hit him hard, but he knew in a few minutes, he'd be plenty warm with all the blows he'd throw at Connor.

Kent watched them spar for a while, inserting a few words of encouragement intermittently, but Tom imagined he didn't care who won. Either way, he'd get his cut of the money. After he left, Tom threw his last punch at Connor. He felt loose and strong, ready to take on the Birmingham Champion.

Connor patted both of Tom's shoulders. "They think you're a gatekeeper, but you're not. You're a champ, lad. Futrell is shopworn. We can do this."

Tom reached for his shirt. "Are you planning on being in the ring with me?"

Connor smiled. "Just imagine him as someone you wish you could put in the grave."

That would be easy. He thought of the man who'd allowed him to be sent to the gallows for an attack he didn't commit. The man bringing all of London to its knees. The London Monster.

— ◦ —

Two hours later, the warehouse was filled with so many people, Tom had to squeeze his way through the crowd behind Connor to get to the ring. The whole town must have been there. He knew Futrell was in the building, but with very little light from the surrounding sconces and chandelier overhead, it was difficult to see where he could be. Tom inhaled deeply to clear his head, the yeasty smell of ale and unwashed bodies awakening his senses.

Connor pushed through, jabbing his elbows at anyone who blocked the way, and lifted the rope for Tom to enter the ring. A few cheers rose from the crowd as Tom skirted under the rope. "He's waitin' to make an entrance, lad."

Tom stood in the centre of the ring and raised his arms. A mix of jeers and praise erupted from the cacophony of voices. A singular voice shouted his name and he turned. It was Stone.

Tom spat in the dirt. He wasn't going to throw the fight for that huff. He knew what he did to Maeve at Parker's, and he was tired of him trying to tell him what to do.

Suddenly, everyone roared, clapping and chanting Futrell's name. Tom turned to see the crowd part and Futrell emerge like a god amongst the beasts. Tom wiped away a drop of sweat that started on his neck and traveled to his chest.

Futrell's second stepped forward. "The greatest boxer of all time! William Futrell, standing six foot two and weighing sixteen stone. The Birmingham Champ!"

They were roughly the same size. He glanced at Connor, who stood just outside the ring with his arms crossed, his eyes narrowed and mouth tight. He crinkled his nose and shook his head slightly at Tom, a clear signal he wasn't impressed with the Birmingham Champ.

Futrell ducked under the rope, and Kent joined them in the centre.

"Open your hands," Kent instructed.

Tom opened his hands to prove they were empty—no rocks or metal objects. Futrell followed. Kent leaned in. "No biting, gouging, kicking, scratching, hitting a downed man or holding the ropes. If you drop down on one knee, you have thirty seconds to recover. Down for more than thirty means it's over. Shake."

Futrell stared at the M on Tom's hand, then grabbed it tightly and didn't let go. He leaned closer until their shoulders were touching, Futrell's mouth only inches from Tom's ear. "A murderer, are you?"

Tom gripped his hand firmly. "Nay. But only because I was stopped."

They shook hands, and Kent left the ring. Tom had a few seconds to size up his opponent. Same strong shoulders and arms. Scarred knuckles. Some on his face. His nose had been broken a few times too. He'd been around for a while. And then Tom noticed he wore silver oval buckles with paste stones on his shoes. He may have come from dining or a party, but he certainly hadn't come from a day of preparation.

They circled each other, arms out and ready. The mob screamed, but Tom blocked out what they were saying. He tightened his chest in anticipation of an unexpected blow and glared into Futrell's eyes, trying to read his thoughts. And then he struck, catching Tom on the chin. His head jerked to the right and a dull pain echoed in his brain. Tom threw a punch and Futrell dodged it. He threw another one and caught Futrell on his cheek, his knuckles hitting him square on the bone.

Futrell stumbled, then righted and came back fiercely with a series of strikes, one of which landed in the centre of Tom's gut. He doubled over to catch his breath.

"Go down on one knee!" Connor yelled over the crowd.

Tom kneeled and counted to twenty, careful not to exceed the thirty seconds allowed. He had to move more, use the ring and his power to overtake him. Connor said he had to be a brawler, so that's what he'd be. He took a deep breath and headed straight for Futrell.

Chapter 16

Sophie and Maeve took a carriage to Blackheath and arrived when the fight had already started. From what Sophie could tell, she was one of less than a dozen women in the room, a fact that made her feel better about wearing her disguise. She tried to peek through the throng to see the fighters, but it was impossible. Smoke from the candles hung in a heavy cloud above, making it difficult to see clearly beyond a few feet. The musty stench of what must have been over two hundred unwashed bodies also filled the air.

"I can barely see Tommy." Maeve tried to pull Sophie through the crowd, but she couldn't budge, stuck behind two large men blocking the way.

The man to her left had his arms raised, shouting terms she thought she might need to know if she were to write an article about the match. But that wasn't what she was there for. She was there to write about the gentlemen who attended such events, wagering carelessly on the barbaric sport.

"Get him with the corkscrew! Duck! Duck!" yelled the man next to her. Just then, a boy of no more than ten or eleven years sidled past him, and out of the corner of her eye, she saw him slip a gold pocket watch from the screaming man's coat, then disappear into the crowd.

"Your watch!" She tugged on the man's arm. "He pinched your watch!"

The man ignored her, too busy shaking his fist in the air and screaming instructions to the boxers. Men were so foolish. That pocket watch was likely worth more than any wager he may have on the match.

Sophie shoved her way to the back and jumped up onto a crate where a few young lads had gathered to watch. She could see over the crowd but not well enough to figure out who was striking whom. "Which one is The Pretty Punch?"

"The one on the left," answered the boy closest to her. "No, the right." He wore clothing that was far too large for him, his breeches tied up with a cord of hemp. "The dark-haired fellow."

They both had dark hair from where she stood. One of them was positioned with his back to her, the width of his shoulders impressive. Then they shifted and she got a glimpse of the other one's back. He was huge too.

The boy elbowed her, almost knocking her off the crate. "A bob says he goes down in the next round."

"What round is it?" she asked.

"Twelfth."

"So, you think The Pretty Punch will lose?"

"Been down a few times. They both have, come to think of it. But the Birmingham Champ's gonna win, he is."

Sophie felt bad for Maeve. She had spent the entire ride to Blackheath telling her what a wonderful boxer Tommy was and all the matches he'd won, so it would be a shame if she were disappointed.

The man in front of them leaned back. "You're wrong, laddie. Futrell doesn't have the neatness and quickness in his style that the other fellow has. This cockerel has pluck. And since they're both skilled, that's what's gonna win this fight."

The boy's mouth twisted as he considered what the man said. "I take back my offer, mate. Aye?"

He stuck out his hand and Sophie shook it. She wouldn't have wagered a bet anyway, especially not one against Maeve's suitor.

Nearly a half hour later, the fight was over, and The Pretty Punch had lost. She waited for the crowd to disperse before she dared venture out and look for Maeve. Sophie finally spotted her waving her hands above her head. "Over here!"

Sophie stepped down from the crate and joined her. "I am so sorry it didn't turn out the way you had hoped, Maeve."

"That cove hit him when he was down. Kicked him twice. Everyone saw it." Her jaw was tight as she spoke, a little vein Sophie had never noticed before throbbing in her neck. "'Twasn't a clean fight."

Maeve's beau sat against the wall with Connor, whose big body blocked the boxer from anyone's view.

"What is Connor doing?" Sophie stretched to see beyond the lingering spectators.

Maeve sighed, exasperated. "Tending to him, I believe."

"Will you go to him?"

"Of course. I want you to meet him, but not like this."

"I understand. I shall wait over here."

Maeve grabbed her hands and kissed her quickly on the cheek before making her way over to her Tommy. Sophie waited against the wall and watched as Maeve fought her way through the men surrounding him. One by one they started to leave, leaving Sophie a clear view of Maeve cradling his head at her breast. She stroked his wet hair hanging down his cheeks and kissed the top of his head. He looked exhausted, his shoulders hunched, the taut muscles in his arms and chest slick with sweat. Sophie found him beautiful in a way. Sadly beautiful.

He sat up and leaned his head back against the wall, his neck stretched and the line of his square jaw visible. An image flashed into her mind of something familiar. Someone familiar. He looked like . . . but he couldn't be . . .

Maeve planted a long, soft kiss on his lips, and Sophie's throat caught. She had done the same the day before. It was Tom.

"Evans! Come meet Tommy!" Maeve waved her over.

But Sophie couldn't move. Her feet remained fixed to the dirt. Tom turned to face her, one eye swollen and a smear of blood under his nose and chin. She swallowed, a hard ragged lump stuck in her throat. Slowly, his shoulders squared, and his lips moved to whisper her name.

She shook her head. Tom was Tommy, Maeve's lover.

Sophie ran out the door and onto the street. She had no idea where she was headed, but she couldn't look at him. Not while the memory of his kiss was still fresh on her lips. Her heart pounded angrily as she quickened her pace to get far away from the mistake she had made.

She almost reached a resting spot near a grocery when a hand reached out and jerked her back. "Look who we have here!"

Sophie recognized the voice and lowered her head, her mind spinning with too many thoughts.

"Dressed as a man, nonetheless!" Dalton's mouth hung open, the hint of a smile creeping into his lips. *"Si magnifique!"*

"Leave me alone, please." Sophie couldn't deal with him right now. She struggled to get out of his grip, but he held tight.

"Ah, ah, ah," he said in refusal. "I believe an explanation is in order."

Why does he have to be here? She had to focus, think straight. She couldn't tell him anything near the truth. She took a deep breath. "I wished to see the fight, so I borrowed some clothes from a friend. I had no desire to be hassled as a woman."

His mouth screwed into a smirk. "You have a fondness for pugilism?"

She was about to answer when her journal slipped from inside her jacket and fell to the ground. He let go of her arm to pick it up. She tried to grab it from him, but he twisted away, flipping the pages and reading her words.

"These read like articles."

She snatched it from him and shoved it back into her coat. "Simply journal entries. That is all."

He stared at her, his hand rubbing his chin. "Does Cuthbert know about this?"

"My journal? Well—"

"No, no. All of it." His hand circled in front of her, indicating he meant her state of dress as well.

"There is no need for him or anyone to know, frankly." She said it with confidence, but her stomach tossed as she spoke.

"They would be horribly disappointed, I would imagine. To know you go about in public dressed as a man, appearing at events no lady should ever attend." He ran a finger along her cheek. "I suppose you wish for me to keep your secret."

She inched her head away, leaving his finger suspended in the air. "I would appreciate that very much. I would never want to cause embarrassment to my family or Bertie."

"No, indeed. That would be horrible." He brought her hand to his lips. "But you needn't worry, *ma petite beauté.* I am quite good at keeping secrets.

A Note

January 1790

The papers are infuriating. Yes, I stabbed Miss Felton, but I did no harm. She was wearing a metal cuirass of sorts underneath her gown, so my blade was stopped from cutting her flesh. I suppose now she will receive dozens of callers requesting a visit so they may comfort her and perhaps steal a peek at her torn skirts, which will undoubtedly be on display in the parlour for all to see. She'll pout and wipe false tears from her cheeks, but inside she will revel in the attention. All my women do. I have singlehandedly graced them with celebrity.

My own mother has expressed trepidation about going out, even in the confines of her carriage. But I see the way she primps before she leaves our home, hoping she will attract the eye of the monster. After all, he only strikes the most beautiful women in London, they say. That is partially true. I do search for lovelies, but they are not always available, so there are times when I must approach those who might otherwise go unnoticed. As it were, I often have better luck with them. They might offer a smile or a nervous giggle after one of my more innocent overtures. Only the lusty ones will listen longer and allow me to express myself more freely.

They all wish for the right to boast, angered when a friend of theirs is targeted instead. It has become a competition of sorts and has made liars out of so many. I am often driven to laughter when I read an account of something I never did. One woman said I approached her in Holborn last Thursday evening, but I was nowhere near there that night. She apparently returned home with a small rent in her skirt and said I called her foul names—many of which she could not repeat—then drew my knife and slit her worn gown. Any fool could see what the little trull was up to. Beyond the attention, she wanted her husband to buy her a bolt of cloth for a new gown, and ruining her own was the only way she was going to get the miserly hog-grubber to spend the coin.

I often wonder about these women whose lies spill from their tongues like pearls from a broken necklace. They spend all their days acting prim and proper, turning up their noses at even the least innocuous social misstep, only to secretly wish they were somehow involved. I would be happy to oblige them, of course. But when I do, they treat me as if I were a scoundrel. A cur. Oh, the sadness of it all.

Only yesterday afternoon, I found myself on Coppice Row, an area known for its eclectic diversity. It is not a street I frequent often, in that I care nothing for the shops that sell tawdry articles of clothing or the bakeries that sell pastry made with lard instead of butter. But I was confident I could walk this street in the daylight without being recognized, for it is a bit of a distance from where I live and find entertainment.

I was dressed finely compared to the other pedestrians, who were mostly covered in pilled wool and knotted linen. Shortly into my stroll, I realized my choice of attire marked me as someone of means and interest, and the last thing I wanted to do was attract attention. I considered turning back to find a hackney to deliver me home, but the crowd behind me seemed thicker than the one ahead so I continued on, hoping to escape their curious glances and questioning stares.

It was then that I spotted her, the whore I followed a month or two earlier as she left the theatre. She was standing at the entrance of a bawdy house across the street. A creature the size and shape of a large bear, towered over her, one foot perched on the wall behind him. I assume he was the bullyboy of the establishment. The whore rested one hand casually on her hip and, with the other hand, played with a curl that hung loosely over her shoulder. That familiar feeling of fear mixed with anger entered my soul like a demon, hot and uncontrollable. I tried to still my racing heart, knowing that if she only turned her head a little to the left, she would see me and perhaps call out, prompting the beast beside her to give chase. I lowered the brim of my hat over my brow and quickened my step, bumping the shoulder of a passerby.

I recalled how even she, a lowly whore, had looked at me with disdain that night I'd approached her. A whore! I do admit that not all the women I approach are amenable to my advances. But a whore?

These are the thoughts that often come to me late at night as they do now. Tangled feelings of rage and desire. I lie in bed, the curtains drawn, only a sliver of blue light streaming in beneath my bedroom door. It's quiet, the silence occasionally broken by the howls from the wind slicing over the roof shingles. I force myself to erase the whore's image from my mind, and I replace it with fine, well-bred beauties. In the darkness, I picture their lovely faces, lowered eyes, and innocently parted lips. The curves of their breasts as they spill invitingly from their gowns draw me in. I can almost smell the jasmine or rose scent that lingers on their skin from their bathwater. It clouds my senses, fills me with warmth on this cold night. My hand slides down my chest in search of that part of me that aches with desire. I lift my hips to thrust into that which is not there, my hand working feverishly to keep up with the racing of my heart. I beg for the pleasure. The pain. Bring it. Bring her. She is mine. She is . . . mine.

Part Three

Chapter 17

January 1790
London, England

Maeve sat in the chair by her window, struggling to read the latest letter from Mrs. Hobart. The words seemed too small, and no matter how close or far she held the paper from her face, they remained a blur. What she managed to conclude, however, was that Emily's fits had become more frequent and violent in nature, requiring supplementary tinctures and herbs. In addition to the six pounds she'd sent for Emily's care this month, she'd need to send another two pounds to cover the new apothecary expenses.

Maeve gazed out the window at the light snowfall dusting the street below. She couldn't bear to think about her daughter's pain and sadness. Was Mrs. Hobart holding Emily close when she suffered from one of her bouts? Did she wipe away her tears with a gentle caress? She wanted her little girl. She should be the one hugging her and drowning her in kisses.

She lifted the lid of her small leather trunk that held all her worldly possessions. At the top lay the tiny, pink-striped scrap of cloth from Emily's blanket. She rubbed her thumbs over the worn fabric, remembering the creamy softness of her daughter's skin, then touched it to her lips, pretending—if only for a moment—it was her daughter's cheek.

She set it aside and stared at the other contents, mostly gifts she had collected over the years. Besides a silver thimble and thread and the book Tom had given her, all the trinkets were from Albert—two ivory hair combs, a pair of lace gloves, a silk handkerchief embroidered with pink and yellow roses in each corner, and her green shawl. She searched for the thimble and thread. Those, she had purchased herself when she realized she needed a place to hide the extra coins she was saving. She set all the items aside and lifted out her only other gown, the blue one. The coins sewn into the hem jingled slightly with the movement.

She didn't need to snip the threads. She knew exactly how much was hidden in the fabric. Eighteen pounds, two shillings. With the extra two pounds Mother Wharton would take from her earnings for Emily, it would take forever before she had enough to leave Parker's.

"Miss Maeve! You in there?" Prudy called with three quick taps on the door. "I have a gent here . . . What did you say your name was, lovey?"

"Richmond," said a mild voice on the other side of the door.

"Mr. Richmond is lookin' for a fair-haired lass like yourself for a bit of play," Prudy sang through the door.

Play could mean anything. Spanking, tickling, chasing, role-playing, or any other fetish one could dream up. Maeve bundled her blue gown in a neat heap, reassured by the extra weight of the coins in the hem, and shoved it back into her trunk. "One minute!"

After everything was put away, she opened the door. Prudy winked and nudged her head at a man Maeve had never seen before. He stood nervously spinning his hat in his hands and chewing the inside of his cheek. He wore a fine green silk coat with grey breeches and a gold waistcoat. When he raised his hand to check his carefully curled peruke, the light from the wall sconce caused the fabric on his chest to shimmer, a clear indication it was sewn with gold thread. She was sure Mother Wharton had noticed it too and had probably charged the cull a price fitting his appearance.

Maeve twirled a strand of her hair and looked up at him innocently. "What type of play do you have in mind, sir?"

Behind him, Prudy rolled her eyes. "You will be delighted, Miss Maeve. He would like us to scold him for all his bad deeds. Naughty gent, this one."

Easy money, Maeve thought. "Then we should get started right away."

They went into Prudy's room and undressed. Mr. Richmond insisted the punishment occur with all three of them naked with the exception of shoes, stockings, and garters. Those should remain on.

He ran to the other side of the bed, where Prudy lay on her stomach, and thrust into her from behind.

"Have you forsaken me?" Maeve asked in her most pouty voice. She smacked the leather strap on the bed. "How could you!"

She thwacked his buttocks over and over. "You belong only to me!"

He yelped and squeaked like a wheel on a cart with each affront until he pulled out of Prudy, then did the same to Maeve. They took turns whipping him until his buttocks was bright red and crisscrossed like a latticed cherry tart. After two good go-arounds, Mr. Richmond dressed, handed each one of them a guinea, then left the room.

Prudy stepped into her petticoat, then turned her back so Maeve could lace her stays. "Sick cull, that one. But at least he was quick. Not like the last one whose prick was as soft as rotten fruit. I spent most of the hour with my mouth full tryin' to give him a stiffy."

Maeve laughed while she dressed. "You know Mother doesn't care for that kind of talk."

"Well, she ain't here. I don't need to talk like a lady." Prudy dipped a rag into the washbowl, then cleaned between her thighs. "I think Mr. Richmond got more pleasure from the strap than the friggin'. Could've given my quim a rest and just tied him to the bedpost for a whippin'."

Maeve laughed. "A guinea is a guinea, I suppose."

"Did you notice the sparklers in his buttons? Emeralds, they were." Prudy tossed the dirty washcloth in the basin and flopped back on the bed. "A macaroni, that one. He could be my keeper."

Maeve hadn't noticed the emeralds, but she remembered the way the light had caught the gold thread on his waistcoat. "He could be. Would you want to be his mistress?"

Prudy inspected the guinea in her hand. "I'd be the mistress to the devil himself so long as he kept me fed and dressed in silks and satins."

Maeve had dreamed of Albert becoming her keeper. She had done everything right. Charmed him with playful banter, complimented him the way Mother had taught her, and remained the ardent lover, even when she wasn't feeling well. But none of it had mattered in the end.

She knew Tommy wasn't a noble, even though he did often visit wearing the clothing of a gentleman. The nobles who frequented Parker's usually insisted they be called Lord So-and-so, unafraid of sharing their peerage identities, their egos stronger than the wrath of their wives. She remembered how her heart had leapt when Tommy had once confessed he had no wife to go home to. He hadn't known it at the time, but it had given Maeve a nugget of hope she kept close to her breast. He might never be her keeper, but he could be her husband. She didn't care if he was a penniless baker or a cobbler. She would live happily as his wife. "I'm tired of rumping for coin. Don't you want to be in love, Prudy?"

"Love? Love's not a word meant for whores."

Maeve hated to think of herself that way. She couldn't. "I'm in love."

Prudy sat up and tucked the guinea into her stays. "You better not let Mother hear of it. She'll throw you out on your arse, she will."

"You're speaking like a ha'penny drab, Prudence." Mother stood in the doorway, hands on hips.

Maeve froze. How much had she heard?

Mother stared down at Prudy. "You will find yourself in a dark alleyway in Covent Garden if you keep that up."

"Yes, Mother," Prudy simpered.

Maeve held her breath, waiting for Mother's wrath to fall on her. But she simply shook her head at Prudy, scowling. "I came to tell you that Mr. Richmond was very pleased with his visit and promised to return. He also invited the two of you to a Twelfth Night masque at the estate of Viscount Sidmouth. You will need better gowns. I will procure them and take the money from your earnings or add them to your accounts."

Maeve breathed a sigh of relief. She hadn't heard their talk about love. Although she was relieved that she wasn't going to be kicked to the street, she wasn't thrilled about owing Mother more money. "Can I not wear my blue gown?"

"That gown is good enough for Parker's, but not for a masque where there will be nobles." She turned to leave. "I expect you to mingle and lure them here with witty conversation and promises of delights. It will be the work you do with your clothes on that matters most. Do you understand?"

They both nodded as she disappeared down the stairs, the jingling of her keys sounding with each heavy step.

"I'm goin' to eat like a pig meant for market at that masquerade." Prudy grabbed the leather strap and kissed it. "Here's to Mr. Richmond, that wicked buck!"

The next night, Mother left a red velvet gown on Maeve's bed with a note stating she would add five pounds six to her account.

The gown showed wear under the arms and along the hem of the skirt, but other than that, it was unmarred. Maeve ran her hands over the black bow on the front. It was made from a heavy satin and twirled in the centre in the shape of a rose. She slipped the gown over her worn petticoat and stays and studied her reflection in the window. The girl who'd owned it before must have been taller and a little thicker in the waist. She pinched the fabric closed on the bodice and thought that with a little mending here and there, it would work nicely for the masque.

She'd never been to a Twelfth Night before, but after every New Year, her mouth watered at the sight of the plum cakes decorated with lacy icing in the confectioner's shop window in town. They were a sure sign someone nearby was planning on celebrating the holiday in a grand manner. Her mouth watered with the memory of the sweet and spicy aromas that wafted out of the shops and into the cold winter air. She'd never thought she would be invited to taste one.

But now she was, thanks to Mr. Richmond.

Maeve wanted to tell the good news to Sophie, but she hadn't visited since Tommy's fight almost a fortnight earlier. She'd left so abruptly that evening, and if Maeve hadn't been so busy tending to Tommy's injuries, she would have gone after her. She hoped it wasn't something she'd said or done.

It had been only days after his fight when he'd allowed a morsel of his life to spill from his lips, giving her a glimpse of what could be. She'd been holding a comfrey poultice to his swollen eye. "I might not see you for a while," he'd said. "With my father away, my brothers will need my help with the shipments."

She'd held her breath when he spoke those few words. No one ever discussed family at Parker's. It was the last thing the men cared to talk about. But she knew it meant that he felt close to her. Close enough to speak of private matters.

"Of course," she'd answered nonchalantly, as if what he'd said were commonplace and knowing she wouldn't see him for weeks weren't burning a hole in her heart. Perhaps he was busy celebrating the holidays. She imagined servants carrying sweetmeats on silver trays, Tommy laughing with his brothers in a room filled with warm, golden light dancing across walls heavy with portraits of family members from generations past. Would she be a part of that someday?

In what she considered a consolation, he'd slipped her ten guineas, a portion of his take of the loser's purse from the fight plus one quarter of the profits. He'd said he would use the rest towards his plan to capture the monster, which was perfectly fine by her. That devil needed to be caught.

It was the most money she ever had at once, but she'd trade it all if he would tell her he wanted to take her away from Parker's and live together with Emily as a family. Instead, he would walk away for weeks, leaving her behind like a forgotten handkerchief.

Now, with the Twelfth Night party only two days away, she had to put thoughts of Tommy aside and prepare to look her best. She had no idea how much debt she had accrued with Mother Wharton, but she was sure it was far more than she had stashed away. If she could entice a few nobles to venture into Parker's, their business could bring her closer to clearing her debt and getting out of there.

Maeve pulled out her thimble, needle, and thread and began to stitch the hem of her red gown. She blinked a few times to clear the clouds from her vision, but they remained where they were, blocking her view of the few tiny stitches she'd managed to sew. The more she struggled to see, the more the pain in her brow grew.

She slid the lamp closer and turned up the flame, but it made little difference. The stitches were impossible to see. She laid the gown over the back of her chair, vowing to work on it in the morning. As she settled into bed, she stared into the darkness, listening to the moans on the other side of the wall. Prudence and Rosie were apparently having a go with a cull who preferred to be called *Master*.

She grazed the tip of her tongue over a tiny sore inside her cheek. A metallic, sharp sting made her flinch. She'd seen them before on the other girls, and sometimes they disappeared with no fuss. But she was a whore, so she knew better.

Chapter 18

Sophie held her mask to her face while Peg tied the strings in back.

Peg stepped back. "How does that feel?"

"Good, thank you."

The mask was made of black and silver feathers that curled around her eyes into points on either side of her head. Bertie had given it to her as a gift after she'd accepted his invitation to attend Lord Sidmouth's Twelfth Night masquerade. The thought of appearing in public as a couple was slowly starting to settle in her chest, as the occasions she would attend with Bertie would naturally increase in the next few months. He was going to be her husband, and it was time she came to terms with it.

She'd done her best to warm to him over the past two weeks. She hadn't shied away from discussing their upcoming nuptials, and she even allowed him to kiss her chastely on the lips once in the parlour when her mother wasn't present. But it was Tom's face that she saw late at night when she lay in bed unable to sleep. Not Bertie's.

He stood at the bottom of the stairs, his mask in hand, wearing a crimson silk coat and breeches with ivory lace at his throat and cuffs. She couldn't help but think her pale pink gown was the worst possible match to his red silk.

The ride to White Lodge in Richmond Park took a little more than an hour. When they'd reached the outer grounds, Bertie's hand found its way through the dark to hers, and she permitted it. His was the grip of someone with hope. Someone with need. It made her heart ache with regret that she didn't feel the same.

The carriage bumped over frozen ruts as it traveled through an archway of oaks. Eventually, the home emerged through the trees at the end of the long frost-covered drive. They inched onward behind a line of carriages and awaited their turn to disembark.

Sophie gazed out the window, her fur cloak hitched high on her shoulders. Torchlight bounced off the grand estate just ahead. "So many people."

Bertie tied on his mask, which was similar to her own except for its less elaborate feathers, then resettled his hand on hers. "I imagine we will know quite a few. And if not, at least we have Dalton and Vivian to keep us entertained."

She eased her hand away. The last time she'd seen Dalton was only two days after Tom's fight in December. They'd all gone to the theatre, and he'd shot her amused glances all evening to remind her that he knew her secret. She'd spent the entire night leaning forward, her hands firmly set on the balcony railing, just to avoid his gaze. It had taken a lot of effort then to escape a confrontation, and she imagined it would take a lot of effort tonight.

The carriage door opened, and the footman reached in to help Sophie down the step. Bertie led her across the wide causeway on his arm and into the entrance hall where a quartet of violinists suffused the air with music.

"This way, please," said a liveried servant with the sweep of his arm.

They entered a smaller hall that led to a large drawing room in the back that served as the ballroom. Dozens of people were already there, drinks in hand, laughing and milling about. The sickening sweet smell of rotten fruit pervaded the air, the telling sign that someone nearby was snuffing. A servant carrying a tray full of champagne coupes approached. Sophie took one and drank half before Bertie even had a chance to offer a toast.

"Is something wrong?" He stared at her half-empty glass.

"Not at all." She signaled to the servant for another glass.

"I know you care little for Dalton and his opinions about social matters, so I will not allow him to upset you tonight. I shall tell him—"

"Cuthbert!"

Sophie closed her eyes at Dalton's voice behind her. She wasn't ready for his little winks and suggestive gazes quite yet. It would take another two or three glasses of champagne for that. A hand furtively skimmed her lower back, and she froze.

"Pleasure to see you, Miss Sophie." Dalton nodded once, his eyes fixed on hers. He wore a green silk mask that covered all but his mouth, a faint trace of brown powdery snuff above his upper lip. "I almost didn't recognize you *déguisé*."

Sophie forced a smile, then nodded at Vivian.

He turned to Bertie. "Is Sidmouth even here? I heard he was in Oxford at the opening of the canal."

"He's returned." Bertie jerked his thumb behind him. "He has yet been able to escape the company of that older gentleman. We are all waiting our turn to make his acquaintance."

Sophie peered around Dalton's shoulder to see the viscount. He was indeed in deep conversation with another gentleman, their heads bowed and nodding as the other spoke.

"I cannot say I recognize him." Dalton clicked his tongue. "A man of business? Another commoner, I suppose, hoping to filch the sterling from his pocket. Always feeling entitled, that lot."

"Entitled?" Sophie did her best to temper her speech and fight the bitter tang in her mouth. Who better to know about entitlement than him? His father was a baronet, after all.

Dalton raised an eyebrow.

Vivian rested her hand on his arm. "I would love a piece of cake. Has anyone yet found the bean?"

Before she could finish her sentence, the music stopped and someone shouted, "We have our Lord of Misrule!"

Sophie turned to find a short, portly man pushing his way through the crowd, his hand raised and a tiny bean pinched between his fingers.

"Apparently so." Sophie turned to Vivian and drank the last of her champagne, willing her pulse to stop racing. Although she was happy about the distraction of the evening's festivities, she wouldn't have minded giving Dalton a lesson in social responsibility.

Bertie leaned into her, his voice more enthusiastic than required. "You love this part, Sophie."

It was true, especially when the person designated as the lord was the lively sort. One year, the valet of her father's acquaintance, Lord Phelps, found the dried bean in his piece of cake and ordered everyone present to trade a piece of clothing with someone of the opposite gender. Sophie had given her violet feathered hat to a pageboy in exchange for his lace jabot. She'd thought it scandalous at the time, but by the end of the night, she saw a few gentlemen wearing ladies' corsets over their shirts and realized how untamed the night could be. She wondered if tonight would end up the same.

The Lord of Misrule was forced to the centre of the crowd, his face ruddy with excitement. He held a mug aloft, its steam rising in silky waves over his head. The scent of apples and spices floated in the air. "Wassail, good folk! Drink hail! And bring on the mummers!"

135

Everyone shouted in salute, and the music began once again. Sophie stepped aside to allow a string of masked mummers to enter the room. They gathered in the centre, all dressed in bright clothing adorned with feathers, ruffles, and jingle bells.

A guiser wearing yellow hose and red garters strode ahead of the group, twirling his hands with great ceremony. "Fair ladies and kind gentlemen, we present you with the tale of a cold winter's night, when a poor cobbler named Tom Foolery wandered the streets innocently in search of his cat . . ."

Bertie handed Sophie a glass of wassail, its warmth penetrating her leather gloves. She closed her eyes to smell the nutmeg and cinnamon wafting from the cider.

"Know you aught of that man?" Bertie whispered in her ear.

"What man?" she asked.

"The man staring at you." He indicated a spot across the room with a simple jerk of his chin. "Over there."

She peered into the crowd but saw no one she recognized. It was difficult, after all, considering almost everyone was masked. "Oh, Bertie. No one is staring at me."

The mummers recited their lines, embellishing every movement with a hop or a flourish of their hands. Tom Foolery lay on his back, fighting off two women poking him with besoms. Sophie laughed as he struggled to get away from both of them by rolling and crawling from one to the other. She turned to Bertie to express her delight, when Dalton whispered, "Such a lovely laugh, *ma petit fleur.*"

Her breath hitched, and a bead of sweat traveled down her neck and disappeared into her bodice. "Would you excuse me for a moment, Bertie? I need to take the air."

"Are you not feeling well?" He settled his hand gently on her wrist.

"'Tis a bit warm in here. I simply . . . need a moment."

"Very well." He offered his arm.

"Alone."

His mouth twitched as his smile faded. "Of course."

She stumbled over her words. "What I mean is, I want you to watch the play for me. You will tell me what I missed when I return, won't you?"

She knew her excuse sounded sloppy, but she had to get away from Dalton, and Bertie would likely invite him and Vivian to join them.

Sophie sidled through the crowd to an alcove in what seemed to be a gentlemen's library in the back of the home. She leaned against one of the tall columns flanking the scalloped arch and removed her mask, allowing the cool air from the open window to wash over her face. She didn't know what to do about Dalton. Who did he think he was, speaking to her like that? And with his wife within earshot. Why wouldn't he simply leave her alone? She should just confess her secrets to her family and Bertie and end this little game.

But she knew she couldn't. They would demand she stop her investigations, even dressed as a woman. Her parents would never let her leave home and would insist she remain under the watchful eye of a more dutiful chaperone than Peg. That would make her miserable. Delving into a world outside her own was the one thing that made her feel alive, like a woman who did more than measure out her life in teaspoons. But if she didn't stop, she would bring disgrace to her family and Bertie. And what would they do to Peg once they discovered her part in all the mischief? Would they send her away? Beat her? Sophie couldn't bear the thought of anything bad happening to Peg. Either way, she was doomed.

"I thought that was you. I've never seen you in a dress before."

Sophie startled from her thoughts. Maeve stood before her in a red velvet gown, her blond tresses curled high upon her head. She was the last person she'd expected to see at the viscount's estate.

"You would make for a good inquisitress, recognizing me behind a mask and gown." Sophie reached for her.

Maeve squeezed her hand. "There's something about your walk that gives you away. Especially as a man."

"I will remember that the next time I wear breeches." Sophie laughed despite her ill mood, then lowered her voice. "Is Lord Sidmouth one of your . . . customers?"

"I don't even know the man. One of Prudy's culls invited us." Maeve shrugged one shoulder. "I've never been to a Twelfth Night masque before. Has everyone gone mad? The gardener is out there telling everyone what to do."

Sophie smiled. If she only knew how wild things could get. "Oh, how I have missed you."

Maeve stared down at their hands, her grip tightening as she spoke. "Where have you been, Sophie? I had no idea where you'd gone after Tommy's fight."

Tommy. Tom. His name pierced a hole in Sophie's heart.

Maeve shook her head. "I shouldn't have taken you there. It was beneath you—"

"No. That wasn't it at all." Sophie wanted to say something about spending time in the brothel but thought better of it.

"Then why did you leave so abruptly?" Maeve tilted her head, her big brown eyes pleading for an answer. "He told me he knew you."

Sophie's heart froze. "Did he?"

"He said you were trying to help him find the London Monster."

Clearly, Tom hadn't divulged the entire nature of their relationship. She nodded, unable to speak.

"If anyone can catch that devil, it's Tommy." At the mention of his name, a delicate smile appeared on Maeve's lips. "Why do you look so sad?"

Sophie struggled to find the words. "There are so many things I haven't told you. I . . . I simply need time."

Maeve nodded slowly. "Is there anything I can do to help?"

There was nothing anyone could do. This was just another secret. She had far too many.

"I been lookin' all over for you, Maeve."

Sophie turned to see the girl who lived in the room across from Maeve's standing in the doorway with a drink in each hand. She took a sip from one, then said, "I got some gents waitin' outside. They want to go back to Parker's."

"Give me one second, Prudy." Maeve turned to Sophie. "I must go, but you know where to find me."

"Of course." Sophie hugged her farewell, swallowing hard to keep her composure. She was the closest person Sophie had to a sister and the one she could hurt the most. "Be well, Maeve."

Sophie's chest tightened as Maeve walked out the door. Seeing her was like unwrapping the bandage from a fresh wound. How could she hurt a girl who already had so much sadness in her life? She was glad she'd promised herself to forget about Tom, as difficult as it was.

The music stopped and the crowd clapped. She had to get back to Bertie.

Sophie retied her mask, ready to do her best to deal with Dalton's antics for the remainder of the evening. She took a few deep breaths and smoothed her gown before entering the hall. The air was steamy from the hordes that still gathered there. She searched the room for Bertie and spotted him standing near the back with Maeve. Her hands were clasped to her chest, and he was shaking his head. Did she know him? She watched their exchange until Prudy dragged Maeve away and out the entrance with two men.

Bertie stood facing the wall, unmoving, his head bowed.

"Bertie?" Sophie placed her hand on his arm, and he startled. When he turned to face her, he was drained of all colour.

"What is wrong? Did something happen with . . . that woman?" She couldn't let him know she knew her. It would bring about a whole host of questions.

Bertie straightened, but his hands remained shaking. "That woman? She . . . she . . . was a harlot. She propositioned me." He placed his palm on his brow. "Forgive me. I should never have said that."

Sophie sucked in her breath. Maeve would never have approached him had she known who he was. "Well, she's gone. There is no need to think upon it any further."

"I need a drink." He tugged on his collar. A trail of sweat dripped down his temple.

"I can get you some wassail. Or champagne." She searched through the room for a servant.

"Nay. I need something stronger."

Sophie imagined all the sermons he attended at church made him feel that being approached by a prostitute was as evil as supping with the devil. Perhaps she may have felt the same before meeting Maeve, but all the fear so deeply instilled in her had dissipated. She tried to think of something to say to soothe him, but as she began to speak, he waved her away, then left her standing alone, edging through a group of partygoers surrounding the Lord of Misrule. After a few minutes, she decided to escape the heat in the curved corridor off the entrance hall.

Light bounced off the walls from the sconces that framed the rows of windows on each side. Around the bend, a couple nestled closely, their soft whispers traveling down the long hallway. Sophie took a deep breath, happy for the time to herself. Life was becoming too complicated. There were too many secrets to hide, too many facts to keep straight, and too many mistakes that could be made. She wished she could step outside of her life and become someone else, if only for a moment.

"Sophie?"

Sophie turned to face the voice she knew so well. The one that came to her late at night or when she sat alone in her parlour, staring at the artificial flowers that marked her future. The one she promised she'd try to forget.

Tom stood at the entrance to the corridor, moonlight from the adjacent window illuminating his silver mask and the shoulders of his blue velvet coat. "I knew it was you."

"Tom?" She wasn't sure what she was feeling. Longing. Despair. Regret. Everything at once.

He slid off his mask, then tucked it into his coat as he drew closer. "I know what you thought you saw that day with Maeve, but I want to explain."

It took her a second to understand what he was saying. Her throat tightened. "Explain that you are a pugilist? Or explain that you have a lover?"

"Maeve is a dear friend. Someone who has been very good to me."

"I can see that. You two seem . . . very close." She didn't want to hear explanations or details. It would only make things worse.

"Certainly not in the way you are implying. It is not like that at all. She is merely—"

She held up her hand. "Please, go no further. This is none of my business."

"It is not what you think." He tried to get her to look him in the eyes, but she couldn't. "If you hadn't left, I would have told you everything."

"That you make a habit of kissing women you care nothing for?"

"What? Of course not."

"You kissed her."

"She kissed *me.*"

She tried to think back to that moment when Maeve leaned over him, his head thrown back in exhaustion, his skin glistening with sweat. Had he kissed her back?

He took her hand, pressing it lightly between both of his. "Maeve told me why you were there. Did you write the article?"

"I couldn't. You told me your name could not be associated with unsavory events."

"And pugilism is unsavory?"

She wasn't sure what she thought of it—a brutal dance choreographed by rules and limits. "Why did you kiss me?"

He hesitated for a moment, then brought her hand to his lips. "I understand you."

Laughter erupted from the hall, and she shivered.

"I know what it feels like, Sophie, to know your purpose in life—even when it goes against everything you've been taught—and not be able to pursue it because the consequences would disappoint those closest to you."

She knew he meant her desire to be a journalist, but that was only a part of what she yearned for. "You have no idea what I go through."

"I think I do. We all have our secrets." He ran his knuckles across her cheek. "You and I are great pretenders."

She swallowed hard, determined not to let his touch disarm her. "That does not change the facts . . . about us. Maeve told me who you are to her."

He looked away, his face somber. "I know what she must have said. I do care for her greatly. But we are friends. That is all we will ever be."

Sophie felt as if a twig had snapped inside her chest. His words would shatter Maeve's dreams. "She told me she loves you."

He sighed in recognition that he knew she spoke the truth. "Do you love your betrothed?"

She stiffened, pulling her hand away. She assumed he and Maeve had spoken that day about their acquaintance, but she hadn't considered Maeve would've divulged that bit of personal information. "That is different. I have no choice in the matter."

"You didn't answer my question."

"He is a good man."

"I see." His finger trailed down her neck. "Have you not thought about me?"

She looked up at him, her heart pounding. He pressed against her, and his fingers settled on the nape of her neck, his hand warm on her skin. She should lie and insist she never thought of him, never thought about that moment at his warehouse when he'd held her close. But her heart wouldn't let her. She closed her eyes.

His thumb traced beneath her ear and over her jaw. She tried to steady her breathing, but it was impossible. He gazed at her, his eyes searching for permission before he untied her mask, the silk strings dangling between his fingers. She held her breath as he lowered his head and kissed her.

Suddenly, nothing mattered but the feel of his lips on hers and the low moan in his throat as she gave in to him. It felt right to be in his arms, warm and safe. Exactly where she should be. His grip tightened around her waist, and his mouth trailed across her cheek and neck. She sighed at the loss of his lips. "Tom," she whispered.

He kissed her again, hard and insistent, his hand firm on her back. Within seconds the music started up again, jerking her out of the moment and reminding her where she was and with whom she was supposed to be. The realization of what she was doing hit her like a frosty gust of wind.

She wriggled out of his arms. "I should go."

He called after her, but she had to leave. Bertie would be wondering where she was.

She scurried down the hall, her head swirling with everything Tom had said, the taste of him still on her lips. She wanted to go back to him, but she couldn't. Too many people would be hurt.

She glanced back once quickly before reaching the end of the corridor.

Her breath caught at the sight of Dalton standing in the threshold, twirling a glass of champagne between long, thin fingers. He eyed her sardonically, a smirk on his lips.

"Poor, dear Cuthbert." He took a slow sip of his champagne. "This puts you in an awkward position, does it not? Perhaps you and I should talk. We have so much to discuss."

She glanced past him at Bertie, who stood on the other side of the entrance hall, tugging his collar away from his neck. "There is nothing to discuss."

Sophie tried to push past him, but he grabbed her arm. "Oh, but there is."

Unable to respond, she speared him with her gaze, then dashed away.

Chapter 19

Cuthbert sat on the edge of the pew, his knees rapidly bobbing up and down and his hands folded in front of him. What if Lord Sidmouth had seen him at the party, the harlot's hand on his arm, and the look of recognition between them? He would surely speak of it in closed circles, perhaps with a smirk on his lips as he exposed Cuthbert for the sinner he was. Would news of it reach his parents? What would they think?

He hoped he'd played it off well with Sophie. She seemed satisfied by his shock at being propositioned. She would surely call off the wedding if she discovered his true nature. She could, after all, claim he was of bad character and therefore end the engagement. His parents would be furious. Furious about the loss of her dowry and the mounting unpaid bills as a result. Furious about the embarrassment surrounding the whole affair. And furious about the debased nature of their son, who falsely purported himself as pious and devout.

If only he could erase his past. Expunge his transgressions. Rid himself of the dark desires that lurked within his soul.

The church bells vehemently clanged above thrice, their vibration penetrating his heart. Even as he sat in church, images of the whores' faces and naked flesh flitted through his mind. Rouged lips and bare white shoulders. Ankles, knees, and thighs. Full round bottoms and breasts for the taking. *I am steeped in lust and lechery*. He squeezed his eyes shut, but the memories of too many past visits remained as if burned into his thoughts with a scorching brand.

It was a new year. Time to make changes. He vowed to stay away from Marylebone, Covent Garden, and the back streets of St. James's Park. Those were the places he seemed to get into the most trouble. This new path would put him on the road to redemption.

He drew a deep breath and headed for White's for a soothing glass of brandy. He had no idea if Dalton would be there, but he was hoping he wouldn't be. He didn't need his crass talk about women or stories of his latest conquests at the brothels in town. And he certainly didn't want to be tempted by sketches of naked women in curious poses.

White's was busy for a Wednesday afternoon. Cuthbert edged through the crowd of men gathered in the gaming room, arguing about something of great interest in the local paper.

Cuthbert leaned over the shoulder of a shorter stout gentleman. "Beg pardon, sir. What is all the fuss about?"

The gentleman turned to face him, a flesh-coloured mole set at the corner of his mouth. Cuthbert tried not to stare, but the little mound bounced as he spoke, drawing his attention. The man tapped the newspaper he held in his hand with two pudgy fingers. "Apparently there was a riot in Westminster. Four candidates turned out for the county elections with only one seat in the House of Commons needing to be filled."

"Too many cocks and only one roost." Cuthbert shrugged. "That hardly sounds like a reason to riot."

"That was not what did it." The man scratched at the mole, turning the thing an angry shade of red. "One of the candidates stood on the husting and proposed to legalize pugilism and other gaming as a way to gain revenue for the city."

"I suppose the crowd did not care much for that."

"That is what one would think . . . but they cheered him on. It was his opponents and their proposers who began the riot. Shouting accusations, name calling. The constables could barely contain the mob."

Cuthbert couldn't imagine how anyone would want to allow that sort of gambling to become legal. Certainly not boxing. Reverend Anthony had given a sermon only weeks ago about that very thing. "For what will it profit a man if he shall gain the whole world, yet lose his own soul?"

The mole-faced man leaned in. "What did you say?"

"Never mind." He swatted his words away. He couldn't remember which gospel it came from, but it had struck him hard at the time. He had thought about the gaming he and Dalton had partaken in the last time they were together at White's, and it soured his stomach.

"He couldn't even call for a vote. A show of hands." He shook the paper, rapping it once on Cuthbert's chest. "But mark me, if this gent can persuade the electors the way he persuaded the crowd, he might find himself in the House of Commons come the election in June."

A tall, thin man wearing a blue coat lined in buff edged between them. "You like my article, do you?"

"You wrote this?" Cuthbert asked.

"Certainly not. I do my best to stay away from riots." He shared a quick laugh with the mole-faced man. "I edited it." He pulled a slender tortoiseshell case from his coat, removed his scissor spectacles, and held them to his face. "See there?" He pointed to his name in tiny print on the page. "I am one and the same."

Cuthbert squinted at the type.

The mole-faced man slapped a meaty hand on the editor's shoulder. "May I introduce you to Mr. Edward Topham, my cousin once removed."

"At your service." Hat in hand, Topham bowed ceremoniously. "Editor of the *World* for three years now. And you are . . ."

"Cuthbert Needham. Pleasure to make your acquaintance." A gust of cold air whipped into the room and stirred the staleness that smelled of spirits and leather.

"I am surprised we haven't met before. White's is my refuge from the daily scramble at the paper." He gestured to the back room with his spectacles. "What do you say to a nice bottle of Cognac to warm us up, gentlemen?"

The mole-faced man brushed his hands down the front of his coat. "It sounds wonderful, but I must take my leave. I am expected home for afternoon refreshments."

He bid farewell and left Cuthbert standing with the editor, his brow raised in question. "Are you game?"

Before they were even seated, Topham ordered a bottle of Renaud and Dualle and had it sent to their table in the back room. Perched in the corner was Lord Greenville, quietly sipping his drink, the gentleman beside him busy prattling on about the upcoming elections. Cuthbert doffed his hat, thankful he was not drunk in front of him at the moment. He didn't need another lesson on discretion from the gentleman.

Topham spoke about everything that was newsworthy at the time—the upcoming elections, the upheaval of the French monarchy, the riot at Versailles, the war between Sweden and Russia, Captain William Bligh's escape from the mutiny on the *Bounty* in the south Pacific and his current unknown whereabouts, the rising price and availability of good horses, the battles between gun sloops in the Baltic Sea, and lastly, the slave trade.

"Did you know that a Negro blacksmith sold for two hundred and sixty pounds in Jamaica? 'Tis the highest price ever paid, as far as I know."

Three hours later, they'd shared two bottles of the Renaud and Dualle—much of which Topham had generously doled out to his cronies milling about—and eaten enough grey-leg partridge and smoked trout to keep them satisfied for days. As Cuthbert leaned back in his chair, his breeches struggled against his waist. He belched once into his fist. "I believe I will never need to read another paper again. You have fed me all the information I should require for months."

Topham laughed and raised his glass in salute, then finished the last of his brandy.

"I knew I would find you here." Dalton entered the back room, his crimson coat lightly dusted with snow.

Both Topham and Cuthbert stood, and Cuthbert made the introductions.

Topham grabbed his hat and shook Cuthbert's hand. "Ah, well, I should be going. Busy day, busy day." He disappeared through the threshold without another word.

Dalton brushed the snow from his shoulders, then sat. "A newspaper editor at White's? Since when do we allow the working class in here?"

"I believe he is related to one of our members. Cousins, or something or other."

"Hmph." Dalton rubbed the back of his neck. "Damned pain. Can't seem to rid myself of it."

Cuthbert knew Dalton hadn't been feeling well lately, but every time he brought it up, Dalton changed the subject. He ran his hand down the buttons on his waistcoat and over his full stomach. "He was an interesting fellow. Full of information."

Dalton lifted the bottle and read the label. "With rather expensive taste." He poured the meagre remains of what was left of the brandy into a glass. "What sort of information?"

Cuthbert shrugged half-heartedly. "News. The French. Riots at Versailles . . ."

Dalton snickered. "And the French claim to be more civilized than us. Beasts, really."

"We had our own riot in Westminster. One of the gents running for Parliament suggested the legalization of gaming. Got everyone riled up, it seems."

"Gaming?"

"Pugilism, to be exact."

"For everyone?"

Cuthbert stared at Dalton. He knew what he meant, but it had never been so clear before now. No one frowned upon gaming amongst gentlemen, but the local bakers and butchers were not allowed to engage in such sport. "'Twas quite a popular notion amongst the crowd."

"I imagine it was. The crowd was likely filled with fishmongers and ferriers, for God's sake, all ready to partake in gentlemen's sport." Dalton swallowed a mouthful of brandy and gazed into his glass. "Have you ever heard of *The Pretty Punch?*"

"The boxer?" Cuthbert asked. If he remembered correctly, he was a local champion. He'd never seen him fight, but he'd heard that he was a large fellow—tall and muscular—who moved gracefully for a man his size. "He lost his last bout with . . . what was that fellow's name . . .?

"William Futrell." Dalton finished his brandy, a smile growing on his lips. "Why do you ask? Wagered heavily on him, did you?"

"You have never taken Sophie to one of his matches?"

Cuthbert sucked in his breath. "Certainly not! What sort of question is that?" In his shock, he knocked over his glass, and a bit of brandy spilled onto his sleeve. He swiped at it angrily with his napkin, but the spot only smeared across the linen and lace.

Dalton scrutinized the stain, pursing his lips in thought. "Simply curious. You might want to attend his next fight with me."

Cuthbert didn't care much for boxing, but the matches were usually over within a matter of minutes, so he didn't mind accompanying Dalton on rare occasion. But he would never expose Sophie to such brutality. Never. "When is it?"

"I believe it hasn't been set yet. But there is talk of a match with John Jackson, The Gentleman. You will go with me when it is agreed." Dalton stood, then doffed his hat with a brief nod. "I must go. If I am a few minutes late, Vivian will accuse me of debauchery. 'Tis a new pastime for her. Crying she has a mutton monger for a husband."

It was true, though. Dalton was an expert in wenching. There wasn't a bawdy house within twenty miles of London where he hadn't engaged in some sort of depravity.

Cuthbert stood to button his coat, wishing he had worn his overcoat now that the sun was merely a sliver along the horizon. The last button gave him some trouble as he tried to force it through the hole. With one last push, it popped off in his hand. "'Tis not my day," he said under his breath.

Dalton grunted in agreement, stretching his neck left and right. "Horrible thing to have a shrew for a wife. But it could be worse."

"How so?" Cuthbert asked, tucking his button inside his coat, his stained cuff peeking out from his sleeve.

"*She* could be the one cuckolding *me*. Now that would be simply horrendous, wouldn't you say, old boy?"

Vivian would never do that. That was simply not in her nature, the way it was not in Sophie's nature either. He was about to say so when Mr. Martindale, the club's proprietor, approached the table and slipped Cuthbert a folded piece of paper. "'Twas added to your bill, sir. We hope you settle your accounts within the month."

Cuthbert nodded, tight-lipped, embarrassed that Martindale would say such a thing in front of Dalton. Out of the corner of his eye, he noticed Greenville cringe. Would he mention the outstanding accounts to his parents? He could only imagine what he owed. Undoubtedly, it was more than Cuthbert could pay and enough to turn his father's face beet red and send his mother into tears. His ears grew hot as he unfolded the paper.

Dalton leaned over Cuthbert's shoulder to glimpse at the new charges. His brows rose as he clicked his tongue. "It seems as if your editor friend has stuck you with the bill, old boy. Not your day at all."

Chapter 20

"I think the evening went quite well." Father dipped the quill into the ink and signed his name in the last of the ledgers. "Sidmouth found my ideas intriguing. I should have his support before the summer."

Tom sprinkled sand over his signature, then set the shaker aside. The tiny office was the only spot in the warehouse where the winter chill hadn't managed to find its way in, yet the frost covering his coat in a light haze had yet to melt. Tom brushed the sand away, then wriggled his fingers to rid them of lingering granules. "Did he agree that legalizing boxing would serve the city?"

"He is a politician, son. He will not agree to anything yet without weighing its popularity first," said Father.

Tom set the ledger on top of the others and piled them to the side of the desk. He hoped Sidmouth would at least consider the idea. He wasn't sure how much longer he could hide his identity as the city's local champion. Until some Londoner beat Futrell, he'd keep the title.

Father grabbed his coat and hat and stood to leave. "Gaining that invitation to Sidmouth's party may have clinched my victory."

It had clinched a victory for Tom as well. After making a few inquiries, he'd discovered Sophie's surname and the location of her family's London home. Seeing her again would be likely now that he knew where she lived.

Tom handed Father his cane and walked him to his waiting carriage. An icy bluster of wind hit him as he stepped outside.

Father rested one foot on the carriage step and paused. "There are a few cases of claret at the warehouse on Harp. Tell Henry to deliver one to Pitt on my behalf in gratitude for the introduction."

Tom watched the carriage pull away and disappear. He hadn't spoken to Henry—or rather, Henry hadn't spoken to him—in almost a week, the misunderstanding about whom, exactly, he was kissing still looming over them like a heavy, dark shadow. It was time to clear things up.

He locked up the warehouse and walked to Harp Lane. Thankfully, the wind was at his back once he turned the corner. The streets were empty the farther he walked away from the docks except for a smattering of people huddled in doorways or those rushing by with determination in their gait, daring to brave the cold. Even the herring gulls showed no interest in leaving their rooftop nests in search of food, their typical squabbling silenced by the brusque gusts. With nothing to distract his attention, his thoughts turned to the other night at White Lodge.

Although he'd seen Maeve and Prudy at Sidmouth's, he'd never approached them. Talking to harlots wouldn't have been the most prudent thing to do under his father's watchful eye. And after hearing confirmation from Sophie about Maeve's feelings for him, he couldn't mislead the poor girl into thinking a simple conversation was anything more than just that. That is what she would do, after all. Mistake the kiss of her hand as flirtation, his smile as an invitation, and the offer of a drink as a declaration of love.

But Sophie—Sophie Carlisle—was a different story. He wasn't sure what she made of his touch.

Tom squared his shoulders and approached Henry, who stood over an open crate, bits of straw spilling over the sides and onto the floor. Even as Tom moved closer, his brother remained focused on the contents. Henry bent to enter descriptions in a ledger, using the stack of newspapers that was piled precariously next to it as a table. It was not the typical shipment of Chinese blue and white porcelain they normally received.

Tom picked up a small snuffbox painted in pink, yellow, and blue with a reclining shepherd and a hare on the lid. "A French shipment? Mennecy?"

Henry didn't bother to look up from his ledger. "And Limoges, Sceaux, Sèvres. They are all here."

Tom nodded, but Henry ignored him. "Father wishes for you to send a case of claret to William Pitt."

"Very well," he answered, expressionless.

Tom set the snuffbox back in the crate on top of a pillow of straw. Although Henry didn't seem amenable to a conversation, there was no way around it. "I want to explain what you saw—"

"I have no interest in that sort of thing. You surround yourself with whores and other reprobates, so I have no doubt what world you have stumbled into." He faced Tom, his cheeks growing red, his head shaking in disapproval. "Imagine if it were discovered, Thomas. Father's chances at Parliament would be ruined. You have already done quite enough to accomplish that."

Tom curled his hand into a fist, the sting of the M at the base of his thumb suddenly returning. "I was not kissing a man, Henry."

He jotted something in the ledger, then clicked his tongue. "And you do not cavort with whores or engage in midnight brawls with miscreants or attack gentlemen in the streets."

"He was not a gentleman! I was saving a woman from the monster!"

"Of course you were."

Henry turned to leave, but Tom grabbed his arm. "The person you saw me kiss was a woman dressed as a man."

Henry tried to twist from his grasp, but Tom held him firmly. "She is a journalist investigating the London Monster. To have access to certain information, she must disguise herself as a man."

A muscle twitched nervously in Henry's cheek. "What is her name?"

"I cannot tell you that. It could ruin her chance of getting published."

Henry seemed to consider what he was saying. "Why were you kissing her?"

No one but Henry would ever ask such a ridiculous question. "We have become close."

Although that may no longer be true.

Henry jerked his arm and Tom let go. He wasn't sure if Henry believed him or not, but he supposed it didn't matter. He'd already made it clear how he felt about him.

Henry leaned back against the crate, his face somber. Everything he was thinking was clearly painted in his pained features. "'Tis so easy for you, I imagine. Doing as you please. Taking what you want."

Easy? Tom drew a deep breath. It would be much easier not to want so much. "I was there when Mother was killed. I could do nothing then, but I can do plenty now."

Henry rubbed his forehead, his face pinched. "I don't mean that."

"You mean . . ."

"Judith. You were right about her affection for me, but her marriage to Chippenham is set."

In some way, Tom was relieved. Henry's distaste for him was tangled up in his lack of progress with Judith. It was amazing what love—or the deprivation of it—could do to a man. "Did you tell her father of your interest?"

"She fears it would prove useless. And cause a scandal."

"So long as she becomes your wife, would you truly care about a scandal?"

Henry chewed his bottom lip and started pacing. "I wouldn't wish to disgrace her family. Or ours."

"Disgrace? She would marry a man she loved and into a family of great wealth. There is nothing disgraceful about that."

"We are not titled."

"A title does not make the man, Henry."

Henry turned abruptly and knocked into the stack of newspapers, sending a slew of them to the floor. They both bent to pick them up, and that was when a caricature of the London Monster caught Tom's attention. Beneath it was the caption, "The Monster Disappointed of his Afternoon Luncheon". The satire was of a large-mouthed ogre holding a knife and fork in each hand and a woman by the back of her gown. Her legs and bottom were exposed except for a large pot covering most of her buttocks.

Henry leaned over Tom's shoulder. "Judith has taken to wearing a copper cuirass over her petticoats."

Tom opened his mouth to speak, but Henry held up his hand to stop him. "Before you ask . . . no, I did not see it. She told me when I suggested she take care until the villain is caught."

Tom studied the sketch. It bore no resemblance to the man he'd seen twice, for it painted him to look like a literal monster. He wondered if this drawing would mislead the public, making it more difficult for anyone to identify him. It could embolden the man since his anonymity would be further protected by such a satirical depiction. He shoved the paper into his coat and ran out the door, bits of straw from his sleeves dancing in the wind.

⟷

Tom hired a sociable to take him to Holborn. There were no closed carriages to be had, so he sat hunched against the wind in an effort to battle the cold. Eventually, the sociable debouched into a wide street, a main thoroughfare, from what Tom could gather. "Stop here, sir."

Maeve had told him of a molly house known as Mother Cluck's Coffeehouse on Field Lane, but he didn't dare mention the name of it to the jarvey. He would find it on his own.

"Young man," he said to a passing baker's boy, who was busy readjusting a sack on his back filled with four large loaves of bread. "Could you direct me to Field Lane?"

The boy looked at him sideways and took one step back, a flicker of alarm in his eyes. "Over there," he said, jerking his hand to the right. "On the way to Saffron Hill."

Before Tom could thank him, he darted off in the other direction. As he walked, he caught his reflection in the glass of a storefront and laughed. His hair, much of which had escaped its ribbon, stood on end as if it had been tousled by a dozen hands, and his cheeks were as ruddy as a ripe tomato. He brushed down his hair with his fingers and retied his ribbon before continuing on his way.

A smattering of shops lined the street, interrupted only by empty plots that had suffered fires or lack of use as told by the bits of old cloth and charred wood scraps. Small children ran after one another layered in rags that likely had once been the clothing of someone much larger. Ahead lay a narrow lane with battered storefronts that edged out to the street in open stalls.

"A penny, sir? For me wee sis?"

Tom peered down at the soot-covered little boy standing beside him. He was no more than ten years of age, and the little girl who dutifully held his hand was all of three or four.

Tom bent down. "I shall give you a penny if you can tell me where the coffeehouse is."

"Are you a moll?" he asked, his face serious.

He drew back slightly, surprised that this child knew of such things. "No. But I have business there. Could you tell me where it is?"

The boy eyed him suspiciously. "Show me the penny first."

Tom reached into his coat and slipped a couple coins from his purse. He held a penny between his fingers just above the child's grasp.

"The end of the street. Where the men have their bubbies out. Not real bubbies, but man bubbies."

Tom did his best to show no shock at the boy's words, then dropped two coins into his open palm. "One for you and one for your sister."

The boy smiled brightly and ran into the alley behind the lane with his sister in tow.

Mother Cluck's was not exactly as the child described. No one inside was half-dressed, but there were plenty of men in gowns, fully corseted and covered in lace. Many wore wigs fashioned to look feminine with scarves or fanciful hats. There were also just as many dressed as normally as Tom.

The bullyboy stopped him with a backhand to the chest before he entered the main parlour. He was shorter than Tom but much thicker around the gut, making them both about the same weight. "What business do ye have here?"

"I should like to speak with Mother Cluck about a certain financial opportunity, if you will." Tom smiled politely as he brushed the bullyboy's hand away from his chest. A small crowd of curious molls lingered nearby, waving their fingers with the obvious hope of gaining his attention.

The bullyboy turned to a molly in a pale blue gown, her face rouged and powdered white. "Get Mother Cluck."

While he waited, Tom surveyed the room. It was much like Parker's, except worse for wear. The furniture was covered in velvets and damask, albeit noticeably tattered and worn, and there was an area for socializing as well as an area for more intimate entertainment in the back. The most notable difference was that although there were no women in the room as far as he could tell, the sound of women's voices was heard far more often than the men's.

"Why wait alone when you can have company?" A petite brunette draped in crimson fluttered a white feathered fan under her nose. She ran her hand over his arm, squeezing it in admiration. "I wonder what a strong gent like you would do with a sweet lass like myself."

Small bits of powder flaked from her jaw as she spoke, revealing a faint peppering of dark stubble.

She leaned into him to curl around his arm like a snake. "We have a lovely little private room in the rear where we could become better acquainted."

He was about to decline the offer when a large buxom woman hobbling with a cane approached in burnt orange satin trimmed in black lace. She was heavily powdered with rouged lips and cheeks and wore her grey hair high upon her head in a mess of curls and black ribbons. All her efforts had had the same effect as putting fresh paint on a crumbling house. It was a horrible waste of time. Tom stared at her, unsure as to whether or not she might actually be a woman.

She planted one hand firmly on her hip. "Are you the cull asking for me?"

"Mother Cluck, I presume?" Tom shrugged off the molly at his arm and doffed his hat.

"If you're offerin' to fill me purse wiv some sterling, then aye."

Tom nodded, smiling. "Is there somewhere we could speak privately, madam?"

"Call me Bessie." She spoke with a cockney accent, clipping her H's and T's and blurring together most of her words.

Bessie waved her cane at the lingering molly. "Get goin'. There's plenty of other men to entertain." She turned to Tom. "Follow me."

She led him to a small room that served as an office of sorts, with a large wooden desk covered in scattered papers and bits of baubles and feathers. On the adjacent wall was a shelf layered in leather and wood artifacts of a sexual nature clumped together, all of which looked like they had been frequently used and were in need of repair or cleaning. He sat in the chair opposite her and cleared his throat. "I am willing to offer you a great deal of money for your services."

She glared at him suspiciously through milky eyes. "Go on."

"I would need a dozen or so of your molls to help me lure the London Monster—"

"The London Monster! Why would ye want to do that?"

He told her of his plan to have them walk the paths of St. James's Park in the evening, unescorted yet protected, so that he may capture the man once and for all.

"And who are these men who are gonna protect 'em?" she asked. "If ye haven't noticed, me molls are not the fightin' type."

"I am still working on that. I know some people who might help us."

She reached between her breasts and slipped out a handkerchief yellowed with age and use, then blew her nose, the trumpeting blare startling. "Before ye say us, ye'd better tell me how heavy ye plan to make me pockets."

Tom thought about the share of the house takings and door receipts he'd earned for the fight with Futrell. After the ten guineas he gave Maeve, he didn't have much left. "Twenty pounds."

"Fifty," she countered without hesitation, tucking her handkerchief back into her gown.

He didn't have fifty pounds. He offered forty, although he didn't have that either.

"Forty, it is!" Bessie leaned back in her chair and rubbed her knobby hands together. "Let me know when you've gathered up your cocks, and I'll have me girls ready."

Tom bid her a farewell and stepped into the street, wondering how he would come up with the money. He had almost twenty pounds left from the fight with Futrell, but that was it. He couldn't go to his father because he would ask what it was for, and Tom wouldn't be able to bring himself to lie about it. There were too many lies between them already. He wouldn't ask for money back from Maeve either. She needed that for Emily.

Tom made his way off Field Lane and back to the main thoroughfare. He could possibly borrow money from Henry or Roger, but they would likely ask what it was for or tell Father.

"Such is my good fortune!"

Tom looked up to find Stone gleaming sardonically, his arms open wide in a false gesture of welcome. "What a coincidence meeting you here in Holborn."

"I have nothing to say to you, Stone." Tom continued walking past him.

He grabbed his sleeve from behind, and Tom shrugged it off.

"You forget who made you who you are," Stone growled between gritted teeth. "Don't think for one second that I believe you threw that fight with Futrell."

"He won anyway. So what does it matter?" He couldn't stand the prick. If Stone didn't back away, he was going to lose some teeth.

Stone leaned in close, his breath coming out in white puffs in the cold. "I could have lost a lot of money on that fight, you son of a whore."

Tom grabbed him by the throat and shoved him against the wall. He spoke as calmly as he could muster. "I don't answer to you."

Stone's face started to redden. Tom released him, his back and shoulders still buzzing with anger.

Stone rubbed at his cravat and coughed. He put up his hand, palm out in supplication. "Relax. I have a proposition for you." He cleared his throat with some effort. "There's a young fighter. John Jackson. He's looking for a match, and you were mentioned. Kent is looking to promote it."

"When?" Father's election wasn't until the summer. He took a deep breath. He needed the money to catch the monster. This would be the last one, he promised himself.

At that moment, four men emerged from the tavern on the other side of the street and joined them. All wore rough clothing, bedraggled and mildewed from years of wear. Judging from their appearance, they appeared to be Holborn locals.

"Problem here, Mr. Stone?" one asked.

Stone waved off their concern and sneered at Tom. "They want it to happen in the spring."

"Fine." Tom turned to leave, and Stone reached to stop him. Tom glared down at Stone's hand clutching a piece of his sleeve. The four men hovered nearby, ready to pounce.

Stone glanced at his cronies, then speared Tom with a glare. "This time, you'll do as I say, or that sweet little whore you spend so much time with will pay the price."

A Note

Who is to sleep? The church bells have been ringing incessantly since dawn to remind us that the queen has aged yet another year. I am expected to attend a ball this evening in her honour—and I will. But for now, I sit on a polished bench near the river, watching the ships adorned in bright colours sail by like flamboyant birds gliding obediently onward in blind allegiance to their leader. At one o'clock the park guns fire, their blasts echoing over church steeples and across the river to the Tower where they are answered by even louder guns. All this noise for a queen who speaks English with a strong German tongue and who no one ever sees.

I leave the river and head back home only to get caught in a crowd. Within seconds, three carriages carrying King George, Queen Charlotte, and the princesses pass by on their way to St. James's. One of the princesses peers out of the carriage light and smiles. I can see from where I am standing that she is likely the eldest of the daughters, the one often politely referred to as plain— eyes too far apart, mouth too small, nose too large. Her eyes lock with mine for a mere second, yet long enough for me to sense she is interested. But she is not the one I shall search out this evening. It will be someone far more beautiful, far more accessible.

My brother once mentioned to me how men should spend more time selecting the right woman to pursue when desiring a conquest. It is a lesson I struggle with each time I search for a paramour. But tonight, I vow to listen.

I carry on as usual until the hour has come for me to call forth my carriage. I have chosen my clothing carefully, for I do not wish to be remembered this evening. Unlike the other peacocks dressed in brightly embroidered velvet coats, I wear an unadorned blue kerseymere coat over a black satin waistcoat and breeches. They are finely made yet plain enough to draw no attention.

At eight o'clock, the ballroom opens, and I am ushered in along with a few hundred other guests. I recognize several faces and make my rounds decorously, complimenting the ladies and talking of unimportant matters with the gentlemen. I am not here to enjoy myself, really. I am only here to observe, to gauge, to calculate. My brother's voice speaks to me as I survey the room, reminding me that much deliberation is necessary when choosing who shall receive my attention after the affair.

His and Her Majesty enter the room with the three princesses, followed by the Duke of Cumberland. The king's scarlet and gold attire outshines that of his wife's, which is dark and austere. Their daughters, however, are adorned in blue, green, and yellow and look like three spring flowers ready to be plucked. The queen greets a few nobles and then falls into conversation with William Pitt, the Prime Minister, leaving her lovely daughters to mingle on their own. What a pity there are so many watchful eyes.

It is an hour or so before I spot the perfect lady to shower with my attention. She is not as finely dressed as the others whose diamond cuffs and gold foil skirts glitter in the firelight, but she holds herself regally with her shoulders back and chin up. I watch as she accepts an offer to dance from an older gentleman whose small dark eyes and pointed nose remind me of a ferret. I silently chastise her for giving in so easily, especially to a man whose proboscis seems especially equipped to sniff out offal. I smile behind my fist at this misstep on her part.

When they finish dancing, she excuses herself and leaves the ballroom. I follow her to the galleries, which are—I note with pleasure—poorly lit and less crowded than the ballroom. A warmth spreads through my chest as I watch her sway her hips in exit. She settles in the back, waving her fan under her chin as she lifts two long tendrils of hair away from her neck.

"Pardon me, madam. But I should like to compliment you on your graceful manner," I say.

She turns to face me, her eyes narrowed to search my face in the dark. "Do I know you, sir?"

She quickly licks her plump bottom lip so it glistens in the distant firelight. I fight the urge to run my thumb over it. "Do you wish to know me?"

"I beg your pardon, sir?" There's a hint of flirtation in her voice.

I am tempted to introduce myself, but in the end, refrain. Before I am able to respond, a girl who looks quite similar, yet moves in a more genteel manner, approaches. "Come, Anne. We should go. The queen has left the ballroom with the princesses to retire for the evening."

I melt into the shadows yet remain close enough to hear their exchange.

My Anne speaks first. "Father said he would meet us here at midnight. 'Tis only eleven o'clock."

Yes, Anne. Stay. Stay with me. I could delight you in many ways.

Her sister, a bit younger, whines. "But I am tired, and I don't care to wait for Father. Mrs. Miel wishes to leave as well. 'Tis only a short walk."

I listen as they argue, damning that young girl to hell for her impudent interruption. Finally, they resolve to leave, and Anne disappears from the gallery without a proper farewell.

I could have had her. At the very least, an unchaste kiss or her hand on my cock.

I follow them out and wait until they pass the court and enter the park, the streetlamps lighting the path ahead. Without a word, I doff my hat a few times to passersby, tempering my anger at the insolent tib who ruined my encounter with Anne. I was so near to taking her in my arms and pressing her close.

There are still far too many people about, so I pace myself, knowing my advance will not go unnoticed should I act too quickly. It is not until we almost reach the end of St. James's Street that two men approach carrying a sedan chair. "By your leave! By your leave!" they shout, and Anne and Mrs. Miel, her chaperone, move to one side, her sister to the other. The young mot stands there stretching her neck to see who is inside the compartment when I recognize my chance to punish her.

"Oh ho. Is that you?" I rush to her and stare into her eyes. She stares back as if I were a leper and not the gentleman I am. "Rude little bitch!" I say.

Her eyes grow wide, and she spits at me, a fine spray landing on the side of my cheek. She turns to run. Anger swells inside my chest, and I strike her hard in the back of her head, sending her reeling forward. The sedan chair blocks Anne and her chaperone from seeing this, but I stay behind, inching out of the light from the streetlamp.

The sister runs ahead shouting, one hand pressed over the spot where I hit her. "For God's sake, make haste! Can't you see that wretch behind!"

That wretch?

Confused, Anne and Mrs. Miel grab each other's arms and stand immobilized until they spring ahead, their heels clacking against the frozen, hard-packed dirt. I wrestle with the idea of disappearing into the darkness, but I can still feel the slobber of that whore on my skin, so I follow them.

"Sarah!" Anne calls to her sister, stumbling then righting herself. Mrs. Miel pushes onward, panting.

Sarah runs to the door of an old baglio at the end of the street, looking back to see where Anne and her chaperone are, when we lock eyes. Her mouth opens in fear and she bangs on the door, pleading for someone to open it. Anne and Mrs. Miel spill towards her.

My rage builds as I draw close. I reach inside my coat and unsheathe my poignard. How dare she think she can call me a wretch! "Blast your eyes, you damned bitch! I shall murder you and drown you in your blood!"

I lunge at her, but she jerks to the side, and I strike Anne in the hip instead. She turns to face me, her brow knitted and eyes teary. The door suddenly swings open, and they rush past a man into the house. He stares at me, clearly bewildered. I slip my dagger behind my back and slowly take my leave, my evening perfectly ruined.

Chapter 21

"Have you been here before, madam?"

Maeve resettled herself in the chair and stared at the young clerk across the desk. "No, sir. This is my first time."

"Good. We do not accept repeat visitors."

Maeve pulled her shawl tighter around her shoulders. She'd heard about London Lock Hospital's strict rules against readmitting patients after they've been discharged. Prudy had told her. But she'd never needed a visit because although she had seen the rash and sores before on the other girls at Parker's, this was the first time she'd ever seen them on her own skin.

"You must go through parish authorities before we can admit you." The clerk leaned back in his chair and rested his hands on his chest, fingers interlaced. "And then, of course, you will need a letter of recommendation from the governor of the hospital as well."

That was hardly discreet. Prudy hadn't mentioned anything about gaining letters of permission to be treated. "I need not be admitted. If I could simply purchase a tincture—"

He smiled falsely. "We do not sell tinctures here, madam. The salts and pills are given to admitted patients."

Maeve thought it would've been as easy as giving her name, visiting with the surgeon, and paying a shilling for a tincture.

"I see," she said, her throat tight.

She stood to leave when the clerk reached into his desk and presented a folded piece of paper. He looked around before handing it to her, then lowered his voice. "There's a physician in Covent Garden who might be able to help you."

She unfolded the handbill and squinted to make sense of the writing.

A speedy and absolute cure for the French Pox or running of the reins, shankers, buboes, or swelling in the groin, without flushing or confinement. Patients experience no hindrance of business while undergoing treatment lasting six to eight days. Guaranteed. 13 Tavistock Street. A lamp lighted in the door in the evening.

Maeve refolded the handbill, then tucked it inside her gown. She was expected back at Parker's by dusk, but with the sun hidden behind a thick blanket of grey clouds, she had no idea how late in the day it was. Had the church bell rung four or five times? Covent Garden market was at least an hour's walk from Grosvenor Place. She'd brought two pounds with her, just a bit more than Prudy had said the cost of treatment might be and, thankfully, enough for a hackney.

The hackney stopped at the market just short of the coach stand, unable to press through the crowded thoroughfare. The jarvey jerked his chin to the right, the horses throwing their heads back impatiently. "Off you go."

She stepped off the footplate and pulled out the handbill once more to look at the house number. Thirteen. That was a number filled with misfortune on its own, but for her, it carried a horrible weight. Albert had left her on September thirteenth almost four years earlier, and she'd been only thirteen when Mr. Daniels at the milliner shop had taken her maidenhead.

She came upon the home, a red brick two-storey place with black shutters on the front window and the number thirteen painted on a wood placard near the door. From all outward appearances, it seemed perfectly respectable.

There was no lighted lamp, but she knocked anyway and waited. Two women walked towards her along the street and shot her accusatory glances. Tingling heat traveled into her neck and ears. She lifted her fist to knock again just as the door opened. A woman wearing a brown cap peeked through the gap and swept a questioning gaze over her.

Maeve's stomach flipped as she considered leaving.

"You looking for the surgeon?" asked the woman.

Unable to find her voice, Maeve nodded.

"Come in, come in, then."

The front room was dimly lit with only two small oil lamps on the far walls. It looked like the milliner's front parlour from years ago with similar faded upholstered chairs—only in green, not yellow—and a side table that had seen years of use.

162

The woman who answered the door pointed to a chair. "Wait here. I'll get the surgeon."

Maeve sat, her hands folded in her lap, her mouth suddenly dry. She poked her tongue at the sore in her cheek, now larger, the sting more prominent than before. She hoped she hadn't made a mistake by coming here. What if the treatment involved cutting or something equally as painful? Or worse, what if the surgeon found her too far gone to cure?

She pressed her thumb into the centre of her palm, now cold and clammy, and glanced back at the door, thinking she could still leave with no trace.

"How may I help you, madam?" A short, slender man wearing a stained apron and his shirtsleeves rolled up entered the room. His hair whirled atop his head in grey and white wisps, partly concealing a pair of dark-rimmed spectacles.

She cleared her throat. "Are you the surgeon?"

"I am. Is there something I can help you with?"

"Well . . . I . . ." She reached into her bodice and pulled out the handbill. "I saw this."

He took it from her and lowered his spectacles to read it, then slipped them off to study her. "Certainly you are here for . . . an acquaintance."

She inhaled deeply and looked away. "I'm afraid not."

He rubbed his forehead with his fingertips. "Very well. Follow me."

He took her to a back room lined with shelves containing herbal tins and jars in various sizes. On a small table by a chair lay three thin, sharp knives and a wooden bowl stained dark from what she imagined was blood.

"Have a seat, please."

She glanced once more at the knives, then sat. She would leave if he suggested bloodletting.

"I only wish to ask you a few questions." He offered her a gentle smile.

She sat, her shoulders still stiff with doubt.

"Your age?" he asked.

"Four and twenty."

"Married?"

"No, sir."

"Have you engaged in sexual congress?"

She nodded, staring at her hands in her lap.

"I see." He pulled over a wooden stool and sat beside her. He lowered his spectacles once again, reached for her arms, and turned them over. "Have you had a rash on your palms or feet?"

"I have. Not a troublesome one, though."

"And your eyes. Has your sight failed you recently?"

She hadn't thought her eyesight related to the matter. "For a while now."

"Mm-hmm." He rubbed his chin thoughtfully. "Have you experienced whites?"

"Whites?"

The surgeon cleared his throat. "A discharge, madam."

She had, but all the girls experienced that. It often went away within a week or two. "I suppose."

"Sores in delicate areas? Pain during urination and release of the bowels?" How did he know? "What do you think it is?"

He took a deep breath and stood. His neck stretched as he squinted to read the labels on the bottles along the shelves. "Poisoned blood. The pox, madam."

Her heart sank. She had hoped it was merely scurvy or at worst, the clap. "Will it require a mercury tincture?"

He pulled three bottles from the shelf, one of which appeared to contain some sort of root. With a knife from the table next to her, he cut it into tiny pieces. "It could. But you would need supervision and to remain in bed for a month or so. Alone, of course." He turned to face her. "But I don't suppose that would be possible."

He was referring to a salivation. She could never afford a month away from her duties at Parker's. Maeve swallowed in a poor attempt to dislodge the knot in her throat. "No, sir."

"Then I can give you this." He poured the contents into a small linen pouch and handed it to her. "Make a tea using a thimbleful every day. You should find relief in a matter of a week or so."

She stared at the little bag, hoping the surgeon was right. "What is it?"

"A bit of sarsaparilla, China root, and guaiacum." He set his spectacles back on top of his head. "You should also refrain from sexual congress until the matter is cleared."

How would she explain this to Mother Wharton? The last thing Mother would want is to be known as the bawd of a poxed brothel. She would instantly throw Maeve on the street if she knew she'd contracted the pox. That would mean Maeve would forfeit her earnings from lying on her back, and Emily still needed her medicines.

"Madam?" The surgeon stood with his palm out. "My payment?"

"Forgive me, sir." She reached into her purse. "How much?"

He smiled. "Thirteen shillings."

Chapter 22

Sophie sat at the dining table, staring at the note Dalton had slipped her at dinner the night before. *Ranelagh pleasure gardens tomorrow. Two in the afternoon.*

It had been almost a month since the Twelfth Night celebration when he'd suggested they speak, so she thought he had simply dropped the matter. But clearly, he had not.

"What is that you are reading, dear?" Mother asked, spreading marmalade on her toast.

Sophie slipped the note back inside the *World* newspaper. "An article about the London Monster. Another attack. This time against a maidservant standing outside the Gordons' home. Kicked her with his knee, it seems, and left her cut and bleeding as a result."

Mother gasped. "That man is the devil's twin, I tell you."

Sophie reread the details in the paper. "He hasn't done that before."

"What?"

"Kicked a woman. She believes he wore some sort of sharp object attached to his knee."

"He is a peculiar fellow, for certain." Mother held up her toast as if to make a point. "Women have no chance when there is a rogue like that walking about."

Sophie wondered if it was the same man. The article did say he swore at the maidservant, cursing and using insulting language, but his method was not typically imbued with such anger from the start. It usually began with a proposition of sorts, albeit a highly inappropriate one.

On another note, she noticed the poor quality of the writing, the lack of detail, and an unnecessary bit of speculation thrown in for good measure. She could have done a much better job with the article.

"Did she get a good look at him?" asked Mother.

"There is no mention of any of that here."

Mother flipped her hand dismissively. "Not that it matters. Not a single description we have heard so far has helped in his capture."

"That is because none of the victims agree on his features. They need a sketching." And she had one. If the papers would only take her seriously, she was sure they would be able to catch the miscreant. But a promise was a promise. She wouldn't divulge Tom's name as her source.

She got up from the table, carefully slipping Dalton's note from between the pages of the *World*. "I am going to Ranelagh to take the air with Peg this afternoon."

"You will catch a chill! Wait for a warmer day, dear."

"Do not worry, Mother. I will bring my fur cloak." Her mother looked unconvinced, so she added, "I have already made arrangements to meet Vivian there . . . to discuss the wedding."

Sophie was certain Vivian wasn't going to be anywhere near Ranelagh or Dalton wouldn't have suggested it. Just as she imagined, her mother's expression changed from disapproving to delighted with the mention of her June nuptials. "Perhaps she can give you suggestions for Mr. Needham's wedding shirt. You have yet to start sewing it."

Honestly, she'd forgotten about it. So many other things had been on her mind. "I will ask her what she thinks."

"Very well. Enjoy the gardens."

She squeezed Dalton's note hidden in her fist and offered a watery smile before leaving.

When Sophie arrived at Ranelagh, Dalton was waiting outside the entrance to the rotunda, alone.

She turned to Peg, who was rubbing her arms for warmth. "I believe that is Mr. Fletcher over there. Why don't you go into the rotunda where it is warm while I bid him a good day."

It was probably better that Peg stay out of sight, just in case Sophie had to give him a piece of her mind. That way, she would have nothing to explain later.

Peg glanced in his direction and shivered. "Your mother may not want you to be seen with him alone."

"Mr. Fletcher is practically family. I am certain she wouldn't mind." It was so far from the truth, she was surprised it glided that easily off her tongue.

Peg agreed grudgingly, then rushed to the rotunda, glancing back once before going in. Dalton stood not twenty feet away, his hands folded on top of his cane in front of him. Sophie took a deep breath, then strode over. "Good day, Mr. Fletcher."

He doffed his hat and smiled. "Indeed it is, Miss Sophie. Shall we take a turn in the garden?"

He held out his arm, and after a moment, she took it. They walked the path along the ornamental lake, where she managed a mild smile at a couple passing by. They nodded back, crunching the stones beneath their feet in a perfect, slow rhythm. She squinted up at the crisp blue sky that teased of warmer weather in the summer months, but at this time only meant that snow was unlikely. Neither of them spoke until they rounded the corner on the far end of the gardens.

"I am glad you came." Dalton stared straight ahead, his rhythmic stride uninterrupted.

"Did I have a choice?" she asked.

He looked down at her and smirked. "*I* know you to be a gambler. You could have rolled the dice and chanced the circumstances of not coming."

She let go of his arm and stopped walking. "What is it that you would care to discuss, Mr. Fletcher?"

"I think you know."

Heat flooded her chest and traveled to her ears. "Quite frankly, none of it is of your concern."

"I beg to differ, *ma petite fleur*. Your betrothed is my closest friend, dullard that he is."

"Leave Bertie out of this."

"That would be impossible, I'm afraid. I would be a horrible chum if I didn't inform him of his future wife's indiscretions." He spoke with false affection.

Sophie steeled herself. It had been more than a fortnight since Dalton had seen them kiss. How could she have been so careless at the party? She'd never meant to hurt Bertie. "What is it you want?"

He rubbed the side of his mouth with his thumb. "What is your paramour's name?"

Paramour? She'd never thought of Tom as her paramour. He was . . . well, not that, exactly. "Why should I tell you? You would only use it to hurt Bertie."

He shrugged and raised an eyebrow. "I suppose I could figure it out myself. He is a well-known pugilist. But you know that, of course." His gaze scanned her gown as if to remind her that he'd seen her in breeches at the fight. But it didn't bother her the way he probably thought it would.

"You would have done that by now if it were that easy." She'd read enough papers to know that Tom's name was never mentioned in any of the articles or she would've seen it. He protected his anonymity with great effort.

"A gambler you are." His mouth curved into a nasty smirk. "You forget that it is I who holds all the cards. Give me his name, or I will tell Cuthbert his betrothed plays the whore with another man."

She moved to slap him, but his hand snapped up to grab her wrist. "Why not put all this anger to better use?"

Before she could respond, he pulled her close and kissed her hard on the lips. She struggled to push him off, but he wouldn't let go. Finally, she stomped on his foot as hard as she could, and he jerked away, hopping and cursing between clenched teeth. She stood back, her lips numb from the attack.

Between grunts, he struggled to speak. "You played the wrong hand, *ma petite*."

Sophie sat quietly in the carriage, having resisted Peg's pleas to speak. She couldn't tell Peg what had transpired because then she'd know the truth about her feelings for Tom and the horrible mess she was now in. It had been hard enough to get her to keep the secret about her writing and masquerading as a man. Adding infidelity to her plight would not exactly keep Sophie in her good graces.

She couldn't believe Dalton's misbehaviour. Well, maybe she could. She'd always thought him a rogue, and now she had the proof she was right. She was proud of herself for fighting back, letting him know he was completely out of order. But the nasty sting of his kiss remained on her lips, and his threat was branded in her memory.

Sophie tapped on the wall of the carriage. "I wish to disembark here."

Peg's face twisted with worry. "What are we doing?"

The carriage stopped, then joggled with the footman's dismount. "*We* are not doing anything. I wish to walk home the last bit. Alone, if you don't mind."

"But the monster—"

Sophie patted the back of Peg's hand. "He never attacks in daylight. That I know for certain."

"Your mother—"

"Tell her I ran into an acquaintance and we chose to walk." The door opened, and she stepped out into the bright sunlight. "I will return shortly. Please do not worry over me, Peg."

The carriage pulled away with Peg peering out the window, her brow wrinkled with concern. Sophie hugged her fur cloak tighter around her shoulders and walked in the direction of her home.

Why did Dalton want to know Tom's name? What did it matter? Telling Bertie he saw her with another man would be devastating enough. His name could be anything and it would make no difference. And why did Dalton care? He clearly wasn't looking after Bertie's best interests. She'd always had the impression that he merely tolerated Bertie and took no great pleasure in their relationship. She'd seen Dalton roll his eyes at remarks Bertie made when he thought no one was looking.

How had her life become so complicated? If Dalton should tell Bertie about Tom, it would destroy him, not to mention his family and her own. What would they all think of her? Bertie would hate her. She was sure of it. As he should. It made the unveiling of her secret life as a reporter seem innocuous.

She stopped to sit on a rough-hewn wooden bench outside an apothecary. The late afternoon sun hung low on the horizon, hidden behind the shops and taverns lining the other side of the street. With the jingle of the door-bell, two women exited the apothecary, carrying the spicy scents of the shop with them into the cold. Sophie inhaled deeply, hoping to clear her mind of the chaos and disorder that now lived there.

She supposed she could give it all up. After all, the only articles she'd ever had published were those regarding commerce or bits of gossip no one cared about. She had earned less than a shilling in total for all of them. They meant nothing. Not like her articles on the monster or her article about Maeve, and she had used her new alias *James Evans* for those, not simply her initials, thinking a man's name would not get her thrown into the Discard pile. But without disclosing her source, they'd ended up there anyway. As would the article on boxing she hadn't yet finished.

But her escapades throughout London dressed as a man were not the real problem. It was something else, something she wasn't sure she could give up.

Sophie stood, brushed off the back of her skirt, and continued on the path home. She quickened her pace, determined to beat the early winter darkness. Suddenly, she was jerked to the side and pulled between two buildings. She was about to scream when her assailant started muttering apologies from beneath his scarf.

"Tom?" she asked, staring into blue eyes she found familiar. A purplish-blue half moon sat below his left eye on slightly puffed skin.

He unwound the scarf from his neck, exposing the rest of his face. "Forgive me, Sophie. I didn't mean to startle you."

She took a deep breath to steady her heart. "Then you probably shouldn't have grabbed me and pulled me into a dark alley. If I didn't know better, I would have thought you were the monster."

He reached for her hand, a smile emerging on his lips. "Please accept my apology. I suppose I was so surprised to finally see you that I acted rather impulsively."

"Indeed." The thumping of her heartbeat in her ears disappeared and her shoulders finally loosened. "What happened to your eye?"

His fingers patted the bruised spot gently. "Would you believe me if I said I ran into a crate at the warehouse?"

She considered the possibility, but the two smaller blue marks beside it made her think otherwise. "No, but you certainly ran into something. A fist, perhaps?"

One corner of his mouth turned up. "Connor's. Couldn't get out of the way fast enough."

So, he had returned to Parker's. As much as she didn't want to be bothered by that, she was. "What are you doing here?"

Tom explained how he'd discovered her surname and place of residence at the party and had been coming here for the past few weeks after leaving the docks, waiting to catch her alone. He hadn't dared venture too close to her home, knowing it would have placed her in an uncomfortable situation. And he insisted he would've never paid a call, announced or otherwise.

She sincerely appreciated his respect for her reputation and her family. But now with Dalton determined to expose her to Bertie, being with Tom so close to her home where they could easily be discovered made her heart race once again.

"I . . . We . . ." she began.

He leaned closer, his smile broadening. "I have been meaning to tell you that our plan is underway."

"Our plan?"

"I have arranged for lures. We will finally catch the monster."

Part of her was excited, but her heart sank regardless. "I am not so sure we should get involved."

"What? Why?" His head tilted to the side, disappointment clearly painted on his face. "I thought you wanted to catch him as much as I do."

"What I mean is, I am not so sure *you and I* should be involved. Working on this together isn't . . . well . . ." She stared at him while he sorted out what she was truly saying.

He was quiet for a moment, his gaze dropping to the ground. "I see."

"I will be married in a few months, and all of this must end." It was hard to say the words because she didn't mean a single one.

"Are you giving up everything? Your reporting?" he asked. "Or just me?"

A strange feeling—regret, relief—grew in her stomach. "Please do not make this more difficult than it already is. I have no choice in the matter."

"Don't give up your writing, Sophie. Publish that story about boxing. Lord Sidmouth is considering legalizing gaming. Your article could be the thing to push the vote over the edge." His voice grew excited, and his eyes shone bright blue. "My father is using it in his platform to run for Parliament."

"Your father is Joseph Hayes?" There was no hiding the shock in her voice.

He nodded uncomfortably.

"I had no idea." His desire for anonymity started to make sense to her. He'd told her she couldn't divulge his name in her articles because it could hurt his father's reputation. A Member of Parliament couldn't be associated with a marked criminal, nor a pugilist. It would be his ruin.

She still couldn't write the article. Dalton could easily use it as evidence that she was masquerading as a man in public, and it would effectually pinpoint Tom as 'the other man'.

"Sophie!"

She spun to find Peg standing at the corner of the building, anguish in her pinched features.

She turned back to Tom. "I should go."

He grabbed her hand. "We are not done, Sophie. I have much to do to before catching the monster, but I will find you. You will share in the glory alongside me."

She watched him disappear down the alley, and she knew with every step he took, he was right. They were not done.

A Note

Late February 1790

Winter. Most people abhor it. I relish in it.

All the false cheer that comes with warmer months disappears as the temperature drops. Smiles fade from people's lips, and their countenances take on the dreariness of the grey skies above. But while they shrink underneath layers of clothing like snails into their shells, I grow. The bitter wind emboldens me. The sound of it whipping through the trees calls to me in a love song. There is something invigorating about the cold that draws me out of my home and into the streets of London in search of another's warm embrace.

I grab my scarf and cane and head to Mayfair. I will not go as far as Hyde Park, for it is early afternoon and it would prove perilous for me to pursue an inamorata in broad daylight. But I feel the urge to be surrounded by others, occasionally brushing shoulders in a crowd, tipping my hat when necessary.

I pass the alehouse on Dover Street and peer into the window of a cutler, where a bladesmith sits on a stool to sharpen a knife against a spinning stone. Every so often, he stops and blows dust from its edge to admire his work. The crossguard is plain like my own, however the ivory hilt is highly decorated with a flowering vine wrapped around the grip. Clearly, it is an ornamental piece and not one meant for use, for one's hand could easily lose its grip on such a curiosity.

I am not in possession of my blade on this chilly afternoon. Daylight hours do not require it. Besides, I would never use one that looked more like an object to be mounted on a wall, than a tool to be used when necessary.

I cross the street where a crowd has gathered to listen to a chanter sing. I faintly recognize the tune as one I've heard before but cannot place the exact location. A party, perhaps? Then I hear the lyrics sung as if in my brother's voice, and I smile to myself. I'm utterly entranced until the chanter sings the final note. If only my brother were still here to guide me, help me as he did when we were younger. To save me from being the wretch I sometimes think I've become. I back away, almost knocking into a cart that a drayman has left carelessly in the pedestrian pathway. I search the crowd to scold the ragabash but only see others as finely dressed as I am.

A few doors down, I am taken by a lovely flower arrangement in a window. The sun casts a bright glare over rose petals that range from fuchsia to crimson, the giant bouquet a startling contrast against the drab browns and greys reflected in the window. I open the door and enter to take a closer look.

"May I be of assistance, sir?" A diminutive but well-postured man appears from behind a curtain to greet me.

"I was just admiring these flowers."

He circles around the counter to touch one of the petals. "I make them from silk imported from China."

"They are quite lovely."

Two women stop to stare through the glass at the flowers, both pointing at the large buds full of colour. The younger one in dark green wool offers a smile, and I doff my hat in response. Her face is plain, but her lips are full of suggestion.

"As you can see, the ladies love my shop. It reminds them of the promise of spring." As he speaks, a small group of women assemble before the window.

"Would you make me a nosegay?" I ask.

"Of course."

The little man disappears into the back room, then emerges moments later with the perfect small bouquet of roses. I raise them to my nose to smell them, forgetting that they are made of silk. He laughs.

"I could not think of a greater compliment, sir," he says. I pay him, and he bows to me as if I were royalty. "Rhynwick Williams, at your service."

As I proceed down Dover Street, holding my bouquet at my waist, I notice something quite extraordinary. These five little buds attract the attention of ladies of all ages, their gazes flitting between the blooms and my face. I chuckle to myself with each flirtatious glance, knowing how successful my next foray in the darkness will be.

Part Four

Chapter 23

March 1790
London, England

Cuthbert unscrewed the jugum, slipped it off, and dropped it into its little red velvet pouch. He smiled to himself, not only pleased that he hadn't had a nocturnal emission, but also proud that he hadn't ventured into a brothel in almost three weeks. His irritability seemed to have lessened, proof that the jugum was doing its work to protect his vital energies. Only three more months of wearing the thing and he would be married.

He dressed and went downstairs to join his parents for breakfast.

"You're looking well, son," his father noted.

His mother set her hand over his with three quick pats. "A few more weeks," she sang.

"'Tis more than a few weeks, Mother."

She shrugged indifferently. "Your father has notified our creditors that all will be squared away in due time."

Father looked up from a fork laden with a thick slice of meat. "Must you discuss such matters over the dining table, wife?"

"It was only a brief mention. There is no need to hide the information from Bertie." She sipped from her cup, then spoke over its rim. "I have noticed a closeness lately between the two of you. It makes my heart sing."

Cuthbert's cheeks warmed. His relationship with Sophie had improved for a while, but lately she seemed preoccupied and showed little interest in their conversations during his visits. "Well, she will be my wife. I should hope we would share a closeness."

He glanced between his parents, who were doing their best to ignore each other, and immediately regretted his statement. The sound of their forks clinking and scraping their dishes echoed in the room.

"I am meeting Dalton at White's later, Father. Would you care to join us?"

"No, no. The rents have come in from Shropshire. I need to go over them with Griggs. Very disappointing, I'm afraid."

Cuthbert hesitated before swallowing his bite of toast. His throat tightened at the truth that they were counting on Sophie's dowry to get them out of debt.

"I thought we were not to discuss money matters at the table," chimed Mother.

Father shot her a punitive look. "*Women* should not discuss such matters at all."

Mother cleared her throat gently and turned to Cuthbert. "Do give my regards to Mr. Fletcher when you see him."

"Of course." The weight of the conversation lay heavy on his shoulders and was only made worse by the additional debt he carried at the club, one they knew nothing about.

The fireplace crackled on the other side of the room at White's, the scent of roasted meat and peppery spices wafting through the air. Cuthbert and Dalton settled into a spot in the back where Dalton assured him they'd have more privacy.

Dalton slid a booklet across the table. Cuthbert didn't need to open it to know what was inside.

"Why must you insist on showing me these?" Cuthbert pushed it back to him. "You know how disturbing I find the pictures."

"Disturbing?" Dalton laughed. "Dear God, *mon ami*, since when do you find the female form disturbing?"

Cuthbert shifted in his chair. "These pictures are not simply of the female form, and you know it." He had spoken under his breath, careful not to let the three gentlemen seated nearby hear.

"What has come of you? Does your betrothed keep your bollocks in a box beside her bed?" Dalton shoved the booklet back inside his coat.

"I am trying to remain faithful until the wedding."

"Looking at pictures of nudes is hardly an act of infidelity." He took a sip of brandy. "Why on earth would you want to be faithful, anyway? Now is the time to rejoice in your freedom to do as you please—without judgment, I might add."

"I have been feeling better lately, and I do not wish to ruin it." He leaned closer and lowered his voice. "I believe it has something to do with the loss of my vital energies through perverse sexual behaviour."

"What?" Dalton twisted up his face, then finished the last of his brandy. "I was hoping we could go to Covent Garden today."

That was Dalton's polite way of enticing him to go whoring. "What about your . . ." Cuthbert wiggled his finger in the direction of Dalton's lap. "Is that not still a problem?"

"Rash is gone. I am in perfect health," he said smugly. "What do you say?"

Cuthbert envisaged one particular whore named Ginny, who used to sell sausages on Drury Lane. She'd told him that she had become an expert on the art of fellatio by practicing on her wares. The image stirred a movement his breeches, making him squirm in his seat. "I told you I wish to be faithful to Sophie."

Dalton signaled the waiter over with the snap of his fingers. "Two more brandies, if you will."

Cuthbert had barely touched his first. "None for me, thank you."

Dalton looked up at the waiter and nodded with a smirk. "Two more."

The waiter walked away with a quick nod.

"Why did you do that? I don't care for another drink."

Dalton exhaled audibly and leaned back in his chair. "You are a good man, Cuthbert. Perhaps too good."

The waiter returned with the brandies, set one in front of each of them, then left. Dalton slipped a small vial from his waistcoat and poured two small drops of liquid into his drink.

Cuthbert raised an eyebrow. "In perfect health, indeed. What is that?"

"A tincture of sorts." He swirled his brandy, stuck the tip of his finger in it, and licked it off. He jerked his chin at Cuthbert's drink. "I suggest you take a swig of that, *mon ami.*"

"What is it with you and forcing spirits on me?"

"Your loyalty to your betrothed is not returned."

A hard knot formed in the pit of Cuthbert's stomach. "What are you saying?"

"There is a rumour that Sophie has been secretly seeing someone else. A ruffian of sorts."

Cuthbert felt the blood rush from his face. The room took on a muted green hue, its details fading with each breath. "A . . . ruffian?"

"I know this is difficult to hear, but—"

"How do you know this?" His chest started to tingle and tighten.

"Does it matter?" Dalton lifted his glass. "Perhaps 'tis not true. Why don't we order something to eat?" He drank a sip, then snapped his fingers once more in the direction of the waiter.

Cuthbert shook his head. Sophie would never be with another man. For a moment, he felt incapable of speech. He finished the brandy in his glass and reached for the second. "I want to know where . . . how . . ."

Dalton gave his hand a small squeeze. "She was seen wearing men's clothing and venturing into seedy areas to write stories as a journalist. I suppose that is where she met him."

"This is . . . this is outrageous. Dressing as a man? Writing stories? 'Tis an absolute lie!"

"Think on it, *mon ami!* Why else does she rebuff your advances? You are her betrothed, after all."

Cuthbert squeezed his eyes shut, trying to erase the memory of all the times Sophie had turned her cheek or slithered out of his grasp.

"A lie? Nay. A farce? Most definitely." Dalton brushed a loose blond curl from his forehead. "Shall we order the eel?"

Heat bloomed behind Cuthbert's eyelids. He couldn't believe any of it. He wouldn't. This wasn't Sophie. His heartbeat thrummed in his ears. "I wish to be alone, if you don't mind."

Dalton stood, paused, then left without a word. The men at the nearby table looked over at him with what Cuthbert assumed was pity. Had they heard their conversation? Who else knew about this? It felt as if a hot coal had lodged in the back of his throat. He finished what was left of his brandy and sat back in his chair, unable to think straight.

The rumours had to be false. Sophie would never do the things Dalton suggested. Never. She was pure. Honest. And her mother would never allow her to behave so crudely.

He rubbed his eyes with the heels of his palms, then stared ahead at a frayed edge in the green brocade wallpaper on the opposite wall. Could he be wrong about her? Images of their time together rushed through his mind. There were days when he'd waited in her parlour for her return from an excursion, excuses spilling from her lips in a torrent of words. She always seemed to brush off his inquiries with the flick of her hand or an offer of more tea. He hadn't found it odd at the time, but if what Dalton had said was true, it would make perfect sense. She was trying to hide a possible rendezvous with this man, this *ruffian*.

The more he thought about it, she was always defending the lower class, making him feel horrible about some of the sentiments he shared with Dalton. Had her affinity for this ruffian turned her away from all that she was? Turned her away from him and their marriage?

His heart grew heavier with doubt with every second that passed.

"Mr. Needham! How good it is to see you."

Cuthbert blinked to clear the tears welling in his eyes, then took a deep breath. "Mr. . ."

"Topham. Edward Topham," the man offered.

Cuthbert studied his tall, slender frame draped in a dark blue coat with fawn cuffs, giving himself a minute to place the name. The editor. "Of course."

He sat down in Dalton's abandoned chair without invitation. "We shared a lovely bottle of Renaud and Dualle a couple months back."

"I believe it was *two* bottles." Cuthbert remembered the hefty bill he was handed after Topham's departure that day. But that couldn't compare to the annoyance he now felt after Dalton's declaration regarding Sophie's infidelity. Couldn't he just leave him alone to wallow in his misery?

"Was it, then?" Topham ordered a glass of brandy for himself and Cuthbert. "'Tis awfully cold outside. Spring could not come soon enough."

Spring. He and Sophie were to be married in late spring. June.

"Awfully busy at the paper now. Between the elections coming up and the London Monster creating havoc, I've had little time to enjoy a drink next to a fire with other gentlemen."

Although Cuthbert wanted to leave, Topham kept him there with stories about the newspaper business over two more glasses of brandy. It was the last thing he cared to hear about, but the man droned on for the good part of an hour. Cuthbert hadn't said more than three words the entire time, but Topham never seemed to notice. Finally, he excused himself, and Cuthbert watched, relieved, as he exited White's and disappeared into the cold.

The door hadn't yet shut when Lord Greenville entered, shrugging off his overcoat and hat and handing them to the eager waiter rushing over to help him. Cuthbert avoided his gaze as he made his way through the room to sit closer to the fireplace.

Alone, he finished the last of his brandy and stood to leave when the proprietor, Mr. Martindale, handed him a note indicating the charge for his, Dalton, and Topham's drinks.

"Add it to my account," Cuthbert said, shrugging on his overcoat.

"But . . ."

Cuthbert hurried out the door before Martindale could remind him of his unpaid balance. He started to head to church. St. Martin-in-the-Fields was but a ten or fifteen-minute walk, time enough to clear his head of all the images of Sophie with another man. But as he turned the corner by St. James's Palace, he decided to walk right past the church and over to Covent Garden instead.

Chapter 24

Maeve forced herself to swallow the tea the surgeon had given her that tasted like water from a footbath. It had been over a month since she'd started drinking the concoction, yet her symptoms only seemed to be getting worse. She'd already spent almost two pounds on the surgeon's curative, and each time she returned to purchase more, he added a little more of this or that, convincing her she should give it another try. But now she was beginning to wonder if the only thing it cured her of was having a fat purse.

She peeked out the side window by the door to watch Connor and Tommy sparring in the alleyway. He usually arrived before dawn—and the customers—but he rarely came inside anymore except to offer her a brief greeting or an update on his efforts to catch the London Monster. Once he'd come to warn her about Mr. Stone. He didn't want her to receive him anymore. At first, she thought he'd said it out of jealousy, but then he'd explained that Stone had threatened to harm her if he didn't agree to lose his upcoming fight, and he thought if she refused him as a customer, he wouldn't be able to get to her. But what other injury could he possibly cause her? Deeper cuts and scrapes around her wrists? Darker bruises between her thighs? None of it mattered. She would suffer all of it if it would bring Tommy closer to her.

Something had changed between them, but she wasn't quite sure what it was. There was no more flirting or small gifts. Perhaps it was only his excitement about his fight at the end of the month that kept him aloof. At least, that's what she hoped it was and not that he knew about her illness. She'd never told Mother Wharton the truth about having the French pox. She'd only said that she had the clap, merely a temporary inconvenience that would be cured in no time. That was why Mother had relegated her to cleaning girl until her little problem was cleared. She didn't think Mother Wharton would disclose that sort of information to Connor, so it was doubtful he knew anything about it, which meant Tommy didn't know either. Nonetheless, Tommy was doing his best to stay away from her.

"There is no time for dawdling. Have you emptied the chamber pots?" Mother Wharton stood next to her at the bar, sour-faced with her arms crossed squarely over her chest. "I believe I can smell them from here."

Maeve left the window to set her teacup on the counter. Paddy whisked it away with a quick wink. "I'm off to do it now, Mother," she said.

"Make haste. Connor will be opening the doors in a few minutes." She sauntered away with the swish of her skirts and the jingling of keys at her waist.

Maeve gripped the bannister to head upstairs. There had been times lately that her legs chose to behave on their own, so she took care to hold fast to the railing. Today, luckily, her legs did as she willed them, so she made it up to the bedchambers without incident.

She knocked twice on Prudy's door before entering, finding her buried under a pile of blankets with only one foot and her head sticking out. Maeve tiptoed to the side of the bed and slid the pot from under it with a soft scraping sound. Prudy stirred, then rolled onto her back.

"'Tis morn already?" Prudy groaned, inching the covers from her face. "My last cull left but an hour ago, he did."

Maeve managed a laugh. "'Tis early, but I assure you 'tis morning."

Maeve opened the curtains, then carried the pot to the window and unlatched the hook to open it. Although it was raining lightly, she shouted, "Gardyloo!" just in case someone might be braving the drizzle and lingering in the alley below. With a quick turn of the pot, she tossed out the contents. She was about to slide the pot back under the bed when she noticed tiny droplets of blood on the porcelain. "You have your courses, Prudy. You're not still entertaining culls, are you?"

"A curse and a blessing, it is. My quim is a bit sore, but I won't give up the coin." Prudy stretched like a cat, her arms high above her head. "I tell the new ones I'm a virgin. A fresh bit. They think they cracked my pipkin, so they slip me an extra shilling or two."

Maeve never slept with culls when she had her courses. It was far too uncomfortable. She slid the chamber pot back under the bed, the little red dots catching the light from the window, and realized she couldn't remember the last time she'd bled. Had she had her courses after the new year? Or was it before? Either way, it had been two months since then. It would make sense, though. The other girls had often complained that a whore's curse often interfered with her courses.

Mother passed by the door, pulling Maeve away from her thoughts. "You have a visitor, Maeve."

She hoped it wasn't Mr. Stone. She didn't want to have to explain she'd contracted a whore's disease to him, of all people. He undoubtedly wouldn't take it very well.

Maeve quickly emptied three more pots from the other girls' rooms, her stomach tumbling at the thought that Mother may have already told Stone about her illness. As she descended the stairs, she scanned the room but saw no one. She took a deep breath to calm herself and made her way to the bar. Paddy stood behind it, wiping it from end to end with a rag.

"Did Mr. Stone enter?" She looked around the parlour.

"Stone? No. But that odd little fellow did. He's over there in that chair." Paddy gestured at the two tall wing chairs set before the fireplace, one visible and the other with its back facing her. "You sure he's old enough to get a cockstand?"

Maeve had no idea who he was talking about. The youngest cull she ever had was seventeen, but he had more hair on his face and bits and pieces then most of her older customers. She peered around the chair and found Sophie hidden by the high back, a gentleman's hat in her lap and her brown woolen clothes glistening from the light drizzle outside. Mother appeared on the stairs, watching with a scowl set heavily in her jowls.

"Soph . . . I mean Mr. Evans. 'Tis so lovely to see you," Maeve said with a quick glance in Mother's direction.

Sophie stood instantly, a worried look on her face. "Shall we go upstairs?"

She leaned in to whisper. "We can't. I'm not supposed to be entertaining gentlemen now. But we can go over here. It should be a while before they start coming in."

Before Sophie could ask her any questions, she led her to the far end of the parlour, where Prudy usually did her table tricks. They sat on the sofa along the back wall away from Mother's view, where she took Sophie's hand in her own. "You seem troubled."

Sophie chewed her bottom lip before speaking. "Not troubled, exactly. But I do need your help."

Maeve leaned closer. "How so?"

Sophie's story flowed from her lips with excitement, her hands waving as she spoke. Maeve had to stop her a few times to ask for clarification as there were parts that didn't make sense, but eventually she understood that she'd decided to write the article about pugilism after all. She wanted to help a local politician running for the House of Commons to win the vote and gain the support of Lord Sidmouth.

"The gent who held the masque?" Maeve asked.

Sophie nodded. "The Speaker of the House of Commons."

"Wouldn't the Members of Parliament like to know I was invited to the Speaker's house?" Maeve giggled. All those important people, members of London society—the most respectable— mingling with harlots. But her laughter faded as she remembered how one person had spent that whole night avoiding her, tearing her heart apart. "So how can I help?"

"You could tell me everything you know about boxing. The names of the fighters, the rules, the gaming. All of it."

Maeve did know quite a bit, some of which she'd learned from the pugilists who frequented Parker's, and the rest she'd learned from Tommy. "There's going to be a fight at the end of the month. You should come with me."

Sophie shifted in her seat. "'Tis becoming more difficult for me to go about dressed as a man."

"How so?"

"'Tis complicated. But I can assure you 'tis all for the best." Sophie offered a quick nod as if to punctuate her sentiment.

"Then come dressed as a woman this time. As long as you're with me, no one will bother you."

"That would be worse. I cannot risk being seen at a boxing match. It would shame my family. And Bertie."

"Please reconsider. Tommy is fighting. It would mean so much to me if you were there."

Sophie shot her a slightly jaundiced look. "I think it better that I do not attend."

Maeve's heart sank. "No one will confuse you for a whore, if that is what you're worried over."

Sophie reached for her hand, her light green eyes fixed on Maeve's. "That is not it at all. 'Tis only that . . . I . . ." She inhaled deeply, her chest clearly rising with the effort. "Fine. I will go with you. I am not sure how, but we will go together."

Although she was thrilled that Sophie had agreed to join her, a sudden wave of nausea washed over her, causing her skin to prickle as if a swarm of ants treaded lightly over her limbs. She moved to stand, but then everything seemed like it was covered in a haze. She tried to blink her vision back into focus but couldn't and fell back on the sofa clumsily. Little white dots of light swam before her eyes against a sea of black.

"Maeve!" It was Sophie's voice. Soft warm hands cupped her cheeks.

186

A buzzing noise like the frantic wings of a nearby insect filled Maeve's head. She opened her eyes and took a deep breath. "I'm quite fine. I simply haven't been myself lately." Bile rose in her throat, but she steeled herself to will it down.

"Is that what you meant when you said you are not supposed to be entertaining customers now? Are you ill?" Sophie's voice was full of concern.

"I lose my balance now and then. A bit of blurred vision does it." Maeve tried to smile through her embarrassment. "I could use a bumper of brandy at the moment."

"Wait here." Sophie disappeared for a minute or two, then returned with a glass, her brow pinched with worry. She handed her the brandy. "How long have you been sick?"

Maeve tried to count the months but couldn't. It was the sort of thing that came and went. The rash had been the first of it years ago, but that had disappeared and only recurred every now and again. She would then feel fine for months until the aches rushed in to hit her like a winter storm. And then, of course, the sores. But she didn't need to tell any of that to Sophie. She'd be better in time if only the tea would work faster. She gulped the brandy, leaving less than half in her glass. Its warmth filled her chest and quieted her mind almost instantly. "Not long. I've been taking a curative."

"Well, it does not seem to be working. Shall I fetch you a surgeon?"

Maeve grabbed Sophie's hand. She couldn't have a doctor examine her, or then Sophie would know she had the French disease. "No. 'Tis nothing. I simply need a little rest."

Mother Wharton approached, a forced smile on her lips. "I would be happy to get you another girl, Mr. Evans. Maeve has other duties to attend to, if you don't mind."

Maeve stood with effort, one hand clutching the back of the sofa for support. "I will see you at another time, Mr. Evans. Good day."

Sophie stood and replaced her cap. With a quick nod, she crossed the parlour and left Parker's.

"I told you I don't care for your unproductive conversations with the culls," Mother said through tight lips.

Maeve lifted the half-empty glass and held it up for her inspection. "He ordered a bumper of brandy."

Mother snatched it away from her, spilling a few drops on the wool rug. "If you think selling a bumper of brandy is going to keep you fed and in a warm bed at night, you are sadly mistaken."

"He was here but a minute. I had no chance to offer him more. I'll do better next time."

Mother turned her attention to a group of men entering the parlour. Maeve had seen them all before. Regulars. They sauntered to the bar, laughing and offering their greetings to Paddy.

Mother straightened her gown, her hand absently running over the keys on the chatelaine at her waist. She nodded once in the men's direction, then forced a smile and lowered her voice. "If you don't, you will find yourself sleeping in a gully, fighting rats over your next meal."

Chapter 25

"You are aware of what happened last year when Wilberforce attempted a motion to end the slave trade, are you not? One of the ship's captains came forward. . . what was his name . . .?" Lord Sidmouth looked to the ceiling, jiggling his finger in the air.

Tom, Henry, and Father sat in Sidmouth's drawing room at White Lodge beside the lit hearth. Although it wasn't overly cold outside, it was damp from almost a week of rain. Sidmouth snapped his fingers at the servant standing by the sideboard, where a decanter of claret gleamed burgundy in the firelight. With the alacrity of a hound eager to please his master, he poured four glasses, then served them on a silver tray.

Tom took a quick sip of wine, then edged closer in his chair, hiding his cut and bruised knuckles in his lap. "Penny, milord. James Penny."

"Aye. Penny." Lord Sidmouth scratched the side of his long, straight nose before continuing. "He'd convinced members that the slaves were treated humanely onboard ships, given pipes and tobacco and entertained with music. No one would lend Wilberforce an ear after that."

Tom remembered that the papers had said he'd lost the vote two-to-one. "All those men had a stake in the slave trade. Of course they voted against Wilberforce."

Father cleared his throat. "In this case, I have faith the opposition is dwindling. More people believe legalizing gaming will benefit our city than those who do not."

"'Tis the electors you must convince, not the people. For they are the ones who vote."

Father set his glass on the small table beside him and smiled, his hands folded over his stomach. "If I may, milord, 'tis *you* we wish to convince."

Sidmouth waved the claret under his nose, then held his glass aloft. "Then, by all means."

Father cleared his throat. "Consider the tax levied on playing cards. The revenue brought in from the stamp duty in the last year alone . . ."

They finished two bottles of wine in the time it took to explain how the monies would be used to increase the number of magistrates and constables at gaming events as well as to improve areas of the city that were in dire need of care. Sidmouth nodded occasionally as Father spoke, Tom interceding only when Sidmouth cocked an eyebrow at something he'd said. Finally, when they were certain he supported the idea, they shook hands.

The valet stood stone-faced as he helped them with their overcoats. Tom slipped his gloves on, relieved that the Speaker hadn't noticed his marred hands. He may have been able to explain the cuts on his knuckles, but one look at the M branded on his palm and their discussion may have ended in a quick escort to the door.

"Parliament will be summoned in June, right before elections. You have little more than two months to secure your victory in your constituency. Should you win, I believe we will see a new London." Sidmouth paused with a sigh. "I only hope this does not encourage gaming amongst the poor. We do not wish to send them the wrong message."

Tom adjusted his hat, fighting back a response. Henry, having not said a single word the entire afternoon, suddenly came to life. "Horse racing, boxing, and cricket are gentlemen's sports, milord. No need to fret over the labour force."

Tom made an effort to hide his smile. Obviously, Henry had never been to a single one of them.

The carriage moved slowly along the boggy road out of Richmond Park, the wheels getting sucked into the mud where there were dips and hollows. Deer scattered as the carriage drew close, joining those frolicking in the open fields. Tom waited to mention Sophie until they left the park and traveled on harder packed roads, where conversation would be easier.

"I have a friend who could write an article to further your cause, Father."

Henry stole a glance in Tom's direction, undoubtedly remembering their conversation back at the warehouse regarding the journalist posing as a man. They never talked about it after that, and Tom could only assume that he'd accepted it as truth. "I believe, once it is published, it will help sway the vote in your favour."

"I suppose that depends on the nature of the piece," Father grumbled.

"It will be flattering, I assure you." But Tom wasn't certain that was true. Would Sophie write a favourable article or one that supported a more privileged stance? Her family was titled, after all.

With the gentle rocking of the carriage, Father nodded off, a soft sigh escaping from his parted lips. They rode in silence, Henry gazing out the carriage light. Tom hated the distance that had grown between him and his brother. Although they had never been close, at least Henry spoke to him every now and then, even if it was only to chastise him for something he'd done. But it had been a long time since Henry had admonished him for having bloody knuckles or a bruised cheek. Tom felt the weight of his disinterest like a cloak made of iron.

"Have you spoken to Judith?" Tom hoped the sound of her name would spark a desire to talk.

Henry remained looking out the window, his voice barely audible. "I have proposed marriage."

"That is wonderful, brother. Did Father approve?"

Henry cringed, his voice still low. "There is no need to tell him until it is agreed upon by *her* father."

Tom never understood Henry. He always managed to do things backward. "What did he say?"

Henry sat back, staring straight ahead. "I did not seek his permission first. Judith is going to present the idea to him to gauge his approval. If he looks upon it favourably, she will send word."

"And then?"

"'Tis not so simple. Chippenham is expected to put up a fight."

"Of course. He needs her family's fortune to lift him out of the ditch he's dug himself into."

"I am not certain her father would go back on his word. Arrangements have been made. A dowry has been set. The bond has been sworn. The penalty would likely be exorbitant if Judith's family broke from the agreement." Henry's face showed no expression. It was as if he were made of granite.

Henry's concern about money was a legitimate one since he had no money to speak of. It would have to come from Father, and he was rarely known to open his purse for non-business ventures. "I will get you the money to pay him off."

Henry turned to face him for the first time, his brow lifted in question. "What? How?"

With that promise, Tom took a deep breath. He would have to win his upcoming fight to be able to pay Mother Cluck and now Henry. Even with a loser's take, he would be far short of what was likely needed. "Leave that to me."

<hr />

The carriage rolled up the drive just as the sun peeked between two thick white clouds. Light glistened from the new leaves on the trees, still heavy with rain.

The crunch of the stones beneath the wheels stirred Father awake. "I must have dozed off," he said, running his hand down his face. He wriggled his nose and mouth a few times before speaking. "Thomas, Roger will likely need your help at the warehouse. Henry, you will come with me. We need to go over the ledgers from last week's shipment from India."

Tom chose to walk to Billingsgate, garnering questioning glances from both his father and brother. But it felt good to be out in the sunshine after weeks of dark grey skies, a hint of warmth on his shoulders and back. The quay was busy as usual with stevedores hauling bags and rolling barrels from the small crafts that ferried between ships and the warehouses. Herring gulls flew noisily overhead, swooping only to scavenge a dropped morsel of grain or runaway piece of exotic fruit.

He hadn't heard from Sophie in several weeks. Not that he expected to, exactly, but he hoped he'd suddenly look up from his work at the warehouse to find her smiling at him once more. He hadn't dared go near her home again for fear someone would see her speaking with him, but he missed her and the way she softened in his arms.

He arrived at the warehouse to find Roger directing four seamen stacking crates in the back. "Thank goodness you are here! We need to move the goods from France over there to make room for the new goods from India." Roger pointed at the far wall with a pudgy finger.

Tom shrugged off his coat and hung it on the coatrack next to the office door. He started to unbutton his waistcoat when he noticed his name scrawled on a letter sitting on the desk. He broke the plain seal, hoping it was from Sophie, but when he unfolded it, Bessie Cluck's signature was on the bottom instead.

A few weeks earlier, he'd sent word to Mother Cluck that he would need the services of her molls at the end of the month, although the day and time was not yet agreed upon. He hadn't heard from her until now.

Dear Mr. Hayes,

You'll have me molls. Strange fellas, they are. Want to help cach the roge. Bring me a diposit of fyve pounds and we shall setle on a date.

Bessie

Tom tucked the letter inside his waistcoat and opened the safe under the desk. While Roger was busy yelling at the men, Tom stole five pounds sterling, added it to his purse, then snatched his overcoat from the rack. "I must go, Roger." He skirted around the crates. "I will help you upon my return."

His brother's shouts followed him out the door until they were drowned out by the noises of the quay. He reached Holborn rather quickly and found his way to Mother Cluck's on Field Lane with no trouble. The warmer weather seemed to bring everyone outdoors except for those who found the parlour of Cluck's Coffeehouse more enticing. He had never seen that many men at Parker's, even on evenings when Mother Wharton offered watered down brandy for half the price.

The molls were adorned from head to toe in feathers and lace, their high-pitched laughter bubbling over their customers' gruff voices. A tiny gentleman wearing a crimson waistcoat and breeches played a tune on the piano in the corner. His head kept the jaunty beat as his fingers danced over the keys.

Tom watched the bullyboy disappear into the crowd to fetch Mother Cluck, stopping only once to lift a man's head by the hair to check if he was breathing. Seemingly satisfied he wasn't dead, he released his hair, then returned with Mother Cluck shortly after.

"Ye got me money?" she asked, not bothering with a proper greeting. She turned back to wave off an anxious-looking couple, he in blue silk and she in white with rose lace from her throat to her ankles. "Got a wedding to 'ficiate."

"A wedding?" he asked, incredulous.

"The captain and Kitty," she replied, as if that explained it. She held out her hand impatiently. Tom removed the coins from his purse and dropped them into her open palm.

"I will need your services on the last day of the month." His fight was scheduled for the twenty-sixth. He figured he'd need a couple of days to recuperate—if John Jackson was as good as the papers proclaimed him to be—in order to take on the London Monster.

She stuck the edge of one coin in her mouth and bit it.

"You'll have the rest when your molls finish the job," he said.

A sudden shriek made them both turn their heads towards the door. One of the molls snatched the periwig off a gentleman, who ducked and dodged his baldhead with each blow, curses spewing from her rouged lips as he cowered from her attack. The bullyboy snatched the wig from the moll's hand and settled it sideways on the man's head before tossing him out the door with the grace of a cat. Tom turned back to Mother Cluck. "I could use him too as part of the deal."

He left the coffeehouse relieved that his plan to catch the monster was in motion. All he had to do now was let Sophie know.

As he turned the corner, a man wearing rough wool and smelling of tobacco and cheap gin approached him. "Ain't you the Pretty Punch?"

Tom recognized him as one of the four who'd come to Stone's side the last time he was in Holborn. "Are you following me?"

The man laughed and smacked him on the chest with the back of his hand. "Came to deliver a message from Mr. Stone."

"I'm not interested." Tom gently shoved him aside and kept walking.

"He says he'll be at the fight."

Tom ignored him. He didn't care if Stone stood ringside. The man meant nothing to him.

"He says if you don't want nothin' to happen to your fancy lady friend, you'll do as he says."

Tom froze. What did that mean? His fancy lady friend. The last time Stone had made a threat, it was against Maeve, but Tom had spoken to Maeve about it. And Connor too, who promised to tell Mother Wharton about the threat. She wouldn't want to jeopardize one of her girls for a bit of coin, would she? Tom was confident that Connor would protect her should the bawd not care. This princock wasn't referring to Maeve, though. He spun around and grabbed him by his shirt. "You tell him, if he touches so much as a single hair on her head, I will send him to his grave."

Chapter 26

It was Friday. Aunt Lydia had sent her carriage for Mother early in the morning for their weekly visit, so the house was quiet except for the occasional sounds coming from the servants belowstairs. Normally, Sophie would be traipsing about London dressed as a man in search of a good story. But those days were over—except for her one last foray into the world of pugilism at the end of the month. She wanted to help Tom and his father, even though her article would likely never see the printed page. She'd do her best to get the story out. It was the least she could do for all his help with her articles on the London Monster.

Bertie arrived at noon, an hour before he was expected and an hour before her mother would be home. It wasn't too unusual for him to arrive early, so she didn't think anything of it until he appeared wearing the crimson silk coat and breeches he normally reserved for formal occasions. Had she misread his calling card?

"Forgive me, Bertie. Are we expected somewhere? I could call for Peg to help me change into a more suitable gown," she offered, confused by his appearance.

He stood as still as a statue, staring at her as if he'd never seen her before. A single bead of sweat dripped down his temple and onto his cheek. He brushed down the front of his fine coat, his cheeks reddening to match his clothing. "I thought you might like to see your future husband dressed like a gentleman."

"You always look the part of a gentleman, Bertie." He had been acting strangely for weeks now, but with their wedding only a few months away, she realized she didn't seem herself as well. It was difficult to concentrate with Tom and Maeve always on her mind and, as a result, she was certain others perceived her as acting strangely lately. Or perhaps she was only imagining their questioning glances and looks of disapproval. Either way, keeping secrets was never easy, and the ones she harboured deep inside were both dangerous and heartrending. "Join me in the parlour."

The silk irises he'd sent her months ago were still in the window, the deep purple and yellow striking in the afternoon sun. They sat on the sofa, close enough so that his knees touched her gown.

"I brought you a gift." He worked a nervous hand into the pocket of his coat and extracted a tiny leather pouch held closed with a black cord. "I hope you like it."

She took the pouch from him and opened it. Inside was a delicate pearl necklace with a gold clasp. "Bertie, I—"

"'Twas my grandmother's."

"'Tis lovely, Bertie, but—"

"I thought it would look charming on your neck. On our wedding day."

Their wedding. It was all anyone ever seemed to talk about these days and the last thing she cared to discuss.

"Here." He reached for the necklace. "Let me see it on you."

He fastened it behind her neck, the slight quiver in his lingering touch unnerving. She leaned away to escape his fingers, but he held fast to her shoulder, his gaze boring into her. She wasn't sure if it was love or hate that she saw in his eyes, but either way, a chill traveled through her from head to toe. He stared at her long enough to make her wish her mother were home.

Suddenly, something seemed to snap inside of him. A shadow spread across his face as the lines around his eyes grew deeper and his jaw hardened. Her stomach flipped just as he lurched forward and kissed her hard on the mouth, his tongue forcing her lips apart. She tried to push him away, but his hands found their way to her neck and shoulder to hold her in place.

"What are you doing?" She wriggled to slide from him, but she was crushed against the back of the sofa underneath his weight. Her mind flashed back to a different time and place—the garden party, the distant voices on the other side of the shrubbery as she scrabbled to get out of that young man's grip. The shock. The fear. The anger.

"Kiss me, Sophie." He nudged his groin into her thigh.

She gasped. "You seem to have forgot yourself!" His fingertips pressed into her skin. Her neck burned where the clasp dug into her flesh.

"I gave you the pearls! Why won't you kiss me?" He shook her as he spoke, his face flushed and angry. Before she could answer, he kissed her hard again, banging her lips against her teeth. The coppery taste of blood told her her lip was bleeding.

She tried to fight him off as one hand found its way down the front of her gown, groping her breast, but she was unable to move or protest with his mouth affixed to hers. She used her forearm to shove him off, but she was no match for his size. She even raked her fingers down his cheek, forgetting she wore gloves.

A knock sounded on the door, and the scurry of a servant's footsteps followed. Bertie's head lifted, and she writhed from his grasp. His hair was mussed, and his coat was creased unbecomingly. Four red splotchy lines ran the length of his left cheek. Sophie scooted away from him to catch her breath.

One of her footmen entered the room, his eyes averted from what he likely misinterpreted as an amorous moment between them. "I beg pardon, but the postboy delivered a letter for you, Miss Sophie."

Bertie turned and wiped his mouth angrily. Sophie stood to retrieve the letter from the footman, relieved to get away from Bertie. The footman made to leave, but she grasped his sleeve, silently begging him to stay. She opened the letter.

I must see you. It was signed *T.*

Sophie folded the note and slipped it inside her sleeve. She pressed her tongue against the growing bump inside her bottom lip, the taste of blood still sharp. "Please have the carriage readied. I need to leave. And have Mr. Needham's carriage brought round, if you will. Our visit is over."

The footman nodded briefly, then disappeared down the hallway.

"Where are you going?" he demanded, his lips trembling.

"That is none of your concern. Especially after your behaviour."

Bertie dropped his head in his hands. "Forgive me, Sophie. 'Tis only that I want us to be close. We will be sharing a marriage bed in less than three months, for God's sake!"

Sophie's throat caught. That may be her fate, but it didn't make the idea seem any more bearable. "Would you have behaved as such with my mother here?"

He shook his head slowly.

"We are not yet married, Bertie."

He opened his mouth to speak but said nothing. He stood, straightened his coat, and grabbed his hat. As he made his way to the door, he turned to her, the distance between them so narrow she could see the flecks of green in his hazel eyes. "But we *will* be married. Soon."

Sophie had her coachman leave her near the fish market just two streets from Tom's warehouse. On her way back, she would stop and pick up some cod to hide her true purpose and keep the servants from talking. As she hurried to the warehouse, her eyes welled with tears. She told herself she was crying because of the acrid smell of coal and salt in the air, but she knew the truth. She took a deep breath and wiped her tears away, her bottom lip throbbing with pain. The Bertie who did that to her was not the Bertie she knew.

How was it that she found herself in this position again? Was she saying something, doing something to invite that sort of attention? She had flirted with that young man years ago at the garden party. She'd also agreed to meet Dalton privately at Ranelagh. And she had allowed Bertie to visit, knowing her mother wasn't home. But when had she ever offered them permission to treat her like a plaything?

In a matter of minutes, she was near the warehouse, dodging her way between the workers and strollers on the quay. Tom stood outside with a large sack over his shoulder, talking to an older gentleman who nodded his head in agreement to whatever he was being told.

"Tom!" she yelled over the screeching gulls and clanging of the ship rigging.

He turned in her direction and smiled. Her chest, which had been as taut as a clock too tightly wound, suddenly loosened. He said one final thing to the older gentleman, threw the sack against the wall, and strode over. Before she realized what she was doing, she rushed into his arms and collapsed against his chest. Her throat burned, and tears flooded her eyes. She couldn't speak. His arms tightened around her, and she felt the light touch of his kiss on top of her head.

"What happened?" His breath was warm in her hair.

She couldn't tell him. He'd think the wrong thing about Bertie. He wasn't a bad person. He was only . . . confused.

She looked up at him but couldn't manage to find the words.

He took his thumb and swiped a spot just under her lip. "Your lip is bleeding."

She tried again to speak but wasn't sure what to say.

He held her away from him, his eyes fixed on her mouth. "Who did this to you? Was it Stone?"

"Who?" What was he talking about? She turned away. "I am uncertain as to how it happened."

He hesitated, obviously trying hard to accept what she said. "Let's go inside."

Several men were in the main part of the warehouse, wedging open crates with heavy black bars. Tom hustled her into the office and shut the door behind them. He leaned against the desk and held her. He didn't push her to speak, only let her rest against his chest until she was ready.

"Did you call me here to discuss the monster? Have you made the arrangements in Holborn?" Her breath began to steady, her voice slowly calming.

He shot her a questioning glance, seemingly disappointed that she wasn't addressing her distress. After a frustrated exhale, he brushed a lock of hair off her cheek and tucked it behind her ear. "I have. We will meet at the end of the month in St. James's Park. But that is not why I asked you to come."

"Ah. You want to discuss the article." She could see his pulse beating strong in the hollow of his throat. "I will be at your next fight to gather as much information—"

"You will go nowhere near the fight." He stared down at her.

"Why? It would be the best way for me—"

"Sophie . . ." He grabbed her hands between his own, his bottom lip caught between his teeth, and shook his head slightly, apparently struggling with the words. "There's a man to whom I owe a debt."

"I am not sure I understand."

In a surge of explanation, he told her how five years ago, he'd been in a brawl outside a tavern with two pickpockets, and a man approached him after seeing him fight. He'd asked him if he would like to put his hands to better use, explaining how he could earn quite a sum of money if he were to become a pugilist. He took him to Parker's to meet Connor so that he could train, and when he thought he was ready, he introduced him to George Kent, the promoter who gave him his first fight. "I made some good money, so Stone believes I owe him in return."

"What does this have to do with me attending the fight?" She was thoroughly confused with his line of reasoning.

"He wants me to take a dive."

It took her a moment to understand what he was saying. "Lose? Purposely?"

He grumbled an assent, then explained further. After he'd won a dozen or so fights over the years and he was the favoured fighter, Stone told him he had to throw the next one to pay him back for his success. That way, the bets would be stacked in his favour, leaving Stone to collect handsomely with a loss. Tom did as he was told, but the dishonesty gnawed at his gut, so he promised to never do it again. "If I win, he will come after you."

Sophie stepped back. "Me?"

"I will not take that risk, so I am going to throw the fight."

Sophie wasn't sure how to respond. How did this man know they were . . . friends? And then it occurred to her. "You said his name is Stone?"

Tom nodded once. "Do you know him?"

It all made perfect sense. Stone took Tom to Parker's because he was a customer there—Maeve's customer—and therefore knew Connor. He must have seen her both at Parker's masquerading as a man and at the fight in December. That was how Tom met Maeve too. Part of her was thankful that he hadn't gone there under other circumstances. "I have never seen him, but Maeve has told me about him. He is a brute of a man, from what I understand."

Tom looked down at his hands. Jagged pink scars crisscrossed his knuckles. She wondered how she'd never noticed them before.

He curled them into fists, then relaxed. "Maeve has told me. She won't let me . . . confront him about her. He pays her too well, and she needs the money for Emily."

Sophie knew the truth of that. Everything Maeve did was for her daughter. "But how does he know about *us?*"

"He has some hackums who follow me on occasion. Perhaps they have seen us together."

They may have been spotted at Vauxhall or St. James's Park. They could be watching the warehouse at that very moment. The thought of them watching her too outraged her. "Well, you will *not* throw the fight. He cannot get to me. I will travel with a companion from now until then, when Maeve and I will go together."

He seemed tortured by her words. "No, Sophie. I won't let you. I don't want him anywhere near you."

She planted her hands firmly on her hips. "I am not your typical fainthearted female who doesn't know how to take care of herself. I would think by now that you realized that."

He pulled her close and kissed her gently on her lips so that she barely felt his touch. When he leaned away, he was half-smiling. "I know that quite well, and that is what concerns me most."

A Note

Late March 1790

I don't usually venture into Holborn, but after my recent encounter with a most disagreeable woman on Grafton Street, I thought a change of venue might be necessary. You would think she'd be grateful for my elevating her into celebrity with my attention. After all, she was plain, middle-aged, and unexceptional in dress. But she stirred up such a fuss that night, a horde of servants from the house she was visiting came rushing out, drawing all sorts of unwanted attention. Luckily, I was able to escape their clutches by slipping into a nearby alley. Frankly, I thought she would accept my offers of affection readily, considering she looked like she hadn't had her skirts lifted in a decade.

In the end, I barely stabbed her in the hip. Perhaps more damage could have been done if she hadn't spun out of my grasp and, in truth, she would've deserved it. After I'd offered my services to her, the ugly prim looked down her nose at me and had the gall to call me a reprobate. I may have called her a name or two as well, using some rather foul imprecations, but what's past is past. Why dwell on the matter?

Today is quite lovely. The sky is a magnificent shade of blue, much like the azure of a bluebird's wing. Although it is officially spring, the flowers have yet to emerge, especially here in Holborn where the colour of choice appears to be brown. Grass is sparse, trees are sparse, and cheer—as it seems—is sparse. I clutch my nosegay with its bright crimson roses at my side as I stroll along the streets in search of a lover, aware that they provide the only bit of colour in this dank town. Unlike my other forays, I walk about in pure daylight. One must be careful here, as thieves are known to favour this area, and I would not dare chance being accosted in the cloak of darkness.

I meander down a narrow street to soon find the majority of the women are haggard-looking, their smiles closed to hide missing teeth. I avoid them as much as I can, but they are everywhere, much like their filthy children. Twice I have had to escape their grubby paws as they reach for my coat, begging for pennies and bringing their stench far too close to my sensitive nose. With this, I realize I should change direction and head to Saffron Hill instead.

Instantly, the air seems to clear, and colour returns. Two dandies in silk walk past me and doff their hats.

"Good day," I offer.

This gives me hope. If they are on this street, perhaps their female counterparts are as well.

After a few paces, I turn and follow them until they disappear into a shabby storefront that boasts itself as a coffeehouse. I watch as other gentlemen enter and exit, many of them dressed as finely as I. Then a woman saunters out and glances in my direction. A woman in a coffeehouse? I find it peculiar but, having no knowledge of the common behaviours of the people of Holborn, I assume it is permitted. Although I cannot see the woman's face clearly, she appears young and slight with a tiny waist and a flirtatious manner. I move closer, lifting my nosegay to my face. She sees me and waves me over with the flutter of her delicate fingers.

My heart lifts with the prospect that she is perfect and ripe for the plucking. I can feel the pulse in my throat begin to race and my cock stir in my breeches. But as I grow closer, I see the dark stubble on her cheek poorly hidden underneath crumbly white powder. A molly.

I turn back around, angry that I have been duped. I smack the nosegay against my thigh as I storm away, my heart racing from the indignity I almost suffered. I decide to head back home and am practically out of Holborn when I see a lovely girl, her blond curls pinned up exposing her creamy white neck. She crosses my path close enough for me to see the swell of her breasts joggle as she walks. She smells like sunshine and soap. I inhale deeply, awakening my senses.

Women are like flowers. Each one carries a distinct scent.

I swallow back my excitement and turn to follow her, resetting the bent petals from my nosegay, careful not to prick my fingers on the blade I've positioned in the middle.

"Beg pardon, miss," I say to gain her attention.

She turns and smiles politely. I realize from her plain clothing that she might be a maidservant, albeit a beautiful one. "Sir?"

"I am not familiar with this area. Would you be so kind as to direct me to Cow Cross?" I only mention this as my intended destination after noticing its name on a sign on the side of a building earlier.

She tilts her head with judgment, her gaze falling over my clothes. *"That's in Jack Ketch's Warren. You don't want to go there."*

I've heard of Jack Ketch's Warren. It is a den of thieves and blackguards. Silently, I chide myself for the misstep. *"Perhaps I have the name wrong. Where are you headed? I could escort you there."*

"There's no need, sir. I'm on Chancery Lane, right over there." She absently waves her hand to the right.

Panic starts to build in my chest. *"Certainly you would like me to join you."*

She looks at me strangely, as if I had said something untoward. She moves to leave, so I hold out the nosegay in presentation. *"Are they not pretty for this time of year? Would you care to smell them?"*

She hesitates, then bends, offering me a rich glimpse down the front of her gown. I whisper, *"Open your legs to me the way petals on a flower bud unfurl to the sun."*

She jolts upright and stares, her mouth hanging open. The colour rushes from her cheeks. I know this moment all too well. She will either slap me or run.

I grab her hand and press it to my cock, but she wrestles it away. In anger, I seize her arm and shove the nosegay in her face, slicing her as she jerks back. A spray of blood escapes from her nose and onto my sleeve. I move to swipe at it and she runs away.

On my way home, I simmer in the carriage, desperate to wipe the damned stain from my sleeve. I will undoubtedly have to explain its presence to the laundress. What shall it be this time? An unfortunate brush with a holly or rose bush? A mishap while polishing my dagger? An encounter with an unusually feral cat?

Before the carriage manages to leave Holborn, I toss the miserable nosegay in an alley already filled with refuse. Hopefully, no one will discover it. I wouldn't want it to be traced back to the vendor who sold it to me, after all.

I grasp the ledge of the window as the coach makes an unsteady turn, one wheel catching a rut that sends me tottering. We are close enough to my home, so I signal the coachman to allow me to disembark. As I alight from the carriage, a public notice blows in the wind and attaches to my leg. I reach to flick it away but am stopped by the sketch in the center. I stare at a crude drawing of Joseph Hayes, a dirty footprint obscuring all but the words

Candidate for the House of Commons. *I rip it into tiny shreds and watch the bits of paper scatter in the wind.*

Chapter 27

Cuthbert thrummed his fingers on the table, waiting for Dalton to arrive. White's was particularly busy that afternoon, full of talk about the fight between The Pretty Punch and Gentleman Jackson that was scheduled to transpire later that evening. Money was already exchanging hands, and bets were entered in the ledger kept at the front. Cuthbert had no desire to engage in any of the gaming, considering he wasn't even sure how he would pay for the meal he'd just finished eating.

Dalton arrived, face flushed and brushing back the blond wisps that covered his forehead. "Forgive my tardiness. Vivian delayed my departure with her need to complain about my lack of interest in her new lace handkerchief. The woman is absolutely *intolérable!*"

Cuthbert had nothing to say to that. His wife wanted his attention. It only made him think of the look on Sophie's face when she told him to leave her home that day after he'd kissed her. She wanted nothing to do with him. "Are you ready?"

Dalton wiggled his brow twice enthusiastically. "To win a fortune? When is a man not ready to do that?"

Cuthbert pushed away from the table and donned his hat. They wove around a few clusters of gentlemen to the door when Martindale stopped them.

"Mr. Needham, if you will." He handed Cuthbert a paper with a running tally of monies owed on his account. Cuthbert's stomach twisted at the total. Martindale stepped aside while he studied it.

Dalton leaned over his shoulder and harrumphed. "It looks like that Topham has done a number on you, my boy. He owes you for those bottles of Cognac."

They did contribute quite a bit to his outstanding balance. "He has been absent of late. I have not seen him here in weeks."

"Well, you know where he works. Send him a friendly letter. Perhaps he'll offer you payment." Dalton spoke in a mocking tone, one that Cuthbert didn't appreciate.

He would never shame himself by asking for money. He'd rather take the scolding from his father for his exorbitant spending. He turned to Martindale and squared his shoulders with as much dignity as he could gather. "I will take this to my steward, and you will receive your payment presently."

Martindale shot him a look full of reservation. "Very well. Until then."

Cuthbert shoved the paper inside his coat and exited, Dalton following behind.

Cuthbert had thought Woodford Green was far enough from the city that he would know no one—outside of Dalton—at the fight. But as the carriages rolled in from the lower road to the quaint little town, he felt that all of London had followed him there.

"I do not understand how you have no desire to place a bet," Dalton said incredulously.

Cuthbert alighted from the carriage and peered out at the clearing. Two men were hammering stakes into the ground, the distance between them measured out in long paces. After all four stakes were set, they tied ropes to them, forming a ring. "One must have money to place a bet. You are well aware of my circumstances."

"What if I were to tell you that the Gentleman will win."

"How do you know that?"

Dalton hugged him around the shoulder as they walked closer to the clearing. "Do you think I would have wagered a thousand pounds if I were not certain?"

Cuthbert almost choked at the thought of that much money being squandered so easily. "But I read the other fellow is far more seasoned. Larger too."

"He is," Dalton offered with no further explanation.

Cuthbert stopped, suddenly wary. "Are you insinuating that the fight is fixed?"

"Let me just say that I have heard some things."

"From whom?"

"Does it matter?" With a gentle nudge, he urged Cuthbert to keep walking. "You should reconsider placing a bet on the Gentleman. It could be the very thing to get you out of debt."

The way the odds were set, he would have to wager at least fifty pounds on Jackson to square his account at White's. If he were to bet more, he could possibly pay off the household debts as well. "And you are certain Jackson will win."

Dalton held up his hands noncommittally. "Do as you wish. I am only telling you what I have heard."

Cuthbert's palms began to sweat. Dalton knew an awful lot about these fights. He frequented them regularly and knew all the pugilists and the lingo associated with the sport. He knew their weights and their arm's reach. He even knew what they ate on the morning before a fight—one slice of bread, no butter, a pint of mulled red wine with a tablespoon of brandy—and that some of them slipped a coin in their left shoe for good luck.

Their conversations were often dizzying, with names and records being thrown about as if it were a science. Some bouts lasted nineteen rounds, thirty rounds, six rounds, and some were over in an instant. Dalton had won quite a bit over the years, so he said, wagering on men named Big Ben, The Brewer, The Cricketer, and The Tinman. He remembered a chat they'd had three years earlier when Dalton had recalled a fight between Mendoza the Jew and a man called The Bath Butcher. He'd described it almost as if it were a beautiful ballet between two brutes who moved like swans on a tossing pond. Cuthbert had always assumed Dalton's fascination had more to do with the gaming than the sport, but as he'd told that story, he considered he might be wrong.

"Fine. Take me to the promoter. I shall wager two hundred pounds on Gentleman Jackson."

The crowd cheered as the fighters arrived. Although they appeared close in age, one was larger than the other. They stripped off their coats and shirts so they were bare to the waist. The smaller one hopped about, stretching his neck left and right, his wiry frame toned and sinewy. The larger one stood beside another huge fellow who whispered in his ear, listening with his forehead bent and jaw set. As Cuthbert studied his wide, muscular back and arms, he began to regret the wager he'd set against him. This man was not going to go down easily, if at all.

"I should withdraw my bet," he muttered, his stomach roiling with nerves.

"'Tis too late for that." Dalton patted him twice on the shoulder. "Trust me, *mon ami.*"

Cuthbert held his breath when the fight began. Each man jabbed at the other, the large one—The Pretty Punch—landing more of his punches than The Gentleman. "This is not going well," Cuthbert insisted.

"'Tis only just begun." Dalton grunted as The Gentleman took a blow to the chin. It was delightfully breezy, yet his forehead dripped with sweat. "An uppercut. But this upstart will give him a good turn. Pull! Pull!"

Cuthbert had no idea what Dalton was saying, but it sounded as if the young contender wasn't doing as he should. The large fellow threw a punch, hitting his opponent square in the eye, and an awful spray of blood emerged instantly. Cuthbert had to look away. "Oh, dear. This is not good."

Dalton elbowed him hard. "Would you stop that? He is going to win!"

But less than twenty minutes later, Gentleman Jackson lay flat on the ground, his face bloodied and his mouth moving but saying nothing. The fight was over, and Cuthbert had lost a fortune.

Dalton's face grew bright red, the hair at his temples drenched with sweat. "That cockerel!"

"What am I to do, Dalton? My father will kill me." How could he have placed himself in this position? His father would disown him. What could he possibly say?

Dalton ignored him. "I bet a fortune on that idiot!"

Cuthbert followed him as he pushed his way through the crowd and over to where The Pretty Punch sat in the shade of a large birch tree.

"What are you going to do?" Cuthbert hoped Dalton had no plan to attack the man, for neither he nor Dalton were near his size. "We should go."

Dalton halted, his eyes bulging with rage. His chest heaved as he spoke. "Go? Do you not understand what just happened, you fool? He was supposed to drop. To drop!"

"Perhaps you heard wrong. Perhaps—"

Dalton grabbed him by his coat and shook him angrily. "It was arranged. It was understood!"

Cuthbert had never seen Dalton so upset, never seen him lose control. His lips were drawn in a tight straight line, and two veins bulged at his right temple as he paced back and forth, talking to himself nonsensically, his blond hair escaping his ribbon each time he rubbed his forehead. By the time he started to calm down, he looked like a madman.

Cuthbert was about to suggest they call for their carriage when he thought he heard Sophie's voice. He stilled, holding his breath to concentrate on its location. It sounded as if it stemmed from the area near the large birch, but there was only one woman over there, and even with her back turned, he knew she was not Sophie. Dalton started to say something, but Cuthbert grabbed his arm to quiet him.

"I hear Sophie."

Dalton's brow raised, and Cuthbert thought he saw his mouth curl up for a second. "Sophie?"

He nodded, hearing the soft inflection in her voice as she expressed her concern for something. "I am almost certain 'tis her."

Dalton peered over the grounds, brushing back his wild hair.

"But why would she be here?" Cuthbert wondered, mostly to himself.

He glanced back at the tree and stared at the small group of people surrounding the fighter. Three large men, the woman, and a young lad, their backs to Cuthbert, stood talking to him. Cuthbert watched them for a few moments, puzzled that no one there fit her description. After a couple of minutes, two of the men patted the fighter on his shoulder and left, laughing and wiping their brows.

The fighter stood and spoke to the woman and the lad, his voice tired but strong. It was not what he had expected either. He spoke like a gentleman, his speech refined and clear. From what he could see, his cheek was swollen and deep red, and there was a bloody cut in the corner of his mouth. He looked tired, but he stood straight and spoke evenly, calmly. The large man behind him handed him his shirt, and he pulled it over his shoulders with some effort.

The fighter reached for the lad's hand and held it. He heard Sophie's voice once more. She spoke softly so he couldn't understand what was said, but he knew that tone well. And that was when he realized that everything Dalton had told him before was true. She was wearing the clothes of a man, but she wasn't there to write a story. He saw it in the way she lowered her head as the pugilist spoke, and the way he stroked the back of her hand with his thumb. She was there for him. The fighter.

He turned and headed for the carriage, too distraught to comprehend the questions Dalton was firing at him from behind.

Chapter 28

"You're certain you are taking it daily?" the surgeon asked.

Maeve was exhausted. It had taken all her energy to get to Covent Garden. She didn't have any left to argue. "Every day. Have you anything stronger?"

The surgeon studied her for a moment, his mouth twisted to the side. "Mercury. But it requires one's ability to partake in a salivation."

Maeve didn't care anymore what it took. She just wanted to feel better. "I'll do it."

"It will cost you."

She nodded tiredly. "I will get the money."

"You will need to be somewhere indoors where you may sweat out the venereal venom in privacy. It can be rather unsightly." He pulled a small vial from a cabinet along the wall. "Two drops in your beverage of choice each day should be plenty."

She reached for the small vial, but he pulled it away.

"First, you must deposit some urine in this bowl for me."

"Why?"

"To ensure there is no pregnancy." He handed her a white porcelain bowl the size of a large melon, then turned his back.

Maeve squatted over the bowl, happy to release her bladder after such a long walk from Parker's. She handed it to the surgeon and waited while he smelled it, then poured what looked like a small amount of claret into it.

"When was the last time you had your courses, Miss?"

A chill ran up her spine. It wasn't something she normally thought about, considering she took great care in making sure to use a pessary after each cull. She imagined the reason she hadn't had her courses in months had to do with her illness, not a child in her womb. "December, perhaps. I'm not certain."

The surgeon exhaled loudly, his hands on his hips. He stared at the bowl, then peered over his spectacles at her. "You are with child."

Her hand instinctively fell to her stomach. Could he be right? Tears welled in her eyes, and she blinked them away. "Are you certain?"

He nodded sadly. "I can give you the mercury, but it will kill the child."

She didn't know what to do. She couldn't have another baby. Mother would throw her out, and then she'd have no way to support Emily. And how would she support this baby? She had no idea who the father could be. Since Albert, she was certain she'd used the pessary every time she'd lain with a man. It seemed impossible. But if the doctor was right, how could she go through with the salivation? She couldn't take the life of her own child.

She rushed out of the room and out the door, unsure of where to go or who to turn to. But as a whore, she knew she had only one home, one place where she lay her head at night. She wouldn't be welcome there once Mother Wharton knew of her predicament, but perhaps she'd show her some mercy and let her stay until the child was born. She could continue cleaning for the next four or five months until the birth. She would do it for a bed to sleep in and a meal each day.

Too tired to walk, she used the coin she was going to spend on a new tonic for a hackney back to Parker's. As she neared the building, she thought about all the babies buried underneath the back steps. Some had been born dead, but others had not. Their newborn cries like purring kittens had been stifled by a pillow pressed firmly to their faces. Afterward, they'd been shrouded in old cloths and thrown into a large pit covered with a foot of earth each time. There had been no burial ceremony, no prayers said. Their bodies were simply disregarded and forgotten as whores came and went over the years. But Maeve promised herself her child would not suffer the same fate.

She inhaled deeply, imagining the tiny fingers and toes of the child inside of her and the soft down that covered his head. In time, she would kiss those gently closed eyes and puckered lips after he fell asleep at her breast. This child would have an older sister to love and who would love him back.

"You comin' in?" Connor startled her out of her thoughts.

She smiled at him weakly and passed through the door. It was crowded for a Monday. The parlour was filled with culls lounging with whores on their laps and drinks in their hands. Across the room, she spotted Prudy performing her coin slot trick on the table in the back.

She stood at the bar and turned to Paddy. "Have you seen Mother Wharton?"

"In there." He nudged his chin in the direction of her private parlour, then winked. "Countin' her money."

She crossed the room and knocked on the closed door. "Mother Wharton, may I speak with you?"

Maeve waited as the sound of her jingling keys grew louder. Mother opened the door just enough for Maeve to see only half her face. "What is it?" she asked, clearly irritated at the intrusion.

Maeve cleared her throat. "I thought you might give me a moment of your time. You see, I have found myself—"

Shouts rang out behind her. "You bloody dastard! You don't have the bollocks to do it!"

Maeve turned to see where the shouts were coming from. Two men—one of which she recognized as Prudy's cull who liked being whipped with a leather strap and the other a stranger who had the wily look of a fox on the hunt—pointed daggers at one another. A circle started to form around them.

"You call me a coward, sir?" The fox inched closer.

Mother shoved Maeve out of the way and ran across the room to the front door, undoubtedly to fetch Connor, who was still outside. But it was all too late. The fox struck at Prudy's cull and sliced his arm just above his elbow. He stared in disbelief as a crimson bloom appeared on his fine green silk coat. Everyone started shouting and racing about the room frantically, snatching up discarded clothing and trying to hide behind furniture.

Prudy's cull lunged and jabbed at the fox unsuccessfully but forced him back, closer to where Maeve stood. They parried each other's jabs, inching their way across the room. Before she found herself in between them, she slipped inside Mother's parlour and shut the door behind her.

The screams and sounds of furniture being thrown about traveled through the door. Something banged against the wall with a hard thud, so she circled around Mother's desk for better protection should the door fling open.

"Someone call the constables!" a man shouted.

"Get help!"

Maeve crouched behind Mother's chair, waiting for the fight to end. Where was Connor?

After what seemed like a lifetime, the shouting stopped and only Mother Wharton's voice could be clearly heard. Maeve couldn't understand what she was saying, but she knew she had to be speaking with an authority, as she used the austere, businesslike tone she reserved for magistrates and priests.

Maeve waited by the desk. It was only the second time she had ever been in Mother's parlour. The first time was when she came to Parker's as a young girl and Mother had told her how lovely she was and how she would surely find a keeper in no time. That was eight years ago, and although she thought she'd found a keeper in Albert, she and Mother had been proven wrong.

The room was tidy yet covered in a thin layer of dust. Maeve imagined Mother must do her own cleaning since she allowed no one to enter her parlour at all. The desk was covered with a leather blotter from end to end. On top were two neat stacks of ledgers and a magnifying glass next to a crystal inkwell sitting on a brass stand. Three quills, all sharpened, stood inside a squat green glass with the initials G. W. etched into its side. Maeve wondered what the G stood for. Georgiana? Grace? Mother didn't *look* like she would have either of those names.

Maeve glanced at the door once before opening the top drawer to see if that was where she kept her coins. She leaned over and squinted at the writing on a piece of paper on top. She thought she recognized the slant of the letters, the evenness of the loops and curls of each word, but she wasn't sure. She removed it to bring it closer to her failing eyes, then, frustrated, grabbed the magnifying glass. It looked like it was from Mrs. Hobart, the woman caring for Emily. She started to read it, her shoulders sinking as she realized it was another request for more money to help with Emily's catalepsy treatments. She turned the letter over and found it peculiar it was not signed. She continued to read, but the final sentence remained unfinished. Maeve looked inside the drawer for another page, but it contained only a wax block, a vial of sand, and some candles.

It was an unfinished letter. Maeve shut her eyes and drew a deep breath. Had Mother Wharton written it? Was this her hand she had been reading all these years? Was there ever a Mrs. Hobart? Where was Emily, if not with her?

When she opened her eyes, the letter was crumpled in her fist, the final words smeared as if they had just been written.

Maeve tossed the letter on the floor and slipped out of the parlour and up the stairs to her own room. She grabbed her two gowns—the red velvet one and the blue one into which her sterling was sewn—and the small leather trunk that held everything she owned, including the tiny pink and cream bit of cloth that served as the only proof that Emily existed. She wasn't going to spend another minute at Parker's. There was only one other place for her to go.

"Do you have the required documentation, madam?" the clerk asked. "A statement from the parish authorities?"

Maeve sat in the very chair she had the last time she was at Lock Hospital, staring at the same clerk. Her voice quivered as she spoke. "I do not, sir. I have come here to beg you for admittance."

"We must follow procedures here—"

"Surely you can make an exception," she insisted.

He started to speak, but she cut him short. "I did as you suggested the last time I was here. I saw the surgeon in Covent Garden, but his tonics did little for me. I need your help."

Just then, a clergyman entered the room, a silver crucifix dangling from a long chain around his neck.

"Father," the clerk said in recognition of his presence.

Maeve stood immediately. "Please, Father, I have no papers . . . I know I should, but . . . I left in a hurry . . . I couldn't stay there any longer . . ."

He held up his hands to stop her. "What are you saying, child?"

She told him her whole story. About her parents' deaths, her aunt taking her in and then sending her to the milliner and how he'd continually raped her, being sent to work at the brothel, Albert leaving her when he discovered she was pregnant with Emily, Mother Wharton's demands of money for Emily's fits—and about the child that lived within her. Everything. After she was done, she felt as if she would collapse right there, too tired to say another word and too disgusted by the words she'd already said.

The clerk gazed at her, his mouth agape. The clergyman rested his hand on her shoulder. "You have a place here, my dear. As the chaplain, I can grant you admittance."

"But what of the Governor's letter of recommendation, Father?" the clerk asked, clearly nervous this was a breach of procedure.

"I can only imagine your hearing is as good as my own. You heard her story. Have you no heart?" He picked up the small leather trunk and her two gowns. "'Tis our Christian duty to help her."

That night as she lay in her narrow cot in a ward beside another two dozen patients, she thought about Prudy and the other girls. She was going to miss them and their wild dreams that someday, fine gentlemen would take them as their mistresses. It was her dream too. But, well, it was only dream. She wished she had bid them a farewell, along with Connor and Paddy, and wondered if she'd ever see any of them again. They had been the only family she'd had since she was sixteen.

A woman two cots over snorted in her sleep, then shifted roughly, the squeaking of her bedstead sharp in the night silence.

Maeve imagined Mother Wharton finding the crumpled letter on the floor by her desk. She would be furious, not because Maeve left, but because it meant she would no longer be able to rob her of her earnings. Maeve doubted the old bawd would tell anyone the truth of what had happened.

How long would the ruse have continued? And how was she going to find Emily?

She slipped her hand underneath her shift and ran it over her belly. It was hard, but not large enough for a child of four or five months. A tear escaped from the corner of her eye, knowing that he may never see the light of day. But she had to fight on. She had to get to Emily. They would be a family. Not as she originally imagined it would be, with Albert sitting beside them at the table as they all shared a meal. But she would have her beautiful daughter in her arms, and she would raise her in a real home. Somewhere. Somehow.

And she thought of Tommy. It had been three days since he'd won his fight against Gentleman Jackson. She smiled thinking about how powerful he looked that day. He was magnificent. Even Connor had said so. But she also remembered the way he looked at Sophie when they stood before him and the fight was over. Her throat started to burn as she realized he had never looked at her that way. He'd reached out at one point and, for just a second, she'd thought that he was reaching for her, but it was Sophie's hand he held in the end.

It all started to make perfect sense. Sophie ran out the day of the fight in December because she realized they were both in love with the same man. She had not been able to face her for those weeks she'd disappeared afterwards to spare her feelings. It was why she had fumbled over her words at the Twelfth Night Masque. She simply couldn't break Maeve's heart.

But nevertheless, her heart was broken.

Chapter 29

"Did you see this, Father?" Tom handed him the morning paper with a page folded back, then grabbed his hat. He had to finish checking in a shipment at the warehouse before dusk, when he was expected to meet the molls in St. James's Park.

Father read aloud. "Joseph Hayes favoured to win the seat in Parliament."

"It appears you have all but won."

Father leaned back in his chair. "I have a slight lead over my opponent. That is not a win, son."

Tom wondered if Sophie had yet written the article on the benefits of employing a tax on gaming. She told him at the fight she would see to it right away, but he knew she had to find the privacy in order to do it, and that would be difficult.

Tom looked in the mirror to straighten his cravat. His cheek was no longer swollen but remained a shade of greenish-yellow, a sure sign he would look normal in a day or two. The wound beside his lip was still pink, but the tenderness and swelling had subsided. His cut and bruised hands were another story.

"I should be going. We shall have all the goods accounted for by this evening." Tom smoothed down his hair. Out of the corner of his eye, he caught his father studying him.

"Did you see here that The Pretty Punch defeated Gentleman Jackson on Friday? It took only nine rounds, apparently." Father stared at him over the top of the paper.

"Did it?" Tom slipped on his gloves, unable to meet his gaze.

"It says here that no one knows who this fellow is, but they believe he is from London." Father lowered the paper and sighed.

Tom doffed his hat. "I should go."

"Thomas, wait." Father stood and set the paper aside. He took two steps closer, then laid a hand on his shoulder. Far off in the distance, a church bell began to clang. Father lowered his voice. "I know why you do it, son. But it will never bring back your mother. There is no need to put yourself in harm's way. There is nothing you could have done to save her. You were a child."

Tom's chest tightened. The image of his mother's twisted neck appeared before his eyes. If only he could go back in time, everything would be different. He swallowed hard. "How long have you known?"

Father huffed and swatted his hand distractedly. "For years now. After the third or fourth fight. It was far too coincidental that you arrived home with wounds the same day of a match."

He couldn't believe what he was hearing. "But I stayed away. I went to . . . a friend's."

"Not in the beginning. And did you not think your disappearance for days afterward was just as conspicuous?" A sad smile touched his lips.

"Forgive me, Father. I never meant to tarnish our name. 'Tis why I only agreed to matches outside of London proper. I didn't want anyone to recognize me." He felt horrible for not being honest from the beginning, but how could he have explained it? No one would've understood.

Father pressed his hand to Tom's cheek. "You are my son, and that is all that matters."

"And Henry and Roger?"

"Those two nick ninnies? They know nothing." He walked Tom to the door. "We shall keep this between us."

Thomas finished his work at the warehouse much quicker than he anticipated, so he headed over to Lloyd's Coffeehouse. He squeezed in between the men who crowded the door and found his way into the main part of the room, where seamen and soldiers were busy avoiding one another. He ordered a coffee and sat on a bench near the back, unable to grab a spot by the large front window. It was loud, as usual, and the smell of coffee and ale pleasantly overpowered the tobacco smoke that pervaded the air.

"The beast must be stopped! He takes some sort of savage delight in the terror and pain of his victims!" shouted an older man devoid of a periwig. He wore plain clothing, yet there was an air about him that bespoke his importance. "No woman is safe from this villain. Our wives, our daughters, our sisters are all prey to this man . . ."

Tom elbowed the sailor next to him. "Who is that?"

The sailor wiped a thin line of foam from his upper lip. "Angerstein. The insurance broker. A bit long-winded, if you ask me."

Tom listened to the older man speak. A fine sheen of sweat broke out on his broad forehead as he wagged his finger in the air. "There have been no fewer than thirty attacks. I have spoken to many of these women myself, some of whom have suffered wounds . . ."

Tom had heard of at least two dozen victims, but he imagined several attacks had gone unreported, much like the attack in Eastcheap.

"I propose a subscription to raise a reward for the capture of the monster, whoever he may be." A general rumble of assent carried through the room. Angerstein reached into his coat, pulled out a small leather pouch, then extracted five gold coins. "I will donate five guineas to start. Who is with me?"

Over a dozen men sidled their way past a group of soldiers to get to Angerstein, each dropping coins on the table behind him. A young lad furiously scribbled their names and pledges on a ledger as they approached.

"There must be fifty pounds there," the sailor said appreciatively, scratching his head. "Fifty pounds. Imagine that!"

It couldn't have been better timing. He was to meet the molls and bullyboys in less than an hour. The reward would more than pay for their services, and he would be able to give his winnings from the fight to Maeve for Emily with a bit left over to help Henry's plight with Judith's betrothal.

He left the coffeehouse as the sun sank to the horizon, leaving the sky striking shades of pink and orange. A cool breeze ran through the trees and over the fresh spring grass in the park. The cows that grazed there were nowhere to be seen, but their muted bellows told Tom they remained somewhere nearby. He waited on the bench where he and the molls had agreed and ran his hand over the dagger he kept under his coat. He hoped he wouldn't have to use it but, if the monster drew his blade, he would not hesitate to do the same.

Just as the sun dipped into oblivion, a parade of molls approached, giggling and prancing their way to the bench. "There he is!"

Tom stood to greet them. "Where is your flashman?"

The brute from Mother Cluck's stepped out of the group, pounding one meaty fist into the other. "Just you and me?" he asked.

Tom glanced around the park in search of Connor. "I am waiting for some more to come."

Two lamplighters walked the path, taking turns raising their long wicks to the streetlamps and giving Tom a clearer view of the molls. They all wore powder and rouged lips and cheeks, but there was no doubt they were men. Tom pulled the flashman aside. "Where are the molls I asked for?" He took one more look at the bits of chest hair peeking out from the tops of their gowns and blanketing their forearms, suddenly concerned his plot to catch the monster had no chance of success.

"The bawd kept the rum molls at the house for the culls." He jabbed his thumb behind him. "These are the geese we got."

They were a sorry lot, but there was nothing he could do at this point.

"Tom!" Connor appeared from the shadows, a half dozen brutes trailing behind him. Tom recognized some of them as the seconds from a few of his past fights. Connor had told him that they had no interest in being paid for their efforts. They only wanted a chance to pummel the monster.

Tom gathered everyone in a circle and told them his plan. The molls would stroll alone or in pairs along the paths while the bullyboys hid nearby ready to strike. "Do not walk too leisurely or he might think you a . . . prostitute."

Several molls tittered. Tom shook his head and exhaled. He pointed to the hairy chests of the two molls standing closest to him. "You might want to drape a shawl around your shoulders, there. We are trying to attract him, not scare him off."

One flipped her hand in his direction, seemingly insulted by his remark, then huffed off to the back of the group.

"Are we ready?" he asked.

One of the larger molls grabbed his arm, then ran her fingers over his shoulder. "You shall come with me." Her voice was deeper than Tom's.

Tom brushed her hand away, hairy knuckles and all. "I imagine you could take care of yourself."

They all scattered in different directions, the bullyboys spacing themselves apart so that the distance between them would leave them in close enough proximity to the molls, should the need arise for action. Tom moved beside a large bush just outside of the light of a streetlamp. He was about to dodge behind it when he heard his name.

"Tom? Is that you?" It was Sophie. He hurried over to her. She stood near the bench, dressed in men's clothing.

"What are you doing here?" he asked in a whisper.

"The same thing you are. Trying to catch the London Monster."

"No. You must go. 'Tis far too dangerous." He led her by her elbow to the lit part of the path.

She shrugged out of his grip. "I have managed to escape the most dangerous part of the night already. You have no idea how difficult it was to evade the attention of my household in order to get here."

"You wasted your time, then. You cannot stay." He searched the coach stand for a hackney and spotted one near the stableyard. He urged her towards it, waving his hand to get the jarvey's attention.

"Stop that!' she demanded as she struggled to bring down his arm. "I am not going anywhere."

"You are."

"I am not," she said resolutely, her words punctuated by the jamming of her hands on her hips. "This is as much my story as it is yours. You said so yourself."

"What?"

"We devised this plan together, and I want to see it through."

He drew her close, torn between being utterly frustrated and incredibly happy that she was with him. "You made no mention of this when we spoke at the fight."

"Why would I? So that you could demand I stay away?" she replied in a huff.

She was right. He would have told her not to come.

"Besides," she added, "this will give me firsthand knowledge of the events that transpire. Imagine the draw of an article written by someone who was there when the monster was taken down. So put away your fears about my safety and let me do my job."

He began to speak, but she placed her finger over his lips. "And before you ask, the answer is yes. I have been traveling with at least one companion everywhere I go, as promised. Tonight being the only exception. Stone would be a fool to attempt harming me."

Although that settled his nerves slightly—knowing Stone preferred to attack women behind closed doors—it did not mean his hackums were not as careful. "I am not certain that is enough for me."

She swatted away his concern with the flip of her hand. He moved to speak again, and that same finger touched his lips once more. "That answer to *that* question is also yes. I sent the article on pugilism to two papers under the name James Evans. All we have to do is wait for a response."

He smiled. "I was not going to ask you that at all."

"Then what were you going to say?"

220

"That you look beautiful, James Evans." He leaned down to kiss her, her lips warm and soft. "Now get behind that bush and do not dare make a sound."

Time passed slowly, the night sky fiercely black with no moon above. Tom leaned against the tree behind the bushes next to Sophie. He had seen the same molls pass by three times since they'd started to carry out the plan, which was over two hours ago.

"I am beginning to think this was a mistake," he whispered. He wasn't sure if the problem lay with the molls, the location, the time, or what, but whatever the reason, it wasn't working. Perhaps the monster was in another area of London. Or perhaps he chose to stay home tonight. The answer could be as simple as that. "Do you think we should leave? Tell the others—"

"Get off me, you rotten fool! Help!"

Tom jumped up and searched the darkness. Sophie stood too, but he urged her back down. "Stay here."

"But—"

"Stay!" he ordered.

"Help me!" came the breathless plea, the voice bouncing with each quick stride to get away.

Tom ran towards the voice. He heard a few grunts and the grumbles of a man angry about being rebuffed. At the edge of the light from the streetlamp, he spotted one of the molls in a scuffle, her arms flailing wildly. Tom jumped over a small hedge and ran to her, his heart pounding heavily in his chest. Why had no one come to her aid? Where were the flashmen?

As he approached, Tom saw only the back of the man. He was dressed in a black coat and breeches and wore his hair loose in curls down his back. Without seeing his face, he couldn't tell if it was the same man with whom he tousled by St. Anne's Church and Eastcheap.

He grabbed him by the shoulders and spun him around just as the moll swung, hitting Tom square in the nose. A sharp crack sounded, sending a searing pain through the centre of his face. He swiped at the blood running down to his mouth, careful not to let go of the man's coat.

"Get away! Get away!" the moll shouted, striking blindly at both of them. Tom tried to block her hands while the monster squirmed out of his grasp.

He managed to lunge at him—with the moll hanging onto his back, pouncing in a frenzy—and knock him down. Tom shifted to shake her off, and the man rolled from under him. As he stood, Tom snatched at his hair. The assailant stumbled a bit, then ran off, leaving Tom clutching a long, curly peruke in his fist.

"What were you doing?" he yelled at the moll, who was sitting in the grass, legs splayed open, her wig tangled beside her, and her rouged lips smeared across her chin.

"It was dark! I couldn't see which of you was the monster!" She started to whimper, and as Tom berated her for foiling the capture, her cries turned into wails.

He brushed off his knees and helped her up. She shoved her wig underneath one arm and smoothed down her skirts. "He told me I should live off the milk of his cock."

The other molls started to gather around her one by one, and she repeated what the monster had said. They stroked her as she spoke, offering words of comfort. "You poor dear."

Tom tipped his head back and pinched his nose. His face throbbed with each heartbeat. Connor jogged up, followed by two other bullyboys. Tom turned to him. "Where were you?"

"The other side of the park. I came as quick as I could." Connor slapped a strong hand on Tom's back, then turned to the moll in tears. She repeated what the monster had said, dabbing at her eyes with a lace handkerchief. "Quit your blubberin'. You hear that every day and think nothin' of it."

If Tom wasn't in so much pain, he'd laugh. He turned to the other two bullyboys whose mouths hung open at the tufts of hair peeking out of the molls' gowns. "And where were you?"

The shorter one tugged on his breeches to nudge them over his gut. "Pissin', I was."

Tom shut his eyes against the pain. He had to be doing more than that to miss a few minutes of scrabbling with the monster.

The taller one ran his hand back and forth over his baldhead. "Fell asleep."

"What?" Tom asked, shocked by his admission.

He shrugged. "Don't know how it happened. Sat down under a tree, and the next thing I knew, this huff was kickin' me to get up." He jerked his thumb at Connor.

Tom left them all standing there—the molls pandering to their complaining sister, and the flashmen taking a scolding from Connor—to find Sophie and escort her home.

"Are you disappointed?" Tom clutched Sophie's hand as the carriage bounced along the cobbles. She'd remained silent since they'd started the drive to her home.

"Of course." She appeared as if she wanted to say more, but she only sighed instead. The moonlight poured through the carriage window, washing them in a blue haze. In the distance, the church bells began to ring.

"I was truly hoping we would catch him," she said, her voice scarcely more than a whisper.

"It was a good plan." He brought her hand to his lips.

She offered a barely perceptible nod, then stared out the window.

"What is it, Sophie? I always feel as if you're not telling me everything, that you're hiding something from me."

She smiled sadly. "I'm hiding so much from everyone."

He wasn't sure what to say. He had far too many secrets as well.

She stared ahead, her profile limned in blue light, her gaze clearly inward. "When I was fifteen, I attended a garden party with my parents. I was excited about wearing my new gown with delicate lace at the shoulders and sleeves. I thought it was beautiful." She slid her hand away from Tom and rested it in her lap. "It was springtime, and the air was perfumed with heady blooms. I'd spent the afternoon flirting and laughing with a young gentleman from Winchester. I truly enjoyed his company." She inhaled deeply and, although they were no longer touching, he could feel her trembling in the seat next to him. "Eventually, we parted, and I spent the remainder of the hour with other guests. Then, as more people arrived, the rooms grew warmer, and I decided to stroll through the garden to take some air. I hadn't considered he would follow me."

Tom's shoulders tightened. He shifted to face her, uncomfortable with where this story was headed.

"The young man had apparently seen me leave and, when I reached the far end of the property, he confronted me. He said I lured him there. That I had invited him with my smile and laughter. He even told me I was dressed like a harlot."

A lump formed in Tom's throat, and his fists clutched responsively.

"He grabbed my arm and shoved me toward the bushes beyond anyone's view. I thought of screaming, but he said no one would hear me—or believe me, for that matter. After all, everyone had seen us speaking with one another. Laughing." She turned to face him, breaking her trance. "I didn't know what to do. And then he pulled back his coat to show me the dagger at his hip. He never drew it, but he made sure I knew it was there."

He took a deep breath to try to temper the heat rising in his chest and into his shoulders.

She sighed. "I don't know how I did it, but I broke away from him and hurried back to the garden path where others were strolling."

He reached for her hand, and she turned to face him. He did his best to sound calm, but he was boiling inside. "Nothing you wore or nothing you said gave him the right to treat you so poorly. That deplorable behaviour belongs to him, not you. Surely you know that."

"Does it, though? I often wonder, if I had only—"

"Sophie, stop. Please." Could she feel the anger vibrating through his body? "A man who asserts his will over a woman is not a man. He is a coward."

She gripped his hand firmly. "I know you think the only reason I want to catch the monster is because I want a story I can publish. But that is not it at all. I want him to pay for what he's done to all the women he's frightened or hurt. I want him to understand that he has no right to make a woman feel she cannot behave kindly or politely without risk of being assaulted. I want him to know. I want all of them to know."

A tear slid down her cheek, leaving behind a silver streak lit by the moonlight. He pulled her close, so her head rested on his shoulder. The carriage rocked steadily, the horses' hooves clomping gently on the cobbles. He kissed her forehead, his thoughts twisting and turning and landing nowhere, yet everywhere. His mother, these women, Maeve, and now Sophie, all victims of a man's brutality.

His lips brushed her skin as he whispered, "I promise you this. I will not stop until I find him. Not ever."

Chapter 30

"I suppose this is the last I shall see of you." Sophie set her hat on top of her trousers in her portmanteau. She smiled at the old milk stains, soil, and tiny bits of debris that yet clung to it. It had certainly seen better days.

She closed the lid and shoved the chest that held her disguise to the back of her wardrobe. It was the second time she'd said those words in a week, but she couldn't have gone to St. James's Park dressed as a woman to catch the monster. It would've been too risky. If only the plan would've worked. The villain would be caught, and she would be able to submit an article of a firsthand account of the capture. In any case, she was grateful Tom wasn't seriously injured in the tussle and no one drew his blade.

So, if her article on pugilism wasn't going to be published, there would be no need for her to go on fooling herself and traipsing around all of London as a man in search of a story that would never go to print.

Peg stood holding a hairbrush, disappointment sewn into her lips. "Are you giving it all up?"

Sophie glanced at the rejection letter for her story about legalizing gaming. She sighed. "I have one last hope. The *World* still has my article. We shall soon discover whether or not my career is over before it starts."

"I know nothing of pugilism, but from what you've told me, I think all of London would do better to pay attention to your article."

She patted Peg on the arm. If only everyone felt as she did. "What truly bothers me is every time I open a paper, there is another article about the

London Monster." She snatched the *Morning Chronicle* off her bed and held it up to Peg. "Look."

Peg took it from her and read. "Who is this Angerstein fellow?"

"Does it matter? Look at the writing. Dull as a butter knife, if you ask me." She knew her articles were better. Vivid. Emotional. Not simply a boring list of facts.

"It says here already fourteen men have been brought before the magistrate, yet not one victim could identify any one of them." Peg shook her head in disbelief.

"Of course not. Those men were likely dragged in there by some greedy informant looking to get his hands on the reward." It was understood that fifty pounds would be paid upon the arrest of the monster, and another fifty would be paid upon his conviction. "Imagine how those poor souls spent breakfast the next morning after their release, staring across the dining table at their wives and pleading their innocence."

Peg's hand flew to her mouth to hide her smile. "If they were allowed back in the house, that is."

Fourteen innocent men! Sophie clicked her tongue. "Angerstein has created a frenzy, I am afraid. Most people would turn in their own sons for one hundred pounds."

"The description should narrow it down, I would think," Peg offered, unconvinced.

Sophie took the paper from Peg and searched for the paragraph listing the monster's features. "*About thirty years of age, middle-sized, a little pock-marked, of a pale complexion, large nose, light brown hair worn tied back or loose in curls, sometimes dressed in all black or a shabby blue coat and straw-coloured breeches, a cocked hat or round hat* . . . Who do you think this is? Or who do you think it isn't?" She slapped the paper down on the bed. "None of it helps."

Peg waved the hairbrush at her. "Frankly, none of it matters. Mr. Needham shall be here shortly, and I need to finish your hair."

She had become so distracted by her rejection letter and the news about the monster that she had forgot about Bertie's visit. She hadn't seen him since he came to the house and behaved inappropriately. Twice she had Peg rebuff his servant when he sent a calling card, but her mother intercepted the last request and accepted it immediately.

She sat at her dressing table and shuddered as if spiders were crawling over her skin. "I am making a horrible mistake, Peg."

Peg stared blankly at her.

"I do not believe I can do it," she said with certainty.

Peg's brow lifted in recognition of what she meant. "Every new bride has reservations."

But Peg didn't understand at all. She didn't know that Sophie's heart belonged to someone else.

"Where are you going, Mother?" Sophie desperately tried to stifle the teacup from clattering on its saucer. She had been on tenterhooks since Bertie arrived.

Mother nodded at Bertie and smiled. "I need to discuss supper plans with Cook. It will only take a minute."

Sophie set her teacup in her lap and watched her mother disappear from the parlour. She had purposefully sat in a chair across from Bertie instead of on the sofa next to him in order to avoid another unpleasant encounter.

He hadn't taken his eyes off her since he arrived as if his gaze alone would bring her back to him. "You look lovely, Sophie."

She managed a weak smile in his general direction.

He spoke softly. "Do you like the flowers? I had the same gentleman make this bouquet."

"They are beautiful," she admitted. They were tulips, this time in bright yellows, reds, and pinks. "But we should have real blooms any day now."

His shoulders sank, deflated by her words. "I thought these might be nice to look at until then."

She nodded vaguely, finding it difficult to look directly at him. They sat in silence for a couple of minutes, her mother's voice barely audible from the parlour. The clock on the mantle ticked away loudly, much slower than her heartbeat.

He cleared his throat and edged forward in his seat. He opened his mouth to speak, then paused, his gaze dropping to the floor. "I know everything," he said plainly.

Startled, she turned to him. His cheeks were flushed, and his heel tapped nervously on the silk rug.

"I know about the boxer. And you."

Sophie's heart froze. Dalton must have told him about the night he saw her kiss him at the party. She could see the pain in Bertie's face, the anguish he must be feeling knowing she loved someone else. "I know not what to say."

He took a quick sip of tea with an unsteady hand. "I would never have believed it if I had not seen it for myself."

Had he seen them together on Twelfth Night too? She closed her eyes, truly sorry he had to witness that kiss. "I never meant to hurt you, Bertie."

"Do you love him?" he asked, a slight tremble in his lips.

She stared down into her teacup, Tom's smile as clear in her mind as if he were standing before her. "Why are you asking me this? Please do not make me say it."

He rubbed his forehead slowly. "I suppose it matters not."

She shook her head. "I had no idea you were watching us that night. That kiss was unexpected—"

"You kissed him?" He clutched his chest and sank back into the chair.

She scrambled for the words. "I thought you saw us . . . at the masque."

"What? The masque? How long have you been . . ."

"Bertie, I—"

He held up his hand stiffly. "Do not call me that! That was from another time. A time when you loved me."

Heat pricked her eyes, and her throat grew thick with shame. She squeezed her lids shut, trying to fight back the tears. "I cannot help how I feel."

"We are to be *married* in little more than two months! This must stop!" His face reddened with anger and disappointment. "Does he know we are betrothed?"

"He does," she whispered.

"I don't suppose that deterred him at all," he snapped.

"He did not know who I was in the beginning. What I mean is, he met me as someone else." She knew she wasn't making sense, but it was far too difficult to explain. "I hadn't told him when we first met. There was no need."

"No *need?* Or no *desire?*" he asked dryly.

She stood and went over to the window. She stared out but saw nothing outside of what was in her own head—Tom in the Old Bailey, Tom at his warehouse, Tom at St. James's Park, Tom at the party. "You are completely wrong about it, Ber . . . Cuthbert. I did not intend for this to happen. You make it sound as if I planned it."

He stood too and paced in front of the sofa, his hand rubbing his forehead, leaving it striped pink. He stopped to face her. "I have been feeling it for a long time now, Sophie. Your . . . your distaste for me."

She shook her head. "I—"

"I saw you turning away from me. I felt it. Postponing the wedding. It had nothing to do with my Aunt Belva, did it? Thrice you changed the date. Thrice!"

"I did not know then. Perhaps—"

"Perhaps, perhaps. Perhaps there is plenty I do not know about you." He snorted derisively, his gaze reproachful. "Have you lain with him?"

"Bertie! How dare you accuse me of such a thing!"

He shrugged exaggeratingly. "I don't know you anymore, Sophie. You take a lover when you are betrothed to another. You kiss him freely, but when I kiss you, *your future husband*, you push me away."

"You forced yourself on me!" She had had enough. "I know I have hurt you. I know I have not behaved as I should. I understand all of that. But none of it was intentional." She reached for his hand, but he pulled away from her. Her heart beat in her throat. "There are so many things I want for my life. And for yours. And love is one of them."

The ticking of the clock marked the silence. He shut his eyes, and the tense lines of his face softened. "We can have that. We only need time."

She sighed. "We have known each other for eleven, twelve years? What we have is friendship."

"What is wrong with that?"

"Nothing. But is friendship enough?" She was certain it was not enough for her.

His gaze dropped to the floor, resignation creeping into his slumped shoulders. "You will grow to love me."

It wasn't going to happen. No matter how hard he wished it, she would never have those feelings of desire or need for him. "Someone, someday, will love you as you should be loved. You are a wonderful man—"

"Spare me the humiliation of listening to you sing my praises while you crush my heart under your heel." He turned back to the sofa. She watched his shoulders lift and fall with each breath he took, his body otherwise still. "I can give you something," he said softly. "I know you are writing. Reporting."

She didn't need confirmation on how he knew that. Dalton's threat that he would divulge all her secrets had apparently come to fruition.

"You masquerade as a man?" he asked mockingly. "I suppose that is how you met the likes of the boxer."

"Do you think anyone would take a woman reporter seriously?" she answered, offended by his sarcastic tone.

"I know someone who might be able to help you get published. An editor. He owes me a favour. He is with the *World*."

The *World*! Her article was likely sitting on the desk of the editor right now. Her heart lifted. This could be her chance. A long time ago, she would have scoffed at the idea of using a less than wholesome method of getting her work in print, but now, after years of dozens of rejections, she just might welcome it. "What are you suggesting?"

Cuthbert faced her and smiled faintly. "I will get you published if you go through with the wedding."

Her heart sank. He was playing a game. Tit for tat. And the stakes were high.

"What do you say, Sophie?"

A Note

Mid April, 1790

Oh, the fools! The fools!

I cannot help but chuckle at the buffoonery of the good people of London. The accusations are flying, my friends. Just read the papers. Early last evening, a clergyman visiting from the north was attacked by a drunkard and dragged before the Turk's Head Coffee House, accused of being me. A clergyman, for God's sake! The poor wretch was brought to the watch house, where they thrust a Bible into his hands and told him to read his last Psalm, threatening him with a hanging to put his black soul to rest. Although I am certain he has committed enough sins to place him in a hair shirt for eternity, I doubt any of them would be worthy of a hanging. He spent the whole night being mistreated by the officiates until the next day two men interfered on his behalf and had him released.

I set the newspaper aside and chuckle to myself, convinced I live amongst a sea of bumbling imbeciles.

What bothers me about all the false arrests of late is that the Bow Street Runners seem more driven than ever to find me. Much of the blame belongs to Angerstein and his reward, however I do admit that my newest flurry of activity may have stirred the pot a bit. I have recently had to cast a wider net, if you will, and more often consider ladies of lower esteem than I normally would pursue. It seems as if less and less highborn women take evening strolls, even in this lovely weather. But I want to make it clear that I take no particular interest in maidservants, fish women, or washerwomen. They simply happen to be the most accessible at this time. One would think they would take more freely to my flattery, looking as they do, but they are no different than their betters, forcing me to punish them for improper etiquette when approached by a gentleman.

The benefit of all the hysteria is that I have become the topic of conversation in every coffeehouse, men's club, and evening party throughout all of London. There is even a play at Astley's Theatre based on my pursuits! As I understand it, it is quite popular and gets full houses regularly. I should love to attend it, but I would be utterly disappointed if the actor playing me were not as distinguished and refined as I. It wouldn't be his fault, of course. That would lie with the exaggerated information in Angerstein's posters and the spurious accounts from the so-called victims. I must admit, however, I rather appreciate the description of me being a 'master of disguise'. I think it suits me well.

I should confess that half the descriptions that make the papers are either entirely contrived or involve another man. I do not pursue my lovers with the help of others. My work is done alone. Nor do I own the drab-coloured surtout coat of a soldier. Please. So, if an attack was made by someone wearing one, it was not I. It is bothersome that there might be imposters out there trying to gain notoriety using my exploits. Many women have come forward saying they were attacked and wounded on nights when I have been sitting at home quietly reading and sipping my brandy. True, other perpetrators have allowed for conflicting descriptions of my person, but I do not care for counterfeits stealing my glory.

There is possibly only one person who might be able to identify me. He is determined to take me down. But why? He has no knowledge of my true identity, so it could not be a personal matter. Strangely enough, I am beginning to admire him. Do not mistake my words—I still loathe the man. Yet, after his most recent effort to catch me in St. James's Park a fortnight past, using lures to draw me to their sides, I find myself thinking about him more and more. I never saw his face that night, but I recognized his voice almost immediately. Smug, confident, determined. It was Hayes. I recall the thumping of my heart when his hands clutched the back of my coat. A flash of fire rushed to my limbs and my throat grew tight. I struggled to reach for my blade, but he'd grabbed my coat in such a way that it drew my arms back. And on top of that, he snatched my favourite periwig, the skite! The whole ordeal lasted but a minute or two, yet it seemed an eternity. It was a clever plan, and if not for that tart slapping and kicking at us like an unleashed gamecock, he might have taken me.

Since then, there have been over a dozen arrests, yet the reward remains unclaimed. One hundred pounds. I stare at the paper once more.

Suddenly, I am struck by genius.

Part Five

Chapter 31

Late April, 1790
London, England

Maeve floated on the water, weightless. Her shift clung to her skin, preventing her arms from moving. She allowed the warm water to flow over her taut belly and legs in soft ripples. The child in her womb stirred, and she smiled.

"You will be the one to set me free," she said.

A small tug on the back of her hair surprised her. She held her breath, thinking it might only be a small fish mistaking her tresses for kelp. But then another tug jarred her, this time with the force of something larger. She tried to fan out her arms to swim away, but they remained paralyzed, stuck to her sides. *What is it*, she wondered. The tugging continued, traveling down her body—her hair, her shift, the exposed skin on the back of her thighs and calves. Water lapped over her nose and mouth. She gasped for breath, choking as she drifted downward below the surface and into the river's dark depths. She stretched her fingers to reach her belly and protect the little life that grew within it, but her hands were unable to move above her hips.

She screamed, knowing the water muffled her cries. No one would hear her. As she sank into darkness, she surrendered her struggle and closed her eyes.

"Maeve!"

A gentle hand wiggled her awake. Winnet, one of the girls in her ward, stood above her, her brow creased with worry. "You're tossin' about like a ship in a storm, you are."

Maeve tried to catch her breath and coughed. She jerked up her hand to cover her mouth, but it was tangled in seaweed. Or was it the sheets?

Winnet sat back on her cot and brushed away the wet mess of hair on Maeve's brow.

"I'm drowning." Maeve squinted up at the sun.

"No, lass. You're fine now." Winnet patted her hand and tipped a mug to her lips. Maeve pushed it away. "The devil found his way into your dreams, nothin' more."

She blinked her eyes into focus at the bright light filling the room. Was it a dream? She remembered the surgeon telling her that she might have visions as the pox worsened. "My bones ache, Winnet. It seems the devil has found his way into them as well."

She struggled to sit up, and Winnet pulled the damp sheets from around her, setting her free. "I'll get Sister Harriet."

Maeve squeezed her hand to stop her and winced, her knuckles as taut as violin's strings. But Winnet broke from her grasp and disappeared.

In minutes, Sister Harriet arrived with a mercury tonic, but Maeve waved it off. "I am with child, Sister."

The nun lowered her head, her face free of judgment yet filled with despair. "Then I shall offer you a prayer."

Sister Harriet sat beside her on a small wooden stool and mumbled softly. Maeve listened to the susurrus of her words, comforted by the sound more than their meaning. She forced a smile. "Would you write two letters for me?"

Sister Harriet left, then returned with quill, ink, and paper. Maeve didn't have much to say, so it only took a few minutes.

"To whom shall I address the first?" The nun held the quill poised over the folded paper.

"Connor MacKenna at Parker's Place on Coppice Row."

Three days after she arrived, Maeve was reassigned to a smaller ward with four beds. Her section was separated by a flimsy curtain draped over a line of hemp that allowed for some privacy from the male patients on the other side. Although no one said it, she knew she'd been moved to the ward for the dying.

The other patients were relatively quiet, with one exception—Martha Little. Maeve had often spilled her porridge when Martha decided to howl unexpectedly, apparently terrified she was being chased by wolves. The inescapable shrieking echoed throughout the room until Sister Harriet or Sister Lucinda quieted Martha with their calming voices, bringing the girl back to her senses.

Martha stood atop her cot, pulling at her hair and wailing.

"There, there, Martha," they whispered, only two beds away. They guided her down, speaking of the light of the Lord and praying for Him to deliver her from her destruction. Martha whimpered softly and settled back into bed. The nuns nodded at one another, seemingly satisfied that they had brought her peace. Before they left, they offered the words Maeve had heard many times since she arrived at London Lock. "The Lord is with you, my child."

Maeve rubbed her sore shoulder. The cot she slept in was no more than a piece of canvas cut from a ship's old sail stretched over a wooden frame and tied at the corners with rope. It made her think of her bed at Parker's, stuffed with horsehair and wool, one of the better beds at the brothel. The other girls had straw or corn husks inside their mattresses and had to replace the stuffing every year when the bugs and musty smell became overbearing. The only reason Maeve had the best mattress lay in the fact that Viscount Yarmouth had had it delivered for the previous girl who had inhabited the room before he became her keeper and took her away. That's when Maeve became Mother's top girl—before she got pregnant and lost her favour. Even then, Mother Wharton never bothered to remove it. When Maeve asked Connor why Mother didn't take it for herself, he said that she slept on a feather bed with silk ticking, one Maeve now imagined she helped pay for.

Maeve shuffled to the washstand and poured water into the bowl. She dipped her hands in the cold water and splashed it over her face. Her son tumbled and kicked inside of her as she bent over. He had to be a boy with such powerful legs. *Who is your father?* she wondered. She sat on her cot and rubbed her ankles, stiff like the rest of her body. The soles of her feet were black as tar from the filth littering the floor.

"You have a visitor, miss." Sister Catherine, the nun who regularly brought food, stared at Maeve's soiled feet and grimaced.

Could her letters have been received so soon? It had only been a few days.

"Would you like me to escort him here?" the nun asked.

"Him?" It was probably Connor.

"The clerk did not tell me his name. Would you prefer I inquire—"

"That won't be necessary." Although she wore only her shift, she didn't care. Connor had seen her in less when she called for his help with a rough cull. "Please send him in."

She raked her fingers through her hair and sat on the edge of her bed.

With her vision so poor, she heard his voice before she saw him, and her insides turned to ice.

"I suppose you thought you could disappear without telling me," he said.

Maeve froze, her stomach turning to lead. It was Stone. "How did you find me?" Bile rose in her throat.

"One of the whores told me. She did not disclose your purpose for being here, but she need not explain. The hospital's reputation for taking in harlots and their victims is well known." His speech was as bitter and condescending as usual.

She realized she was rubbing her wrists, remembering the painful rawness after one of his visits. "What is it that you want?"

"Your face has not yet begun to turn. No wens." He ran his knuckles across her cheek. "Do you know what you have done, *ma petite pute?*"

His quiet tone was strange, one she'd never heard before. She inched away from his hand. She didn't think he would try to hurt her with Martha in the room, but she would be ready if he did. "I have done nothing."

"Nothing?" He chuckled, then inhaled deeply. He spoke softly, but his eyes bore into her with malice. "You dirty jilt. How long have you known?"

She glanced around the bed for a weapon. Anything sharp. "No more than a few months, I swear."

He leaned into her. "You're lying."

She looked past him at Martha, who lay on her side facing the wall. The gentle rise and fall of her chest told Maeve she was fast asleep.

"Look at you." His mouth turned downward in a scowl. "The little Irish lass with a lusty voice, yet was a rose never blown upon. At least that's what the bawd had said."

She didn't doubt that Mother had told the culls that she was a virgin when she arrived. It wasn't true, but it was a sure way to bring in a brace of shiners to add to her coffers. "You found me pleasing."

"You flatter yourself," he said dryly. "Had I known you were diseased, I would have never laid a hand on you."

She had no idea when she'd contracted the pox, but she knew she hadn't arrived at the brothel tainted. "For all I know, *you* gave it to *me.*"

He smacked her hard with the back of his hand, sending her crashing back on the bed. Her head hit the wooden frame just above her ear, and a burst of white light flashed through her skull. She moved to touch her temple, then his fingers wrapped around her throat. She inhaled sharply with the pain and smelled the sweet apricot scent of snuff on his skin.

"*You* blame *me?* Need I remind you that I am a gentleman?" He spoke between gnashed teeth, releasing her neck with a jerk. He ran his hands through his hair and paced back and forth in front of her cot. Although she normally appreciated the closed curtain that gave her privacy, she didn't now.

She knew nothing about Stone other than his strange proclivity for finding sexual pleasure in torturing her. She had assumed he was a nobleman or at least gentry, but only through his speech and fine clothing—not his behaviour. She slid closer to the end of the bed near the wall where her washbowl sat. Underneath the rickety stand was a pitcher just out of her reach.

He rubbed his face harshly with both hands. "You have ruined my life. What will become of me?"

She thought about the years of having her hands bound, her mouth gagged, and her throat squeezed until she saw spots before her eyes. She knew what would become of him, but she honestly didn't care. "We are one in the same. Hand in glove. Maggots will feed from your corpse just as easily as they will mine."

He stopped pacing and stared at her, his brown eyes dark with what she imagined was fear. His anguished features faded as his face paled. "Then, I suppose, I shall see you in hell."

Chapter 32

"I am looking for Edward Topham." Cuthbert stopped at the desk of the first lad he saw in the *World* offices. The gangly boy pointed to the back of the room past four rows of people sitting at wooden desks, all busy either reading through a loop or writing furiously. The scratch of their quills on paper found their way into his spine and up to his neck. He shuddered.

Although Sophie had told him that she would not accept his offer to help her get her work published, he wasn't going to surrender his fight. He knew she was truly telling him that she chose the boxer over him, but he'd detected a note of sadness when she spoke, which made him think regret yet lived in her heart. That gave him hope. More so, he hadn't had the proof of his devotion in his hands at the time he'd made her that promise. With Topham's assurance she would be published, he was certain she would change her mind.

Cuthbert edged between the desks to an office in the back with Topham's name and position engraved on a brass placard on the partially open door. He knocked lightly three times before entering. Topham sat at a large desk piled high with papers. Beside it stood a rusty bucket crammed with scrolls. Two stately leather armchairs faced the desk, separated by a small table holding a crystal decanter of golden liquid. Cuthbert cleared his throat to gain his attention.

Topham looked up from his work and lowered his scissor spectacles. Cuthbert waited while the man's face moved from acknowledgement to recognition. "Ah, Needham, is it?"

Cuthbert smiled, relieved that the editor recalled their acquaintance. "It is, sir."

"Forgive me for my hesitance. My only place of reference for our association is the club." Topham skirted around his desk and offered him a seat in one of the leather chairs. "What brings you here?"

The editor retrieved two crystal glasses from his desk, poured them both a drink from the decanter, then sat in the nearby chair.

"I have not seen you at White's in a while." Cuthbert held the glass to his nose and inhaled. Cognac.

"Ah, well. We have been quite busy here of late. You heard about the London Monster's latest attack. It seems the old fellow struck Mrs. Harlow again. This time in Pall Mall."

"Again?" Cuthbert thought that must be rare. And particularly unlucky for Mrs. Harlow.

"The first time was in January outside of Brooks's Club. Both times her clothing was cut, but this time she was also wounded." Topham sipped his Cognac and sighed. "He has a penchant for piquerism, this one."

"Twice. That is remarkable." Cuthbert knew Mrs. Harlow as the lady bookseller he often purchased novels from for Sophie. "Were her wounds severe?"

"Enough to drive the poor woman to her bed. 'Tis my understanding she is not yet accepting visitors."

Cuthbert shook his head. "Did she get a good look at the fellow?"

"Ah, well. She described him, all right. Dark hair, average height, long nose. Similar to the others, but without specificity." He tipped his glass to peer inside. "I fear the villain will never be caught."

Cuthbert finished the last of his Cognac, which he noticed was not the same quality as the Renaud and Dualle they'd shared at White's. "You do enjoy your Cognac, Topham."

Topham poured Cuthbert another glass, then sipped his drink with a smile, eyes half closed. "I recently enjoyed one made by the Barraud family. I can still taste the kumquats and walnuts on my tongue."

Cuthbert wondered who'd paid the bill for that one. "You are a man with good taste."

Topham smiled and set aside his now empty glass. "I assume you are not here to discuss my fondness for Cognac."

"No, sir. I am here to ask you for a favour." He didn't want to sound too desperate for fear of scaring him away from the idea, so he said it plainly. "I want you to publish an article written by my fiancée."

"Your fiancée?" he asked skeptically. "An article written by a woman?"

Cuthbert shifted in his chair. "She is quite intelligent, I assure you."

He smiled condescendingly. "And what is it about? Scandals for the entertainment of the fashionable world? I do love that."

The *World* was known for being a paper of amusement, publishing articles on fashion and folly, sports, and other entertainments. Scandal was often a topic of discussion, done with humour and speculation. He took a large swig. "Not exactly."

"No?" he asked, amused.

"I believe she has written a piece on pugilism." He hated to even say the word. The image of her holding that boxer's hand at the fight in Woodford Green was branded in his memory. But this was the only way to get her back. To make her love him again.

"What does a woman know about pugilism?" It was more of a statement than a question. "What would my readers say if they knew I had published an article by a woman—on gentlemanly matters, nonetheless? I would be laughed out of town, I am sure."

"Perhaps you should read it first. I can have her send it to you—"

He stood, clearly indicating their meeting was over. "There is no need, Mr. Needham. I have recently accepted an article on that subject by a talented writer, I am afraid."

Cuthbert stood too. "But—"

"Our principle concerns are fine writing and pleasantry, the first requirement much more important than the latter. This gentleman writer manages to accomplish both."

Cuthbert's mouth was suddenly dry. This was his last chance. Topham had to agree to publish her. Didn't he understand that? He swallowed the last of his drink. "You owe me, sir."

"Owe you?" Topham asked firmly.

"For . . . for the Cognac," he uttered, wiping his sweaty palms down the front of his breeches.

"Ah, well. I see." He reached underneath his desk, only the hump of his back visible from where Cuthbert stood. After a few seconds, the screech of an unused hinge broke the silence. Topham offered him a small blue pouch jingling with coins. "Twenty pounds will have to do, as I will not publish your betrothed's article."

<hr/>

Cuthbert lumbered down the street, mumbling to himself about the unfairness of the world. At this point, the least of his concerns was repayment—in coin—

244

for the bottles of Cognac he and Topham had drunk. He needed to get Sophie back, lure her out of the clutches of that boxer. He stood to lose so much. His debts had accrued to an amount that would be quite difficult from which to rebound. Add that to the debt his family had gathered over the years of dwindling rent rolls from their properties, and the total was staggering. Sophie's dowry was the only way to climb out of the financial abyss he and his family had created, and his parents never neglected to remind him of it.

But for him, it was so much more than that. He had always imagined he and Sophie would be together as husband and wife. Even at twelve, the first time he kissed her, he knew they would marry. Over the years, Dalton had tried to convince him to take a mistress, and he had considered it once, but although she was lovely, she did not have the grace and intelligence of Sophie. She had even sworn her love for him. But when he'd kissed her, he felt nothing more than the tightening of his breeches.

Sophie had to realize her mistake and come back to him.

He stumbled over some cobbles, and a hand reached out to steady him. "My dear boy, take care."

Lord Greenville smiled at him weakly, that familiar look of concern in the creases of his eyes.

"The pavers have done a sloppy job with the causey." Cuthbert straightened his coat, a little lightheaded from the Cognac. Greenville reared back slightly, crinkling his nose, an obvious indication that he detected spirits on Cuthbert's breath.

"Indeed." Greenville tilted his head to the side. "Would you care to join me? I am on my way to Hyde Park. I understand the tulips are in full bloom. 'Tis a lovely way to spend the afternoon on such a day as this."

"I . . . cannot . . . presently, milord."

"Are you quite certain?"

Could the man know where he was headed? What he planned to do? Cuthbert tugged at his cravat, which suddenly felt like it was wound too tight around his neck, then nodded.

"Very well, then. Do give my regards to your parents for me, will you?" Greenville tipped his hat and continued down the path.

It took Cuthbert only a few minutes to get to his destination. He pushed through the doors that had become far too familiar over the years and searched for the bawd. She was busy speaking to another gentleman in the corner, likely arranging the payment for the service of one of her girls. Before he could gain her attention, the fair-haired girl with freckles across her cheeks grabbed his arm. She was already in a state of dishabille, wearing only her underclothes and a necklace made of glass baubles, ready for business.

"Back for more, lovey?" she asked in a hard Cockney accent. She hooked one finger in his cravat and loosened it from around his neck. He'd been with her a few times, but only for oral pleasures, nothing more. This time he wanted something different. She kissed him, and he recognized the strong yeasty taste of porter on her tongue.

"Take me upstairs," he said plainly.

Neither of them undressed fully. He merely lowered his breeches and removed his coat. He'd freed her breasts from her stays and lifted her petticoat, leaving her stockings as they were.

"That's it, lovey. You've a cock like a beast, you do." The glass beads of her necklace jounced with each thrust.

"Shhh." He covered her mouth while maintaining his rhythm. He didn't care for her unsavory comments, especially not with that accent. With his other hand, he squeezed her breast, wondering if Sophie's would feel the same. After only a minute or so, the entire tryst was over, and he felt empty.

He slid out of her and buttoned up his breeches.

"Did you like that, lovey?" She remained on the bed, her breasts still exposed and her legs dangling off the side. "I can play the whore pipe for six pence a tune." She whistled through the gap in her teeth, then licked her lips.

"I dare say that will not be necessary." He shrugged on his coat and reached into the blue velvet pouch Topham had given him, then dropped a shilling into her open palm.

"A bob," she said appreciatively, then slid it in her stays. "You come back to me, lovey. Just ask for Biddy. I'll treat you right, I will."

But he didn't want to come back. He wanted to stop visiting whores. He opened his mouth to tell her, but the words stuck in his throat. He wiped at a tear that escaped the corner of his eye and turned to leave, but the girl caught his arm and pulled him close.

"There, there, now. Let Biddy give you a good hug. That will cheer you up, lovey." She rocked him in her arms as they lay on the bed, his head on her chest. His eyes grew heavy with the steady swaying, and he soon settled into sleep. He woke unsure of how long they had lain there and was shocked when a church bell rang twice in the distance.

"I should go." He grabbed his money pouch from the bed and shoved it into his coat before leaving.

He sat in a pew near the back of the church, his head cradled in his hands. *What have I done? Is this God's punishment for my sins? Has He taken Sophie away from me?*

How would he ever be in God's good graces again?

The weight of the pouch at his breast made him realize what he could do to gain God's favour. He pulled it out and bowed his head to the cross on the altar. "I beg your forgiveness. Count not my transgressions but, rather, my tears of repentance . . . my sorrow for the offences I have committed against you."

"May I be of help?" Reverend Anthony's hand rested on Cuthbert's shoulder, the weight of it no more than that of a small bird.

Cuthbert didn't know how to respond. He could never tell him the truth of what lay in his black soul. He offered the reverend the blue velvet pouch, promising himself that this would not be the last of it. Although he knew his mother paid tithes to the church regularly, he had never done it in his own name before. He needed to clear his soul and his heart in order to bring back Sophie and gain esteem in God's eyes. "I want to help the church."

Reverend Anthony accepted the pouch, weighing its heft in the palm of his hand. "This is quite generous of you."

Cuthbert's thoughts tumbled. He was unsure of what to say without saying too much. "We have been members of the church since my great grandfather built a home here in London."

"So I understand." The reverend nodded once.

"What I mean to say is . . . that St. Martin-in-the-Fields holds a special place in my heart. I only hope that . . . I am in the church's heart as well."

The reverend waved his arm out gracefully to the expanse of the church. "All God's children have a place in His home and in His heart."

Cuthbert took a deep breath, somewhat calmed by the reverend's words. He was certain he did the right thing by giving him what was left of the twenty pounds Topham had paid him. It was sure to cleanse his soul of at least some of its sin. He shook the reverend's hand and bid him farewell. His shoulders straightened as he approached the exit, feeling a little better about his future.

Reverend Anthony called to him, his gentle voice echoing throughout the large chamber. "Mr. Needham?"

Cuthbert turned to face him and froze. Inside one hand was the empty pouch and in the other, a cheap glass bauble necklace.

He hadn't explained the situation well. He knew that. And the reverend certainly saw through his flimsy account of what happened. The crux of it was true. He was robbed. But his excuse that it was a pickpocket—and not a prostitute who had plenty of time to make the switch while he lay in her arms—was beyond implausible. What type of pickpocket replaces a stolen item with another?

Not only was he out the twenty pounds, but he'd embarrassed himself in front of the reverend. He hoped he wouldn't share the story with his mother. He wasn't sure he could handle her inescapable questioning.

He sat on a bench in Hyde Park wondering how he had found himself in such a hopeless position. It seemed like only yesterday that Sophie had softened to him, allowing chaste kisses in the absence of her mother. What had gone wrong? When had that fool come into her life?

He sighed and peered up at the trees now adorned with the bright green leaves of spring dancing in the breeze. Spring. A time for weddings. They were to be married in a couple of months. Had she told her parents of her affair with the boxer? Were they scolding her for her behaviour? Who knew about her infidelity besides him and Dalton? Vivian? Her maidservant?

He stared across the park lawn at the couples strolling arm in arm on the far path. They seemed happy, the men standing tall and confident and the women smiling up at them in awe. It was everything he wanted. Sophie on his arm, admiring his wit and intellect as they talked of their day.

In the distance, two petite women—one older, one younger—walked by, seemingly in a hurry. He watched the younger one as she stopped to right her hat when the wind blew it askew. He knew that gown, blue with green striping on the skirt. He slowly stood and squinted, noting the dark curls that hung over one shoulder. It was Sophie.

Where was she headed with such urgency? Could she be going to see the boxer?

He raised his hand to get her attention. He thought of shouting her name, but something made him refrain from doing it. Instead, he chose to follow her.

Chapter 33

The hysteria to catch the London Monster was everywhere. Tom felt it in the judging glares of men and women as he walked to the warehouse. No one was safe from being accused. Fear had spread throughout the city like fire in dry brush.

From his winnings, he'd paid Mother Cluck the rest of the forty pounds he'd promised her, but he wasn't happy about it. Her moll had ruined everything. In truth, he couldn't blame her for the way she'd reacted that night. It was dark, and with no experience in defending herself, she must've assumed her wild flailing was the right way of handling the attack. If only she had permitted him to take over. But it was too late for that.

When he reached the docks, Tom paid a newsboy a penny for a paper. A frontpage article indicated the London Monster had attacked another woman—a servant girl—only two days before on the Strand along the north end of the Thames. She had apparently been approached by a group of four men, one of whom carried a nosegay. He'd asked her to smell it, but she declined, as the flowers appeared artificial. He insisted, so she eventually acquiesced and was stabbed below her eye with some sort of sharp instrument. They laughed and left her standing in the street, bleeding from her wound.

That sounded nothing like the man he knew as the monster. Tom doubted he would travel with others to commit his crime. The three times he'd encountered him, he'd been alone. And using a nosegay to cut a woman's face? He entered the warehouse and tossed the paper on a crate.

Someone in the back was whistling a cheery tune with a bouncing melody.

"There you are," Henry said, taking a break from his tune. He hugged a ledger to his chest and joined Tom, grinning from ear to ear.

It was not in Henry's nature to whistle or walk in such a buoyant manner. He was the morose brother of the three of them, always pouting over paperwork or agitated over business matters. At best, he was stoic.

"You certainly are in a lively mood, brother." Tom stared at the little yellow flower bud sticking out from the pages of his ledger.

"Am I?" Henry beamed.

Tom smiled. This was not the Henry he knew. Where was the brooding? The tension? The timidity? Tom snatched the yellow bud and held it to his nose.

Henry stole it back, then tucked it carefully between the pages once more. "'Twas a gift."

"A gift? From an admirer?"

"Judith, actually." Henry tried to contain his smile, but it was useless. He was spilling over with cheer. "She gave it to me this morning."

"You paid her a visit?" Judging from Henry's behaviour, it seemed like it went well.

"I paid her *father* a visit. He has approved of the marriage, and since you gave me the sterling I need to pay off Chippenham, I expect we should be married this summer."

Tom couldn't believe it. Henry had actually followed through on his plan to win Judith's hand in marriage. "Then it was money well spent."

Henry chewed his bottom lip, studying Tom. "I wish you would tell me where you acquired it. I hope it was not ill-gotten."

Tom remembered what Father had said about keeping his sport a secret between the two of them. "I came upon it honestly, I assure you."

"Not from Father?" Henry asked, his brow raised.

"Not from Father." Tom knew Father would probably not have approved of Henry besting a nobleman, especially with the upcoming elections. Coming between the marriage of two noble families was not something anyone would dare do under most circumstances. "Did Father offer his consent?"

Henry's face dropped, the corner of his mouth twitching slightly. "I plan on telling him tonight."

"You have yet to tell him?" he asked incredulously.

"I thought it might be a good idea to have you there, speaking on my behalf, should I need you."

Tom sighed. This was the Henry he knew. "You can do this on your own, brother. Tell him that the Forsythes have agreed to the marriage. You have gone about it unconventionally, but tell him that your heart drove you to this point. Surely, he will understand that." Father had married their mother for love. It was not an arranged affair, and his love for her had not died the day her life was cut short. But Tom was thinking about his own heart and how the joy of falling in love was not so simple. "I will be there if you need me, but I have faith that you will do well on your own."

"And if Father should know about her arrangement with Chippenham?" Henry asked.

There was a possibility that he could know. It may have been announced in the papers. "Tell him it is taken care of. The bond will be returned to Chippenham with the forfeiture of the marriage, and you have reimbursed a portion of the dowry Judith would have provided the family. In time, the rest will be paid."

"But what if—"

"Henry." Tom set both of his hands on his brother's shoulders. "You now have the opportunity to marry the girl you love. Do not allow your fears to prevent it from happening."

Tom spent the whole day at the warehouse, first going over the shipments of sugar and rum from the West Indies and then the coal from their colliery up north. Normally, this warehouse didn't accept the coal, but Roger had said with the opening of the Oxford Canal, they could no longer keep the amount of coal coming in at the warehouse on Harp. It was good news for business, but it left Tom covered in soot as if he were a chimney sweep.

He ran a rag over his face and forearms in a futile attempt to remove the black scuffs from his skin. His back was sore from the lifting and shoveling, but it felt good to use those muscles he hadn't used since the fight. It had been three weeks since he'd beaten Jackson and earned the winner's purse. He was glad he was able to pay Mother Cluck easily and give his brother the money to pay off Chippenham's family but, other than that, the purse didn't mean anything to him. The monster was still roaming the streets, stabbing innocent women.

He headed home out of Billingsgate and decided to take the back alley near Pudding Lane to beat the setting sun. All of London seemed to be rushing home. Carriage wheels clattering over cobblestones, and fishwives and milkmaids hawking their wares produced a cacophony of noise. One street over, Tom heard the shouts of a dustman collecting waste from door to door, his bell clanging to announce his arrival. As he approached Lombard, the noise grew even busier, but he no longer smelled the fishy stench of the docks or the sour odours of the Thames. He inhaled the night air, knowing he was closer to home.

Just as he was about to turn the corner, he was grabbed from behind by several hands and dragged back into the alley. A sharp blow to the gut doubled him over, his breath catching with the pain. The shadows of the narrow passageway and the dusk hid the four faces of the assailants, but he knew who they were regardless.

He struggled to get out of their grip, his right arm finally breaking free from the hold, allowing him to throw a hard punch in the face of one of them. The cockard's head jarred back with a crack, and he fell into a pile of rubbish. Before Tom could turn to deal with the others, a pointed kick to his side forced him onto his knees. He gulped air, and a red flash of searing pain filled his gut.

Two of Stone's hackums stood on either side of him, close enough to be taken down. Tom thrusted his elbows back, jamming each one in their knees, forcing them to stagger backward. Tom shot up as the fourth man lunged to tackle him. A blow struck him in the chest, but he'd been hit harder. He punched him, clipping his jaw and sending him reeling. The man he'd knocked into the pile of debris stood wobbly and launched himself headfirst. Tom whirled to the side to escape his grasp. Just as he gained his footing, the other three bombarded him with wild jabs to his face and ribs. He sank to his knees with the blows, then collapsed.

One of them grabbed a fistful of hair and jerked Tom's head back. "Did you think he'd let you walk away?"

Tom squeezed his eyes shut. A burning ache below his ribs prevented him from standing. "What do you want?" he choked.

"Oh, I think you know," said the one whose voice he recognized from their encounter in Holborn. He wondered if Stone was nearby.

Tom peered up at them through lids that were already starting to swell. He wriggled his jaw side to side to see if it was broken. It moved smoothly, yet agonizingly. The bruising would be bad. "Tell him I shall do as he says as long as he leaves the girl alone."

"'Tis too late for that."

Chapter 34

Sophie's feet couldn't move fast enough. She had to get to the hospital to see Maeve before dusk when they no longer allowed visitors.

"Make haste, Peg," she urged, tugging her arm.

"I am moving as quickly as I can," Peg said through laboured breath.

They pushed through the doors of the hospital just as the sky turned pink. At the end of the hall sat a clerk behind a large wooden desk. He was busy speaking with a young woman who wiped at her tears, a child at her hip.

"Your mother would not care for this at all," Peg said, hardly amused.

Sophie remembered her own shock when she'd received the letter from Maeve indicating where she had gone. She had no idea that Maeve was that sick, certainly not with the pox. She'd heard of the horrible effects of the disease but had never known anyone to have it. Of course, it wasn't exactly a topic discussed in polite company.

"This is a charitable hospital, Peg," Sophie whispered.

"One for harlots and men sunk in debauchery." Peg shivered with disgust.

The woman and her child turned from the clerk, tears traveling down both of their faces. Sophie stepped aside, imagining only the worst. She cleared her throat as she approached the desk. "I am here to see one of your patients. Maeve Hannigen."

The clerk checked his pocket watch. "You will have only a few minutes to visit. We close shortly."

"Wait here, Peg." She left her maid on a bench near the door.

She followed a nun through a large corridor filled with patients end to end. Some lay curled inward moaning, and others sat on their cots, staring into space. Sophie pulled her handkerchief from inside her sleeve and held it over her nose and mouth to block the stale reek of illness.

The nun led her to a maze of smaller rooms separated by makeshift curtains. She tugged aside the dirty oilcloth to reveal four beds, three of which were occupied with frail bodies. The nun pointed to the cot closest to the wall.

Sophie's heart caught at the sight of Maeve lying on her side, paler and thinner than she remembered. Her shift had fallen from her shoulder, exposing sharp knobs of bone. Her gold tresses lying over her pillow were now tangled and as dull as tarnished brass. Other than a small washstand holding a washbasin and a wooden bowl containing a paltry amount of porridge, the little room was bare.

Sophie sat beside her and gently laid her hand on her hip. "Maeve?"

Maeve's chest rose with a deep breath, her eyes blinking open slowly. She pushed herself up on one elbow and rubbed her brow with the back of her hand. "Sophie?"

Sophie forced a smile. It had only been a few weeks since they had seen each other, yet the vibrant, beautiful Maeve she remembered was not present in this empty shell.

"I came as quickly as I could." Sophie helped her into a sitting position and brushed her hair away from her face. "I had no idea—"

"I imagine how I must look. I wish I had never sent you that letter." Maeve inched up the shoulder of her shift. "I know what you must think of me."

Sophie pulled her to her breast and ran one hand down her back, her fingers trailing down the tiny knobs of her spine. "I only wish you had told me sooner. I could have fetched you a surgeon—"

"There was no hope then, as there is no hope now," she whispered. "'Tis the price of playing the whore."

Sophie didn't know what to say. But none of this was Maeve's fault. She was cursed with misfortune when she lost her parents to consumption, and it only continued from there. "Perhaps you can take a stronger tonic."

Maeve smiled feebly, her mouth twitching with the effort. She took Sophie's hand and placed it over her stomach. Sophie inhaled sharply.

Maeve looked up at her. "A tonic would kill my baby."

Sophie ran her hand over the hardness of Maeve's belly. A tear fell from the corner of her eye, and she quickly wiped it away. She reached for the bowl of porridge, measured out a small amount on the spoon, and held it to Maeve's lips. "You must eat."

Maeve grimaced and turned her head away.

"For your child?" asked Sophie.

With some prodding, she eventually took the bite that Sophie offered. She fed her two more spoonsful until Maeve pushed away her hand. "Please. No more."

Sophie set the porridge back on the washstand. It was clear that Maeve's unborn child would not survive much longer without nourishment, but in the end, she wasn't sure Maeve would survive to give him life.

"I asked you here to tell you some things," Maeve started. She took a few laboured breaths before continuing. "Mother Wharton has been taking the money I gave her for Emily. She forged the letters from Emily's caretaker."

Sophie was shocked. "How do you know this?"

Maeve told her how she found the unfinished letter in the bawd's private parlour. That was what made her leave Parker's with only a few belongings and come to the Lock Hospital.

"I don't know where she is. I am not even certain Mr. and Mrs. Hobart even exist." She wiped a speck of porridge from the corner of her mouth with a trembling hand. "She needs her medicines, Sophie."

Sophie remembered seeing Mother Wharton with her keys on a noisy chatelaine around her waist, Maeve joking that she never allowed anyone into her parlour because that was where she kept her riches. Apparently, she kept her secrets there as well.

Maeve rested her hand on Sophie's. "I thought you might be able to find her. Perhaps post something in one of the papers."

Sophie couldn't believe the bawd could be so cruel. "She may have been sent to the Foundling Hospital in Bloomsbury. If that is the case, they should have a record of her."

Maeve's eyes lit up. "Do you think so?"

"'Tis certainly a possibility. I will do my best to find her, and when I do . . ." She ran her hand over Maeve's hair, the words caught in her throat. ". . . you will be reunited as a family. You must have faith."

Maeve rested her head on Sophie's shoulder. "I think you know I might not live to see that day."

Just then, Bertie appeared from behind the curtain. Sophie was about to ask him what he was doing there, when Maeve pulled from her arms and straightened. She stared at Bertie with shock.

"Albert?"

Bertie's faced paled, and his mouth fell open, his eyes darting between her and Maeve. "I . . . I . . ."

Maeve fumbled with her hair, a faint blush spreading over her cheeks. "How did you find me?"

Was Maeve hallucinating? Sophie stared at Bertie, then glanced between them, the reality of what was happening settling in. Her heartbeat thrummed in her ears. "Albert?"

"How rude of me." Maeve smiled at her. "Sophie, this is my Albert."

Bertie's hand shook as he removed his hat, his sober gaze fixed on Sophie. "I . . . I should explain."

Sophie stood slowly, her mind spinning with the stories Maeve had told her about the married viscount from Hampshire who left her when he learned she was with child. At the time, Sophie had thought him a coward, a brute. And now, as she stared at the man she thought she knew almost as well as she knew herself, she realized she was right.

Then it occurred to her that Bertie had been unusually upset at the masque after Maeve approached him. Now she knew why.

Sophie wanted to tell Maeve how he had lied to her about who he was. He wasn't a viscount as he'd told her, at least not until his father passed on his title. He certainly wasn't married either. He wasn't even from Hampshire. He was a liar, a user, an imposter. But then a tear flowed down Maeve's smiling face, a gleam of hope in her eyes, and Sophie realized she couldn't tell her. She took a deep breath and did her best to hide the quiver in her voice. "'Tis a pleasure to meet you, *milord.*"

Bertie's brow knitted in confusion. "What? I—"

"Maeve has told me quite a bit about you. It was so nice of you to come here to pay her a visit." Sophie was sure her mouth was tightened into a scowl when she said it, but as long as Maeve couldn't see it, she didn't care what she looked like.

"Sophie has agreed to help me find Emily." Maeve struggled to rise, so Sophie threaded her arm through hers to help lift her into a seated position. "She has your eyes, Albert."

Sophie waited for him to respond, but he only opened and closed his mouth, the lack of recognition of his own child's name evident in his half-hearted shrug and loss for words.

"Your daughter," Sophie said with a firm jaw. She saw the discomfort in Bertie's flushed face and desperate eyes but didn't feel one bit of remorse for her tone.

"A daughter," he said under his breath. "Her paternity was never proven, you see—"

Sophie speared him with her glare, then turned to Maeve. "Would you mind if I spoke to Ber . . . Albert for a moment?"

She slid the curtain back behind her and led Bertie out of the little room to a small alcove on the other side. He started to speak, his brow covered in perspiration, but seemed to think better of it.

"You will not hurt that girl anymore," she said.

"I wish you would permit me to explain—"

"What could you possibly say?" she asked.

He spun his hat in his hands while he paced back and forth in the narrow space. "I didn't know what to do. I didn't have the money to support the child. I wanted to do the right thing. Honestly, I did. But my family would have never allowed it. Please believe me, Sophie—"

"You never wanted to do the right thing!"

Bertie froze, his faced screwed in anguish. "She's a harlot! What do you expect me to do?"

"I don't even know who you are." Her heart raced in anger. "All this time I admired you. Going to church so often to *lighten your spirit with His grace*, as you'd say. But what did it do for your tainted soul?"

Bertie's mouth tightened into a straight line, his jaw set. "Do not speak to me of a tainted soul. You have been bedding a blackguard for months while playing the innocent."

She slapped him hard, leaving a bright red print on his cheek and her hand stinging. She tried to control her breath, but it was impossible. "This is your chance to be the man you never were. Now go in there and beg forgiveness, and pray she gives it to you before she draws her last breath."

Sophie marched home, leaving Peg a few paces behind her. She still couldn't believe what had just happened. *All this time, all this time . . .*

"You are making it impossible for me to keep up with you!" Peg called from behind.

As hard as Sophie tried, she found it difficult to slow her pace.

"Tell me what has you so upset!"

Sophie stopped to face her. "I cannot discuss it. At least, not now."

She turned to resume walking, but Peg caught her arm. "Were you expecting Mr. Needham there?"

"No, I was not," she said, irritated.

"But you're mad at him," Peg offered. It was a question disguised as a statement.

"Truly, Peg, I do not wish to discuss it."

Peg looped her arm through Sophie's. "Then find peace in our walk, or your mother will be sure to smell the scent of displeasure and assail you with questions."

They walked in the dark, choosing paths with lit streetlamps. It was not a good time to be out with the London Monster still loose. A slight breeze stirred the trees on the other side of the street, and she took a deep breath to calm her racing mind. She had to admit the night air and slower pace were soothing.

"How fortuitous to run into you here." Dalton appeared from nowhere.

He was the last person she wanted to see, and it was evident in her tone. "I do live around the corner. But you know that."

"My dear, have I caught you at a bad time?" he asked, full of sarcasm and clearly detecting her foul mood.

Sophie stared at him fully, not troubling to hide her distaste for him. "How well do you know Bertie?"

He drew back, ostensibly surprised by the question, then the corners of his mouth turned up. "It appears we have something to discuss." He turned to Peg. "You needn't bother yourself, dear. I can escort Miss Sophie the rest of the way home."

Peg began to argue against it, but Sophie sent her away with the assurance that Dalton was a suitable escort and she would follow shortly. She wasn't particularly thrilled with the notion, but she had to find out what he knew.

"What is this about?" he asked, a hint of pleasure in his curiosity.

"I thought you might know how he spends his days. You two share an awful lot of time together, after all." She wasn't going to divulge the crux of what she had learned, but with some careful probing, she wondered if he would give her a clue as to whether or not he was aware of his past indiscretion.

He made a sound that was probably supposed to be a laugh but sounded more like a growl. "Should we not be discussing how *you* spend *your* days?"

She knew he was referring to her relationship with Tom, but he could no longer hold that over her head. "Bertie knows about everything, thanks to you."

"Aye, he does. But that is of little consequence to me." He peered ahead in the distance, his expression stern. Sophie followed his gaze to Peg, who had just disappeared around the corner. "What is of consequence to me is how important you are to the boxer."

"How is that any of your concern?" Heat bloomed under her skin. A vivid memory of their last kiss filled her head, Tom's lips warm and sure. Dalton must've discerned what she was thinking in her face because his lips twisted into a sneer.

He grabbed her hard above her elbow and pulled her into a narrow, arched passageway between two buildings.

"Let go of me!" She tried to tug out of his grip. His fingertips dug into her arm, holding her steadfast. "You have forgot yourself—"

"*Écoute moi*, you little whore," he said in a venomous whisper.

She leaned away from him, but he held tight and shook her still.

"You are the reason I am out a fortune," he spat.

"I have no idea what you are talking about!"

"Did he do it for *you?* Was he trying to impress you?" he asked, his face only inches from hers.

"Who? What?" He wasn't making sense. She wriggled her arms to get him to release her, but he wouldn't budge.

"The boxer. He was supposed to take a dive. But you were there," he said through clenched teeth.

Finally, the story was coming together. Tom had told her that Stone had expected him to lose his last fight, but at her urging, he hadn't listened. Dalton must've known and wagered against him.

He pulled a small blade from inside his coat and pointed it at her.

Sophie's heart pounded. "If anything should happen to me, Peg will tell everyone that she left me with you."

"And I will let everyone know how I tried to save you from an attacker. With the monster yet free, the constables will believe my story of heroism."

He was right. He could blame the monster for his crime and get away with it. She started to scream, but he slapped his hand over her mouth, muffling her cries. She squirmed in his embrace as he dragged her farther into the shadows. One of her shoes fell off in the struggle, and her stockinged foot met the wet ground. A sharp pain started in her heel, and she realized she must've stepped on broken glass. Tears blurred her eyes as he led her deeper into the darkness.

His hand shifted slightly so that one of his fingers pressed into her mouth. She bit down as hard as she could, catching the flesh and bone between her teeth. He jumped back with a curse and, when he let go, she screamed.

Between the dark and her tears, it was difficult to see. She pressed her hand against the wall to gain her bearings and shuffled a few feet before she stumbled into something hard and unforgiving.

Dalton grabbed her by the throat and shoved her against the brick wall. Her head hit with a thud, flooding her ears with a dull ringing. She took a deep breath to still the noise.

Dalton froze at the sound of footsteps of someone in approach. She attempted to cry out, but his grip was still firm, so her pleas for help couldn't travel far.

"Let go of her, Stone."

She was sure it was Tom's voice. He had got his name wrong, but at the moment, she didn't care what he called him.

The hand at her neck squeezed tighter. Her head filled with white-hot light as she gasped for breath. She felt Dalton half-spin in the direction of the voice. She kicked at his shin with her slipper, but her toe only met the fleshy part of his calf.

Through the faint light from a distant streetlamp, she could make out Tom's silhouette not ten feet away.

Dalton shoved her to the ground behind him. She landed hard on her hip, sending a flash of pain down her leg. The edge of his blade gleamed slightly as he directed it at Tom.

Tom took a few careful steps. "I told you I would kill you if you laid a hand on her."

Dalton snorted derisively. "It seems you are not fit to fight off a cat. Should I thank my men for your condition?"

His men? Tom took another step closer, and Sophie gasped, her stomach catching at the sight of him. His skin was blackened, and one eye was swollen almost completely shut. His nose and chin were smeared with blood, and his hair fell over his shoulders in messy strands. He had the look of a feral animal.

"You have gone too far, Stone." Tom lunged, knocking him to the ground. Sophie heard the clang of Dalton's knife as it jangled over the uneven cobbles, but it was too dark to see where it went.

They rolled and scrabbled over each other, grunting with each blow. Sophie couldn't tell who was who in the dark.

"I made you who you are, you ungrateful cockard!" Dalton grumbled in a strangled voice.

The crack of three more blows sounded, and Sophie squeezed her eyes shut, praying they were not directed at Tom. Suddenly, the only noise was someone's heavy, tired breathing. No scuffling. No straining. No hitting.

A pair of hands cupped her shoulders, and she flinched.

"Tell me you are not hurt," Tom said with laboured breath. She slowly opened her eyes. He was a bloody mess.

She rubbed the back of her head where a lump was starting to form. "A bit. I may have stepped on glass."

Sophie lifted her foot so he could see. The heel of her stocking was torn and smeared with blood. Tom's jaw tightened.

She touched his cheek gently. "How did you find me?"

"I assumed he would have to go somewhere near your home if he wanted to get you alone."

Now that she thought about it, it was no coincidence that Dalton was standing outside only two streets from her home. And she had foolishly sent Peg away.

"His lackeys made me believe I was too late." He kissed her forehead. "I would never have forgiven myself if Stone—"

"That was Dalton Fletcher," she said.

He looked at her strangely. "Perhaps to you. But I know him as Stone."

"Mr. Stone? Maeve's . . ."

"Aye."

First Bertie and now Dalton. She was beginning to wonder what was truth and what was fiction.

"There he is!" someone shouted. A flurry of footsteps grew closer to the narrow passageway.

Four Bow Street Runners dressed in bright red waistcoats approached, holding torches high above their heads, their metal emblems on their truncheons flashing in the firelight. "We heard your screams, miss."

Sophie blinked to make out their faces. They glanced at Dalton lying on the ground only a few feet away and Tom huddled by the wall. One of them asked, "Is he dead?"

A heavyset man with a barrel-shaped chest shone his torch over Dalton's chest. "Nay. Still breathing." He turned back and stared at Tom, then jerked his head in his direction.

Another one grabbed the back of Tom's coat. "Get away from the lass!"

"He's not the one . . ." she said, panicked. "You misunderstand—"

"Look at this piece of filth." The bearded one nudged Tom with his truncheon. "A lowly foot pad if ever I've seen one."

Tom stood, wiping the blood from his nose on his sleeve.

The bearded one held his torch near Tom's face. "What's that on your hand?"

Sophie's head throbbed. She opened her mouth to tell them they were blaming the wrong man, but a Runner interrupted her.

"'Tis a brand," the heavy Runner said. He seized Tom's hand and flipped up his palm to study the letter. "For murder."

Tom snatched his hand away, balling it into a fist. The two Runners in the back started whispering.

"Your name?" the bearded one asked. The two in the back stepped closer.

Tom's glance darted between them. "Thomas Hayes."

The bearded Runner jerked back. "Well then, Mr. Hayes, you're under arrest."

A Note

Early May, 1790

I am astounded! Perhaps that is the wrong word. Amused. I am amused.

Only a few days past, I walked into the magistrate's office to report my sighting of the London Monster. A different clerk sat at the desk this time, chewing on the end of a cheroot in a most unappealing manner. He was in desperate need of grooming as he wore a ghastly beard that covered the entire bottom half of his face. I had a sneaking suspicion that what lay beneath the messy growth was not entirely pleasant either.

My skin tingled as I sat in front of him, artfully retelling the story of one of my latest encounters with a rather stout young woman in Edgeware Row. Of course, I left out details that only I—or the monster— would know.

"She was carrying a basket on one arm, when a man wearing a greatcoat approached her. I thought nothing of it at the time and kept walking," I said.

The clerk scribbled on a piece of paper as I spoke, occasionally stopping to spit bits of tobacco onto the floor beside him. I offered him a stern look of disapproval each time, but as he was unlikely accustomed to good manners, he ignored me.

"What was in the basket?" he asked.

What a foolish question, *I thought. I happened to know she was carrying radishes, but I didn't dare offer that information, for only someone next to her would have seen what was inside. "How would I know that, sir?"*

I watched his clumsy thoughts work their way across his features like an ox lumbering across an uneven field.

I continued. "The man said something to her, and she pushed him away." What I'd actually said that night was, Now, who shall treat with a glass of gin first, you or I? *I thought I'd been extremely polite, making no mention of her enormous wobbling breasts, which were barely contained in her gown.*

"Go on," he urged, still scribbling. A small bit of brown juice escaped the corner of his mouth as he spoke.

Unable to look at the mess on his face, I focused on the French lace cuffs of my shirt. "And then he slashed his knife across her breasts and ran off." In truth, I may have said a word or two before I drew my blade. Perhaps about fucking her nasty cunt . . . or something of that nature.

I plucked a tiny blue thread from my sleeve before continuing. "Just as the culprit ran away, I thought I recognized the fellow as one Thomas Hayes."

"Your name, sir?" the clerk asked, the cheroot bouncing between his lips, causing flecks of tobacco to vanish in the brown forest on his chin. Didn't he know that no one wears a beard anymore except criminals and farmers?

I offered him a name. I do not recall what it was, but it sounded pleasant on the tongue.

That was only days ago. And now they have him. I could burst into a paean!

I sit here reading the paper, a cup of tea in my hand. This is horrible news for his father, as the elections are little more than a month away. But the arrogant arse deserves it. There will be no win for him this time if I can help it. Imagine discovering that your son is found in an alleyway with a woman, presumably after he attacks her. There are other details, of course, but none so entertaining.

I chuckle to myself. Truly, I am a genius.

Chapter 35

He couldn't do it.

When Sophie left Cuthbert standing in that miserable hospital with Maeve, he panicked. He didn't go back inside the curtain to claim paternity of his daughter. He couldn't even look at Maeve. He waited for what seemed like an eternity, sweating in that small alcove until he was sure Sophie was long gone from Grosvenor Place and thoroughly on her way home, and then he left.

He was a coward. Sophie had all but said it. And he always knew it.

He had to admit that when he'd received the letter from Sophie this morning, for one brief moment he thought she had reconsidered abandoning their engagement. It was a foolish notion, but he didn't want to face the breadth of what had transpired between them. What she now knew, and what it meant for his family. He set the letter down, unable to finish reading.

How would he tell his mother and father? He had no idea if Sophie would tell her own parents the truth of it. That he'd fathered a child with a whore.

He wiped his brow with a shaky hand, picturing the look on his mother's face when she discovered all his sordid secrets. The Carlisles were sure to find out soon and send notice of their desire to discuss the dissolution of the marriage settlement.

He sat at his dressing table and stared at the letter, her beautiful hand filling the pages with words he dared not read. He would put it someplace where he could almost forget it existed, perhaps under the floorboards with his jugum. He started to fold it, then noticed Dalton's name near the bottom. Did she know that he was the one who'd told him about her and the boxer? He carefully unfolded the letter and read.

When he was done, he wasn't certain he believed it. Some of it made sense, of course, but not the part claiming Dalton had attacked her. He would never behave so devilishly. Certainly, he may have been irate at losing such an exorbitant amount of money on the fight. He'd witnessed Dalton's reaction after the boxer had won, but any man would be angry at such a loss. Even Cuthbert felt the sting of losing the wager he set against the arse. But to be incensed enough to attack Sophie for it seemed absolutely false. Even the part about Dalton being a *Mr. Stone* who kept a bevy of rogues beside him to carry out his orders seemed unlikely. Dalton avoided people of that lowly nature the way the sun avoids the moon. Whores were a different story, of course.

Cuthbert leaned back in the chair and sighed. He hadn't heard from Dalton in a couple of days, but that wasn't unusual. They could go a week without seeing each other.

Two impatient taps on the door pulled him out of his reverie. "Bertie? Are you in there?"

His heart pounded at Mother's voice. What could she want? Had she heard from the Carlisles? He lifted the loose floorboard beside his bed and tossed the letter in the hole. He took a deep breath and let it out slowly before opening the door.

She entered, pulling on her gloves. "I am going into market this morning and would like you to accompany me. We could pay a visit to the Carlisles while out."

Her voice was steady, lighthearted. If the Carlisles had contacted her, she wouldn't sound so cheerful.

"That is nowhere near Kensington." Heat rose into his neck. "Regardless, you cannot go unannounced. Really, Mother."

He couldn't let her go. Everything would be revealed. The lies, the debauchery.

"Surely they would be delighted to see us," she insisted.

"Well, I cannot join you. I . . . I have already made arrangements . . ." he stammered, thinking she wouldn't go without him. She had only visited a handful of times without Father over the twelve or so years they'd known them. He held his breath while she considered her plans.

Mother sighed. "Very well. Next time, perhaps."

Since he had to leave the house to keep up the pretense, he grabbed his coat and headed out the door. Just as he reached the front gate and thought things could not possibly get worse, Lord Greenville's carriage pulled into the drive.

Cuthbert used the walk to Dalton's to imagine all the sordid stories spilling from Mr. Holier-Than-Thou's superior lips. There was no possibility of Mother leaving the house now that Greenville had arrived, blessing her with his presence. Mother was likely sitting in the parlour with a teacup politely poised before her mouth, awaiting to hear one of Greenville's boring tales about the latest party he attended, complete with a list of the other self-important people in attendance. But Cuthbert was sure Greenville had other intentions. After all, he had seen him at his worst, drunk and speaking of wicked matters. He imagined Mother spilling her tea on her lap, her eyes bulging with every dirty detail. But truly, did any of it matter?

He reached Dalton's house, shaking his head free of Greenville and hoping to clear up Sophie's claims about the attack.

A servant answered the door and insisted that Dalton was not taking visitors at present. Before Cuthbert could ascertain the reason, Vivian skirted around the threshold, her eyes pink and puffy and her cheeks blotched. "Mr. Needham."

Cuthbert removed his hat. "Forgive me for the intrusion, Mrs. Fletcher, but I thought your husband might be up for a visit."

She dabbed at her eyes with an embroidered handkerchief, her mouth quivering with emotion. "I am afraid he is unwell."

"Ill?" he asked, careful not to suggest something sinister.

She glanced behind her once, presumably to ensure that no one was within hearing distance. "Injured, actually."

"Oh dear," he said under his breath. Could there be some truth to Sophie's accusations? He swallowed hard. "What happened?"

"A . . . misunderstanding." She wiped away the new tears that sprung forth at the question and shook her head. "I . . . I cannot speak on it further. Good day, Mr. Needham."

The door shut with a decisive click, marking the truth.

After spending several hours at White's and drinking more than his fair share of brandy, he didn't think he could ever go home. How would he explain himself? He'd lost his fiancée, his best friend, and his future all in the matter of a day. And none of that even included what Greenville had likely told his mother.

He lay slumped over the table with his head on his arms, wondering when his ruin had started. Was it the day Dalton had convinced him to go to Parker's for the first time? Was it the moment he'd met Maeve with her enticing smile and voice that promised sin? Or was it much earlier, when he was a lad of twelve and decided that the beautiful, clever girl with the green eyes of a cat would someday be his wife?

A quick tap on his shoulder forced him to sit up. Lord Greenville stared down at him, his perfectly coiffed periwig tied neatly in back with a large blue bow. Why was this damned man always a whisper away when Cuthbert felt his worst? Cuthbert moved to stand, but Greenville rested his hand lightly on his shoulder. "May I be of assistance? Shall I have my carriage brought round for you?"

Words of concern? False, no doubt. "Thank you, milord. But I think you've done enough."

Cuthbert knew he shouldn't have said that, but why should he go on pretending he didn't know what the man was about. Greenville stared at him strangely. "Before I leave you, Mr. Needham, you should know that although I do not approve of your behaviour and the nature in which you have found yourself," he said, twirling his hand in Cuthbert's general location, "I believe there is hope for you yet. Just remember, appearances—when not guarded—are often a glimpse of the unseen. You, young man, are giving us all quite the view." He tipped his hat then walked away.

This time, Cuthbert didn't care if Greenville told his parents he saw him deep in his cups at White's. He had so much more to be concerned about. His head dropped back down on his arms.

"Mr. Needham." Martindale jammed the latest tally of expenses under Cuthbert's arm with a derisive snort. "I am afraid we can no longer add anything to your account until it is paid in full. I will honor it today, considering your . . . state . . . but today is the last, unfortunately."

Cuthbert lifted his head and stared at the numbers scrawled on the paper. *What is another eighteen pounds when I owe hundreds?*

"Very well." He shoved the paper inside his coat. He pushed up from the table, his arms and head feeling heavier than usual, and shuffled out the door. Two men sidled around him, jostling him left and right in the process. He belched loudly in response to their rudeness, then lumbered down the steps to the street.

With only a paltry amount of sterling in his pocket, he hired a hackney to Covent Garden. He couldn't remember getting there and assumed he must've fallen asleep during the ride. He shoved his way through the door of the brothel, the smell of damp furniture and tobacco smoke in the air.

The bullyboy stopped him abruptly with his hand placed firmly on his chest. "You're a bit brandy-faced, mate. Don't want no trouble."

Cuthbert mumbled his assent and staggered to the back. Three whores stood together, the fair-haired one with her back to him. He tapped her on the shoulder, and she turned to face him. She grinned broadly, the small gap between her two front teeth fully exposed. She crinkled her nose, the spray of freckles on her cheeks lifting slightly. "Back again, lovey!"

"You stole my money," Cuthbert said sloppily, wagging his finger in her face.

She stuck it in her mouth and sucked, batting her eyes flirtatiously. Just as his breeches tightened, she plucked it out. "I'll make it up to you, I will."

"I do not want you to make it up to me. I want my money back." He wasn't sure if his words came out the way he intended, but judging from her pout, he assumed the message was received.

"Come now, lovey. Let Biddy make you forget all about your troubles." She threaded her arm through his. "Would you like that?"

She snuggled into him, running her hand down his cheek and over his chest. Her touch was soft but sure. How many times had he wished that Sophie would stroke him the same way?

He clutched her hand and pressed it to his groin. "Bring the other two girls with you."

When he opened his eyes, it was dark outside. Biddy and the other two whores lay naked in a tangle of sheets beside him, their bodies contorted in ways that any man would find a curiosity. He stared at their breasts and the tufts of hair between their legs but didn't feel the burn of desire that he normally did when he looked at Dalton's sketches or dreamed of women late at night. Perhaps he had finally been cured of his sexual maladies, indecent thoughts, and ache to pleasure himself. Or was he now numb to what had become mundane.

He bent to put on his breeches, and a wave of dizziness struck him. Bile rose in his throat, and he seized the chamber pot just as he retched. One of the girls fidgeted and moaned in her sleep.

Cuthbert slid the pot back under the bed, dressed, then slipped out the door.

He walked home, the sounds of the night marking his steps. *Bang, click, screech. Bang, click, screech.* Someone on the next street tinkered in his shop—a farrier or a blacksmith, perhaps—sending high-pitched metal clinks into the night sky. The scrape of a shovel was followed by the acrid, earthy smell of burning coal. Cuthbert wondered who these people were up so late.

Did they live in tiny nearby hovels or in a single room above their shops? Was there anyone out there who cared that they were not yet snug in their beds? Did they have wives with soft white arms that held them close when they needed it?

As he neared his home, the sounds faded. The house was dark and quiet. He went upstairs to his room, where Raymond had been kind enough to light a fire. He wondered if his parents knew. Perhaps they'd paid the fagetter his due. He doubted it.

He undressed, then lifted the floorboard beside his bed. Sophie's letter glowed in the dark as if lit from within. He opened it and read it once again at his dressing table, her words even more striking the second time. It was strange that although he knew what to expect before he read it, the words seemed to hold more power with truth behind them. He folded it back up and stood before the fire, his head still heavy from the brandy.

"I am humiliated, loathed, and now . . . impoverished. What have I left?" he asked as soft as a prayer.

He flung the letter into the flames and watched it burn, the edges curling and crumbling. A fine plume of smoke twirled upward, then vanished.

"Farewell, Sophie," he whispered.

He walked back to the loose floorboard and crouched to replace it. The red velvet pouch containing his jugum sat in a sad little clump inside. He lifted it out and untied the silk string that held it closed. Spermatorrhoea. That was what it was intended to cure. But as he weighed the metal ring in his palm, he realized it was hopeless. Or perhaps he was hopeless. He had proven it only hours earlier in the arms of three whores. He would never change. And in time, everyone would know exactly who he was.

He walked back over to the hearth and threw the jugum and the pouch beside the ashes that were now the burnt letter. In seconds, the velvet danced in the flames and the jagged metal ring turned black.

Chapter 36

Tom sat against the wall of his cell with almost a dozen other prisoners, his hands bound in chains. Although it wasn't the same cell he'd lived in only nine months earlier at Newgate, the accusation was *exactly* the same. Unfortunately, so was the all too familiar stench of urine and stale bodies that permeated the air.

He wondered who had accused him of being the London Monster. He was told that someone had identified him by name. It could be Stone, but even with the pummeling he'd given him, he didn't think Stone would want him locked up and unable to fight. That would only ensure that he'd never get his money back. Could it be Sophie's betrothed? Did he know of their acquaintance? Or was it someone from John Jackson's camp who wanted revenge for Tom winning the fight? For that matter, it could be anyone associated with the past fighters he'd defeated.

Or it could be one of his father's political opponents, someone desperate to ruin his campaign now that he was predicted to win. He hoped his arrest had not made the papers. He couldn't stomach his father losing the election because of him.

The prisoner next to him tapped him on the arm. "What you in here for, mate?"

Tom stared at the man who looked as if he hadn't seen a meal in weeks.

"Crimes I didn't commit," he offered, intentionally vague. If they thought he was the London Monster, he wasn't sure what they might do.

"Me too." He exposed a jagged smile like a picket fence with every other post kicked in.

Another prisoner chimed in. "Aye, we're all innocent, ain't we?"

A few of them laughed, their mirth ending in a series of coughs.

Tom rested his elbows on his knees, his head in his hands, the chain on his wrists jangling with the movement. He knew Sophie could clear him of the attack on her, but how could she prove he wasn't the London Monster?

"What's that there, mate?" The skinny prisoner next to him wriggled his finger at his hand. Was he ever going to escape that accusation either?

"An M," he answered dryly.

The other prisoners stared at him, their bodies suddenly rigid.

"I suppose that's for another crime ye didn' commit." But this time, no one laughed.

Tom woke the next morning to the clucking of hens. He glanced past the bars of his cell and down the narrow hall, expecting to see a brood of chickens flapping their wings in a desperate attempt to be freed, but nothing was there. Slowly, the clucking turned to shouts and the occasional word. Whatever was happening had attracted the attention of several rather boisterous women.

His stomach growled, the pang of hunger finally hitting him. The rectangle of murky light that landed on the floor opposite him from the tiny window high on the wall told him it was well after dawn, yet no gaoler had delivered food. Not that he would eat it anyway.

He listened carefully to the voices nearby, all seemingly female, but he couldn't decipher what they were saying.

Minutes later, the jingling of keys announced the arrival of two guards. They stopped in front of Tom's cell, their hands resting on the daggers at their hips. The taller one with the puffed-out chest pointed at him. "You. Up."

Tom knew when prison guards requested one's presence, it was not usually to share a cup of chocolate. He stood slowly, steeling himself for the likely beating to follow. The prisoners who were awake sluggishly lifted their heads to watch him edge around the open gate.

The tall guard grabbed his arm and shoved him ahead. "You're a lucky devil, you are."

They led him down the dank passage and past a number of other cells, all filled with bedraggled, half-starved men. Those leaning against the bars stared questioningly as he walked by.

His heart thundered in his chest. He thought they might be taking him out to the yard to be shot, but it was Sunday, and executions—even unlawful ones—were not allowed on the Sabbath.

"I have not yet been tried." He hoped the guards were not the dishonest type.

The tall one was about to utter something when he stopped. Tom watched him work out an idea in his head. The guard studied him through slit eyes. "Ain't you the boxer?"

The shorter one straightened, eyes wide. "Aye," he said, dragging out the word. "I seen you twice. You really should've taken down that huff in December. What was his name?"

The taller nodded with recognition. "Future."

Tom's shoulders started to relax. "Futrell."

"Aye. That's the one!" The shorter guard sucked in his gut while tugging on his coat. It was that little shuffle smaller men often did in his presence to demonstrate they too were not capons. "But the last match with you and that Gentleman . . . you really got him good, you did."

Tom harrumphed. "I hope you did not wager against me on that one."

"You were favoured. I made ten bob," he boasted, grinning from ear to ear.

Tom managed a smile, somewhat convinced his immediate fate was not death. "Where are you taking me?"

The tall guard smacked him on the back of his shoulder. "To the magistrate. Got a whole clutch of women sayin' you ain't the monster."

They passed through the gate to the Old Bailey, the memory of standing in the exact same spot only nine months earlier so sharp, he could still smell the pungent, rancid meat from the butchery that was no longer there.

The shorter guard unlocked a heavy wooden door. "Lift your hands."

Tom did as he said, and the guard removed his chains.

"In there." The tall guard stepped aside to let him into the poorly lit room. He blinked his eyes to adjust to the darkness. Inside, standing two deep, were a dozen of the molls from Mother Cluck's Coffeehouse. And Sophie.

Tom wasn't sure whether he should laugh or fear for his life. He glanced at the magistrate, who looked completely overwhelmed by the unusual group before him. A few of the molls dabbed at their eyes as he walked in farther to face the magistrate. They were all dressed in fanciful gowns, their wigs neatly coiffed and decorated with baubles and bows. The feisty moll who'd batted him wildly that night the monster attacked, waved coquettishly with her handkerchief pinched between her fingers.

Sophie smiled at him with worried eyes.

The magistrate cleared his throat. "These women have come to your defense."

Did the judge not realize they were not women? He wore no spectacles, and with only two sconces on the wall behind the molls, Tom realized they probably appeared only in silhouette to the man. Tom pressed his lips together to hide his amusement.

"They say you attempted to rescue that one when the monster accosted her." He jerked his hand in the direction of the feisty moll, who now batted her eyes in what he assumed was an effort to appear harmless.

"'Tis true, milord." He grinned at Sophie, grateful she had been so clever.

"Did you get a good look at the culprit?" The judge squinted dubiously at him.

"I have seen him several times. Miss Carlisle drew a rather accurate depiction of the man and left it with the constable's office a few months ago," Tom replied.

"I could draw you another, if you'd like," Sophie proposed. "With Mr. Hayes here to assist my memory, I am certain I can sketch his likeness precisely."

With the sweep of his hand over his desk, the magistrate offered her paper, a quill, and ink. She limped over, clearly suffering from the cut in her heel. Tom took her by the arm and pulled a chair up to the desk for her. After ten minutes and some descriptive reminders, Tom stepped back while she presented the judge with the London Monster's likeness.

"He is a gentleman, milord." Tom watched while the judge studied the sketch. "I have heard him speak."

"A gentleman! Not according to his victims, I assure you." He shifted uncomfortably in his large leather chair. "If we were not in the presence of ladies, I would speak clearly regarding his rather profane execrations."

"What I mean, milord, is his manner of speech is . . . educated."

The judge's brow furrowed, seemingly unconvinced that the monster wasn't lowborn.

Sophie stood with effort, the smell of lavender and honey swirling over to Tom's nose. He inched closer beside her and surreptitiously inhaled to capture more of her scent. He would never tire of it.

She straightened with confidence. "I know it might be hard to believe, milord, but often those perceived to be true gentlemen are not always as they seem."

She'd said it resolutely with an obvious tone of sadness and regret. Tom wanted to take her in his arms but fought the urge, knowing the inappropriate nature of such a gesture could make the judge rethink Tom's respectability and reliability as a witness.

"Very well." The judge turned to Tom, Sophie's sketch in his hands. "Go with the guards and they will see to your discharge."

The molls waved and blew kisses as the hackneys drove them away. Tom wrapped Sophie in his arms and pressed her to his chest. *Will you ever be mine?* he wondered.

"I cannot believe it worked." She smiled up at him. "They were so excited to plead your case."

"I noticed you rounded up the more attractive ones." Not all of them were the molls he used to lure the monster in St. James's Park. These were more practiced in the art of being feminine.

"I had the hairier ones stay behind." She laughed. "When I told them what it was for, they were happy to come. They didn't seem to fear being arrested for unnatural behaviour. I even offered them a pound each, but not one of them took it. They felt horrible for botching our plans that night."

"And the bawd? I refuse to believe she allowed her molls to leave without some sort of payment."

"She set her price, of course. But I told her I would write an article instead about how she was instrumental in trying to catch the monster. I assured her it would help her in the future should she ever find herself dealing with legal matters regarding her . . . employ."

"And she agreed?" He couldn't believe it. That woman was as greedy as a nun was charitable.

"She did," she said with a shrug.

"And what did you tell the magistrate about Stone?"

Sophie sighed. "I told him . . . I knew him, and that there was no attack."

"What?" He dragged his fingers through his hair. She couldn't have let him go.

"I couldn't, Tom. I have known Dalton for years. I know his wife. His parents."

Frustration boiled within his chest. "How did you explain your injuries, then?"

He gently grazed the back of her head with his fingertips, feeling a knot the size of a walnut.

"I said he'd been drinking and I was trying to get him home, but we stumbled . . ."

"The man was going to kill you, Sophie."

She shook her head sadly. "I have to believe he would never have done it."

Tom inhaled deeply to calm his racing heart. Stone would've killed her. He had something to prove.

"After you were arrested, I had the constables help me get him in a hackney to take him home." She paused, clearly uncomfortable with the memory. "I delivered him to his wife and told her the truth. I know she believed me. She saw the marks on my neck and my torn gown. It will be up to her as to how she chooses to handle it."

Although Tom didn't agree with her decision to let him go, he had to trust her judgment. She apparently knew him better than he did. He'd never pictured Stone with a wife. With any luck, she was a shrew who'd make him wish he'd been sent to Newgate for what he'd done.

He kissed the top of her head and pulled her close. "I pray we have seen the last of him."

"He would be a fool to attempt to harm me again. I think he understands that now."

"When I think of how he treated Maeve, and then what he was going to do to you—"

She suddenly stiffened in his arms. "Maeve is in the hospital! London Lock. I forgot to tell you."

His heart sank, knowing that only the syphilitic went there to either be cured or to die. He listened while Sophie spoke about her sickness, why she left Parker's, and how she needed Sophie to find Emily, the truth of Maeve's circumstances almost too horrific to believe.

"We shall find her," he assured her.

He thought of the first time Maeve had nursed him back to health after one of his fights. She'd sung words of comfort as she pressed poultices to his injuries with gentle hands. He hadn't sensed her true feelings for him back then. He wondered how much he'd hurt her every time he proffered her a book or coin instead of his affection. How did God choose who would love whom? And why were some left with no one to love them?

"I shall do everything I can to help her." Tom waited for the next hackney to push ahead in line. The carriage traveled up the street slowly, the horse long in the tooth.

"Thank you for all you have done for me," he said. She had risked so much for nothing in return.

The jarvey jumped off his bench and lowered the footplate. Tom helped her up the step, supporting her as she favoured her injured foot. She seemed pensive, a small frown visible between her brows.

"Please tell me you are who you say you are." She touched his face, her green eyes pleading. "It seems that everyone I thought I knew has turned out to be an imposter."

He saw the doubt and fear in her tentative smile and felt the uncertainty as she grazed his face with the tips of her fingers. "I promise." He kissed her softly on the lips. "I am the man who loves you."

A Note

May 1790

Damn fools!

How could they let him go? The magistrate who cleared him of the charges should be tarred and feathered. They had an actual firsthand account—my firsthand account—of an attack, and yet they set him free.

The papers don't even know what to make of it. Him. Me. What have you.

No one can agree as to whether there is one of me, several of me, or if I even exist at all. Hopefully the Public Ledger *will convince everyone that I never existed. That I was merely a pickpocket who may have injured a woman while slicing her gown in search of sterling, giving rise to a phantom creature kept alive by the wild imaginations of a few lonely women in desperate need of attention. Perhaps this Miss Barrs, who lied about being attacked and was discovered to be a fraud, will send the Bow Street Runners on their way in search of real criminals.*

Of the eleven attacks recorded in the papers so far this month, I have only been involved in eight, I can assure you. The other three were either completely fabricated or committed by a charlatan yearning for my notoriety. In all eight cases, there were only six in which I drew blood. Nothing serious.

A few men were arrested. I thought it might be clever to remain at home while they are rotting in gaol. That way, the Runners and all of London would assume they found their man. But the past few weeks have proven difficult for me. I blame it on the season and all the young ladies parading about in low-necked gowns, displaying their wares brazenly. They draw me out of my home, offering a feminine ear into which I may whisper my true desires. Unfortunately, this inability to temper my urges is what confirms to the Runners that they have not caught their man after all.

Tonight, I venture onto Jermyn Street, where I have had success before, but I leave my nosegay behind. I used it only a few times until one of my imposters stole my idea and employed it against a woman in Salisbury Square. This evening, my method will be different.

The street is relatively busy—naturally an effect of the mild weather. A petite young lady, perhaps a maidservant, with dark hair and fair features hurries ahead of me in the direction of Leicester Square. I follow her, avoiding the glances of passersby. As the crowd thins, I approach her. My groin aches with lust as I grow near.

"Do you wish for company tonight?" I ask, only a few steps behind.

She glances over her shoulder but continues to walk quickly. "No, sir."

"But surely a lovely lady as yourself would care for an escort." I rub my hand over my breeches with anticipation. I am as hard as stone.

"I wish to be alone," she says, not bothering to look back this time.

My rage starts to build. "And why is that? Do you find yourself above me?"

She begins to move faster, the back of her skirts bobbing with each step.

"I will plunge myself into you. Taste you. Would you like that?" I am ready to throw her on the ground and give her my cock until she screams.

She starts to run, and I chase her. "You dirty slattern! I could split you in two!"

I reach into my coat and unsheathe my blade. She stumbles slightly, and I grab her arm. She tries to spin out of my grasp, so I slice her across the hip. She calls out, but no one is nearby. I rush after her, and then a man in his nightclothes emerges from his home, holding a lit candlestick.

"Who goes there?" he shouts into the night.

I back into a dark threshold and wait while he shines his light in all directions. Seemingly satisfied nothing is amiss, he reenters his home and shuts the door behind him.

"Damn him! I had her!" I mutter to myself. I peek around the wall, but she is nowhere to be seen.

My heart thumps in my throat. Why did she deny me? I unbutton my breeches and grab myself roughly. They all think they are better than me. I would be the best lover they ever had. They don't know what I can do. I stroke faster, sensing relief is imminent.

No one understands the madness that dwells within my soul. I am a man. Only a man. Not a monster.

I close my eyes and moan as my hand fills with heat.

Chapter 37

Sophie sat at her dressing table, reading the letter from Mr. Edward Topham, editor of the *World*. Peg stood behind her with her hands tightly clasped as if she were about to burst with curiosity.

"Well, then." Sophie folded the letter back up and slid it under her oil lamp.

Peg exhaled, deflated, her hands untwining. "Do not give up, dear. One day, someone is going to recognize your talent and publish your work."

She turned to face Peg. "They *are* going to publish it. It was accepted."

Peg inhaled sharply. "That is wonderful news!"

Sophie sighed. "I suppose so."

Peg rested her hand lightly on Sophie's shoulder. "Then why are you not happy, dear?"

Sophie stared at herself in the mirror. Why wasn't she happy? The article was going to be in the paper tomorrow, according to Mr. Topham's letter. He had praised her writing and the personalization she'd added to the piece. He liked her style, he said. Or at least, he liked James Evans's style and wanted to feature her articles regularly. She would finally have her work in print. Monthly? Weekly? But one windfall wasn't going to surmount all the other calamities and heartbreaks in her life.

It was strange how it didn't seem to matter that much to her anymore.

She patted Peg's hand and smiled. "I have to go to Bloomsbury."

"Very well. I will get my things." Peg started out the bedroom door, but Sophie called her back.

"There is no need for you to come with me. I will call for the carriage." With Dalton no longer a threat and the London Monster known only to attack in the evening, she didn't worry about going out without an escort. "I only need you to tell my mother we are going to Smithfield. She will want some hindquarters for dinner tonight. 'Tis the perfect alibi."

"How will you get about on your own?"

Sophie wriggled her foot. "I barely notice the pain anymore. You did a lovely job nursing it."

Peg studied her through squinted eyes. "I can see right through that compliment. I will let you be, but you will need one of your father's canes if you plan on traipsing about."

"Very well." Sophie stood, careful not to put too much pressure on her foot. She tested it with a bit more weight, the bandage wrapped around it helping to cushion her heel.

"'Tis late. Will you at least tell me where you are headed?" she asked, her face painted with worry.

"I am going to help a friend."

The Foundling Hospital was situated on Guilford Street. Sophie hobbled, with the help of her father's silver-tipped cane, through the gate and down the long path to the main brick building flanked by two imposing wings on either side. A few people milled about, but she saw no signs of any children in the large courtyard or inside the endless rows of windows.

She was guided to a small office, where she waited for the secretary. The room was dark, lit only by two small oil lamps on either side of the desk and the grey light streaming in the window. Papers littered the desktop, and some lay on the floor behind the clerk's chair. Sophie's stomach turned at the thought that the record keeping might not be as efficient as it should be.

"Forgive me, madam. I am afraid there was a bit of a scuffle in the dining commons amongst the lads." The secretary, a portly gentleman, circled around the desk, his stomach gliding over it and knocking a few more papers to the floor. "You know how children can be when one thinks he has not received as much white soup as the other."

She had no idea how children could be, but she was relieved to know that they were on the premises and hopeful that Emily might be there as well.

"How may I be of assistance?" He settled into his chair with a breathy huff.

"I am looking for a little girl. She was brought here on December tenth in eighty-six at the age of four months. Her name is Emily Hannigen."

"And you are . . .?" he asked, his fingers steepled on the swell of his stomach.

"A friend of her mother's."

"And where is she?"

Sophie straightened in her chair. "She is ill. Unable to be here."

He tugged his waistcoat over his protruding belly. "Well, madam. I am afraid I am unable to assist you. We keep all information under strict lock and key unless ordered by the vice president or treasurer. As the secretary, I can only provide information regarding the child to the mother."

"But she cannot come. She . . . is . . ."

His brow rose in question. "Did she provide you with some sort of trinket that would identify you as a person worthy of this information?"

"A trinket?"

"Mothers typically offer some sort of token that only a family member or she herself would have possession of to prove a relation to the child, therefore allowing access to the child's records," he explained.

Sophie's throat started to burn. "There must be another way."

"Perhaps you can acquire it from her when you see her." He shuffled through the mess of papers before him, demonstrating his loss of interest in her plight.

Sophie shambled down the length of the courtyard, feeling as helpless as a leaf caught in a swirling eddy. Maeve had only provided her with information, not a trinket, and with the sun sinking below the horizon, she'd never make it to Lock Hospital in time to see her. She could ask her about it tomorrow. Perhaps she could write a letter Sophie could present to the Secretary. Surely that would suffice.

While she rode home, she wondered what had become of Emily. With her catalepsy, she worried that her caretaker might not be giving her the proper attention she needed. Sophie prayed that wouldn't be the case and that the hospital was doing what was necessary, or if she was with a family, they thought of her as one of their own and treated her thus.

She arrived home to her parents waiting in the parlour, Peg behind them, unable to meet Sophie's gaze.

"Where have you been? You should be resting your ankle!" Mother nervously ran her fingers along the strand of pearls at her neck. Sophie had told her she twisted her ankle the night of the attack and fallen into some thorn bushes to explain her torn dress. Peg had seemed suspicious, but Mother accepted it all as fact.

Sophie glanced at Peg, whose lower lip was now trembling. The excuse that they went to Smithfield Market clearly hadn't worked this time. "I have been at the Foundling Hospital, if you must know."

"*If we must know?*" Father asked, his voice a bit louder than usual. "Have you no sense, child? You cannot go about without a care in the world, as if the monster is of no concern—"

"What were you doing at the Foundling Hospital?" Mother asked.

Sophie took a deep breath. It was time to tell the truth. About everything. "I am searching for a little girl. The daughter of a prostitute who—"

"A prostitute!" Father shouted. "What on earth—"

"Have you gone mad?" Mother interrupted.

They spoke over one another, no one listening and everyone talking until Sophie put up her hands. "Quiet!"

Peg's eyes grew as round as saucers.

"If you will only allow me to explain." She told them about masquerading as a man to gather information for her writing, meeting Maeve outside the theatre, seeing her regularly at Parker's, attending boxing matches, submitting her articles, and researching the London Monster. She even told them about the article that would be published tomorrow. When she was done, her parents sat on the sofa, their mouths agape, clearly unable to utter a word.

But she hadn't finished. She took a deep, steadying breath. "And I should let you know that I will not marry Bertie."

Her mother blinked her eyes in shock. "What?"

"I have already told him." Her insides quaked with nerves, but Tom's last words to her before she rode off in the hackney gave her the strength to continue. "I am in love with someone else."

"In love?" Father asked distastefully, as if she had just told him she had the plague.

Mother draped her arm around her. "You are speaking foolishly, dear. You simply need a good rest—"

"No, Mother. I want to have purpose. And Tom understands that."

"Tom? Who is this Tom?" Father rubbed his forehead anxiously.

"Mr. Needham would make the perfect husband. He loves you." Mother squeezed her around the shoulders in a conciliatory manner. "I can see it in the way he looks at you, dear."

"But *I* do not love *him*." Although her heart galloped with her declaration, she was relieved all of it was out in the open now. She was tired of pretending. "There are things . . . unforgivable things . . ."

"What could be so unforgivable?" Her mother laid a gentle hand on hers, warm and tender. "If it is what I think it is, you need not allow it to upset you. Many men take lovers."

Father turned away, then mumbled an excuse to leave the room, having something to attend to in his study. Peg followed, padding away as quiet as a mouse.

"No, Mother. I could possibly forgive that." Maeve's watery smile when Bertie walked through the chink in the curtain at the hospital flitted before her eyes. "There are secrets I cannot tell you because they do not belong to me, but you should know that I will not marry a man for whom I have no respect. You must trust me on this."

"I see," Mother said, head bowed. "Are the Needhams aware?"

"I am not sure what they know, but I made my position quite clear in a letter to Bertie. Perhaps he has shared my feelings with them." There were still plenty of things she hadn't divulged. Nothing about Dalton and the attack, for they would surely go straight to the magistrate. She'd told that messy lie about the thorn bushes when she'd returned that night looking as if she were dragged behind a cart. And she couldn't tell her parents anything more about Tom. At least not yet.

"I suppose a conversation must be had between the families, considering your wedding is . . . *was* only a few weeks away." Her mother fiddled with her pearls as she instructed the footman to bring the carriage around. She turned, offering her a tight smile. "We will discuss the rest later."

It was late into the evening when her parents returned. Sophie lay on her bed in her nightclothes, her mind stirring with endless possibilities about how the Needhams would take the news. Could they deny her request to end the betrothal? Would Bertie be present during the discussion, and would he argue against the dissolution? Would her parents—or Bertie—mention her affection for Tom? Even if everyone agreed and the marriage was called off, there were no guarantees that her parents would allow her to see Tom ever again.

The door slammed downstairs, jarring Sophie out of her thoughts. She slid on her slippers and, favoring her injured foot, shuffled downstairs with the help of her cane to find her parents in Father's study.

"Sit," he demanded without looking at her.

She sat on the edge of her seat and listened patiently while her parents relayed the conversation they'd had with the Needhams. They explained that since no banns were posted, no laws were broken. Unfortunately, though, the

Needhams insisted that some of the terms of the promised dowry must be honored. Father agreed, although reluctantly, he said, since Sophie was the one to call off the marriage. There was no mention of Bertie's indiscretions, so Sophie assumed Bertie had not told them the truth. However, his deceit didn't matter to her as long as she was no longer bound to marry him.

"Forgive me for the trouble I have caused you both," she said, truly sorry for the humiliation they must've felt that evening but relieved that it was over. She stood to leave, and her mother called her back.

"We want to know who this Tom is," Mother said resolutely.

Sophie returned to her chair, resting her hands on the knob of her cane. "His name is Thomas Hayes."

"That tells us naught. Who is he?" Father said, insisting.

She couldn't tell them he was a pugilist. That would end the conversation immediately with a final mandate never to see him again. "He is the son of Joseph Hayes, the gentleman running for a seat in the House of Commons."

"A commoner?" Mother asked, scandalized.

"A gentleman," she answered.

Father leaned back in his chair and sighed. "Of commerce. He owns a colliery, I believe."

"And invests in shipping," Sophie offered quickly as she shifted in her seat. "You know him, Father?"

"Not personally. But I heard him speak a few months ago about a desire to legalize gaming. But I fear it will only—"

Sophie shot out of her seat. "Say no more, Father. Read my article tomorrow, and then we shall talk."

Upon her mother's insistence, Sophie left the house the next morning with Peg by her side. Although they hadn't forbade her from seeing Tom, they hadn't permitted it either. Peg's presence was a clear message that Sophie would never leave home without a chaperone from here on out.

The ride to Billingsgate seemed eternally long, Peg peppering Sophie with a thousand questions along the way.

"You said he is tall. I always find the tall ones dashing." Peg patted her hair, primping in a way that made Sophie want to laugh. "And his brothers. Are they tall?"

Sophie took a deep breath, hoping the onslaught of questions would end soon. "I have only met one of them. But he is nearly as tall."

In a matter of minutes, the carriage stopped at the docks. Peg gasped, obvious worry in her creased brow. "Look at all the men."

With a smile, Sophie waved it off dismissively, then accepted the hand of the footman helping her down the step. Peg could be so prudish.

They walked to Tom's warehouse, Peg nudging her every now and then when one of the stevedores made a coarse remark, but Sophie waved that off too.

"'Tis awfully loud here." Peg shook her head disapprovingly. Between the screeching gulls, the clanging of ship rigging, the cursing and grunting of the dockworkers, and the fishwives shouting their wares, Sophie had to agree.

"Follow me." Sophie gripped Peg's hand tightly and led her through the chaos to a young lad who stood atop a crate selling papers. "Do you have the *World?*"

"Aye, miss. Tuppence." He flashed his palm.

She handed Peg her cane while she searched for two pennies. "Here you go." She dropped the coins in his hand in exchange for the paper, then continued to the warehouse.

Tom stood with another man just outside, shading his eyes and pointing at the Thames. Sophie's heart skipped. "Tom!"

He turned in her direction, his mouth emerging into a smile as he recognized her.

"Is that your gentleman?" Peg asked slowly, clearly awestruck.

Sophie nodded.

Peg squeezed her hand. "He's a fine one."

Tom doffed his hat as they neared, still smiling. "This is a pleasant surprise. How are you feeling, Miss Sophie?"

"Quite well." She appreciated the display of formality in front of Peg, but he seemed too businesslike for a man who'd declared his love for her a few days ago. "This is my maid, Mrs. Margaret."

Peg held out her hand for a kiss, a pink blush in her cheeks.

Tom kissed it and then Sophie's. "Please come inside, ladies."

The warehouse was dark, so it took Sophie a few seconds for her eyes to adjust. She turned to Tom, desperate for a few moments alone. "Would it be a bother if Peg waited in your office while we spoke?"

"Of course not." He extended his arm towards the back in invitation.

Sophie rested her hand on Peg's arm. "Would you mind?"

Peg shot her a sharp look of reproach but followed Tom to the office anyway. When he returned to Sophie's side, she handed him the paper.

He unfolded it.

"Page three. Halfway down," she instructed. She waited anxiously while he read, her heartbeat in her throat.

"Is this your article?" he asked incredulously.

"James Evans's article, actually," she quipped.

His features lit up, eyes glistening. "You did it, Sophie."

She kissed him on the lips, catching him by surprise. "Do you like it?"

He seemed unsure how to respond. He touched his fingers to his lips, and she knew he was thinking about the kiss and not the article. He smiled sadly. "'Tis remarkable."

She watched him scan the article once again. Out of the corner of her eye, she saw Peg peek around the doorway of the office. She knew it would only be a matter of time before her maid insisted they leave. "We need to visit Maeve."

He seemed surprised by the change of subject. "I was hoping to go today, but a shipment that was delayed finally arrived."

"Tomorrow, then?" She couldn't help but feel something was wrong. It was as if he found her presence a menace.

"First thing," he agreed.

She explained she'd gone to the Foundling Hospital and was told she needed a personal item from Maeve in order to enquire about Emily. He merely nodded as she spoke. "I thought a letter might do."

He tilted his head to the side, his blue eyes questioning. "Do you think it was a good idea to bring your maid here?"

She suddenly felt nervous about what she had done. Had she misunderstood him when he said he loved her? Did he no longer want to see her? Now she wasn't sure she should tell him the news about her broken betrothal to Bertie. "Would you like for me to leave?"

He grabbed her hands and held them to his lips. "Of course not. I simply think it might not be in your best interest if your maid knows about our . . . friendship. You are promised to another, after all."

Her stomach tumbled. "Did you mean what you said to me in front of the Old Bailey?"

He took a deep breath and let it out slowly. "You know I did, Sophie. But I understand it doesn't change anything between us."

"And if I told you it did?" she asked cautiously.

He looked at her sideways with what was unmistakably hope.

Her heartbeat slowed to a pace of calm resolve. "I am no longer betrothed."

Chapter 38

"Are you not having breakfast?" Henry balanced a slice of toast elegantly between two fingers.

"Not today. In a hurry," Tom said, swinging on his coat.

Roger lumbered past him. "In a hurry for what? To engage in more mischief, I presume. A tavern? Brothel? Which one is it, Thomas?"

His acerbic comment would have rubbed Tom wrong in the past, but nothing would upset him today. Sophie was no longer spoken for, and that was all that mattered. "Both, perhaps," he answered cheerily.

Tom shut the door behind him and dashed down the front steps, having promised to meet Sophie at the Lock Hospital when it opened. The breeze was delightful, and thin white clouds scudded across the crisp blue sky. Normally, he would've enjoyed the walk, but he didn't want to arrive a single minute late this morning, so he hired a hackney.

Father had been elated with Sophie's article yesterday, especially after its effects were confirmed in another paper today. The *Oracle* praised Father's forward thinking and predicted his win in the House as almost guaranteed. The author even used a quote to support the idea from the Prince of Wales stating that The Pretty Punch was one of the finest pugilists he'd ever seen. Father had shot a quick glance at Tom and smiled to himself when he'd read it. Tom had no idea when the prince had attended one of his matches but, with his approval, the electors would not likely vote against him.

Tom arrived at the hospital a few minutes before the doors opened. He had never before been nervous about seeing Sophie, but something about the possibilities that lay ahead made his insides buzz as if he might not be able to contain his joy when she appeared. He considered entering but politely declined the clerk's offer, unable to imagine sitting still on one of the benches in the hall. Tom stood outside and checked his pocket watch. It was a quarter of an hour past, and Sophie had yet to arrive.

He wondered if they'd be able to find Emily quickly enough. From what Sophie had said, it didn't seem like Maeve was faring well. As long as he had known her, she had never been sick. Of course, she may have been, but Maeve was not one to complain. After all she'd endured at the hands of Stone and all the other men who'd used her, she had never once grumbled an objection about the way she was treated. It always came down to the money, of course. Even when Tom offered to take care of Stone, she wouldn't let him. It was the one thing about which he wished he hadn't listened to her.

And now she carried a child, its father likely unknown. He hoped that fact would keep her strong, fighting.

He paced in front of the entrance, his emotions being tossed about like leaves in a storm. He was torn between his anguish over Maeve's condition and his excitement over seeing Sophie.

Sophie showed up a few minutes later, her green eyes lit as if from within. She whispered something to Peg, who remained in the carriage.

"Did you miss me?" Sophie asked.

He wanted to take her in his arms but, with too many people around, he squeezed her hand instead. "Only the way a winter garden misses sunshine."

She squeezed his hand back, and they stepped through the archway of the hospital.

"The Prince of Wales is an enthusiast, it seems," she whispered on the way to the clerk.

He leaned closer, his voice low. "So I've heard. I have no recollection as to when he attended one of my fights."

"You would not have seen him. He goes in plain dress, apparently, with only one man in tow."

"And you know this how?" he asked, amused.

"I am a reporter. I have my ways," she answered, smiling. She approached the desk and spoke in hushed tones with the clerk. He said a few words, then signaled for a nun to escort them back to a small alcove partitioned with curtains.

Tom sucked in his breath when he saw Maeve. She looked like a small child underneath the bedclothes, not the vivacious, hearty woman he remembered.

Sophie pulled back the sheet and gasped. Maeve's hands were tied to the sides of the bedframe. She swung to face the nun in retreat. "What is going on here? Untie her at once!"

"She has fits of anger and must be restrained," the nun insisted, her lips finishing in a tight line.

"I'll do it." Tom tugged out the knots and freed her hands from the binding. He snapped open the curtain for the nun to leave. "For a charitable hospital, I find your manner of treating the patients rather *uncharitable.*"

He stood back while Sophie roused her from her sleep with soft words and a few strokes of her hair. Maeve coughed, her breath coming in ragged spurts. She stared at Tom, but her face remained blank, showing no sign of recognition.

He approached the bed gingerly, and she squinted at him. "Tommy?"

She was the only person to call him that. There was a time when it had bothered him but, at the moment, it warmed his heart. "Aye. 'Tis good to see you, Maeve."

She struggled to sit with Sophie's help. Her hand fluttered over her messy hair like a butterfly unsure of where to land. She tried to manage a smile, but it seemed impossible. Tom felt completely helpless.

Sophie rested her hand on her back. "How are you feeling, dear?"

"The Lord spoke to me last night and promised to join me with my parents."

Tom exchanged glances with Sophie.

"Have you been eating?" Sophie motioned towards a bowl of porridge that sat untouched, two flies darting over it in a frenzy. Tom swatted at them unsuccessfully.

"I have no desire for food."

"Your baby needs you to eat," Sophie whispered.

Maeve shook her head slightly, then licked her parched lips. "I hope . . . I hope you two find happiness."

Tom shared a look with Sophie, regret filling his gut over what he could never have given Maeve. "I—"

Maeve's hand slowly lifted to stop him. "I know you care for each other. Nothing would make me happier than to see two people I love so dearly with one another."

Tom knew how hard it must be for her to say those words. It made him all the more grateful for her blessing. He sat beside her and held her hand. "We are going to find Emily."

A tear escaped the corner of her eye, her lips trembling. "If I could only see her before I die."

"Do not speak of your death, Maeve." Tom knew she wouldn't live much longer, but it pained him to hear her acknowledgement of her fate. "We will find Emily and bring her to you as soon as we can, but you must do your best to stay strong until then. For her and for your unborn child. Would you promise me that?"

She stared up at him, her eyelids dipping over her pupils. "I cannot keep anything down. A bit of ale, perhaps."

His chest ached. "I will make sure you get all the ale you need."

Sophie ran her hand gently down Maeve's back. "The secretary at the Foundling Hospital says we need something from you that proves you are her mother. Do you have anything like that?"

Maeve closed her eyes, her breath hitching. "Under the bed. In the box."

Tom reached under the cot and pulled out a small leather trunk closed with a brass clasp. He set in on her lap and watched her shaky hands fumble to open it. Her fingertips ran over a few personal items—a pair of gloves, a neatly folded handkerchief, hair combs, the book he'd given her with some of its pages folded back—and settled on a square of rose and white fabric. She held it to her lips, then pressed it to her cheek.

"I pinned a piece of cloth just like this one to her gown when Mother took her away. It came from her blanket." She handed it to Sophie, a gleam of hope in her eyes.

Tom watched Sophie struggle to find the words. "This is perfect."

He had spent years under Maeve's care, her gentle hands applying poultices to his wounds or helping to stop a nosebleed after a fight. As he stared down at her hollow cheeks now with the pallor of sickness, he felt helpless, unable to give her the same care she'd given him.

He kissed her forehead and said goodbye, hoping it wasn't the last time he'd see her. As he approached the desk at the entrance, he spied a nun who had just finished stripping an empty cot. "Sister?"

The nun turned to face him, her expression somber. "Sir?"

"Maeve Hannigen is a friend of mine. Could you see to it that she is given ale regularly? A bit of charity." He pulled out his purse and extracted two pounds. "Please."

She smiled sadly, accepting the coins. "I'll make sure she is cared for."

He waited outside for Sophie by her carriage, his heart foolishly filled with hope. After a few minutes, she emerged from the building and joined him. He had just helped her onto the footplate when a boy of twelve or so with gangly arms and legs approached.

"Are you Thomas Hayes?" the boy inquired.

"Who is asking?" Tom wondered if the papers had finally connected him with The Pretty Punch.

"I have a letter for you, sir." He pulled a folded note from the inside of his shirt and handed it to Tom. Before Tom could offer him a penny, he ran off.

"What is it?" Sophie asked.

He scanned the letter, his pulse increasing with each word. *I hope your stay in Newgate was a pleasant one this time around. Did you really think I would allow you to cause me so much trouble without retaliation? Until the next time . . .*

There was no signature, of course, but it didn't need one.

Chapter 39

She couldn't believe what she'd read.

Tom was quiet most of the way to the Foundling Hospital, but Sophie could sense he was boiling inside. Although they had always vowed to catch the man who'd almost let Tom hang for his crimes, she realized their efforts were suddenly more urgent. *Until the next time . . .?* What would the monster do next? Get others to insist he attacked them? Go to the papers with more false accusations? Come after her?

Tom insisted he didn't want to discuss it—possibly because Peg was with them—so Sophie stayed silent, but horrible scenarios flitted through her mind. Would the monster dare to harm him?

When they finally reached the hospital and alighted from the carriage, she tried to broach the subject.

His voice was steady when he spoke. "We mustn't lose sight of why we are here. Do not allow that man to throw us off course."

She wondered how he could think about anything else, but she knew he was right. They were there for Maeve. And little Emily.

The secretary at the Foundling Hospital pursed his lips while he scrutinized the small swatch of fabric in Sophie's outstretched hand. She couldn't figure out what exactly he expected to find on the cloth.

"'Tis awfully small," the secretary noted.

"For God's sake, man, it is all we have," Tom snapped, his leg bouncing up and down rhythmically.

The secretary sighed and pushed up from the desk. "I shall only be a moment."

He disappeared out the door, and Sophie set her palm on Tom's thigh to stop his leg from bobbing. Her chest swelled with hope. "We could find her, Tom."

He pressed her hand to his lips. "Sophie . . . you understand Maeve will not last much longer."

Sophie shut her eyes. She didn't want to be reminded about her friend dying.

Tom gently cleared his throat. "I wish to marry you and take care of Emily. As a family."

She stared at him, uncertain she had heard him correctly.

He shuffled in his chair. "We can raise her as our own. Give her a life better than anything Maeve could have ever dreamed for her. I . . . think she would approve."

These were the words Bertie should have said to Maeve and never did. And here was a man who had no reason to care for this child but did it without hesitation because he couldn't deny his huge, generous heart. Her eyes flooded with tears.

He continued, hesitant. "I hope I haven't misread your . . ."

His face dropped as she shook her head, unsure of what to make of him.

He steeled himself. "Forgive me. I see I have misspoken."

"Not at all." She rested her hand on his and spoke through tears. "It is only that I have never known a man like you."

The secretary waddled back into the room, a small stack of papers tucked under his arm. "It appears your Emily Hannigen does not exist."

That couldn't be possible. All foundlings in London were taken to this hospital. They had to have a record of her. She was about to insist he look again, when he resumed.

"However, on the same date, an Emily *Needham* was entered into the records. This token," he said, holding up the pink and white striped cloth, "matches hers."

Sophie blanched. Maeve had given her daughter Bertie's surname. She hadn't even considered that.

"But children are baptized and given new names upon arrival. Her name is . . . Mary." He shuffled through the papers and settled on one. "She was taken to Bedfordshire to live with the wet nurse. A Miss . . . Hobart."

So, the Hobarts *did* exist. Maeve would be happy to hear that. It was unfortunate, however, that they'd never received the money Mother Wharton had stolen from Maeve to help Emily.

"And her illness?" Sophie asked. She hoped she didn't suffer much. She would love to tell Maeve her catalepsy wasn't as bad as she thought. She reached for Tom's hand.

"Her illness?" he asked, seemingly perplexed.

"She has fits. She requires herbs to help her sleep. And for stomach disorders." Sophie waited while he scanned the records, page after page, his lips pressed together in concentration.

"The child is healthy. The reports from the inspectress indicate 'she is a lively girl, fair-haired with hazel eyes and a pleasant disposition'. There is no indication of illness—"

"Are you certain? She suffers horribly from catalepsy," she insisted.

"I assure you there is no mention of that in here. Something as serious as catalepsy would be documented."

Could Maeve have misunderstood? She turned to Tom. "Do you think Mother Wharton lied to Maeve?" It was the only thing that made sense.

Tom let out a long breath. "If she did, then the woman has a black heart."

"So, she is well. And in Bedfordshire." Sophie's chest filled with light. The little girl who was almost four years of age, was perfectly healthy. She couldn't wait to see Maeve's face when she shared the good news.

She decided she would tell her mother she had to leave for Bedfordshire first thing in the morning. If only Maeve could stay strong a few days longer, she could reunite her with her daughter. Then Sophie would make arrangements for the adoption.

"Not exactly, madam." The Secretary folded his hands over the papers and frowned. "The child died two months ago from influenza."

That night, Sophie lay in bed, her cheeks stiff with dried tears. She had promised to meet Tom at the hospital to visit Maeve in the morning, but she wasn't sure how she was going to face her. What could she possibly say? Maeve seemed hopeful. How could she destroy that?

She struggled with every possibility that could've changed Maeve's fate. Every thought she considered began with *if only*. If only Bertie had taken responsibility for his daughter years ago, she and Maeve would have been cared for properly and lived healthy lives. If only Maeve had known that Emily was never sick, she would've never fallen prey to Mother Wharton's deception. If only Maeve had discovered the truth about Mother Wharton's deception earlier, she would've escaped Parker's sooner and reclaimed her child. Or, at the very least, if only they had started looking for Emily three months ago, they may have found her before she grew ill. If only . . .

When dawn broke, she felt as if she had been run over by a horse and cart, her limbs aching and stiff as boards. She moaned and lifted her arms to stretch, cracking her spine and shoulders back into place. She pressed her palms to her dry eyes, tired from staring into the dark while she searched for answers. But it had all been for naught. Nothing could change the truth.

Peg hurried behind her, complaining from the moment she disembarked from the hackney a few streets away. "'Tis a pity your mother took the carriage. I am short of breath!"

"'Tis no wonder! Perhaps if you did less talking and more walking, you would be fine." She hadn't meant to sound so ornery, but with no sleep and her mind and heart heavy with what lay ahead, she simply couldn't help it. Although Sophie had taken the cane upon Peg's insistence that morning, she barely needed it. Her heel was feeling much better. She realized her pace was quick, but she worried that Maeve had little time to spare. "We are only one street away from the hospital now."

The air smelled of rain. A couple of men scurried past, casting anxious glances at the heavy clouds. Sophie peered up at the grey sky before entering the hospital. *Rain. How fitting*, she thought. *Rain hard and wash away all of Maeve's pain.*

"And all my guilt," she added under her breath. Even with Maeve's sweet acceptance of her relationship with Tom, she couldn't help but feel guilty for all the happiness she felt when he was near.

Tom stood at the entrance, pacing, his head bowed and arms folded across his chest. He didn't see her approach.

"Are you ready?" she asked, startling him out of his concentration.

"Sophie." He doffed his hat at Peg as well. Sophie could see the sadness in his eyes. He was dreading this visit too.

They left Peg on the bench in the hall and followed the nun back to Maeve's small corner behind the curtain. She was slouched against the wall at the head of her bed, her hands loosely folded in her lap and her eyes glazed over. At least her wrists were not bound this time.

Sophie settled next to her on the bed and reached for her hand. Maeve's head lolled once in a sloppy effort to face her.

"Did you find her?" she asked drowsily.

Sophie's throat was thick with despair. Tom rested his hand gently on her shoulder. She blinked back tears, then swallowed hard, willing her voice to come. "We did."

A soft moan escaped Maeve's lips, her fingers twitching as she tried to squeeze Sophie's hand. "Tell me."

Sophie knew at that moment what she would do. What she *should* do. "She was never ill, Maeve. Your sweet girl is healthy and happy. A precocious little darling, they say. Clever and beautiful."

Tom's hand stiffened on Sophie's shoulder. She looked up to gain his understanding, and he kissed the top of her head.

For a brief moment, a hint of colour returned to Maeve's cheeks, and the corners of her mouth quivered slightly upward. "Her catalepsy?"

Tom spoke softly. "None of that was true. The bawd . . . Your daughter is perfect."

"She lives in Bedfordshire with the Hobarts, who take wonderful care of her," Sophie added. "She is quite happy in the countryside."

"The countryside," Maeve whispered dreamily. "Will you bring her to me?"

Tom knelt beside them. "Of course we will. We will ride to Bedfordshire and bring you your daughter."

Maeve rested her head on Sophie's chest, her thin breath ragged. Sophie stroked her hair as she hummed a tune she remembered her nurse singing to her when she was a child. It was a popular tune that everyone knew. Perhaps Maeve had even sung it to Emily the first four months of her life. Eventually, Maeve's breath slowed, settling into a deep rhythm.

Neither she nor Tom spoke until they walked out the entrance. Peg stood a few feet away, obviously sensing they needed privacy.

"You did the right thing," Tom said.

She hadn't been sure of it at the time, but when she saw the gleam in Maeve's eyes after she'd told her her daughter was alive and well, she knew.

The next day, the postboy arrived with a letter from the chaplain of London Lock. *Maeve Hannigen and her unborn child died during the night and are now at peace with the Lord.*

Sophie stood outside the warehouse with Tom, waiting while he read the letter from the chaplain.

"I find it hard to believe." He pulled Sophie into his arms. Peg, after wiping away Sophie's tears all morning, turned the other way, softening to the outward display of affection. Tom tipped up her chin. "You gave her such a gift."

"I hope so."

He kissed her softly. His embrace was warm, and his skin smelled of the spices he had been unpacking inside the warehouse when she arrived.

He bent to kiss her again, but they both turned towards the shouts of a paperboy. "London Monster caught! Read it here first! Tuppence a look!"

Tom rushed to the lad and bought a paper. He held it so Sophie could read along. "It says they will transport him today from Clerkenwell Prison to the Bow Street public office."

"We should go," Sophie said, recognizing a sense of urgency in Tom's eyes as they quickly scanned the page.

"Do you think you could manage the walk?" He tucked the paper into his coat.

She lifted her skirts to show him her healed foot. "I am as good as new."

Chapter 40

A huge crowd had already formed by the time they arrived. People were shouting with their fists raised in the air, blocking the way of carriages attempting to pass through the thoroughfare.

"Perhaps you two should stay back." Tom glanced at the office entrance as they stood across the street.

"Not on your life," Sophie said doggedly. "I wouldn't give up this moment for anything."

Tom grinned down at her. "Then on we go, lady reporter."

She turned to Peg. "Wait here."

They squeezed through the mob in time to see two thick-armed Runners cordoned by a parade of other patrols lead a frightened, dark-haired man wearing a threadbare blue frockcoat inside.

He seemed shorter, smaller than the man Tom remembered. As he was shoved ahead, the man stopped to square his shoulders, which made Tom think the only thing he had in common with the monster was the stiffness of his posture. Over the past nine months, he'd wrestled with the man twice, squeezing his arms around his neck and torso, close enough to smell the lye and sulfur used to bleach his linen shirt. He remembered the peruke that he tore from his head, dark brown and curled with care, that disappeared at some point after their scuffle. *This* man wore no wig, his natural hair bound with a simple dark ribbon at the base of his skull, a sparse tendril hanging limply beneath. But even if he'd had a wig on, his eyes seemed too dark and small, his nose too long to be the monster's.

Elbows jabbed Tom from both sides, forcing him a couple feet closer. The Runner shouted for everyone to move back, but no one listened.

Could he be mistaken? It was dark both nights they'd tussled, as well as that evening in Eastcheap when he'd witnessed him bothering that young maid.

He stared at the man swallowed by the swarm of patrols surrounding him. For a brief second, the prisoner caught his eye, but he quickly broke the connection when he was jostled from behind. That's when Tom realized his instincts were right. The monster definitely would've held his gaze. There was no doubt about that.

"'Tis not him," Tom said resolutely.

"Are you certain?" Sophie asked.

"Positive. That is not the man." He grabbed Sophie by the hand and wended his way through the maze of onlookers. They shoved through until they managed to make it inside. A group of spectators whispered and pointed as the man he knew was *not* the monster stood in front of a desk.

A corpulent patrolman in a scarlet coat with gold buttons sat at the desk blocking further entrance into the room. He eyed the prisoner, a quill poised between his thick fingers. "Name?"

One of the Runners shunted him with a tight grip on his arm. "Rhynwick Williams."

Two well-appointed ladies—one dressed in green, the other yellow—stood to the side, swiping at their eyes with handkerchiefs as the Runners thrust him into a larger chamber. "'Tis him!" asserted the one in green.

Several people gasped.

Tom pulled Sophie forward until they stood before the desk. "You have the wrong man. That is *not* him," Tom insisted.

"And you are?" he asked skeptically, his cheeks wobbling.

The shouts from outside forced Tom to raise his voice. "The real monster is taller and broader-backed. He often wears a dark peruke—"

"How do you know this?" he asked, a smirk on his lips.

He was about to answer when Sophie interrupted. "There is a sketch of him with the magistrate at the Old Bailey."

Tom sighed, knowing that did them no good at the moment.

The guard jerked a pudgy thumb towards the woman in green. "Miss Porter says it is him. And she was one of his victims."

Tom remembered reading about her and her sister being attacked the night of the queen's birthday celebration. But Miss Porter was wrong.

"You must believe me. I saw him attack women three times. I was there. He is not the man."

"Your word against hers."

300

He turned to Sophie, alarm surging through him. "Did you not bring your sketch to this office?"

Sophie's eyes lit up. "Do you think they kept it?"

"There is only one way to find out." He sidled through the crowd to the back wall, and there it was, dangling precariously by one pin. The bottom corner of the paper was ripped, but the older sketch was unharmed. He tugged it off the wall and slammed it on the guard's desk. "Here. This is the man."

The guard tilted his head to the side, his lips puckered in puzzlement. "You cannot see the face."

Sophie had drawn all his features except his eyes, which she kept in shadow. Frustration bristled through Tom's chest. "But you can see enough to tell that the man you arrested is not the monster."

"Like I said, the lady says he was the one who attacked her." He huffed loudly, then leaned back in his chair, resigned.

Tom was dizzy with anger. How could they ignore such proof? And then he remembered the note he had tucked in his waistcoat. They could compare Williams's writing to the script on the letter. He reached inside in search of it, but it was gone.

Visions of his mother's lifeless body passed before him. Another man was going to get away with his crimes.

He led Sophie outside, edging past a knot of spectators and away from the chaos and screaming.

"What was the point? My accounts. Your sketches." He raked his fingers through his hair. All the nights he'd spent looking for the devil had been in vain. He didn't want to see another man blamed for the real culprit's offenses. He knew what that felt like, the hopelessness of no one believing your pleas of innocence. He had almost hanged for it. Twice.

Sophie laid a gentle hand on his arm. "Why stop? We should continue to pursue what we know is true."

"No one will believe us, love. You heard the patrolman."

She smiled at him sadly. "Perhaps this is our purpose. Perhaps this mishandling of the truth is what we were meant to expose."

Tom exhaled, his skin tingling with anger. She was right. There had to be a reason they were brought together. A reason he didn't die at his own hanging and she was there to make sure it was recorded in history.

"Now that my articles will be published regularly, I will be able to write the stories I was always meant to write." She wrapped her arms around his neck, her touch soothing. "Your truth. Maeve's truth. Emily's truth."

"And now Rhynwick Williams's truth." He rubbed a finger over the M branded at the base of his thumb. And one day, his mother's truth. For the first time in his life, he didn't feel alone in his purpose. He might not be able to catch every blackguard that terrorized the streets of London, but he would certainly try. And he would not allow the truth of the crimes to be brushed aside like crumbs from a table. The victims deserved to have their stories told. His mother deserved it. And Sophie could do her part to make sure it was done. "It might require a lifetime to do it. Are you willing to give me that? A lifetime?"

She stared up at him, her eyes brimming with tears. He wasn't sure what put them there—the fumbled arrest, the loss of Maeve and Emily, her broken betrothal. So much had happened since they met, and much of it sad.

But then she tipped her face up to him, her lips slightly parted, and he knew those tears were for him and the hope of their future together.

He kissed her as the church bells rang in the distance. Her lips were warm and tender, just like her heart.

Her grip tightened around his neck. "I can think of no better way to spend the rest of my life."

A Final Note

June 15, 1790

It is time for me to go. The countryside awaits.

I leave my valet to finish the packing of my trunks. There is not much to do, considering my winter wardrobe will remain here in London while I summer in Dorset. The timing could not be better.

Honestly, I had nothing to do with the flower maker's arrest. Unless, of course, you interpret my serendipitous idea to approach some of my paramours with a silk nosegay as an intentional clue to snare the man. But I assure you, none of that was part of my plan when I purchased the flowers from him this past winter.

I am elated that someone else is in custody, however. I would not do well in a dingy gaol cell. The dampness, the grime, the smells of urine and sweat. I find none of that appealing. And I certainly find standing at the gallows with a noose around my neck even less alluring. Nay. Better him than me.

But even as I sit here in my comfortable chair by the window, looking out over the gardens, I must admit I feel unsettled. The man I truly want to pay for my crimes yet walks free. When I first saw him, he was but a boy. A clumsy, gangly boy. I hadn't known his identity prior to his botched hanging, but before they'd covered his face, I recognized his blue gaze staring fiercely out at the crowd of onlookers.

How long has it been? Ten years? Twelve?

How better to hurt the man who stole my love from me than to hurt his son! After all, a father's heart beats within his son's chest. Joseph will likely win a seat in the House of Commons in the elections only ten days henceforth. His fortune grows from his collieries. A working man is he.

I trace my fingers over the emerald necklace in my lap. The diamonds sparkle in the sunlight streaming through the window, sending tiny rainbows of light dancing on the far wall. The spray of colour is quite lovely, as was she. I slide the stones across my lips. I had never meant to take it or her rings, but I had to make our encounter appear as a robbery. That was my brother's suggestion when the event turned sour. It had never been my intent to kill her. I had only wanted her attention. Her affection.

I was merely a man in love.

"Lord Greenville?"

I slip the necklace into my waistcoat in a pocket close to my heart and turn to my footman. "What is it?"

"Your carriage awaits, milord."

If you enjoyed *The London Monster*, please consider writing a review on Goodreads or Amazon. This helps other readers discover the story. Thank you!

Goodreads:
https://www.goodreads.com/book/show/55851589-the-london-monster

Amazon:
https://www.amazon.com/London-Monster-Donna-Scott-ebook/dp/B08M4D6T9N/

If you would like to be informed about new releases and special offers, please sign up for my Newsletter at http://eepurl.com/g06zzz

Historical Note

The London Monster terrorized the streets of London one hundred years before Jack the Ripper. Although they shared an aura of perverse sexuality and their targets were women (the Monster's were beauties, and the Ripper's, prostitutes), the London Monster is not known to have ever murdered anyone. He had a propensity for cutting and stabbing his female victims in the hip or groin, not necessarily to kill, but—it is believed—to teach a lesson or punish. This method created hysteria that spread throughout the city, which ironically gave the surviving women celebrity status and turned ordinary men into vigilantes.

His reign of terror lasted two years, from March 1788 to June 1790. Within that timeframe, he attacked approximately 56 women. This number remains in question, however, because many believe some of his attacks were not reported and others were fabricated.

Over time, the monster's *modus operandi* evolved. As the story goes, he approached women with a comment, many times of a sexual nature, which was met with reproach and disgust. His actual words were said to be so indecent that the women who reported his attacks wouldn't repeat them. In the testimony of the Porter sisters—Anne and Sarah—they accused him of using "very gross," "dreadful," and "abusive" language so, out of decency, much of what he said was never disclosed in the court transcripts. He would insult, abuse, and cut his victims with a knife, sometimes slicing through their gowns and into their flesh. In several reports, he had a sharp object connected to his hand or knee that he would use strategically in the assault. Most of the time, the point of impact was in the hip, thigh, or buttocks, some suspecting those areas were targeted with sexual intent. These attacks led women to wear copper cuirasses underneath their skirts, which covered their backsides, should the monster attack. It wasn't until April of 1790, that one of his victims was sliced through her nose when he asked her to smell a nosegay with a sharp object hidden inside.

Men everywhere started to worry over their wives, sisters, and daughters, demanding that the villain be caught. As a result, John Angerstein, a wealthy insurance broker and art collector, offered a reward of 100 pounds—50 pounds for the capture and arrest of the monster and the remaining 50 pounds once he was convicted. This brought about a slew of vigilante monster-hunters roaming the streets at night, accusing and restraining innocent men throughout London. Angerstein pasted posters all over the city with various descriptions of the monster, all obtained from the victims and witnesses, and none of which quite matched. He eventually acknowledged the frenzy he created over finding the monster, ironically stating that "it was not safe for a gentleman to walk the streets, unless under the protection of a lady".

Because of this mania, historians believe many of the attacks may have been fabricated. As the monster was known to attack only beautiful women, several women were suspected of slashing their own gowns and mildly injuring themselves to gain social celebrity. Essentially, it became a statement of one's great beauty and, thus, an "honour" to have been selected by the man. These victims often reclined in their parlours, inviting curious visitors to take a peek at the gash or scratch where blade met flesh. During the height of the hysteria, the reports were numerous.

Because his victims rarely described him in the same manner, his capture became that much more difficult. In the end however, a twenty-three-year-old unemployed artificial flower maker named Rhynwick Williams was arrested as the London Monster. A day later, he was examined by the justices at the Bow Street public offices. The Porter sisters were the first to give evidence against him, identifying him as the same man who used coarse language to offer indecent proposals that eventually resulted in an assault. He was tried at the Old Bailey and, although he had at least seventeen character witnesses testifying on his behalf and several victims agreeing that he was not the man who attacked them, he was pronounced guilty by a unanimous jury and sent to Newgate.

If not for the support of the Irish poet and conversationalist Theophilus Swift, who came forward to argue his innocence, Williams may have rot in prison. In a matter of months, he was released with the help of Swift, who proposed Williams's innocence and claimed his accusers were frauds. He was retried in December and found guilty once again for "the misdemeanor of willfully and maliciously cutting people with intent to kill and murder them". He was sentenced to six years in Newgate prison and required to pay two hundred pounds and two sureties in one hundred pounds each upon the conclusion of his prison term. In December 1796, he was finally released and lived a normal yet obscure life.

In time, the people of London forgot about the monster and his depraved crimes. Many believed Williams to be innocent, yet his fate was already sealed. What *is* unanimously agreed upon is that the London Monster was a man with perverse sexual desires and a vulgar tongue who—although he never seriously injured anyone, and no one died from his attacks—posed a grave threat to the stability of the city and general welfare of its people.

Acknowledgements

I owe deep gratitude to the professionals, friends, and family who helped bring this novel to light.

First, I am grateful for the support of the D4EO agency for believing in this story and welcoming me aboard.

My incredibly talented editor, Jessica Cale, deserves recognition. With her ever-discerning eye, she patiently corrected all my mistakes—both historical and grammatical. Any errors remaining belong solely to me.

Jenny Quinlan is responsible for the beautiful cover. I'm always amazed how she can turn the germ of an idea into something so special.

Thank you to Anna Meadmore, curator of the Royal Ballet School Special Collection located at White Lodge in Richmond Park, the novel's setting for Lord Sidmouth's Twelfth Night Party. After months of overseas correspondence, we were finally able to meet in person, and she was kind enough to devote her time to giving me a tour of the grounds and structures while sharing wonderful stories about the history of the lodge.

Many thanks also go to Michael Hellyer and the other archivists at SMITF Church for their assistance with my endless inquiries concerning Saint Martin-in-the-Fields and the Reverend Doctor Anthony Hamilton, Vicar at the time Cuthbert would have been desperately (and ineffectually) praying for his own salvation.

Additional thanks go to Dr. Elena Roth of the Bascom Palmer Eye Institute, who answered all my questions regarding the effect of neurosyphilis on the body, specifically as it relates to eyesight.

Gary Johnson of the Newspaper and Current Periodical Room at the Library of Congress also proved most helpful answering questions about 18th century newspaper editors and content.

Much gratitude goes to Jan Bondeson, author of *The London Monster: A sanguinary Tale.* This book is undoubtedly the single best resource on the London Monster. Not only is it filled with colourful details about the attacks, victims, and trials, but it directed me toward other highly useful resources on the subject. I truly appreciate our correspondences and the articles he sent me.

My beta reader and biggest advocate, Lisa del Valle, has offered me unwavering support for this novel and all the others. I thank her for her honesty and enthusiasm over the years.

I am indebted to Julie Edelstein for her guidance, talent, and criticism. She is the first person to see my work, and it's her stamp of approval that allows me to continue.

The encouragement given by my sweet father Georgie, who left us a while ago, still lives within my memory.

Finally, my mother, husband, and sons have believed in me from the beginning. They are my heart.

A Note from the Author

While this is a work of fiction, I have described the London Monster attacks as they were reported according to legal documents and historical newspapers. Rhynwick Williams was the only person ever arrested for the crimes committed by the London Monster. Many historians, however, argue he was falsely convicted due to numerous conflicting witness accounts.

Although there are transcripts from the trial, the women who reported the attacks were either unwilling to repeat the words the monster said to them, or the Old Bailey clerks recording their testimonies felt their words too vulgar to transcribe. With only a few actual quotes from the transcripts, I took the liberty of creating the monster's dialogue based on reports that he used obscene foul language of a highly sexual nature. For plot purposes, I shifted some of the attacks earlier or later depending on where Tom and Sophie were in the story yet kept the nature and location of the attacks historically accurate. The attack on the Porter sisters—Anne and Sarah—was on January 19, 1790, the night of Queen Charlotte's birthday party. Although I've placed the London Monster at the party as a guest, there is no proof he was in attendance.

Tom, Sophie, Cuthbert, Maeve, Dalton, Lord Greenville, and related characters are purely creations of my imagination. Some peripheral characters such as Lord Sidmouth, William Pitt, and the pugilists—William Futrell, Tom Johnson, Isaac Perrins, Jude Green, and John Jackson—are historical figures.

Parker's Place is also fictional, though created in the image of many brothels in the late 18th century. Mother Cluck's Coffee House is loosely based on Mother Clap's Molly House, a prominent rendezvous spot for London gay culture at the time.

In order to place my characters in the same room together with Lord Sidmouth, I created a Twelfth Night Party at White Lodge. Historically, White Lodge was actually in horrible disrepair in 1790, when Sophie, Tom, Cuthbert, and Maeve attended the masque. Additionally, the property wasn't gifted to Henry Addington, 1st Viscount Sidmouth, by grace and favour of King George III, until 1801.

The comment made by the *World* editor regarding the sale of a slave in Jamaica refers to an event that took place in mid-May of 1790, five months later than indicated.

The caricature, *The Monster Disappointed of his Afternoon Luncheon*, of the monster holding up a woman by her gown, was not published until May of 1790, five months after it was indicated in the novel.

Angerstein's reward for the capture and conviction of the monster was created on April 15, 1790, two weeks after it is indicated in the novel.

The monster mentions a clergyman being attacked outside of the coffeehouse. Although this happened, the correct date was April 29th, 1790, a couple of weeks later than indicated in the story.

To discover the historical inspirations behind the novel, please visit my website www.donnascott.net and please follow me on . . .

Facebook: Donna Scott-Author
Twitter: D_ScottWriter
Instagram: DonnaScottWriter

Also by Donna Scott, *Shame the Devil* and *The Tacksman's Daughter*:

Questions for Readers

1. Character duality plays a large role in this novel. Which identity for each character—the one carefully hidden or the overt one—is most revealing? Explain.

2. Although Tom is clearly troubled by the memory of his mother's murder, his brothers seem to have moved on. Why do you think Tom still suffers from the pain of losing her, so much so that he dedicates his life to fighting?

3. Sophie is driven to find the monster for several reasons, one of which is her own painful memory of an uncomfortable encounter at a garden party. But as she looks back, she questions her own behavior during the confrontation. Why do you think women do this even today?

4. Is Cuthbert a sympathetic character, or is he repulsive? What are the factors and influences that shape him? Explain.

5. Throughout the novel, Sophie questions traditional female gender roles. What do you anticipate her future with Tom would look like?

6. Although we never meet Maeve's young daughter, she plays a significant role in the novel. What does the discovery of her whereabouts tell you about London in 1790?

7. All the characters in the novel are flawed, yet some thrive while others languish. What are the distinguishing factors that determine their fates?

8. The monster's *Notes* give us a glimpse into his psyche. Where do you think his motivation to attack women comes from and, after his identity is revealed, do you imagine him continuing his predatory behavior?

Donna Scott is an award-winning author of 17th and 18th century historical fiction. Before embarking on a writing career, she spent her time in the world of academia. She earned her BA in English from the University of Miami and her MS and EdD (ABD) from Florida International University. She has two sons and lives in sunny South Florida with her husband. Her debut novel, *Shame the Devil*, received a First Place Chaucer Award for Historical Fiction and a Best Book Award from Chanticleer International Book Awards.

Manufactured by Amazon.ca
Acheson, AB

11505039R00177